SISTERS OF BELFAST

Sisters of Belfast

a novel

Melanie Maure

HARPER

NEW YORK • LONDON • TORONTO • SYDNEY

HARPER

This novel is a work of fiction based on some historical events and locations. Any references to real people, events, establishments, organizations, or locales are intended only to give the fiction a sense of reality and authenticity, and are used fictitiously. All other names, characters and places, and all dialogue and incidents portrayed in this book are the product of the author's imagination.

HarperCollins books may be purchased for educational, business, or sales promotional use. For information, please email the Special Markets Department at SPsales@harpercollins.com.

FIRST EDITION

Designed by Jamie Lynn Kerner

Library of Congress Cataloging-in-Publication Data has been applied for.

ISBN 978-0-06-334155-5 (pbk.)

23 24 25 26 27 LBC 5 4 3 2 1

For my mother, Patricia Maure, who gave me unwavering love and the joy of literature.
For the mothers and babies robbed of this same birthright.

SISTERS OF BELFAST

Prologue

AELISH, EASTER 1941

AELISH MCGUIRE'S TEN-YEAR-OLD WORLD LIES BROKEN. All around her, confusing mounds of debris. She coughs, choking, scarcely able to breathe through brick dust, soot, shock. Her mussed long hair and wide eyes are caked with black, turning the room into a disorienting haze. How did she get from the bedroom she and Izzy share to the living room plunged in darkness?

If not for the stabbing ring in her ears and the muffled howls from the streets, Aelish would believe she is still dreaming, that she's fallen through the looking glass into a shaken version of Alice's Wonderland. Something dense crashes to the floor nearby. The floorboards convulse. Aelish curls into her trembling legs, covers her ears.

Sweeping her arms out around her, Aelish pleads for something to hold her. She finds her mother's hand. How small her own is compared to Mammy's. She clutches her mother's fingers to the thin cotton of her nightdress and strokes the smooth thumbnail, removing the grime. Aelish marvels at the perfect half-moon where nail turns to skin. The warmth of Mammy's skin calms Aelish as she spins the cool wedding band on Ma's ring finger.

"I just can't shake this awful feeling, Patrick." This is what Ma said earlier that evening. "It feels like the ground is rumblin' under my feet. Something bad is coming. They're not done with us yet."

Ma never called Da Patrick unless she was sour at him for having a pint too many at Flannigan's Pub, or if he refused to go to Sunday mass. Aelish's da had not been to Flannigan's in weeks and had been going to mass without a fuss ever since the air raid sirens began wailing through Belfast.

"Don't be daft, Sarah Jane." Listening from her bed, Aelish had pictured Da touching Ma's cheek. That's what he did when Ma worried. "Hitler has no more interest in Ireland. Besides, I heard he's not fond of Irish stew. Too much mutton." Da tried to make Ma laugh. There was silence.

As the ashes settle around her, Aelish can see that the front of their home has become an open mouth screaming into the street. Some of Da's books are splayed open, shredded and lying next to Ma's dented teakettle. The full moon's light plays a trick on Aelish's young mind by softening everything it touches, attempting to turn all the jagged calamity into smooth, polished silver. Her father is across the room under a chaos of bricks that once was the fireplace. She spies a child-sized gas mask lying face up and full of dirt near her father's fingertips. When Daddy made Aelish practice wearing the dreadful mask, the rasping of trapped breathing sounded like a terrified rat trying to scratch its way out. Not once did Aelish get past the count of five before ripping it off her head, gasping, frantic.

It being over there with him near the pile of bricks and not on Aelish's face where it should be fills her with that same sticky feel of telling a lie. She turns away, tries to rub soot off her nightdress, dabs the stinging trickle of blood at her temple.

And there is Isabel, Aelish's twin, lying in the doorway, her flannel nightgown twisted, gas mask pushed to the side of her sleeping sooty face. Izzy often showed up to the supper table with it strapped to her head, giggling a hollow sound behind the snout, bothered by nothing. Unaware of how much it troubled Mammy.

Da would scold Isabel for acting the maggot while trying to hide his grin from Ma. Ma would rub the worried patch of skin on her brow. To Aelish, Isabel's being older by minutes meant that Isabel took all the brave feelings and left Aelish a hollow shell of bother and butterflies.

"Isabel!" Aelish calls out, then coughs, spitting a grimy paste. "Stop fooling around. Get up!" Aelish wonders how long Izzy can stay that way, what with her leg in such a funny position. Aelish is helpless against the violent rattle in her legs and arms. People scream and cry out from the street. Aelish crams her knuckles into her ears, wishing they still felt full of water—every noise muffled. A streak of orange shoots over Isabel's head and disappears into the street.

"Lassy Mog!" Aelish calls out as their cat vanishes into moonlit mayhem. She hopes there is enough milk to put out for Lassy Mog. She doesn't want him being outside, hungry and alone. Aelish clamps her eyes shut against all of this, tries to lock her jaw against teeth that bang like lose shutters bullied by wind.

She rocks side to side, singing, *"I see the moon and the moon sees me . . . ,"* desperate for this stampeding reality to swerve around her shaking body. Aelish cracks open her stinging eyes, looks up to a moon that burns a torchlight over the blackened ruins of the city. She believes that is where God lives—nestled and watching from one of those holes on the moon.

"God, I promise I'll be good, forever," she whispers. "Please wake them up. Please make the sirens stop."

One last worry scurries through her head—Mammy loves to paint, and she will never find her paintbrushes in this terrible mess.

A moment before she crumples to the living room floor with the rest of her broken family, Aelish looks down and sees her mother's silky hand is no longer attached to her thin arm.

AELISH, EASTER 2016

THIS IS WHERE AELISH MCGUIRE'S EIGHTY-FIVE-YEAR-OLD MIND is—back in 1941 scrambling through the dusty rubble of history—as early-morning spring light trickles through the soaring stained glass of Belfast's Saint Patrick's cathedral. It settles onto the backs of Aelish's hands, painting a holy bouquet of rose and violet. She wriggles her fingers, a well-worn tactic for fetching herself from recollection, and she expects the sound of rusted door hinges.

These are not my mother's hands, she thinks; *Ma's hands never had the chance to throb with age.*

"What made you decide to become a nun?" A young woman, very dear to Aelish, floats this question into the hush of the cathedral. "What if the same thing happens to me as it did to you?"

Aelish knows it is rare that women of this day and age would consider taking a solemn religious vow, living a cloistered life.

Squinting through milky eyes and smudged glasses, Aelish drinks in the girl's smooth curtain of auburn hair, sharp nose, and almond-shaped eyes that turn down at the edges, her face a collection of sharp angles assembled in perfect symmetry. The likeness of this young woman is undeniable. And she has her grandad Declan's eyes.

Aelish worries her hands with a button on her knitted jumper, then reaches for the crucifix between her flaccid breasts. Most days, touching the heavy worn metal of the cross is a comfort. Today, she is haunted by the phantom weight of her ma's hand entwined with her own.

How much do I tell this precious child without veering her away from God's plan? Aelish immediately feels the fool, believing even for a second that she has the power to change such a thing—God's plan, that is.

It is fitting and painful that these questions should rise today of all days, it being Easter Sunday. The thought of digging through the rubble of her life, rolling back the great stone that both hides and protects her from the past, is cumbersome, depleting. She fears the deformity of decay.

Aelish lifts her head, attempts to straighten the stoop in her stubborn backbone. It's a losing battle. She settles instead for a sideways glance at the young woman with peach skin. It is difficult to look at her familiar features and not be swallowed, brittle bones and all, by grief and a long-toothed shame.

Aelish clears the lump from her throat with a strange croaking noise. She wants to declare it was a deep abiding love for the Lord and His church that guided her decision to join the sisterhood, but she does not dare add more deceit to her life—not this late in the game.

"A war," she utters, uncertain if she's thinking of Hitler's senseless bloodshed marching across Europe or the blitzkrieg that was happening inside her young heart—either way, she says, "That's what made me decide to become a nun."

Aelish anticipates that shouldering this millstone of truth will hurdle her straight back into that Easter of 1941 and her childhood home on Donegall Street—the confusing stench of a burning city, sirens slicing the smoky air.

Instead, the church pew beneath her bony bottom begins to pitch and roll gently side to side. And rather than the miasma of a burning city, her memory sends her back to her first sea voyage in 1955, a bloom of ocean minerals, a sea breeze to cool her cheeks. Aelish grips her arthritic hands around the steely recollection of a ship's rail while her heart curls around the desperation she'd had to sail to Isabel, to Declan across the Atlantic.

She closes the folds of her eyelids, wanting to hide the remorse rising in her chest. She hears Sister Mary Michael's words—true forgiveness is releasing hope that anything from the past can be different than what it was. Aelish is still so laden with that hope it hurts.

PART 1

1

AELISH, APRIL 1955

SEA PASSAGE FROM BELFAST HARBOUR TO POUCH COVE, NEWfoundland, gives Aelish six days to pore through every word in Isabel's letters. She is—they are—twenty-four, and Aelish wishes she and Izzy could have experienced their first departure from Ireland side by side.

Sometimes she reads her twin's words by the light coming through the porthole in the narrow cabin. Today, one of the more pleasant days, she has journeyed to an upper deck and hears Izzy's voice speaking to her on the wind as she reads.

> *Declan and me have a small cottage near the harbour, and the sound of the ocean meeting the cliffs wakes me in the morning and puts me to sleep each night. The only thing missing is you, Aelish.*

She ends every single letter with this same declaration. The life Izzy describes drips with colour, reminding Aelish of one of Ma's many paintings with cobalt skies and emerald seas. All those painted images were turned to ash in the bombing fourteen years ago. These losses twinge from time to time; invisible slivers under a lacy emotional skin.

According to the letters, Isabel and Declan emigrated to Newfoundland, Canada, where Declan found work on a fishing boat with one of the many Irish folks settled in this faraway place.

Often, Aelish must stop reading, clutch the paper to her chest, remind herself to breathe. Mostly she reads about Izzy's small wedding by the sea, witnessed by two strangers: a Mr. and Mrs. Doolin. She is angry with herself for not feeling Isabel move so far away, mad with Isabel for moving across the world, and mad with Declan for taking her there. Resentful of this Mr. and Mrs. Doolin, imagining them as thick-skinned and unfriendly.

Aelish makes herself read it over and over, surrendering to the hurt in her chest. *I believed I only needed her,* she thinks. And now, standing at the railing of the ship, the wind turning her veil into a snapping black sail, unsure if her twin sister will survive the lung fever, Aelish recalls all the times Isabel snuck through the dark orphanage dormitory so they might share a narrow cot and a thin itchy blanket.

Only now does Aelish recognize her sister's clinging squeeze—the way she draped herself over Aelish's back—perhaps to avoid being swept away by a sorrowful wind. Isabel was gritty and defiant during the day, but ghosts came to call when the lights went out. *This was when she needed me.* Aelish wraps her arms around her belly at this thought, yearning for that chance to comfort Izzy once again.

"Sofia! Get away from there, or I'll tell Mammy." The worried voice of a young girl pulls Aelish out of her remorse. Not too far away, a second younger dark-haired girl clings to the ship railing with her button nose just above the black metal. Her eyes scan the horizon, transfixed, even as her older sibling calls to her, fearful. The young one turns to Aelish and flashes a grin with holes in it. With the keenness of a fox, she takes Aelish's habit in from head to toe, then she sticks her tongue out. Aelish feigns shock, placing a hand over her smile, a smile that feels as rusty as an old bicycle chain.

"Sofia! I said get off there." The older sister yanks the collar of the little one's dress, dragging her down the deck, fighting every step. Their cross words are swallowed by the lumbering of the ship's engine.

Aelish leans her forearms on the rail; Isabel's letter flutters in her hand. It sounds, a frantic fragile bird held by a leg. This is one of the last letters Izzy sent. In it, she speaks of wishing for children and how these longed-for children would have an aunt Aelish, the only living relative who could tell them stories of their grandad and grandma.

Declan's letter to Sister Mike, the one pleading with Aelish to come to Newfoundland, confirmed Izzy's wish has come true: not just one child but two. The weight of Izzy's second wish—for the children to have an auntie—weighs heavy and tangled in Aelish's arms. It requires burying all the hurt, all the resentment, and keeping buried what could destroy everything.

As she thinks of the babies, only three months old, there is a peculiar stir of excitement loosening something in Aelish. A gust of wind snatches the letter from her fingertips. Holding the crucifix at her chest and stretching over the railing, Aelish grabs at the air as the paper flys away. The cold metal across her hips and how dangerously far over she is reaching do not register. The back of her robe goes tight as if a rock has been dropped onto its hem. Teetering backward, Aelish's feet land on the metal of the deck, her teeth clacking together. She drops to her knees and comes face-to-face with the little girl named Sofia.

"You gots to be more careful," she says, wagging a short rosy finger so close Aelish sees the swirl of her young fingerprint.

"My sister gets mad when you's not careful." Aelish hugs the child's pointy shoulders, pinning her arms to her side. Tears sting her eyes as she breathes in the smell of salt and sweat from the little one's black hair.

"Thank you, may God bless you, child." Aelish holds her at arm's length and says, "You remind me of someone extraordinary." Aelish pulls the girl into her arms once more, and the little one wriggles her way out of the embrace as quick as a fish.

"I don't like hugs," she exclaims, fists balled at her hips. She sticks her tongue out, spins around, and skips away. Aelish closes her eyes and listens to the sound of shiny black shoes tapping along the deck. The feel of Isabel's breath on her neck, the touch of Izzy's hand in hers; it's all so awake. Kneeling at the lower rail, she searches the roiling surface of the ocean for Isabel's letter. Aelish rests her forehead against the rail and begins to recite the Lord's Prayer.

As a young girl in the orphanage, she had always imagined her prayers—all the little girls' prayers—drifting up and getting trapped in the rafters of the stark white dormitory ceiling, the words banging and frantic until, exhausted, they fell to the floor lifeless, never reaching their destination. She could almost feel them under her feet sometimes, small prayer skeletons crunching underfoot.

Out here, praying into the wind, her lamentations soar. She still doesn't know their destination, but she does know they are free. She hopes they can avoid the sickly patch of clouds the nose of the ship points toward. A frightful slash of lightning bursts from its belly. Raindrops bounce off the deck, wetting her ankles as she makes her way across the deck, headed for her stifling cabin. Another stab of lightning, much closer this time, fills the sky and lifts the fine hairs on the back of Aelish's neck just as she pulls closed the deck door.

AELISH, 1941

THE FLOORS, WALLS, AND HIGH CEILING IN THE GIRLS' DORMITORY at the Sisters of Bethlehem Orphanage were bone white. Even the yellow sun shied away from all that white.

As clean as the young girls at the orphanage kept the long room, scrubbing with oil soap on hands and knees, Aelish still tracked dust bits swimming in the line of sunlight. A plain-looking nun sat next to Aelish on her bed, the woman's short legs barely reaching the floor. When Aelish sneezed and wiped her nose across her sleeve, Sister Mary Michael pulled a starched hanky out of her robe.

"Blow your nose, child." Sister Mary Michael's voice was soft. When Sister talked, Aelish smelled the cigarettes the nun snuck under the giant oak tree in the yard behind the abbey and the rose water she used to cover it. Aelish wanted to ask the Sister if prayers could make it through the ceiling or if they got trapped, but she didn't want to bother the nun with these things. Not while a war was hurting so many people and there was so much to worry about.

Shortly after the bombs hit Belfast, Aelish was one of many girls delivered to the abbey and greeted by Sister Mary Michael on the front step. She would gather them in through the wide front doors and instruct them to call her Sister Mike.

Sister Mike's hands cupped in her lap looked to Aelish like a pale bird's nest waiting for an egg. It was hard to tell how old she was.

"Your sister Isabel will have to stay in hospital until she's well enough to be here," Sister Mike said. "Her leg was badly hurt. She's a lucky girl. You both are."

"I don't feel lucky," Aelish replied, hoping not to sound bold.

Sister Mike's round face squished out the edges of her white wimple, and she turned a little red like she was embarrassed.

Aelish held the white hanky out to return it, but the Sister curled her hand over Aelish's and lowered it to her lap. Sister Mike made a soothing clucking sound and petted the long tight braids Aelish wasn't used to wearing. Reaching up, Aelish itched the sore taut valley of scalp between the braids.

Clomping footsteps as loud as a horse came down the narrow aisle between the beds. Aelish's eyes scanned for shelter. There was a dense prickly stone in her belly whenever Sister Edel, the Mother Superior, entered a room.

"Sorry to interrupt your little chitchat, Sister Mary Michael, but Aelish must come to the chapel. Now. Don't dawdle." *Clap-clap.* Aelish flinched at the sharpness of Mother Superior's palms cracking together. To Aelish, it sounded like heavy wooden beams snapping overhead.

"The good Lord and morning prayers will not wait for you, Aelish McGuire," Mother Superior announced; Aelish could not look away from the bits of white stuff gathered in the corners of the woman's mouth.

Kneeling on the floorboards of the chapel, the rough wood grain bit at the bare skin of Aelish's knees. She looked at the looming stony-eyed Virgin Mary statue holding her grey dead son, then clamped her eyes shut, but not soon enough. She pictured Daddy's arm sticking out of all the smashed fireplace bricks, her gas mask at the end of his fingertips.

Aelish rubbed her eyes, then looked up at the colourful stained-glass Saint Patrick in the window to her left, holding his shamrock and staff. Da's name was Patrick, but everyone called him Paddy. Because everyone loved Da. A ball of gum formed in her throat. She struggled to breathe.

With hands under her chin and eyes squeezed tight, Aelish moved her lips, pretending to pray the Hail Mary like all the other girls. She would not cry, not here, not in front of Jesus and Mary and certainly not in front of Sister Edel. On the inside, she screamed and begged a different prayer.

Please don't take Izzy away. I promise to be good. Please, God. Over and over she pled, her fingernails digging half-moon bites in her palms. She would do anything, make any promise to keep Izzy safe.

That night at bedtime Aelish folded twenty-one acorns into the cotton hanky Sister Mike had given her. One acorn for each night she and Izzy had been apart. She placed the bundle under her spine.

The collection of acorns kept her from falling into sleep and the nightmare place where Mammy had no hands and Da's forehead was broke open. As Aelish's anxiety flared, so too did the stinging, itchy patches of skin in the crooks of her elbows. In her distress she itched them raw. The room smelled of burned dirt as the peat in the fireplace smouldered.

Aelish wondered if Izzy had the same nightmares lying in hospital. But how could she? Isabel didn't squirm away when Da tried to slip the gas mask over her head, nor did she trip and fall, running back to get her doll. Isabel did all the right things.

Clare, the red-headed girl in the next bed, kicked her covers to the floor and whimpered at something in her dreams.

"It's alright, shhhh," Aelish whispered across the narrow aisle. "They'll come back for you." This girl was older and in the orphanage before the bombs hit, before Aelish arrived. Despite being older, she plugged her thumb into her mouth and sucked herself to sleep every night. Most mornings, Clare would wake with a scowl, angry as a wet cat. "What are you looking at?" she'd often snap. And before Aelish could tell her that her hair was pretty, the colour of cinnamon, the girl would spit, "Are ya a feckin' eejit? Stop starin'!"

Aelish decided not to cover Clare up. Instead, she wrapped herself tighter in the blankets and moved the acorns out of the way just for a little while. Rolling onto her side, she stared at the wrinkled toes of her brown boots tucked under her cot. They were given to her when she arrived at the abbey barefoot. Aelish wondered where *her* shoes were, the ones she left near the front door of the house. Did Izzy manage to get her shoes on? Aelish couldn't recall, not without picturing her sister's twisted leg.

As she rubbed the strange aching knot in her thigh, she changed her mind about angry red-haired Clare. She slipped out of bed, picked the crumpled blanket from the floor, and covered her up once more, feeling glad she was not Clare, who was all alone. She then scurried to the farthest end of the room, navigating the rows of head-to-toe cots. Slipping past the altar holding the Virgin Mary and using all of her might, she slid open one of the windows, pressed her lips to the crack, and hastily prayed. *I'm glad I still have Izzy. I have my teaspoon. Please let Isabel come home soon.*

AELISH, APRIL 1955

FROM THE BED IN HER SHIP CABIN, AELISH CAN TOUCH THE DOOR handle with her stockinged foot. The same way she could—but never dared—reach out and touch Clare in the next cot at the orphanage.

It is day four and all the letters from Izzy fan out on top of her, a patchwork quilt of written emotions threaded together with Aelish's guilt. Izzy's words were a comforting weight on her, all night. This is the first time she has slept outside the abbey since the age of sixteen when she and Sister Mike journeyed to the neighbouring parish rectory to clean. Aelish rolls away from the mauve light coming through the porthole as well as a pang of memory—returning with Sister Mike from their cleaning to find Izzy gone. The note left behind is a hieroglyphic in Aelish's mind.

Dear Aelish,

I had to leave. I hope to explain it to you someday. Your life can be good and safe here. You belong at the abbey. I don't. I'm sorry.

Love,
Izzy

Aelish clutches the sheaf of paper resting on her chest, wondering if Isabel might not have run off if Aelish had had the guts to refuse Sister Mike's cleaning duties that day. If she'd had Izzy's nerve, she might have faked having a dose of something, stayed at the orphanage with Izzy. Aelish presses down on knowing that everything would be different if she had even a fraction of Izzy's nerve. In the farthest corner of her mind stirs the wondering: *Would I have even chosen to join the sisterhood if Izzy had not left me behind?* Aelish shivers and brushes this questioning aside. Nonsense.

Her Bible and crucifix rest side by side on a shelf at the foot of the bed. Veil and habit hang lifeless on a hook fastened to the door—it is meaningless material until she fills it out with body and spirit. Both of which have been feeling wrung out as of late. Aelish is uncertain if all the space she feels in the cramped cabin is a freedom or a free-falling. She is used to the swaddling regimen of the abbey, rising at 5:00 a.m. for vigils and morning prayers, lauds, and vespers. She misses Sister Mike's natural way of calming things around the abbey and she wonders if Sister Mike has continued with Aelish's Bible study students in her absence. She misses them, especially the gaunt, runny-nosed home babies—Molly and the other little ones who come from the mother and baby home down the road.

When Aelish was a young girl, she attended school with some of these children. Their frailty had pulled at her. When she became a novice nun, she decided to volunteer teaching Bible studies during their lunchtime at school. And when she noticed some of the children missing, Aelish broached the idea with Sister Edel of bringing Bible studies directly to the mother and baby home—to the little ones who, for whatever reason, could not attend school.

"You've got no business in that place, Sister Clare," was Sister Edel's brusque reply. Aelish had gotten somewhat used to Mother Superior's abruptness—as much as one could get used to a mule kick—however, something was different that day. Sister Edel did not present her usual looking-straight-through-you dismissiveness. Instead, she fixed on Aelish and said, "I am very certain the Soeurs du Saint Sacrement running that mother and baby home have no need of an overly ambitious novice the likes of you under their feet. Besides, those unwed mothers and their illegitimate children are in need of far greater teaching than you could ever give. Do I make myself clear?" The memory of that galvanizing glare sends a chill through Aelish. She flicks the door handle with her toes and says to the letter in her hand, "I wonder if Sister Mike would feel differently about it, now that she's Mother Superior?" She makes a mental note to broach the subject upon returning to life in the abbey. For the first time in years Aelish feels like she is talking with Izzy.

A bone-deep craving for coffee with cream brings Aelish to her feet and reaching for her habits, old and new. She smiles, empathizing with what drives Sister Mike to smoke. Looking at her Bible, she promises her God and herself, "I'll pray right after I find some coffee."

2

ISABEL, APRIL 1955

THE PATCH OF FRESH SPRING GRASS IN THE HOSPITAL COURTyard is only a few paces wide and long but calls out to Isabel to be strolled upon—if Isabel had the breath to walk more than three steps.

"Is Aelish coming for sure, Dec?" She pulls in a gulp of air. Her lungs burn from stringing together more than a few words. She leans back in her wheelchair. Clad in his enormous green fishing wellies, Declan sits with his ankles crossed, one long arm dangling over the back of the wooden bench, the mask that's supposed to be on his face hanging from his pinky. Envy for the ease in her husband's body is raw. Under his other hand is a folded newspaper, the headlines between his fingers announcing Canada's new prime minister, Lester B. Pearson.

Isabel thinks to ask what the B stands for, and what it means here in Canada to be Liberal, then her mind swings back to the lawn. Compared to the cliff face their cottage sits on with its sharp grey edges, the postage stamp of lawn holds a greenness she is craving. A greenness she grew up in.

"Sister Mike sent a letter the day Aelish left," Declan replies. "Iz, you have to eat something, get your strength up for when she gets here." He pulls out a jackknife and begins to shorten his fingernails in thin shavings.

"I'll eat something if you stop wearing those god-awful wellies everywhere. They smell like the outhouse door on a fishing boat."

He grins and waggles his feet. Studying his face, Izzy is sad to see that the worry over her and the twins is fossilizing around his eyes. The skin on his fingers is cracked from the salt water and rough ropes on the boats. As with most men, however, all of this only adds to his handsomeness. *Not fair,* Izzy thinks, contemplating her stretch marks and pendulous breasts.

She pokes a finger into one of the lumps of hospital food on the tray balanced on her lap and tastes it; they may as well be piles of dung as far as her appetite is concerned. She tears a corner of the square white bread and places it on her tongue; the texture reminds her of all those holy communions standing at the altar with her mouth open like some starving baby bird. Humiliating; that's how she saw it. All of it—the communion, the kneeling, the time spent in the dingy confessional box spewing counterfeit sins just to have something to say.

"I haven't seen that in a while," Declan says, admiring his wife. "You were smiling. It can't be that bread. It's no soda bread from home."

"Church. I was remembering church." Declan waits while Izzy takes in a breath. He leans forward, arms on his knees. "In confession, I got bored telling the same sins over and over." Another wheeze. "So I started telling Father McManus I robbed banks and stole the crown jewels." Isabel coughs into her hanky, examines it: no blood. "He actually laughed, ya know, on the other side of the curtain when I confessed to rubbing nettle on Mother Superior's knickers."

"You didn't!" Declan grabs Izzy's leg as he laughs.

"That's exactly what Father said." Through the years, Isabel has come to appreciate that particular priest's decency. Father McManus was most certainly Aelish's first crush, although her twin would never fess up to such sinful lust.

She can't figure out why she has never told Declan that story before. Isabel has loved his laugh from the first time she heard it in the schoolyard. It has saved her again and again. Laughing is difficult for Isabel; it draws on her lungs as a straw draws liquid. She covers her mouth, shakes her head, and grips Declan's strong fingers.

He rubs her back in slow circles, stifling his laughter. As is their way, they are breaking all the rules. This time by being so close and touching one another while she fights tuberculosis.

"The twins miss ya, Iz. I know they're only little, but they miss their mammy."

Isabel lays a hand on the fullness of her breasts, the ache at the mention of her babies. It was a few short weeks she had with them in their tidy cottage before she got sick. Isabel collapsed to the kitchen floor one morning shortly after settling the babies in their bassinets and has been in hospital ever since.

"Bring them, Dec. I want to see them."

This is the third time Isabel has pleaded with him, knowing her request is both dangerous and impossible. Not asking would make her a terrible mother. An absent mother—her worst fear. Declan presses his lips together, scratches at his reddish stubble. Izzy is aware of pushing on her husband's bruised heart when she asks a second question.

"Will your folks come, Declan? To help?" Isabel does not pray; however, these days, she lobs hope into the air whenever she can, not realizing it can land on others sharp side down.

Like most people Isabel knew from her childhood in Ireland, Declan's parents are simple farming folk. However, they chose to disown their only son when he chose a life with Isabel, who, according to them, was a girl with neither parents nor moral fibre.

Declan's jaw tightens; he flicks a small pebble off the bench. Rarely does he speak aloud the pain his choosing Isabel has caused.

He doesn't have to. Her husband's emotions are behind glass—nothing hidden. He changes the subject.

"Aelish will be here in a matter of days, Iz. Then maybe the two of you can finally put the past behind you."

Isabel picks up the tray of food and holds it out for Declan to take. The smell turns Isabel's stomach, reminding her of orphanage food and the nuns—circling sharks keeping the silence.

"What did you say in that letter to get her to come all this way? I've written so many letters and never got a single reply. Why now, Dec?"

"Because I told her you needed her. You've always needed her. But goddammit, Isabel Kelly, you're just too feckin' stubborn to admit it!" Declan doesn't often take a tone with Izzy; he's the soother, the calm in the storm. She sits back in her chair, surprised and somewhat amused by his attempt at being the fiery one. "You have to tell her what happened after you left the orphanage. No more secrets." He slices the air with his hand.

"I didn't leave." Izzy clutches a handful of the blanket covering her legs.

Anger drains Isabel's energy. The soft skin at her temple pulses. Declan's hand on her shoulder slows the throbbing in her head.

"You know I didn't mean that the way it sounded. But that's what I'm talking about, Iz."

Isabel stares at her husband, waiting for him to finish his thought. Declan Kelly's thoughts float, his words meander, often infuriating Isabel. She folds her hands, waiting, holding back. Declan scratches his forehead, then says, "It's not Aelish's fault whatever happened. You can't be cross with her for not answering your letters when you've never told her what happened after the orphanage. And you know they didn't tell her. She'd feel different if she knew everything."

"Would she?" Isabel asks, sensing the spiky fear under her shell of scepticism. *Maybe I never wanted to find out what Aelish would do or choose,* she thinks to herself.

"Well, when she gets here and the two of you talk, you'll see that I'm right." He taps himself on the chest. "Just this once, I'm right."

As she studies his eyes, the way the outsides of them turn down, she remembers how giddy she was the first time she told Aelish that she loved Declan. That confession to her twin sister was more precious than when she spoke *I love you* to Declan himself. Isabel was spooning Aelish in the darkened dormitory and Aelish stiffened at the news, locking Izzy out, then scurried away to kneel at the foot of that damned statue of Virgin Mary. *Virgin, my arse,* Isabel thinks.

Declan sits up, puffs his chest out, and wags a finger at his wife. She notices the grime of dock work under his fingernails. "Even the blind chicken gets a worm from time to time," he declares.

Laughter doubles Isabel over into a raspy bout of coughing just as the nurse steps out into the courtyard.

"Oh, dear, Mrs. Kelly! That's enough for today." The nurse with her hair strapped back in a bun under her cap strides across the lawn. Declan stands, fumbling with his mask, transformed into a helpless boy by the sight of his struggling wife.

"It's time for you to leave, Mr. Kelly. And how many times do I have to tell you to keep at a distance from your wife?" Spinning Isabel's chair, the nurse begins pushing. When Izzy grabs the wheels, the nurse's ample belly bumps into the back of Isabel's head. "Mrs. Kelly! We need to get you inside."

Yanking on the right wheel, Isabel spins the chair back toward Declan. His head is lowered. His brown work pants are stained and in desperate need of repair; his green plaid shirt is untucked on one side. And, dear Lord, those boots. Isabel has never loved him more.

"You're right," Isabel tells him. "She will choose me—when Ay knows everything—she will choose me."

The nurse spins the chair and pushes Isabel through the open doors. Isabel covers her mouth and smiles when he calls out, "This blind chicken sure does love you."

At the same moment, Isabel notices something that has been lifeless for a very long time. It starts with a flickering in her spine. The rope is fluttering, soft as a butterfly drying its wings. Isabel closes her eyes and thinks, *I'm here, Ay. Waiting for you. Just like you waited for me. Aelish. Aelish. Aelish,* she calls in her mind as the nurse lectures over her shoulder.

ISABEL, 1941

THE NUN SENT TO FETCH ISABEL FROM HOSPITAL AND DRIVE HER to the orphanage could barely see over the wheel. She pulled through the iron gates with extreme caution, looking in every direction, then headed up the long stony drive. The nun drove slower than cold molasses, Isabel's young frustration growing hotter by the second. Isabel poked at her leg and swallowed hard. Making her leg hurt even more than it always did was the only way to keep the anger in front of her tender, frightened underbelly.

The abbey sat back at a distance from the road with its top-floor windows peering empty-eyed over a high stone wall. The orphanage was strung out to the side of the abbey. It reminded Isabel of the withered leg on the stray dog she used to sneak scraps to—it was a pest, an afterthought to most on her street.

Aelish, Aelish, Aelish. Inside her head, Isabel repeated her sister's name. She pulled on the rope strung out between them, knowing this was how she drew Aelish near, no matter the distance. Peering out the windscreen, Izzy did not see her sister. A bubble of sour worry floated to the top of her stomach. Maybe the thread they share got shook loose when the house fell, and now Aelish no longer hears her.

"Is this the right place?" she asked, sitting forward, head swivelling in every direction. "Is my sister here? You brought me to the same place, right?" Isabel's fingers gripped the seat and the flesh of her leg. Two painful tears spilt down her face. Sister Mike reached over and laid a hand on top of Isabel's gripping fingers.

"Don't!" Isabel yanked her hand away and turned to the side window.

"There she is," Sister said softly, jutting her chin. "See there, on the front steps."

Isabel bit the inside of her cheek as two more tears found their way past her anger. Aelish came down off the steps, running out of control. She caught the toe of her boot on something in the grass and fell to hands and knees. She examined her scraped palm for a second, then was off again, running toward Isabel. Aelish was jerked forward when she grabbed at the door handle before Sister Mike had brought the car to a halt.

"Aelish!" Sister scolded. "Good Lord, save me. I've only begun to drive, and I don't need to kill a child doin' so." She touched her lips to the cross hanging at her chest.

Isabel forgot about her leg and tried to swing it out the door. She cried out. Aelish dropped to her knees, wrapped her arms around Isabel's waist, and buried her face.

"They're liars, Ay." Isabel was the only one to shorten her sister's name. "Everyone's lying," she said again. "They haven't even looked for Ma and Da."

Izzy felt dampness from Aelish's eyes and nose soaking through her hospital housecoat and onto her tummy. Isabel fiddled with a loose thread at the nape of Aelish's dress, wondered why she was wearing someone else's clothes. Isabel expected to get out of her hospital gown and into her own dress and jumper.

"We have to go back home," Izzy announced. "They won't know where we are. Ma will be worried sick."

Aelish lifted her head, her nose running, her nostrils red and cracked. Isabel's mouth went dry. Aelish knew something Isabel did not; this terrified Isabel. And Isabel did not want to hear it.

"Get out of my way," Isabel shouted, pushing Aelish's shoulder, sending her onto her bottom with a thud.

"Girls!" Sister Mike scurried around the open door and helped Aelish to her feet, then turned to Isabel, knelt in front of her, hands folded in her lap, not daring to touch her. "Isabel, child," she said tenderly. "Don't do that. You and your sister must look after each other now. You must love one another through this."

Now. This. These two words took Isabel's life by the edge and flipped it. Isabel stared at the scuffs on the toes of her twin's brown boots. They were much too big for Aelish. Aelish would never say so, she would never complain about wearing someone else's sloppy boots.

"Why are you wearing those nasty boots, Ay?" she asked, disgusted. "They don't fit us proper."

"Sister Mike says we'll grow into them," Aelish replied, stepping one foot on top of the other. "And when we outgrow them, we'll get new ones."

"I don't want new boots!" Isabel shouted, pounding on her leg. The enormous pain turned the world watery. Isabel panted her way through the agony, and when it cleared, Aelish was holding Isabel's curled fists against her face, one on each cheek. "Where's Mammy and Daddy?" Isabel pleaded. Aelish's tears pooled in the shallow dips of Isabel's knuckles, and her nose dripped in strings to her dress. Aelish took a shuddering breath.

"They're in heaven, Izzy." Her voice cracked.

Aelish took a furtive glance at Sister Mike, who was running her fingers over the knotted rope hung at her waist. Sister Mike nodded and closed her eyes, all slow and owl-like.

"Straight to heaven, no purgatory. I swear it's true. Sister Mike and Father McManus said so," Aelish assured her and drew a small cross on her chest. In the exact spot on Isabel's chest, it felt as though a rod was being pushed right through its centre.

Sister Mike had wrestled a small wheelchair out of the boot and set it beside the twins. Isabel kicked it with her good leg, barely missing Aelish. The chair rolled back but not nearly enough to take the bite out of Isabel's raging heartache.

"How would you know." Isabel spat her words at Sister Mike. As she pulled herself off the seat of the car and into the chair, she grunted, furious and trapped.

Refusing to be pushed across the stones to the front steps, Isabel felt her arms ache and the palms of her hands began to blister.

Izzy, don't leave me. When this thought swept into the back of her mind and the rope pulled taut between the twins there came a sliver of relief—Aelish could feel Isabel determined and scheming their escape from the orphanage.

ISABEL, APRIL 1955

ISABEL DESPISES THE STIFF HOSPITAL BED THAT MAKES HER HIPS ache, the mint green curtain that the nurses insist on drawing tight around her, the masks they wear that leave her feeling dirty and shunned.

"Goddammit, I wanted to be well when Aelish arrived," Isabel whispers.

She'd had a setback the day after her visit with Declan and had been too weak to fight the doctor, who decided it best to sink a tube into her chest. The acid of her anger rises, eating away at her belly, chest, and throat. She is ravenous to be at home wrapped around her husband and babies, sunken deep into the valley of their secondhand mattress.

She had wanted to be able to talk to Aelish for hours, show her how good life is in Pouch Cove, spring and summer being irresistible. Izzy wanted the tenacity to convince her sister to stay. To share a life. Here. Her tuberculosis had other plans—one day, making her believe she was mending, the next day, making her claw for air.

Isabel turns her head side to side, hoping to rid the fuzziness in her brain, a murky sand pouring out one ear and then the other.

"No more sedatives," she mutters, wiping a hand across her dry lips.

The nurses try to convince her these pills calm her nerves, help her recover, but to Isabel, weakness, vulnerability—hers or anyone else's—is unbearable. Being feeble leaves her at the mercy of others. Her abhorrence of helplessness is why she is not trapped in a wheelchair from childhood as was predicted. It is why Isabel escaped those monsters posing as nuns, why she's been fighting the drink. It's also the reason she's twice refused her sedatives and a third time hid the bitter pills under her tongue, only to spit them under the neighbouring bed.

When the sedatives hit her bloodstream, they scoop Isabel up, mind and body, and toss her back into every powerless moment of her life.

She can still recall how the nurses talked around her broken ten-year-old body. "Pulled from the bombing! Little one's lucky to be alive, even if she ends up with a gamy leg," they said. "Poor little lamb, she'll never be the same; you can be sure of that," they predicted.

"No more sedatives," Isabel asserts once again and lifts her arms over her head, circles her wrists. She does this just because she can, and despite the effort it takes. In bringing her arms back to her sides, the tube protruding from her chest shifts to the right no more than the width of a matchstick. With that tiny deviation comes a searing pain ripping through her breastbone, turning the room blinding white. Isabel glances down, certain she will see her chest splayed open. Everything looks the same. Nothing to explain the bonfire lit in her right breast. The squeak of nursing shoes comes down the hall outside her room. Isabel tries to speak, and nothing comes out. Despite knowing the pain of it, Isabel reaches over and slides the metal food tray off the table to draw attention.

"Mrs. Kelly!" The dark-haired nurse charges to Isabel's bedside, ready to scold. By the swift change in the woman's eyes peering over her mask, the nurse understands her patient is in distress. Glancing down at the tube, Isabel hopes to point her in the right direction. A small crimson circle has bloomed around the bandage stuck just above Isabel's right breast.

"Oh my, Mrs. Kelly. What's happened here?" Lifting the corner of the bandage, the nurse clucks her tongue. "Well, that's no good. No good at all. We're going to have to get Dr. Fitzgerald back in here to stitch that back up." The nurse squeaks across the room, returns with a syringe in hand.

Isabel's eyes feel too large for her head.

"No," Isabel's protest is a faint whistle through a dry reed.

"You won't want to feel those stitches being repaired, my dear. Trust me. Now stop fussing." The nurse dexterously plunges the needle into Izzy's arm. The giant hand of helplessness scrapes her off the bed, hurdles her into flashes of being lashed with the stick, kneeling on coarse salt, lying in blood-soaked bedsheets. Izzy tries to hold fast to the mint green curtain breathing around her while her body lurches back, caught in the memory of falling. Tumbling from her wheelchair onto the fresh earth of her parents' grave, clawing with her childhood hands through the odour of damp dirt, the wailing of a woman a few burial mounds away, and Aelish wrapped around Izzy, a protective shell. The sedation finally and mercifully presses her far beneath all of this.

3

AELISH, APRIL 1955

AELISH IS AS TATTERED AS THE BROWN BAG SHE CARRIES down the walkway from the ship. Despite being on steady ground, she sways, her insides tilting. Throughout the final three days of sea passage, Aelish prayed nonstop, often lying belly down on the floor of her room, the ship pitching on an ill-tempered sea. She worried about the two young girls she met on the deck and said a few extra devotions, petitioning Saint Agnes and Saint Christopher for their safety. The waters finally calmed as the ship neared St. John's Harbour in Newfoundland.

It is early morning, and the sunrise on the harbour's edge is blinding after the cabin's confined dimness. Aelish shades her eyes, watches the gulls swarm the fishing boats returning, loaded with an early-morning catch. When her sight adjusts, she wonders if the ship's captain mistakenly turned them around at some point, bringing everyone straight back to Belfast Harbour. The craggy land rising behind the wharf, the weather-worn fishing shacks around the bay confuse Aelish with their alikeness.

Her bag suddenly seems too heavy despite its meagre contents, so she sets it at her feet, rubs her low back. With eyes shut, she hopes to slow the sloshing in her stomach. Something bumps Aelish's hip and knocks her into a teetering sidestep. Catching her balance at the edge of the dock, Aelish see the young girl, the sassy one who saved her from falling into the ocean, whizz past, her jet-black hair in a wild tangle. She runs into a flock of milling gulls. They explode in all directions, shocked by her uncaged energy.

"My apologies, Sister," a woman calls from behind. "They've been cooped up and horribly misbehaved." The woman's complexion has a pea soup–tinge, and her hat sits crooked on a messy nest of brown hair. She has the look of a soldier returned from battle.

"Go fetch your sister before she falls into the water, Lord help us," the tired mother says to the less rambunctious older child at her side.

"Maybe we should let her fall in," the girl mutters as she stomps down the dock.

"My apologies once again, Sister. Please pray for me—patience, Dear Lord, patience." The worn mother attempts to smooth her hair as though Aelish deserves a tidy presence. *You should see what mess lies beneath this habit,* she thinks.

Aelish folds her lips together, not wanting to smile amid this poor woman's trials, but she can't help but feel a twinge of excitement thinking about Isabel's children.

"Of course I will pray for you. Patience, peace, and perhaps some time alone with a warm cup of tea," she says. "Or would you prefer something stronger than tea?" The woman blinks and recoils slightly, then her stiff shoulders drop.

"Yes, indeed, Sister. Perhaps one shot of whiskey . . . and an extra for that one." She points to the wild one, deftly dodging her older sibling. The laughter Aelish shares with the bedraggled mother is refreshing. The woman's colour has returned to her cheeks by the time she gathers the pile of bags around her and trudges away.

"Thank you, Sister. God bless you," she calls back over her shoulder.

"And you as well." Aelish means to call after her, let the woman know about the generous rip in the back of her skirt, but decides to save her that one extra bother.

"Aelish?" a man calls out. For a moment, it's confusing to hear her name. *I wonder how anyone in this strange place would recognize me.* And then she looks down at her robe. *I'm a penguin among seagulls.* Aelish doesn't visually recognize the tall thin man walking toward her; however, the tingle on her arms is full of remembering. Declan's hair is still a chestnut mop with thick chunks poking out from under his knit cap. As he steps closer, Aelish can see his eyes still hold the youth of their childhood, but the worry in them makes her clasp the cross at her chest.

"How is she? How is my sister?" she blurts before even acknowledging him.

"She'll be relieved to see you. Izzy's been asking after you every day since Sister Mike told us you were on your way."

Declan folds Aelish into his embrace and squeezes her to his chest. Her spine stiffens, she has no idea what to do with her arms, and then her eyes well with all the relief of hearing her sister is alive. There is also the terrible despair of not having felt the protective shelter of a man's body since the age of ten. Aelish peels herself out of his arms before her body has the mind to let go and collapse at his feet. Declan steps away, hastily scoops up the worn bag.

"Let me get this for you. Is this all you have?" He holds the baggage at arm's length, then smirks. "I guess you don't need a heap of clothes, do ya, Aelish?"

That mischievous smirk turns him back into a teenager. *I should correct him,* she thinks, *let him know my name is now Sister Clare.* But something young inside enjoys hearing him repeat her birth name.

The last time he said her name was in the frigid schoolroom—they were fifteen. She and Izzy had gotten their first period the day before—Izzy in the morning and Aelish in the evening. Izzy was always first.

The pier under her sensible brown shoes lists to one side, and Aelish sidesteps, catching herself. She is relieved Declan is looking skyward and not seeing her mind wander back to their childhood.

"Well, ya don't see that every day!" Declan swings her bag toward the end of the pier. "There, do you see it? It's an albatross." Spotting the large seabird perched on a post, Aelish nods, unsure why the excitement. It looks to her like an overfed seagull. "We don't see those here, not much at all. Did ya know they can fly for days on a single flap of their wings? Wings as wide as this dock." Declan whistles and reaches his arms out. "My ma would say it's a good omen. Storms been giving the fishing boats a right lashing lately, maybe a sign of friendlier seas."

The comfort of his conversation is both peculiar and intoxicating. Aelish brings a hand to the heat on the back of her neck.

"Is that so?" she replies, trying to cover the anxious need to see Isabel. She was never good at hiding anything. She turns away, shades her eyes again, hoping to also conceal the wonder of how different her life would be had she not shoved Declan away all those years ago. All because she was a foolish embarrassed girl. The warmth from her neck crowds her face.

Declan tromps ahead in his tall green wellies, and Aelish hurries to keep up with his long stride as they head toward a collection of vehicles onshore. Wanting to have faith in Declan's mother—her belief in good omens—Aelish looks back to the albatross, sees it is indeed rather majestic, and hopes it is more than just a seabird come to rest.

AELISH, 1946

"FRESH AIR IS THE BEST WAY TO KEEP THE LUNG FEVER AWAY," Teacher had proclaimed. Open windows all around the school room lets the frigid air barge in. At fifteen, Aelish dreamed of being a teacher just like Ma, but vowed always to have a warm, cosy classroom for her students, complete with blankets and hot tea.

So far, no one in the class had gotten tuberculosis, not even the home babies. The small boy seated next to Aelish, who may have been eight or a very runty ten, swaddled his arms over his rasping chest. His nose was running again, and he reached his tongue up to catch the wet trail coming from his left nostril. Aelish worried about them, the home babies, the kids who came from the mother and baby home over the hill. Teacher made them wait outside until all the other students were seated before letting them file into the desks at the back of the room. Some of them shivered year-round, sickly with dark circles under their eyes. The other kids didn't talk much to these little ones, as if they were the cause of every bad thing that happened in Ireland. Aelish always tried to include them.

"Can you help me with my reading again at lunch today, Aelish?" The sound of Declan Kelly's adolescent voice created a riot of extra goose bumps across her arms and shoulders. And evaporated any thoughts of the home babies.

Declan Kelly was a year older. Aelish had kept a secret from Izzy for an entire year and regretted it. What Aelish didn't tell: the first time she saw him, a spinning sensation filled her head, and her heart suddenly felt two sizes too large.

Despite his never getting the math problems correct and speaking his words backward while reading, Aelish liked Declan Kelly's smile from the start. It was warm and kind, and it made Aelish feel as though he might understand her, maybe even like her. She looked forward to tutoring him more than anything else.

She turned her head slightly and nodded, not daring to turn away from Teacher and get in trouble. School was easy, safe for Aelish, and she wanted to keep it that way. When Aelish turned forward again, Isabel was staring at her with narrowed eyes, tugging on the cord between them.

The teacher's bell tinkled. Everyone in the room folded their hands, closed their eyes, and bowed to pray before lunch. For a time, Aelish was silent, only mouthing the words so she could hear Declan's voice rolling over her shoulder. She hurried through her lunch, tasting nothing, the dry soda biscuit lodging in her throat. For once, she was relieved Izzy decided to eat with two other girls. The space that had been swelling between her and Izzy as they matured usually left her feeling transparent and vulnerable. But not that day.

"Are you ready, Aelish?" Declan stood in front of Aelish's desk, a reader hanging from his long fingers. There was dirt caked under his nails. A fast glance at his thin face was all that Aelish could manage, but in that shy glance, she noticed a light dusting of dark hairs on his upper lip. It seemed they'd sprouted overnight.

"Yes, always." Aelish bit the inside of her cheek, wanting to cut through her stupid words. Her hands shook as she pulled her chalkboard out. Declan slid into the desk next to hers and turned sideways, his legs so long that his kneecaps brushed Aelish's thigh. Aside from the two home babies hovering near the door, not wanting to go out into the cold in their tattered jumpers and flimsy hobnail boots, Aelish and Declan were alone.

"Did you practice reading the chapter I gave you last night? Were there any words you didn't understand?" Declan's eyebrows drew together, and his mouth hung open slightly. Aelish had to look away—from his discomfort, his sincerity, what she hoped was her future.

"Let's go back over what we did yesterday. You did so well with those words," she offered, wanting to save him from any humiliation.

He began to trace a finger over the words while reading aloud in a slow, disjointed march. Aelish watched his hand slide over the page.

Staring at the dirt under his wide fingernail, she wondered what sort of farm he lived on. Sheep? Cows? Definitely not pigs, because he didn't smell like the other boys whose families raise pigs. Declan smelled of the sea, Aelish had noticed this before. It was strange and wonderful that he would smell of something she loved when she knew he came from a farming family. This thought caused her stomach to tighten, and she wondered if Declan could smell the orphanage on her—a cloud of dusky incense wafting off her skin and sour mutton from her breath. The odour of her first monthly. Aelish turned her breathing into a thin shallow stream, covered her mouth, crossed her legs, then stuffed her fingers into her armpits.

When Declan came to the end of the page, he looked up at Aelish, his eyes so wide, white showed all around the moss-coloured ring. Aelish thought it was the purest kind of hopefulness she'd seen.

"Did I get them all right this time?" he asked, hesitant and eager.

Aelish had not heard every word he read, but she would rather be swallowed into the earth than tell him she had been too busy thinking about how he smelled to pay attention. She lied.

"That was perfect, Declan. Just perfect." She made a mental note to add lying to her list of confessions for the day.

Declan's grin lifted his oversized ears, and excitement brightened his eyes. Before Aelish could look away—not that she wanted to—Declan leaned over and pressed his lips to hers. He stayed there long enough for her to feel two of his warm breaths on her upper lip. Aelish was a statue bolted to her seat. Declan pulled away slowly, folded his lips over his teeth. He glanced down at the reader in front of him and pushed it forward on the desk with one finger. The place where his lips had touched hers buzzed, and she feared having a spell right on the spot. The swish in her ears was deafening.

"I would be an eejit and a waster for the rest of my life if it weren't for you helping me, Aelish. I might not have to stay on my da's farm if I can learn to read better and maybe go to college."

Stuffing her hands between her thighs, she resisted the overwhelming urge to take his hand in hers. Forever. Instead, she pushed her feet against the wood floor and blurted words that brought an instant spiky regret.

"You smell like the ocean."

The horror of her confession blazed in her body. Declan tilted his head as though he didn't hear correctly. It was all Aelish could hope for—that he did not just hear those stupid stupid words. Then she lied some more.

"My sister . . . she said you smell like ocean," Aelish uttered, and much too loud.

Aelish pressed her knuckle between her front teeth. The room reeled. Dust motes grew to the size of moths floating around Declan's head. There was an odour of onion as a trickle of sweat rolled from her armpit.

"Isabel talked about me?" He tilted his head.

Declan's confusion turning to curiosity sent Aelish's heart plummeting. *What have I done?* She wanted to run out of the room, but her legs were fused to the chair. She couldn't leave. She had to get Declan to go before she exploded into a million mortified fragments.

"Read the new chapter tonight," she said, abruptly shutting the reader.

He pulled back. "Oh, okay. But I was hoping we could do more . . . today. I like being your student." Although not sure, Aelish thought he sounded hurt. He stood, paused. "I mean it, Aelish, you're a real good teacher. Thank you."

She stared straight ahead, silent. He rose and walked away, hands crammed in his pockets. She blinked back the burn in her eyes until he passed the two home babies nestled together in the doorway and stepped outside, likely in search of Izzy.

The weight of her head, the squeeze on her heart, it was all too much. She folded her arms on the desk and buried her fevered face. Aelish imagined Declan searching the schoolyard for her twin sister and wondered how it was possible to have the most wonderful thing and the most crushing thing happen all at once.

AELISH, APRIL 1955

DECLAN'S OLD TRUCK ROLLS TO A STOP IN FRONT OF ST. JOHN'S sanatorium, then backfires. He pats the dashboard, consoling an old dying friend.

"She may be in rough shape, but she just doesn't give up," he says, staring out the cracked windscreen. Aelish knows he isn't talking only about his rusted-out truck. Her legs grow antsy, unable to wait another minute.

"Aelish, hold on," Declan calls as she hurries to the front doors. "Slow down." He catches her with only a few strides, squeezes her arm. "I need to tell you—Izzy's had an operation." The word *operation* stops her.

"But she has tuberculosis. What operation? Why would they operate on Izzy? I thought you said she was up and about? Eating?" Aelish says, turning back to Declan, feeling misled.

Declan buries his hands deep in the pockets of his stained work pants. He stares down at the toes of his sloppy boots, looking like the boy she sent out into the schoolyard.

"Just two days ago Izz was doing so well, but she got worse just like that." Declan snaps his fingers, startling Aelish. "They . . . the doctors said it would help. They said they do it for most people with consumption around here. In Newfoundland and Labrador, the doctors can't seem to get this god-awful plague under control." Losing patience, Aelish heads up the steps for the doors.

With a shaking hand, she takes a mask from a fresh young nurse who studies Aelish's veil, likely wondering how the string will fit around the cumbersome materials.

"I'll just hold it like this." Aelish places it over her nose and mouth. The suffocation is swift. The thin layer of paper over her mouth becomes the stinking rubber gas mask of her childhood—the gas mask that did nothing to save her family. Biting down on the tender inside of her cheek stops the mind movie of Isabel lying in the decimated doorway of their Donegall Street home—her flannel nightgown twisted around her body, Da buried under busted bricks, and Ma's hand being strangely far from her arm.

"I can't wear that." Aelish shoves the mask back at the nurse, then kisses the crucifix hanging from her neck.

The timid nurse is left holding the mask out in front of her as Aelish walks through a set of swinging doors. Declan is tying his mask as he walks behind. Glancing back and seeing it strapped over his mouth and nose, Aelish wheezes.

She stops, a hand to her throat, when she spots Isabel in the farthest corner of the room. Her sister's body hardly creates a bump under the blankets. The sight of her twin makes no sense. Her skin is ashen. There is a tube poking out of her chest. The sound of Isabel's breathing is watery and desperate.

"She has good days and not so good days. Sometimes they give her sedatives to keep her calm . . . better recovery. That's what they say." Declan's eyes well, his voice full of apology.

When Izzy turns her head, it's with the effort of pushing a mountain. She blinks several times, then smiles. Her lips move to form the name *Aelish,* but her voice is too feeble to carry any sound. Aelish convinces her legs to walk, and there it is—their connection—growing stronger with every step, the rope thickening.

The bellows of Aelish's chest suddenly feel collapsed; the world around goes grainy. She's plugged in, once again, to the inner workings of her twin. *What suffers her suffers me. I deserve this discomfort for turning her away all these years.*

For the first time since donning the black robes five years ago, Aelish is swallowed by the urge to rip them off so she can breathe, so that there is no barrier between them.

Then Aelish hears Sister Edel's chastising voice say, *Your life belongs to the Lord.*

Instead of crawling into the bed and holding Isabel like she wants to, Aelish takes her hand. It's as thin as the letter that slipped from her fingers, only to be swallowed by the ocean.

"I've missed you." Isabel's chest heaves between each word. She squeezes Aelish's fingers; the feebleness of it is overwhelming. Even the whispers of red in Izzy's dark hair are dull.

"I've missed you too, Isabel, and I'm Sister Clare now." Aelish fingers the knotted rope hanging at her waist. Despite Isabel's weakness of body, her willfulness courses up Aelish's arm in prickles.

"You will always be Aelish to me," she says.

This defiant declaration is soon broken by Izzy's ragged cough. Aelish covers her mouth not to keep the disease away but to contain her anger. *If you had stayed with me, I could have kept you safe.* These words sit on the tip of Aelish's tongue, a bitter taste.

"We can't stay too long," Declan mumbles from behind his mask. "The nurses keep our visits short; besides, your face isn't covered, Aelish . . . I mean Clare . . . Sister." Declan twists his knit cap in his hands.

"Go meet the babies, Aelish." Isabel draws a raspy inhale. "Go hold them for me and come back tomorrow and tell me how beautiful they are. Tell me how they smell."

The softness that settles through Izzy's being, the mothering words she uses transform her into a perfect stranger. She is a woman experiencing a magnitude of love of which Aelish has no concept. When Aelish touches her sister's cheek, her eyes close. Izzy presses into her twin's palm as if resting for the first time in a long while.

"I'll pray to the Virgin Mother for you, Izzy. I'll ask her to bring you back to your children." Perhaps too tired to fight, Isabel nods her head. "Mother Mary knows the pain of being separated from her child. She'll look after them."

"You need to look after them, Aelish. You need to," Isabel says with eyes still closed, then her chest drops into a shallow, even rise and fall. Her grip on Aelish's hand goes limp. Declan touches Aelish's shoulder, and she is surprised by her wanting to lean into his touch; instead, she draws her shoulders back, lifts her chin.

"She does that when the sedatives kick in." Declan looks to the floor. "She just falls asleep. We better go, let her rest." Aelish draws a tiny cross on Isabel's forehead, on her slightly parted lips and her chest. "Let's go meet your niece and nephew," Declan says.

Walking away from Isabel's room is an arduous swim against a swift current. At the same time, there is a strange warmth in Aelish's chest. It's then she realizes she is thinking of Isabel's babies, wanting to see their identical perfect mouths, fingers, and feet. She is longing to know this smell that soothes her sister.

Patrick and Sarah, Aelish hears Izzy say from the secret corner of her mind. It's been so long since she has heard Izzy from the inside, it makes her jump a little.

Declan glances at her, then asks, "You okay?"

"What are their names . . . the babies?" Aelish asks.

"Izzy insisted on calling them Sar and Paddy. Sarah Aelish and Patrick Declan. After you and your parents, of course."

Aelish plunks down into a plastic chair in the hall, likely set there for just such a purpose—to catch the weight of anguish. She wants to cry. She wants to laugh. But does neither. Instead, she sets her forehead into her palms and listens for more of Izzy's voice in her head. There is only silence. And the prodding ghost of the acorns she kept wrapped in Sister Mike's hanky and tucked under her young spine. The biting memory of acorns is replaced by the tentative touch of Declan's hand. Feeling his touch, Aelish thinks, *It's strange to miss something you never had.*

To help wipe away the awkwardness, Aelish gathers herself tall, nods at her new brother-in-law, and heads for the front door. On the way out, she turns to Declan and says, "We'll need to have a chat with her doctor about those sedatives. Izzy's way too stubborn for the likes of those. She'll fight them all the way, and that will do her more harm than good."

AELISH, APRIL 1955

EVERYTHING NEAR THE EDGE OF THE OCEAN IN THE VILLAGE OF Pouch Cove is scoured by salty sea air. Even the bold red and bright blue houses fight to hold their primary hues. The outside of Isabel's simple square home is no exception. The white clapboards are bubbled and cracked, having been painted over and over. Aelish has never tried to imagine what Izzy's home would look like; in fact, she didn't know if she had a home. Praying for her soul every day, she not once thought to ask that Isabel have the warmth and shelter of a house.

"Home sweet home," Declan says, opening the front door, standing aside. "And just a heads-up, if ya want to get on with the locals, it's pronounced 'pooch' Cove, not 'pouch.' Although I'm sure they'd cut you a break, being a nun and all." He points at her veil.

"I'll keep that in mind." When Aelish hears mewling sounds of helplessness from in the house her heart gives a strange blissful lurch. Disturbed by the tingling across her breasts, she pulls the robe away from her chest.

Unlike the dull, worn outside of Isabel's home, the inside looks like one of Ma's paint palettes all messy with colour. Bright knitted blankets lie across tired furniture. Hand-braided rugs of sunny yellow, turquoise, and emerald are like tossed puzzle pieces over scuffed honey-coloured floorboards. The kitchen walls are the colour of butter. So taken by the colourful space, Aelish doesn't notice the plump woman sitting in a wooden rocker by the front window until she speaks.

"How did ya find the missus today, Declan?" She holds a tiny cocoon in the crook of each arm as she glides forward and back. The woman is all roundness—round face, round cheeks, round eyes, a perfectly shaped snowy bun on her head, and a round torso to hold it all.

"She's stubborn and giving them all a hard time," Declan says, then splays a hand toward Aelish as if she is a long-lost artefact. "This is Izzy's sister Aelish—I mean Sister Clare." Declan snaps his fingers at his mistake. "This is Mrs. Doolin from up the hill."

"How'd you do, Sister?" the woman says in an accent that sounds Irish worn down at the edges. The woman dips her head as a sign of respect. "And please call me Gabby. This one"—she juts her chin at Declan—"insists on calling me Mrs. Doolin, but that was me mother-in-law." She raises her eyes to the ceiling. "God rest her, but she was a mean-spirited goat and a genuine pain in most everyone's arse, and I'd rather not be compared."

"Fair enough, Gabby it is, then. And may Mrs. Doolin's goat-ish soul rest in peace," Aelish says, then feels the room sway. The swishing in her skull forces her to clutch the back of a wooden chair. "I'm afraid the crossing got the better of me."

Declan grabs Aelish's elbow, then guides her onto the chair. "I'll get you some water," he says, then walks a few steps to the kitchen sink and the multitude of baby bottles lining the counter-top. Studying his back steadies Aelish like the horizon did on the swaying ship.

"Take off those boots, young man. This is a house, not a fishing boat," Gabby calls out as any good mother would, then turns to Aelish and asks, "Would you like to hold him?"

"Pardon?" Aelish rubs her palms together, feeling a slick of sweat on them.

"Him? Or her?" She holds the cocoons out, first the blue, then the pink. Seeing them suspended, unsecured makes Aelish suck in a breath. "They're an armload both at once, and I take it you've not had much practice with the little ones, have ya?" She leans forward and hoists herself out of the rocker with a grunt. When Mrs. Doolin holds out the pink bundle, the first thing Aelish sees of her niece is one impossibly dainty, rosy finger sticking out of the folds of cotton. Her heart lurches.

"Go on now, Sister," Mrs. Doolin says with a grin, "I'm sure you've carried heavier burdens than these dear-hearts. Go on."

Aelish slides an arm under the blanket. Her arms feel weak and fierce at once. The warmth coming from this tiny creature envelops Aelish. Looking nervously from the cheery older woman to the sleeping infant against her chest, Aelish scarcely draws a breath, afraid that it will disturb this perfection. The baby curls and uncurls one tiny finger. Aelish kisses the precious dimples across the back of her hand.

"Who does she favour?" Declan's voice startles Aelish; she jerks, scaring the baby. Her niece gives a drawn-out squeak.

"Certainly not me at the moment," Aelish says, watching the babe's scalp shift from pleasant pink to an angry ruddy red. Her squeak turns into an astonishing roar of discontent. Aelish hurriedly passes the child into her father's arms.

Declan balances his little girl on the length of his forearm, his long thumb and fingers wrapping right the way around her skull. He strides to the door and slips out of his boots.

"Hey, precious girl," he coos. "You hush now, or you'll scare Auntie Aelish away." Declan glances up and grins. "We just got her here, and we don't want her to leave, now do we." Aelish is hypnotized by his soothing sway-bounce. So too is the wee girl, as the noise from inside the blanket falls silent. Gulls cry from the harbour below. She looks down at the tips of her tight black shoes peeking out from under the hem of her robe. Her toes are cramped, bound. She longs to stand barefoot on the soft bumps of the hand-woven rug under her feet. Suddenly Aelish remembers watching Ma paint in the kitchen just two days before the bombs fell. It was a garden of violets she was bringing to life. The sound of her brushstrokes across a canvas, soothing. "I love the smell of purple," Aelish told her mother. When Mammy laughed that day, it made Aelish shoulders and arms feel soft, just as they do now. It dawns on Aelish: *That was the last day I felt safe outside of God's fortified walls. Until now.*

"Sister Clare? Are ya feelin' okay?" Gabby Doolin asks. At the sound of her chosen name, Aelish's shoulders turn rigid again, eyes blinking against the light in the room that is suddenly too bright.

"I think I need to have a lay-down if you don't mind." She pries the tight material away from her chin, wanting nothing more than to be somewhere private and remove all the binding.

"We're a little shy on space, so you'll have to use our room." Declan points to a door at the end of a short hall. "I haven't been in there much since Izzy's been away. I've been sleeping here on the couch with these two close by. It's just easier."

"I can see it's taking a toll on you, young man." Gabby looks Declan up and down. "Tommy tells me you've been a bit careless around the fishing boats. Sleeping on your feet. You wanna watch yourself there. And eat that casserole I put in the fridge."

Watching the woman ooze motherly tenderness at everyone, Aelish is embarrassed by her earlier predictions. The woman is anything but thick-skinned and unfriendly.

"Come, Sister." She cups Aelish's elbow, leading her down the hall. "I'll get ya settled in." As they walk, she pats Aelish's forearm. The familiarity of that simple gesture, the comforting scuff of the woman's slippers make Aelish want to cry. There is a desperate ache to remain at her sister's side, be near Isabel's children, Isabel's life, and the people in it.

AELISH, APRIL 1955

AELISH CALLED SISTER MIKE EARLIER IN THE DAY FROM THE general store on the way home from the hospital. She let her know of her safe arrival, news of Isabel's condition, and so many still suffering from lung fever on this rugged edge of Canada. However, she decides to fight the weariness and write to Sister Mike of all the things there was no time to say. Sitting at her sister's dressing table with pen and paper, Aelish writes.

My Dearest Mother Superior,

The scratches and broken corners of my sister's dresser, the haze on her mirror tell me this item came to her well used. Everything in this room looks worn out. Everyone here looks tired—Izzy, of course, and poor Declan. The babies are the only ones with any energy, especially when they cry. Oh, Sister Mike, the sound of their crying is a strange choir and will take some getting used to.

I look at myself in the foggy glass for the first time in years, and I pray the Lord does not mistake this for vanity. How silly of me to even assume our intentions could fool our God. My wimple and veil are set aside, and I have the same tired look as my sister's belongings. The only difference being the lightness all around me.

My sister's life is humble, and some would even say poor. But the lightness I feel here in her house is something I've not experienced, at least not since being a little girl at home with my parents.

Is it wrong to have such a feeling when my sister is so desperately ill and when I am away from the abbey, my daily communion with the Lord?

Perhaps it is the exhaustion from my travels and the stress of feeling helpless in the face of Izzy's illness that has me muddleheaded. I know I do not have to ask this of you, but please pray for Isabel, her two precious children, and her husband. I will write again soon with updates. If it is God's will, there will be positive reports.

Sincerely and with the love of God,
Sister Clare

Setting the pen aside, Aelish glances at her reflection one more time. She does not see herself; she sees her twin sister. *It's always been that way,* she thinks, being mistaken for Isabel; rarely was it the other way around. Everyone saw Isabel.

A flat, wide hairbrush sits on the dressing table; tangled in its bristles are a few long strands of auburn hair. When she runs the soft brush through her own wavy chestnut shoulder-length hair, Aelish closes her eyes and imagines she has more.

The bristles against her scalp are an intense pleasure; she shivers. An image of her twin sister and Declan forms in Aelish's head as slow as a ground mist rising. He runs the brush through Isabel's silken hair as she sits in front of the dressing table. In Aelish's imagination, her sister carries the look of a contented cat, and when he bends to place a light kiss upon her scalp, a cascade of warmth runs down Aelish's back and pools at the bottom of her backbone. The sensation is familiar. Simultaneously soothing and unsettling; difficult for Aelish to house in her black-and-white world.

"We were fifteen," Aelish says, her voice more in than out. Her thoughts are falling backward.

By that age, a fissure had grown between the twins. A fissure which cracked into a gaping canyon when, without permission, Isabel unloaded her confession onto Aelish. Isabel didn't ask for permission, ever. Isabel rested her forehead against the back of Aelish's skull in her narrow cot, in the dark of the orphanage, and all the images of Isabel's day at the shore with Declan slid directly into the space behind Aelish's eyes. The tang of sea air filled up the hollows of her nose. Seagulls crying and waves stumbling onto shore rolled into her ears. When Isabel whispered all the details of what she and the boy had done on the sand, tucked behind a tall black rock, the sort of rock Aelish and Izzy would have played on as little girls, Aelish was gripped by an aching deep in her belly and hips. Her body froze in place. Aelish was forced to clamp a hand over her mouth, unsure if it were her or Izzy's body spinning and throbbing. Pictures of the two of them in the sand, doing what they did, bumped through Aelish's teenage body even as she shuttered her eyes tight and prayed. She got out of bed, leaving Isabel behind, and padded to the statue of the Virgin Mother standing guard at the far end of the dormitory. There she knelt in the shadow of Mary and the snake. There she prayed the words she would most regret: *Dear Virgin Mother, please show Isabel the error of her ways.*

"Aelish?" a deep voice calls through the door. She tosses the brush onto the dresser and sends some of her sister's scant treasures toppling to the floor. "Is everything okay in there?" Declan asks.

"Yes, yes, of course," Aelish says much too quickly.

"Could I bother you for something? I think little Paddy's blanket is in there, and he won't settle without it."

Uncertain how she didn't hear it before, she suddenly realizes the babe's wailing has filled the house. Glancing around, Aelish sees a crocheted blanket in the corner. She scoops the blanket up and opens the door. Declan takes a step back, his eyes widen, then he quickly glances down. That's when Aelish remembers: *I am exposed.* She wants to run back to the bed for her veil. Desperate to cover her self-consciousness, Aelish reaches for her head.

"You look . . ." Declan stammers. "Just like Izzy. I forgot."

Him staring as though Aelish were something extraordinary unanchors her. The weaving feel of sea legs returns, forcing her to clutch the doorway. Wee Paddy's cries take on a new pitch of shrill desperation.

"Sorry to bother you. I'll let you rest." Declan shrugs, surrendering to fatherhood. "That is, if you can with all the complaining going on out here." Declan stops, his back turned, the blanket dangling in his hand. He asks, "Did Izz ever talk about how she was feeling?" Declan turns and studies Aelish with worried eyes.

He scrubs the patchy stubble on his face. "In the letters she wrote you, did she ever say anything that seemed off?"

Aelish scans her memory, but the time spent poring over Izzy's letters on the ship is hazed with seasickness. "Besides marrying you and having twins?" Declan chuckles at her attempted humour.

"Did she talk about not . . ." He hesitates, then drapes the blanket over his shoulder. "Not doing so good?"

"I only found out she wasn't well when I read the letter you sent to Sister Mike," Aelish replies. He shakes his head a little as if he is about to clarify himself. Just then, Sarah joins her brother's unhappy chorus from the living room.

"Duty calls," Declan says as he heads down the hall to his children.

Follow him, pursue the subject, says the strong voice in Aelish's mind. But the part that knows Isabel from top to bottom and senses that her sister's pain is beyond that of lung fever is too tired . . . too scared.

"Let me help," she says. "I think I'm too tired to sleep."

Declan glances over his shoulder, and relief softens the lines across his forehead. "Thanks, Sister Clare, but only if you're sure." When he uses her chosen religious name, there is a dropping disappointment in her chest, followed by a stab of guilt.

With Paddy on his chest Declan paces and bounces and shushes around the dim-lit living room. By the look of the orange strokes threading the horizon, it is early dusk.

"God bless their innocent souls," Aelish whispers, swaying Sar side to side, caressing her downy cheek.

Declan begins to sing. The sound stops Aelish mid-sway.

I see the moon, and the moon sees me
Shining though the branches of the old oak tree
Oh, let the light that shines on me
Shine on the one I love

Aelish joins him, singing softly,

Over the mountain, over the sea,
Back where my heart is longing to be

The clench in her throat threatens to end the lullaby, but Declan carries on.

Oh, let the light that shines on me
Shine on the one I love

One of Aelish's tears plops onto wee Sarah's forehead, runs down the side of her silken temple. Aelish places her lips to the damp spot on the baby's high round forehead.

Declan continues to hum as he sets a quieted Paddy into the wicker bassinet. When he takes Sarah from Aelish's arms, a coldness rushes into the spot where she held the infant. With the babies tucked into baskets, Declan's thin back rounds and his shoulders droop.

"Go sleep, Declan. I'll clean up the bottle factory in the kitchen."

"If you don't mind, I could use it. Have to be up and on the boat before the sun. Mrs. Doolin will be back soon to mind the babies."

"Go on, then, you do look like death warmed, dear brother-in-law. And I'll do my best to help Mrs. Doolin, although I'm afraid I'm a bit thick when it comes to babies." The embarrassment of being uncovered has softened.

Declan starts to walk away, his stockinged feet dragging, then he turns back and says, "Do you remember that day in the schoolhouse, you were helping me read—" He pauses, scratches his eyebrow, obscuring half his face. "And I *thanked you?*" His smile is uneasy. Aelish feels a burst of chaos inside, one she's not felt since that very day he *thanked* her. Touching her short hair, she wishes it were long again—like Izzy's. "I'm sorry," Declan continues. "I'm sorry I did that. It was wrong and I never should have kissed you. I'm sure you didn't tell Izzy, 'cause I never would have heard the end of it. You probably thought I was an eejit boy. Hell! I was an eejit boy." He shakes his head, chuckles, acting the way an adult should when reminiscing about childhood shenanigans—a foolishness long since gone.

Aelish is shocked at the feel of tumbling disappointment. *I'm sorry I did that . . . It was wrong.* Shocked to feel the messiness of fifteen all over again. *I never should have kissed you.* Shocked at how quickly she then tucks it all away, dismisses his words with a wave, and a forces smile that pains her.

"I still can't wrap me lame brains around how much you look like my Izz," Declan says, heading to the bedroom. Wanting to push that apology down further, Aelish is tempted to change the subject, ask Declan what he meant about Izzy not doing so good, but the way he shuffles, lethargic, toward his room—their room—lays her words aside for another time. Instead, she sits on a chair between the bassinets and attempts, with prayer, to block out his remorse for kissing her. Soon her prayers turn into a humming, then soft singing.

I hear the lark, and the lark hears me
singing from the branches of the old oak tree.

4

SISTER MARY MICHAEL, MAY 1955

"SHOULD I HAVE TOLD HER, CHARLIE? DID I DO THE RIGHT thing? Aelish refused to open all the other letters Isabel sent." Sister Mike watches Charlie Rose pry a rotting board off the garden shed behind the abbey. Sweat stains the back of his shirt in a half circle. He's gotten thicker, she notices. His waist, arms, and shoulders bulkier. *We are in our late fifties, after all,* she surmises.

"This whole shed should be pulled down, a new one built. I can do it as quick as ya like. It's been here so long I think Jesus built it," he says, clearly ignoring Sister Mike.

He throws the decaying wood aside, and Sister Mike jumps to the right to avoid being nicked on the ankle. "Watch yourself there, Sister." Although she cannot see it, there's a smirk in his voice.

"You know we don't have the budget for a new shed. Answer me, did I do the right thing telling Aelish about that letter from Declan? It came to me; it was written to me."

Charlie grumbles as a second board disintegrates in his hands.

"Rotten," he declares, slipping his gloves off and slapping them against his thigh. When he turns to Sister Mike, it's as though he is surprised to see her still standing there. *The man is exasperating on his best days,* Sister Mike thinks.

"Oh, for the love of Pete, Fiona," Charlie exclaims, running a forearm across his sweaty brow. "Why are ya asking a daft bugger like me? Go ask God or a saint or somethin'. It's not my business. You're not my business . . ." His voice drops when he adds, "Haven't been for a very long time." Sister Mike knows the man does not realize he's used her given name—Fiona. He does it from time to time when he's bothered by something. The deep fold between his heavy dark eyebrows announces that today, she is the bother.

"I'm sorry, Charlie. You're right. I should not be bugging you with this sort of thing. It's just that—" She pauses, weighing her words. "You've always had such good judgement."

"Why are ya callin' her Aelish, by the way? Isn't she Sister Clare?" He points out Sister Mike's blurred perspective, having stood too close to the twins all these years. To add more salt, Charlie mutters, "I thought I had good judgement too at one point. Guess I was wrong." Just as his careless tossing of wood had, these words force Sister Mike back a step.

It's been years since his hurt has shown itself. She thinks to ask him why he chose to stay on as caretaker all these years if his pain is so close to the surface, then thinks the better of it. *I don't need to hear it.*

Charlie pulls a rusted nail from one of the boards and deposits it into his shirt pocket. Sister Mike is walking away, leaving him be, when he says, "What did Sister Edel say."

It's not a question. His tone is gruff, impatient. Keeping her distance, Sister Mike replies, "Nothing much these days, and even if she was speakin', I wouldn't ask her. If I'm lacking perspective, she's completely blind." Charlie's chuckle lightens her heart just a bit.

"I'd want to know," Charlie says, then shrugs. "And I think Sister Clare would have wanted to know if her sister is in a troubled way."

"Yes, but what if while Sister Clare is in Newfoundland, she decides to leave the sisterhood and stay with Isabel?" Sister Mike is a bit shocked by this buried fear. But then again, that's the reason she came to Charlie; like that rusted nail in his pocket, he has a way of pulling the truth, even if it hurts.

Charlie holds his back as he stoops to pick up his hammer from the grass. When he stands and locks eyes with Sister Mike, she pulls off her glasses and pretends to clean them. The man becomes a blurry Charlie-looking outline.

"She's a grown woman." His voice sinks with sadness. "She'll choose whatever her heart wants. But I don't have to tell you that." The fuzzy outline of him bends again. Sister Mike puts her glasses back on when she hears the screech of more obstinate nails being dragged out of wood. Charlie is down on one knee, turned away, gloves on.

Sister Mike reaches out to lay a hand on his shoulder but, at the last second, pulls it all in—the touch, the affection, the need to fix the heart she broke all those years ago. Taking two steps back, her hands locked together and where they belong, she says, "Thank you, Charlie. You're a good man."

Charlie stops, a nail head in the claw ready to be wrenched. Sister Mike watches his shoulders expand and soften with each breath. He does not look her way when he says, "If ya don't mind, I'd like to get this done. And I'm sure you've got plenty to do, being Mother Superior and all."

Sister Mike knows using her title puts her firmly in her place, a safe distance from unhealed wounds, unpulled nails. And although she knows she would choose this life again and again, she cannot ignore the sting of being shoved away. It reminds her that everything she holds dear, although godly, sits on a cliff of human fallibility.

As Sister Mike walks across the lawn still damp from yesterday's rain, she stops to slip out of her sandals and burrows her toes into the grass. Reaching into her robe, she feels for the missing folded letter she carried for several days before giving it to Sister Clare. A single sheet of stationery should not have been so heavy.

She is unsure whether she is relieved or anxious it is gone, across the ocean.

An image of Aelish as a panic-stricken ten-year-old child clutching a bundle of acorns wrapped in a hanky rises in her mind, Aelish's young face a collection of sharp worried angles that would become part of her beauty—their beauty—as the twins aged.

Young Aelish pleaded for answers. "When will Izzy be well enough, Sister? Why can't I stay in hospital with her? I must take care of her now . . . Mammy and Daddy are gone. They're gone, right? To heaven?" During that time, with Hitler's war creating so many orphans to care for, Sister Mike had been hollow, void of answers. Instead, she held the girl tight, loosened her braids, and rocked the child to a fitful sleep, acorns clutched in her small hands.

Sister Mike looks back at Charlie Rose and whispers, "Mother Mary, go with Aelish's heart." As an afterthought, she adds, "And be here with mine." She pulls open the abbey door, thinking: *These walls cannot keep out our history or our heartbreak.*

SISTER EDEL, MAY 1955

WHILE DR. GIBBS, THE OLD FOOL, FLITS ABOUT HER BED, TAKING her blood pressure, pressing a frigid stethoscope against her chest, Sister Edel searches for any bodily residue—vigorous movement in her legs, arms, lungs—of the last few walks she took in the rain with Sister Mary Michael. Could it really have been some ten years back? It seems her muscles have turned amnesic.

"Breathe deep, very gooood," Dr. Gibbs coos, as though she's six, not sixty-three.

Sister Mary Michael stands in the corner of the room, nodding whenever the doctor assesses the obvious. She's not needed here.

Sister Edel is quite able to comprehend doctor-speak, especially coming from a simpleton like Gibbs. And then it dawns on her: the fumbling doctor asked Sister Mary Michael to be in the room as a buffer of sorts, perhaps as his moral support. Something about this pleases her.

Dr. Gibbs snaps the metal closure on his black bag. She notices the slight tremor in his left hand. *Fear or drink?* she wonders. Then takes note of the tracks of thin red lines on his bulbous nose. *I'd be off my nut to believe there isn't a generous flask in that bag,* she surmises.

It is the fourth time this year Sister Edel has had to tolerate his irksome presence in her room. She watches the saggy waddle under his narrow jaw—it looks very much like his tired leather medical bag. Lying supine and as wide as a road, she longs to be free of the rheumatism, which as a child was an annoyance and has since become a cage.

"Well, you'll likely never walk again, but you can certainly get some exercise moving your arms around." The man swings his scrawny limbs around like an imbecilic windmill. Stunned, Sister Edel decides his stupidity deserves no comment. Even Sister Mary Michael looks amused, a casual hand covering her mouth.

The man looks down at the hefty nun while pinching his dimpled chin. She knows what he is doing; she has dealt with blowhard priests day in and day out for decades. If she could stand, she would step nose-to-nose just to see the old doctor waver in his attempt to intimidate her, reduce her—and in her own bedroom of all places. The gall.

"Well?" she says. "Have you poked and prodded enough?" Sister Edel speaks dismissively. She's heard it all before and is rather bored with the medical soapbox routine.

"Sister Edel, you must take better care of your health." He has the nerve to reach out and pat her hand. "Your blood pressure is much too high, and those lungs don't sound good at all." Doctor Gibbs glances at Sister Mike. *The two of them are in this together,* Sister Edel thinks, *determined to put me in the grave.*

"She still smokes!" Sister Edel points at Sister Mike.

"This I know, and the reports are showing that smoking is indeed a bit harmful." The doctor clasps his lapels, stands a bit taller. "But I'm not here to see Sister Mary Michael. She is not the one with shortness of breath, headaches, and back pain."

"It's a touch of a cold. That's all there is to it," Sister Edel announces. She points at Sister Mike. "I'm sorry this one wasted your time, Doctor. She had no business bothering you to come out here." Sister Mary Michael places two fingers over her lips and looks out the window.

"I'm sure her concern is genuine. Please take the medications I've left on your bedside table. They will help with the swelling around the—"

"It's not swelling, it's fat." Sister Edel enjoys the feeling of hushing the man, even at her own expense. Flustered, Dr. Gibbs fetches his bag from the dresser, plunks his hat onto his head, and opens the door.

"See to it she takes the medication, Sister Mary Michael." The doctor walks out of Sister Edel's room as most do, slump-shouldered and chastised.

"No one need tell me when to take my medicine!" Sister Edel hollers this just a bit too loud down the quiet hall. A punishable offence for anyone else. Although she wishes she could stand and stare down Sister Mike, her nimble days have gone the way of seeing her own feet—a thing of the past.

Sister Mike is standing, hands folded. The nun's petiteness and her calmness bring Sister Edel's blood to a boil. It feels as though two puny persistent fists are punching the back of her eyes, first one and then the other. Pressing her thumb and finger into her eyelids slows the thumping.

"Why don't you rest, Sister," Sister Mary Michael suggests. Sister Edel's insides burn a little every time she is no longer referred to as Mother Superior. *Isabel McGuire took care of that,* she thinks. Her temples throb again. "Would you like me to read you the letter Sister Clare sent from Newfoundland? Isabel's babies are bright, happy, and determined to wear their auntie Aelish out." Sister Edel feels the clawing of her fury at the mention of Isabel McGuire.

"No. I do not want to hear about that girl and her illegitimate children." If Sister Edel could cross her arms over the mountain of her bosom, she most certainly would.

"Isabel and Declan are married—were before the children came along. They're hardly illegitimate."

"I bet they've not been baptized." Judging by Sister Mike's stunned, obtuse look, she's not given this devastating possibility much thought. No surprise to Sister Edel. *I've seen houseplants that are more observant,* she thinks, then shakes her head.

"I have no idea if they are baptized or not. That's up to their parents. And none of your business."

"Isabel McGuire doesn't have the sense God gave a goose," Sister Edel retorts. "Her leaving here was the best thing that could have happened. She belonged elsewhere, not here. She's an unfit mother if ever there was one."

"Shame on you!" Sister Mike exclaims. She points to the door and what—who—lay beyond. "None of these girls, past, present, or future, *belong* here. And what is this 'elsewhere'? You have no idea where Isabel went from here, what she suffered after this place."

Sister Edel looks out the window for a moment. An image of Kathleen's wide grin, the angelic sound of her singing voice rises like a speckled living photograph in her mind. It's been happening more and more as she lies ageing, petrifying.

"Sister Edel? You have no idea, right?"

Sister Edel clears her throat. Clears Kathleen. Clears Isabel McGuire. She still thinks of Sister Mary Michael as her subordinate and is bothered by her disrespect. What's more acute: she feels nettled head to foot by Sister Mary Michael's long-standing and blatant favour of Isabel McGuire, a girl determined, from day one, to throw her life into a handbasket headed straight for hell. Even though Sister Mary Michael is the acting Mother Superior, she has no idea what it takes to uphold the virtue of this place, let alone a good life, a good family. Sister Edel must blink away the picture of Kathleen once more. A bulky silence follows. Sister Edel knows they both went too far, but she is not about to admit it.

"Leave me be, Sister Mary Michael." She refuses to address her as Mother Superior. "I'm tired, and I need to rest. And you need to examine the enormous blind spot you've always had when it comes to those girls."

Not one for too much of a battle, Sister Mary Michael lets out a deep breath and turns to leave. She stops, one hand on the doorjamb. Keeping her back to Sister Edel, she hangs her head and, just above a whisper, says, "I cannot believe we are still goin' around about this after all these years. The McGuire twins are no longer girls."

Sister Edel watches as yet another person exits her room crestfallen. First that mealy Dr. Gibbs, now Sister Mary Michael. The voice reminding her *These people are here to help you* is far off and muffled by a thick layer of hardheadedness. Sister Edel closes her eyes, screws a mental lid onto the idea of remembering Kathleen. She then resumes the search within the unbending corridors of her being for any traces of those last aimless walks she took with Sister Mary Michael.

SISTER EDEL, 1945

SISTER EDEL HAD SLIPPED INTO HER RAINCOAT AND WELLIES, grabbed an umbrella, and was waiting, overheating. "You're slower than the second coming," she pointed out to Sister Mary Michael, who careened around the corner into the vestibule of the abbey, glasses askew. Sister Edel was the mother superior and could not imagine that Sister Mary Michael would one day take her place.

"I was helping one of the . . ." Sister Mary Michael paused. "The girls with—"

"You mean the twins," Sister Edel interjected. Any flimsy excuse for tardiness always created a crawl of frustration inside, particularly if it had to do with the McGuire twins. "Why do you insist on coddling those McGuire girls? They are no different from the others. At fourteen, they should be self-sufficient." The Mother Superior's irritation bloomed when she noticed a rather large splatter of something on Sister Mary Michael's chest. Likely from breakfast. "And speaking of self-sufficiency—you could stand to take a bit more pride in your appearance." She pointed at the mystery food, disgusted. "You're a mess."

Sister Mary Michael scratched at the stain, raised her finger to her nose, and announced as though solving a complex puzzle, "Oatmeal. And the pride cometh before the fall."

Sister Edel pushed the door open and stepped outside, no longer able to witness the discombobulated spectacle that was Sister Mary Michael. She'd been watching it since childhood, and it never changed.

"Remind me why we are out on this terrible day walking about aimless?" Sister Edel asked. The umbrella burst open like a jack-in-the-box, its insides caught by the wind. The Mother Superior stumbled forward, nearly falling to the muddy ground. Sister Mary Michael's smudged glasses were not near smudged enough to mask her amusement.

"It's good for our health to take a daily stroll," Sister Mary Michael informed her. "And it's a good way to show thanks for the war being over. We are free to roam!" She swept a hand up the lane as though Sister Edel had never seen the place before. "Besides that, you've been under too much pressure, and Dr. Gibbs says your blood pressure was far too high at your last check-up."

"You're a nun, Sister Mary Michael, you're not allowed to lie. I'm getting fat, and Dr. Gibbs has instructed you to walk me like some old heifer in the field."

Sister Mary Michael fell silent. It would have felt less painful if she'd laughed, or agreed even. Sister Edel's ankles and knees sang in pain with every step. Looking out across the hills of green spotted with grey knuckles of rock, Sister Edel wished she were able-bodied enough to stroll through them.

"I know they've started calling me Smelly Edelly," Sister Edel announced, pushing down on the childish hurt hovering below her starched surface. Sister Mary Michael remained quiet. They passed through the front gates and turned right onto the narrow, broken road. A mob of sheep huddled in the centre of the road ahead, seeming uncertain or content. With sheep, one cannot tell.

"They're children," Sister Mary Michael finally said, as though her superior needed a reminder. Tightening her grip on the umbrella handle woke the arthritic flare in Sister Edel's hands.

"They're spoiled," she corrected. "I know it's that Isabel McGuire. It's always her. There is something wrong with that child. She has not an obedient God-fearing bone in her body." She paused, then added with certainty, "Yet."

Sister Mary Michael put a hand on her arm and pulled her to a stop just shy of the tight flock of sheep. Sister Edel was taken aback by the firmness in the nun's grip, the set of her thin jawbone, her boldness. Sister Mary Michael removed her glasses; a bead of rain hung from the end of her upturned nose. She was always the pretty one, with her wide eyes and cherry lips. Not even a wimple and veil could cover it. Sister Edel pulled her arm away, looked to the huddle of sheep before coveting set in.

"They are anything but spoiled," Sister Mary Michael stated. "And yes, there is something wrong; they've got no parents. No grandparents, no family. Isabel has every right to be angry. I worry Aelish has not been angry enough. Don't you see?"

The Mother Superior watched as the nun—her subordinate—shrank to proper size, recognizing the overstepping.

"I see everything I need to see," Mother Superior declared, straightening her spine. "And I see you favouring two young ladies, one of whom is headed down the wrong road. We've all had our losses. Might I remind you that this was not our first war." She circled her hand between them. "And then there was that little thing called the Spanish flu." Sister Edel waited for Sister Mary Michael to argue against these tragedies that had taken parents and friends from both their younger lives. "There is no excuse for ungodly behaviour. The Lord giveth and the Lord taketh away."

The rain ceased, and Sister Edel pulled the umbrella closed with a snap, then used it to jab one of the sheep in the rump. The ewe gave a disgruntled bleat.

Stopped in the middle of the flock, Sister Edel turned to Sister Mary Michael trailing behind. "And you would do well to remember our job is to shepherd these young ladies toward a holy life of service, humility, and obedience." Narrowing her eyes, she poked the thin nun in the chest the same way she had the stubborn sheep, then added, "No matter the cost. Do I make myself clear?"

Firmly back in her place, the subordinate rubbed her chest and agreed, "Yes, Mother Superior."

As Sister Edel bent to pat the fleecy head of a spring lamb hiding in the depths of the flock, she thought about how she and this nun, dripping in the rain beside her, had known each other since childhood, with Sister Mary Michael the younger, weaker of the two. And how at some point in their twenties as young nuns Sister Mary Michael had seen fit to side with the despicable Father Michael O'Flanagan—a staunch supporter of the IRA and a man who dared call the Pope an enemy of Irish independence. The boldness was unimaginable. So Sister Edel distanced herself and set her course to become Mother Superior of the Sisters of Bethlehem, certainly a divine order. And just as many of her beloved saints had, she took on the alienation—a small price to pay.

Deep in thought on the paroxysms of sainthood, she was jostled sideways as the ewe rammed the top of her head into Sister Edel's ample thigh. The pain glowed; she felt the bruise forming under her robes. Sister Mary Michael laughed openly, clapping her hands together and holding them against her chest, clearly delighted. The Mother Superior cracked the ewe over the skull with a hollow *whap*.

"Daft creature!" she growled. She fought the urge to wallop Sister Mary Michael as well. Instead, she spun and marched toward the abbey.

"This is nonsense. We're wasting time wandering as aimless as these dense animals."

The sound of Sister Mary Michael's amusement would stalk her the remainder of that day. The rain started again, falling in pebble-sized drops. When she opened the umbrella and Sister Mary Michael sidled next to her right shoulder, Sister Edel switched the umbrella to the left, leaving her companion unsheltered.

SISTER MARY MICHAEL, MAY 1955

SISTER MIKE WALKS THROUGH THE CHAPEL TO THE TABLE adorned with rows of red votives flickering like rubies, waiting to be conduits of prayer. She picks up a match and draws it across the grit of a match box. The sound intrudes on the reflective, at times airless silence.

On her way to the chapel, the intention had been to pray for strength in keeping her hands off of Sister Edel's holier-than-thou throat. The way she treated poor Dr. Gibbs is unforgivable. But as she stares at the flaming match, the sound of the McGuire twins at ten years old sobbing at their parents' grave site pushes itself up from the back of her mind, where it has been buried for years.

Their little-girl crying had twisted together into one mournful call in the summer air, joined by the moaning cries of a woman just a few mounds away—no doubt a war widow, or perhaps a newly childless mother.

The heat of the flame reaches her fingertips before she has a chance to light the red votive dedicated to the twins—to all the orphans and those swallowed up by the evil appetites of war some fifteen years ago. She shakes the match and curses under her breath, dropping it into the bowl of sand. This time, she tries holding off the memory of the twins crying out for their parents in the dirt until the prayer candle is lit.

Today Sister Mike cannot keep the tendrilous thoughts of the Belfast Blitz at bay. Squabbling with Sister Edel has stirred up more than just a dust of frustration. It has been many years since she's felt that dark nostalgia. Perhaps it's age; the halfway mark of her life come and gone.

She recalls how the blitz had brought a bereft flood of children pouring into the Sisters of Bethlehem Orphanage, more than they could handle. She stares at her freckled fingers. Her skin remembers taking each of those lost lambs by the hand, leading them in through the tall wooden doors. Their fingers clutching at hers. Those doors must have looked like a giant's throat to the little ones, she thinks. She often thought of these orphaned children as lightning trapped in a bottle as she watched them at night writhe and bind themselves in blankets. And they smelled, all of them, of brick dust.

Sister Mike takes off her glasses, sets them on the pew seat, and rubs the sides of her nose, attempting to stave off more memories.

"Is this what you had in mind? Is this how you wanted the little children to come to you? I highly doubt it." She looks up without her glasses; Jesus is a bleary and silent shadow hanging on the crucifix. "Obviously, I still have a bone to pick with you," she says.

With every child that arrived or every little one she fetched from hospital during that time, there rose more anger and despair. As she presses in on her temples, the smell of nicotine on her fingers awakens the bear of need in her body. It is an ambling, undeniable craving, one that no amount of prayer can nullify. It is her awful-smelling, yet shamefully soothing cross to carry.

Coming to kneel, Sister Mary Michael presses her fists to her brow. The second her eyes close, the twins appear—not as the grown women they are, rather as the dispossessed little girls they were. *Why these two girls?* she wonders. *What is it about them?*

With a moment to be still, she recalls Isabel McGuire in the car seated next to her during the drive from hospital to the abbey. A clarity comes, sodden with sorrow.

When the Spanish flu killed Sister Mike's da some thirty-five years ago, her mother could not get out from under the boiling grief. No amount of praying, coddling, shushing, empty-promising could penetrate that wall of her mother's fiery heartbreak.

The anger roiled off little Isabel McGuire the same way, that of a full-grown woman in deepest despair, and it never receded. Sister Mike moves her folded hands down to her chest, hoping to ameliorate the familiar dismay.

"I fear for her, Dear Lord." Sister Mike is muddled as to which of the twins she speaks of. The inexplicable foreboding does not subside.

Sister Mike tries to blink away the image of Aelish, who, as a girl, was the meeker, timider of the two, wrapping her thin quivering body over Isabel's fury at the graveside. Young Aelish was a blanket on a flaming log, unaware that she was being burned through. These two girls, identical in the flesh yet worlds apart in spirit, managed to wend their way into the left and right chambers of her heart. Unlike any others.

"Was I weak, Lord? Blindly involved? Was Sister Edel right? Please don't make that true; I couldn't humble myself to that depth. Did I not trust in your mercy and strength to care for these children?" There is no answer, only the rapping of rain against the tall windows of the chapel. The exhaustion in her thighs drops Sister Mike back onto her heels. She surrenders tight-clasped fingers into the lap of her robe and stares at the rows of stubby red candles.

Faithlessness coils around her ankles. Just as it did after losing her father to that flu in her early twenties, then her mother to the wake of grief a few years later. She knows the exact moment when this fissure of faithlessness reopened. A moment she cannot forget. Will not seek forgiveness for.

Again she pictures the twins entwined in the dirt and grass at their parents' grave, small featherless birds fallen from the nest. And she sees herself . . . turn away from them when she should have lain with them. That was the moment.

"I just couldn't bear it. I'm so sorry," she whispers to the girls, to God. Sister Mike holds her throat, folds herself in half and sobs. When the sobbing is through, Sister Mike does not pray the rosary or do the stations of the cross or seek out Father McManus for confession. None of this she deserves.

Instead of all of that, Sister Mary Michael cleans her smudged glasses with the hem of her robe, pulls the packet of cigarettes from her pocket, and decides she'll go for a walk. She openly blesses that she no longer has to drag Sister Edel along the road like some surly ox.

5

AELISH, MAY 1955

THE FOUR WEEKS SINCE AELISH LEFT IRELAND AND HER HOME in the abbey have been a blur of sleepless nights, hospital visits, cooking, cleaning, feeding. Even the blood in her veins is exhausted, yet at the same time, a sweet new aliveness tingles her skin.

Unlike her room in the abbey overlooking the stations of the cross, the window in Aelish's makeshift bedroom in Isabel's home has a view of the sea. Declan cleared out the small pantry off the kitchen, apologizing for its modest size. The slatted wood walls of her accommodations are infused with the comforting aromas of bread and root vegetables. It holds a comfortable cot, a chair, and a table with one leg shorter than the rest. Aelish pushes on the corner of the table and smiles. Each time she sits to write, it dips to one side, reminding her a bit of Izzy's lopsided walk. Lopsided or not, it was a miracle her twin could walk at all. And perhaps more stubbornness than miracle.

Aelish visits Isabel every day, watching over her dogged convalescence—a steep hill of recovery that dips periodically. Despite the dips, Izzy remains determined to be home and well soon.

Aelish hears Mrs. Doolin in the next room fussing over Paddy, who has recently learned to roll over. Aelish rubs her sandy eyes, then clasps her hands behind her back, stretching out the demands of carrying two babies.

"Fresh air," she says, "the best medicine." She slips into her coat, reaches into the pocket, and feels the familiar loop of beads nestled, waiting.

"Mrs. Doolin, would you mind if I stepped out for a breath of sea air?"

Gabby is seated on the floor with the twins. Aelish is not sure how she got down there and even less certain how she will get up.

She waves Aelish off. "We're right as rain here, Sister. Tide's out—it's a good time to treasure hunt," she says, clutching the babies' round bellies. They squeal with glee, and the sound sends Aelish out the door with tiny bubbles coursing across her skin.

Arriving at the water's edge, she turns into the wind, glances down at the small crabs skittering about. A penny-sized triangle of amber glass twinkles among the rocks and swaths of kelp crisping in the sun. It has been worn smooth, made matte from sand and salt.

"Izzy will like this." Aelish drops it into one of her wellies.

The fishing community's old Catholic church sits at a precarious angle, clinging to the hillside. *I promise to get there and receive communion after a visit with Isabel today,* she vows before perching on a large stone for morning devotions. Crabs dart like tiny thieves between the rocks, and gulls drift overhead. She ponders Declan's question about Isabel, whether she mentioned "not doing so good." Although Izzy did not write of any struggles, Aelish intends to broach the subject on today's visit now that her sister is stronger.

Halfway through the third decade of the rosary, she hears shouting. Aelish continues to pray, assuming the fishermen on the pier to be the source of the noise. The indecipherable ruckus becomes more precise. Aelish is startled to hear her name.

"Aelish!" Declan is standing on the dock, waving his arms. His gestures shoot Aelish up from solitude. The rosary slips from her fingers, snakes down through the wet stones to the sand below. Hearing Declan shout her name . . . "Aelish!" . . . she freezes, gripped by a flash of the night the bombs destroyed her home. Da hollering at her as she ran back into her room to save Miss Molly, her baby doll with button eyes and yellow yarn hair. She tripped on the way back to the front door. Everyone waiting for her—for Aelish—her gas mask hanging in Da's hand.

"Aelish! It's Izz," Declan shouts through cupped hands.

Declan's voice breaks through, pulling her from the ruins, the remorse of the past.

Aelish glances down at the rosary Sister Mike gave her the day Aelish became a novice. Leaving it behind, she scrambles up the sharp rocks and hopes the tide won't pull the beads out to sea.

AELISH, MAY 1955

DECLAN IS SHEET WHITE. AELISH GRABS HIS ARM, AND HE COVERS her hand with his. His skin is hot despite the crisp air.

"What is it, Declan? Is Izzy alright? The twins?"

"We have to go." He still has Aelish's hand as he strides up the dock, tugging her along. Aelish stumbles in Izzy's floppy wellies.

"Declan!" Aelish pulls her hand out of his grip and trots to keep up. "What's happening?"

"Maggie stopped in on her way home and said Izz had a rough night and that I should get over there as soon as I could."

"Who's Maggie? What did she mean by 'a rough night'?" Covering herself with the cross, Aelish reaches for her crucifix, then remembers it's coiled in the sand.

"Maggie's a friend of Isabel's. She's a nurse and was on shift last night. Izz couldn't breathe last night." Aelish's gut coils tight as they run for Declan's truck.

"What about the babies?"

"Mrs. Doolin," Declan says as he slides in behind the wheel.

It takes two hands for Aelish to pull the heavy door shut. When Declan turns the key, the truck groans. He tries three more times, then slams his palm on the cracked dashboard so hard Aelish fears the lorry might fall to rusty hunks.

"Goddammit! Ya goddamn scut! You're useless!" he hollers. Declan wraps his hands around the wheel, shakes it. He stares straight ahead. Aelish keeps silent in the nearness of his anger. She begins to petition Saint Jude under her breath.

"What are you doing?" Declan asks, softening.

"Praying to Saint Jude." She continues her petitions.

"Can he fix this heap of junk?"

"Something like that," she says. "He's the patron saint of lost causes."

For a moment, there is silence. Aelish's eyes are still closed, and she wonders if Declan thinks she's crazy. And then she hears him chuckle, and his chuckle turns into a full gale of laughter, the kind that sits like a tipsy lid on sadness.

"That's perfect," he manages to say. This time, when he turns the key, the depleted truck sputters to life. "Well, I'll be! Ol' Saint Jude knows his way around trucks," he exclaims. Declan pulls his cap off, runs his forearm across his brow, and then uses his cap to wipe the tears from his jaw. He leans over, squeezes Aelish's hands still folded in her lap. Staring at his hand, she notices two open blisters on his thumb the size of a sixpence; the creases of skin across his knuckles are streaked with grime of some kind.

"Thank you, Aelish." His eyes are glassy, round, his voice laden with sadness.

"'Twasn't me. It was good ol' Saint Jude."

When Declan takes his hand back, drops the truck into gear, and pulls out onto the dirt road, Aelish notices how cold her hands are. She hopes stuffing them into the folds of robe between her thighs will re-create that same warmth.

"I mean, thank you for being here, for all of us. I don't know how much longer I could have done this by myself." Declan shakes his head, rubs his palm on the steering wheel. "We really need you."

"I'm nothing special," Aelish says, looking out the window. "Just another broken-down thing for Saint Jude to look after." It's all Aelish can think to say that will let her tuck away everything but her concern for Isabel.

The colourful seaside houses flick past the truck window as they roll toward St. John's sanitorium. The sickening worry for her twin sister feels as dense as the stony outcroppings holding these homes to the earth. She wishes she'd have felt this same impenetrable worry for Izzy that final night in the abbey basement—the night she let her twin slip away. In truth, she did feel worried—overwrought, in fact—just not for Izzy.

Declan's truck backfires as it rolls, lethargic, into a parking spot outside the hospital. Aelish jolts. At the memory? At the sound? An exhausting ache runs through her hands from grasping the door handle, fending off the past, and bracing for what is to come. She tents her fingers and presses them into one another, listening to the engine's *tick tick tick* as it cools itself off. She puts her shoulder into the truck door, jumps out, and runs toward the hospital. Declan calls out, "Izzy really needs you. More than she needs me, most times."

Shivering, Aelish stops at the top of the steps, a hand splayed on the hospital door. It is not the frigid sea breeze that grips her. Rather, it is the dank, chilled memory of standing in the abbey's laundry and turning away from two things: Isabel's moment of naked need and a precarious turning point in her own life. Aelish glances over her shoulder and sees a pale, worried Declan trudging up the steps. Crowded around him are the ghosts of a life she did not choose and shimmering memories of the night she let it all go.

AELISH, 1952

IT WAS AELISH'S TURN FOR NIGHT DUTY WHEN IZZY SHOWED UP, begging her to leave the convent. All new Sisters took a weekly shift watching over the young girls in the long white dormitory as they struggled to sleep, twisting and turning from unrelenting rootlessness. Aelish wiped moist palms against her robe before pushing the dormitory door open and stepping into the hallway, yellow-glass wall lights casting eggs of light. A mouse skittered across her path, disappeared into a knothole. She wished to be that uncomplicated.

The day before, her favourite Bible study student, Molly, a peaky little thing from the mother and baby home, had informed Aelish, "That Isabel lady, the one who looks just like you, Sister Clare, stopped me on my way here again and said she needs to see you tomorrow night." Aelish did not need to ask where. This was the third time Isabel had made Molly a carrier pigeon, and each time Isabel had failed to show up at the basement door.

To Aelish, seeing her sister, if she indeed showed up this time, would be a storm full of swirling debris, chunks of heartbreak, gritty anger, howling sadness. And in the eye of the storm—a longing she refused to acknowledge.

Aelish tiptoed barefoot past Sister Edel's office. When she slipped back into her shoes at the doorway to the laundry, they suddenly felt two sizes too small, strangling her feet. She descended the narrow steps, which seemed to grow tighter around her. The room was buried deep beneath the building, making it impossible to hear anything, yet still, she cringed as she wriggled the steel bolt on the door out of its tight hole. Aelish felt sixteen again, nervous and out of control. It was a stinging reminder of waiting at the same door for Isabel to sneak back into the abbey after her day at the beach with Declan—the day that had changed so much.

With the door open, the night wind grabbed at the sleeves of her robe. There was a rumble off in the distance that seemed to touch down in Aelish's belly as she stepped across the leaf-littered field, the rusty scent of autumn filling the night.

Aelish's heartbeat was frantic. Only moments before, she had been clear about what she wanted to say, and suddenly, every step was collecting confusion, and now she was questioning, *Should I be angry with Isabel for putting me in this position, or excited to see her after four years?*

"Damn you, Isabel," Aelish muttered. Remorse for damning her sister grew as she drew nearer to the skeletal hem of ash and birch and Scots pine.

An owl with a strange warble called from the dark. It called again, sounding even stranger, as though something were lodged in its throat. Despite feeling like an exposed nerve, Aelish began to giggle, pressing her veil over her mouth.

"Isabel, stop that! You'll get us caught," Aelish hissed into the trees.

Isabel stepped from the shadows, and when Aelish saw her twin's smile, she ran to her. Wrapped in Aelish's arms, Izzy felt no bigger than a branch. Her angular features were made even sharper by thinness, and when Aelish held Isabel away, the round heads of her shoulder bones cupped into her palms.

"Isabel, you're nothing but a rope. What's wrong?" Aelish pulled her close again, wanting to nourish her. Isabel's fingertips dug into Aelish's back, into something vital.

"I was ill for a while," she whispered. "But I'm okay now. Thank you for seeing me, Ay."

Holding her at arm's length again, Aelish stared into Isabel's eyes. The sharp smell of stale alcohol rode on her twin's breath, on her skin.

"I had to see you," Isabel said. "I couldn't leave without seeing you."

Her words took the wind from Aelish's body. *Leave? Again?* As Aelish's emotional squall picked up, so too did the wind in the trees. Branches and leaves rustled anxiously against one another.

"What do you mean?" Aelish asked loud enough to be heard over building gusts of wind.

Both Isabel and Aelish turned toward a splashing sound. A curtain of slashing rain drove across the lawn toward them. They jumped at the crash of a nearby tree losing a limb.

Grabbing Izzy's hand, Aelish pulled her across the lawn. The downpour turned the grass and dead leaves into a sopping rug. Isabel hopped along, swinging her lame leg.

Aelish closed the laundry door and rested her back against it as if holding off a monster—a beast threatening to take Izzy away, yet again. Isabel peeled away strings of long wet hair clinging to her forehead. Aelish's veil was drenched and weighed on her head. Aelish had not missed her long hair until seeing Izzy twist hers and wring rainwater onto the hard-packed dirt floor.

"Why did you come here?" Aelish asked, feeling like a bad tooth from head to foot.

Isabel didn't answer, eyes wandering the room. She ran a trembling hand over the ironing table next to them, then pulled away as if scalded. Trancelike, Isabel walked over to the deep cast-iron sink against the wall, turned her back on Aelish, and leaned on the lip of the basin.

"That smell has never left me," she whispered. Unsure what she was talking about, Aelish waited in silence. She knew better than to push her sister too much. "The mustiness. That stinking lye.

I can't get it out of me after all these years. The cruelty and beatings by that old bitch Mother Superior I could handle, but this stench!" Isabel slapped the edge of the sink, startling Aelish. "It takes me down every time." Even in the dimness, with her back rounded, Aelish could see the bumps of Izzy's spine pressing through her damp sweater. Isabel shook, and Aelish heard her sniffle. "I've tried to stay close to you, Ay, I hoped you would change your mind about this place, but I can't do it anymore."

It was the first time Aelish really saw all those years of pain suffocating her sister like a cruel vine. She had become skilled at holding Isabel's anger, her rebelliousness, her strength even. Seeing Izzy's naked wounds, however, drained Aelish, leaving her desperate to know what had happened to her twin while she herself was safe in the abbey.

"What are you saying?" Aelish asked, reluctant. Aelish reached down for the cord at her waist, a series of knots that helped her hang on. Sweaty palms made it slippery. Isabel grabbed Aelish by the elbows and stared, first into one eye and then the other. A foot of thunder stomped the earth, rattling the high windows. The twins screamed, grabbed on to each other. Aelish began to sob. Isabel gently turned Aelish around, belly to back, then wrapped her arms around Aelish's shoulders. Resting her chin in Aelish's neck crook, they swayed. Aelish was washed by an urge to rip off her veil, feel her twin's chin on a bare shoulder.

"We're grown women now, Aelish. I have so much to tell you. Come with us."

Aelish opened her eyes, her back clenched. "What 'us'?" she asked.

"You remember Declan, right? We've saved some money, and we're leaving Ireland. It's a new start." Isabel's thin arms squeezed tighter.

Aelish's mind jostled with panic and questions. She wriggled out of Isabel's arms, clutched her rosary. The feel of the crucifix jabbing her tender palm brought the room and her reality into sharper view.

"But you aren't married." Aelish took a breath, then asked, "Are you?"

"No, not yet. But soon, maybe once we get to where we're going."

Aelish remembered the day she took her veil, her vows. Standing in the cavernous cathedral in a donated white wedding dress—alone.

"Without me? You'll be married without me?" Aelish's body sparked into angry coals.

"No!" Isabel exclaimed, reaching for Aelish's hand. Aelish pulled away. "Not if you come with me, Ay. That's why I came, why I had to see you. I don't want to leave without you."

The pure hope in Isabel's eyes told Aelish her sister had no clue the enormity of what she was asking. No idea the depth of the vows Aelish had taken and to whom. At the same moment, Aelish heard the petrified little girl inside herself—the one she believed was finally safe and quiet—pleading: *Do you want Izzy to leave you here again? Don't you want to be by her side when she marries?*

"What do you think this is, Isabel?" Aelish waved a hand toward the ceiling, then held out her rosary. It swung in front of Isabel's nose, and her red-rimmed eyes tracked it side to side. "Do you think this is a part-time job? Unlike you, I have a purpose."

Isabel recoiled as if slapped. Aelish, however, could not stop herself. Just like she could not stop herself from ripping clumps of hair from mean Clare's head after Isabel ran away from the orphanage.

"This is a life," Aelish exclaimed, tugging at the knotted rope cinched at her waist. "This is a vow, a marriage, a sacrifice that actually means something. After you left the first time, I started again." Aelish knew she was lobbing bombs that shook her twin. "And you expect me to throw all of that over just so I can run off with you and your childhood sweetheart? Are you daft, Isabel? Or just selfish? Or is it the booze that's coming out of your skin?"

Isabel looked nervously over Aelish's shoulder toward the stairwell. "Lower your voice," she said, wiping at her tears. "I didn't come here to make fun of your life. I know how much it means to you. There are some things we need to talk about." She touched the edge of Aelish's wet veil. The tenderness of her gesture threatened to melt the anger which, at that moment, was the only thing holding Aelish upright.

"If you knew how much all of this means to me . . . how much you mean to me. How dare you ask me to choose." Aelish knew what she was about to say was an unstoppable train of hurt. "Isabel McGuire, you are the most selfish person I know. You think of no one else but yourself." An image of Declan, his kind smile, flashed in Aelish's head. Brushing a finger over her lips, she felt that one kiss. "Does Declan know how selfish you are? Does he have any idea what he's getting into?"

Isabel backed away, but Aelish could not stop herself.

"Ma and Da would be ashamed of you." She knew these words were indelible as soon as they hit the musty air.

Isabel's head jolted back, shocked. She brought her hands together, pressed against her mouth. Hurt poured from her eyes. A swath of lightning turned the room blue for an instant. They simultaneously ducked and dropped to their knees, heads covered. When Aelish peeked between her elbows, she was faced with her sad, scared reflection.

"I know you, Aelish, and I know you didn't mean that." Isabel lowered her hands into her lap, fidgeting with her fingers. "And I'm going to stop drinking, I am."

Aelish's throat burned from the acidic residue of her words, the crucifix hanging at her neck suddenly heavy and rugged.

"I'm sorry, Izzy. I'm still so angry that you left me."

"Left you?" Isabel's eyes flashed. "I had no choice! You, on the other hand, chose this." Isabel slapped the packed dirt floor, and Aelish imagined it to be the sound of slapping dead flesh. "You chose these awful people! How do you think that made me feel? Beatings and berating and praying to lifeless statues over me, Aelish!" Isabel pounded her fist against her chest, then wiped her sleeve under her nose.

After a long rain-cloaked silence, Isabel's piercing glare softened. "We can start over, Ay. Like it's supposed to be. You and me. You can't tell me there isn't some part of you that wants to be out there"—she waved to the high windows, then stroked the sleeve of Aelish's robe—"instead of trapped in here."

Isabel stood and pulled Aelish up. They didn't let go of one another. "Come with me. Please," Isabel begged. "Let's at least go somewhere it's safe for us to talk. I didn't want to leave you." She pulled Aelish into her arms. Aelish felt a heart pounding, unsure who it belonged to.

"I'm scared," they confessed in unison. The twins separated and stared at one another. Aelish was shocked that Isabel would feel frightened without her. She began to wonder, to picture the two of them away, somewhere. Aelish never imagined it—would not or could not—but with Izzy in front of her, she was brave enough to see gossamer ideas, feel them filling out her skin with effervescent possibility. *Maybe we'd have a tiny house, a garden like Ma's with root vegetables and wildflowers,* she thought.

As if reading her thoughts, Isabel said, "We can have a beautiful life, Ay." Isabel kissed Aelish's cheek. "There's no love for you in these brick walls."

"You filthy heathen!" Sister Edel roared from the stairwell.

ISABEL, 1952

THE MOTHER SUPERIOR'S WAVE OF FURY MADE LANDFALL ON Izzy's chest. Sister Edel was stuffed into the stairway door, a metre stick gripped in her fist—a menacing storybook ogre if ever there was. If not for the shock, Isabel would have laughed aloud.

"Get thee behind me, Satan," Sister Edel growled, pointing her stick at Isabel. "Thou art an offence unto me for thou savourest not the things that be of God."

"Shut yer gob, you ol' cow," Isabel yelled back. "You and your God don't scare me anymore; in fact, you never did, so mind your own business." Isabel waved off the blustering nun. "Go pray to whoever would have such a sour cuss like you."

Turning back to Aelish, Isabel grabbed her shaking hands. Never had Isabel been less frightened by Sister Edel. Her love of Aelish was an eclipse over everything else.

"You have a choice now, Ay. It's not too late," Isabel whispered, hopeful.

For a split second Isabel was confused as her head yanked back, Mother Superior's thickened fingers buried deep in her dark hair. Isabel clawed at Sister Edel's iron hand. Aelish stepped away, palms stacked over her mouth.

"Get. Thee. Behind. Me. Satan," Mother Superior chanted through gritted teeth, pulling Isabel toward the door by her hair. Mother Superior was not a young woman yet had the strength of a bull. Isabel heard the woman's teeth grinding like stones in a river.

"Stop it!" Aelish pleaded. "Stop it, both of you."

Isabel was more astonished when Aelish lunged at the Mother Superior, grabbing her wrist, twisting her splotched skin. Sister Edel's grip weakened, and Isabel pulled away and spun to face the nun, both panting. Isabel swiped a lock of hair from her eyes, then spat on the floor at Mother Superior's feet.

"That's what I think of you and this place. And everything you've done." Isabel then grabbed the crucifix hanging at Sister Edel's neck and yanked, almost toppling the heavy woman. Isabel held the crucifix in the air. It swung on a broken rope from her clenched fingers.

For a moment, the room—the world—fell paralyzed. Isabel stared at a pathetic pleading Christ, heard him begging her not to do what she was about to do. She saw the identical beseeching expression in Aelish. She opened her fingers, let the rope slither from her hand. All three women stared at the wooden cross lying prone in the dirt. Isabel stepped onto the crucifix with the heel of her scuffed wet boot, locked her gaze on the Mother Superior, and rotated her foot back and forth, grinding it all into the earth. Aelish pulled a startled hiss through her teeth. Isabel's insides seethed when her twin chewed at her knuckle in the helpless way she did as a child.

"Isabel! Stop, please," Aelish begged. She kissed the cross hanging at her neck. "Father, please forgive her."

"What?" Isabel cried out, incredulous. "Forgive me? Do you ever say that same prayer for this miserable old cow?" Isabel clamped tight her jaw to fight tears, but it was useless. She tilted her head and stared at Aelish. "You have no idea what they did, do you? They didn't tell you the truth."

There was a loud crack when Sister Edel's stick hit Isabel's arm and splintered in two. Isabel did not flinch. Sister Edel held the broken remains of her discipline. It shook in her fist. Sweat poured down the woman's bulging face, her skin the grey of dishwater. There was no mistaking fear in the woman's eyes as Isabel turned and stood half a head taller.

Sister Edel bunched the front of her robe, her mouth opened and closed, noiseless. Then she groaned.

"All this," Isabel announced, spreading her arms wide like a ringmaster at the circus, "is a feckin' joke."

Isabel picked the broken piece of stick off the ground, examined it as if it were a contaminated thing, then stepped close to Mother Superior. She heard Aelish begging in her mind, yanking on the rope. The Mother Superior gasped, rubbing her left arm. Isabel held the stick so close to Sister Edel's nose it made the old woman cross-eyed.

"Never again," Isabel declared. "Do you hear me? Never. Again."

Isabel snapped the short stick over her knee in a flash, then threw the two splintered pieces of wood at the Mother Superior. One of the jagged ends pierced Sister Edel's doughy cheek, just below her left eye. Instantly, a deep red rivulet trickled from the puncture. Isabel was mesmerized by satisfaction as blood soaked the nun's snow-white wimple at her chin. The heavy nun cupped her cheek, then collapsed.

"Sister Edel!" Aelish screamed as she dropped to her knees beside the panting nun. Mother Superior's eyes rolled, untethered. Her stubby fingers clawed at the veil.

"Off . . . off," Mother Superior hissed.

Watching her twin try to set the woman free, Isabel was struck with the nightmares she suffered after Hitler bombed the Belfast harbour, night terrors of families trapped under collapsed roofs and fractured stairways. People scratching desperately at debris to find loved ones—people who deserved to live. She felt none of that heartbreak for Sister Edel.

Aelish shook as she removed the fastening pins, then paused—Isabel knew that Aelish did not want to see what was under that covering. She slid the veil away, and a curtain of silver hair fell to Sister Edel's shoulders. Isabel was stunned by the transformation. The woman was not beautiful. But for a flashing moment, Isabel saw that she was vulnerable. Helpless. Human, not beast.

Digging fingernails into her palms, Isabel was brought back to her bitterness, cultivated by years of being treated, by this woman, like a human stain.

"Leave her, Aelish," Isabel commanded. She stepped toward them, wanting to pull Aelish from the trap. "She's had it coming. Think of all those poor girls she tortured through the years. Don't you remember Becky? This woman made her sit with pee-soaked sheets on her head. Don't you still hear little Becky crying? Innocent—every single one of them—innocent and helpless, and . . ." Her voice broke. "Lost. And all she did was lay a beating on us for being sad, and in the name of God, no less. Let's see if her God saves her now."

Isabel watched Aelish move a lock of silver hair out of the Mother Superior's eyes. Isabel's heart dropped. The woman's mouth hung open, showing immaculate teeth.

"Izzy, go upstairs and wake one of the other Sisters," Aelish ordered. Isabel shook her head, locked her arms around her chest, and rubbed the outsides of her shoulders to quell the shivering, the bewilderment of her sister holding an ounce of pity for such a dreadful person.

"Come with me, Ay. Let's be free of this place." Isabel bent down, examining Sister Edel like a specimen. "She'll be okay. Her colour's coming back, look." Sister Edel's breathing slowed, but her eyes remained hazy, unfocused.

"Kathleen." The Sister's voice was a croak. "Why?"

Isabel backed away from the sour smell coming off the nun and asked, "Who the hell is Kathleen?" Isabel looked to Aelish, who stroked the Mother Superior's sagging cheek.

"I don't know, Isabel, just go get help this minute."

Isabel did not recognize the commanding tone of Aelish's voice. She back stepped toward the door, her chest in a breathless knot. Isabel blinked rapidly, swiped her tears.

"That woman deserves to suffer," Isabel whispered. "Just like

I did." She pressed one hand to her heart. "Please, Aelish, come with me, choose me."

Even as the words floated out of her mouth, Isabel felt the rope between them go slack. Aelish had let go of her end. And Isabel had walked out the basement door, glancing back only once to see Aelish buried under the crumbled fortress of Sister Edel.

ISABEL, MAY 1955

IT MIGHT BE THE DISEASE STRIPPING ISABEL'S DEFENCES AWAY, the medicines in her body, but in this state, she has no separation from what Aelish is thinking. Her remorse. Aelish's ruminating about the abbey basement on that last night—to the pungent stink of lye and sham holiness. Izzy claws the bed, pulling herself up from Aelish's emotional undertow. And when she rises to the surface, she feels her twin sister rushing toward her bedside like the colour red.

Izzy turns away and looks out the window as a nurse walks into the room. It is a depleting endeavour. One tear spills out the corner of her right eye. Maggie, Izzy's favourite nurse and friend, checks a chart held by a clipboard, then looks at the upside-down watch pinned to her chest.

"Time for your sedative, Izzy."

Izzy takes a run at speaking, pleading. "Please wait, Maggie. My sister is coming. I can feel it."

Maggie touches Isabel's blanketed toes. Despite being Izzy's age, she does not look old enough to be a nurse, and the freckles across her nose do not help. Maggie glances at the chart once again, then back over her shoulder.

She bites her lip, then says, "Okay, but if she's not here in twenty minutes, I'll be back."

Just then, Izzy hears Aelish in the hall, arguing with the flinty black-haired nurse. The sound of her twin racing to her side is all the sedative she needs.

AELISH, MAY 1955

AELISH REFUSES THE MASK. THE EXHAUSTED NURSE GLARES AND purses her lips, exaggerating the pinched verticals lines around her mouth.

"Suit yourself, Sister." She emphasizes *Sister.* "But don't the Lord help those who help themselves?" She strides away and mutters, "Foolish woman."

"God works in mysterious ways, even for fools," Aelish remarks.

Aelish hears her twin before seeing her. A gurgling sound comes from Isabel's corner of the room. Aelish's throat fills with liquid, making her cough. Declan stops, turns his worried eyes on Aelish.

"Can you do this?" he asks.

Aelish must look away from his masked face. She turns him around by the arm and gently pushes him through the door. The nearer she gets to Isabel, the more Aelish feels the fire in her chest, the rod of pain in her backbone. Taking a deep breath—for Izzy—then another and another, Aelish steps to the bedside. Izzy's chest slows its heaving. A bit of colour pinks her waxy cheeks. Her eyelids slide open like blinds on a darkened room.

"Izzy," Aelish whispers, taking Isabel's hand. "Izzy, I'm here." A single tear slides out the corner of Isabel's eye and gets caught in the silky strands of hair at her temple.

"You." Izzy pauses for a breath. "Should have a mask."

"So I've been told. Never mind that."

Isabel's ashen skin—the drastic change since their last visit—

is incomprehensible. Aelish presses a knuckle to her lips to control a sob.

"Your babies miss you, Izzy. They are happy as clams, but they miss you." Mentioning them materializes their warm helplessness against her chest.

"How do they smell?" Isabel asks. She closes her eyes. They inhale at the same time, conjuring the scent of innocent downy heads.

"Like peaches and sweet cream," Aelish says.

Isabel says nothing for so long Aelish believes she has fallen asleep. Her chest rises and lowers evenly, and the wet sound diminishes. Running a thumb over her sister's palm, Aelish feels raised tracks. When she turns her hand over, there is a pale map of puckered scars. Aelish's mind spins, wondering how and when this happened. *What are these scars from? Why wasn't I there to clean these wounds?*

Izzy opens her eyes and looks to Declan. He steps closer on the opposite side of the bed. Izzy holds up her other hand for him to take, and when he winds his long fingers into hers, it's like the thick and thin tendrils of a vine coming together. Aelish feels like a shameful voyeur of their connection, yet at the same time, so entangled she cannot get free. Isabel's voice in Aelish's head is strong and loud and unhindered by sickness.

Please don't leave them, Aelish.

Aelish blinks, startled. Embarrassed. Declan continues to smile at his wife, worried but unaware of that voice.

"Paddy rolled over yesterday, Izz," Declan says. "Sar's almost there, but she's a bit chubbier."

"Hmmm," Isabel replies, saving her breath.

Aelish brushes away a strand of hair stuck against Izzy's forehead. Her skin is slick and cool. Her lips begin to move, but no words emerge. She tries again, and this time her voice is unmistakable.

"Aelish." Her grip grows more assertive. Declan glances at Aelish with some surprise. "Don't let my babies be"—Isabel takes a ragged inhale—"without a mammy. Don't let them know"—another gasp—"what that's like."

"Izz!" Declan whispers. "Don't talk like that. Don't. You'll be home in no time. You've just hit a rough patch." Declan pulls the mask down to his neck and kisses the inside of Isabel's wrist as he pleads with her. "Sar and Paddy need you; I talk about you to them all the time . . . all the time, I promise."

Aelish's hands shake as she leans into the edge of the bed for support. Isabel moves her eyes from Declan to Aelish, back and forth as though weaving them together in her mind.

Aelish hears her twin inside her skull, again loud and persistent.

Don't let them know our pain.

"Isabel McGuire," Aelish says sternly, hoping to sound like Da, trying to ignore her twin's persistent tug on the rope. "I pray for you and your family, and I know the good Lord is watching over all of you. He will provide and heal." Aelish words are dry chaff. There is no moisture in her mouth suddenly.

"You're right, Ay." Aelish is stunned by her agnostic sister's words of agreement. "I've prayed for you to come." She takes a breath. "And you did. Now I'm praying you'll take my place."

"No one's takin' any places around here. Do ya hear me!" Declan says, raising his voice. "You're not going anywhere, you're my sweet stubborn *cailin dubh,* my dark-haired lass."

Isabel ignores her pleading husband, stares at Aelish, and folds her dry lips over her teeth. Her brows draw close.

"Say you'll take my place, Aelish."

With a tumbling mind, Aelish fears she might be having a spell. She slides a hand down to the knots hanging at her side—a series of strong knuckles. Touching each one, she says under her breath, "Chastity, obedience, poverty, enclosure. Mother Mary, pray for us."

She finds her footing and thinks: *I know the good Lord would not have me choose.*

"I will," she says to Isabel, uncertain if this is a lie. "I'll help take care of the babes until you're ready to come home."

"No!" Isabel tries to lift her head from the pillow. The grasp of her hand is fierce, and Aelish sees the white indents she is making on Declan's hand as well. "Promise me. Both of you," she manages to say before falling into a spasm of coughing, a fine spray of blood landing on her nightdress.

Declan rests a hand across his wife's forehead. Her watery eyes are locked on Aelish's. Her voice rings in Aelish's head, pleading—*Say it, say you will.*

Moving under some invisible pull, Aelish's vocal cords vibrate, her tongue rolls, her lips form words that terrify her. Saying them gives her twin permission to leave her yet again. Saying them tears her carefully constructed world apart. Aelish knows saying them out loud means they cannot be unsaid or taken back. *That's the way it is with us.*

"I will, Isabel. I will take your place."

Declan runs his fingers through his sandy hair, shakes his head. As if unable to stop the promising, Aelish continues, "We won't let those little ones go through what you and I did, Izzy. We promise." Aelish feels as though her words are being cast down a long hallway. Declan stares at her from miles away, dumbstruck.

"Right, Declan?" she asks.

"This is daft," he says as he kisses Izzy's hand again. "But anything to make you feel better, Izz. I promise you our kids will not know what that's like, because you'll be home soon."

Isabel's arms droop. She runs her tongue over cracked lips. Aelish tips a small cup of water to her sister's mouth, and like a weak sparrow, she sips, her eyes never leaving Aelish's. Isabel's pale green irises churn with relief and grief.

"Time to let Isabel rest," the nurse commands as she walks into the room. The spattering of red on Izzy's nightdress stops the nurse in her tracks. She balls her hands onto her generous hips and narrows her eyes at Aelish, unmasked and foolhardy. Declan slips his covering up as if silently chastised. The nurse dons her cover, approaches the bed, takes Aelish's arm, and begins to pull; nun or no nun, the woman is taking control.

"Sister, you are reckless. Now, you must leave," she orders.

"'Reckless.' There's hope for you after all," Isabel whispers. A surprising satisfaction swells in Aelish's chest as she watches her wearied twin give a crooked grin.

Pulling her arm free from the nurse's grip, Aelish steps back to Izzy's bedside and takes her hand. Aelish traces those unfamiliar scars on Isabel's palm, and with her cheek pressed to Isabel's, she feels Isabel's lips move. One word passes into the tunnel of Aelish's ear, then slides downslope to puncture her heart.

"Teaspoons."

6

SISTER EDEL, JULY 1955

Dear Sister Mike,

Having Isabel home is a miracle, and the fact that we were able to celebrate our twenty-fourth birthday together is an added blessing. When we spoke on the phone about her frightening setback and incredible recovery, brought about by God's will, and perhaps a helping of Izzy's bull-headedness, I did not get the chance to tell you the entire story.

The day after she made me promise to be there for her children, I was terrified, so full of doubt. I returned to the rocks I'd been praying on. I asked our Holy Father for a miracle.

Something sharp dug into my heel then as I sat with my sadness and fear. I removed my boot and turned it upside down, and the tiny piece of amber sea glass I'd meant to give to Izzy dropped into my hand. And then, clumsy as I am, it slipped from my grip and disappeared between the rocks. When I looked into the crack to find it, there tangled in a thick strand of seaweed was my rosary, the one you gave to me. When I pressed the crucifix to my lips, the taste of salt seemed to give life to the miraculous . . .

it made miracles seem more earthly. Am I making any sense, Sister? Oh, how I miss our talks over tea.

I prayed with all my heart that Isabel not be washed out to sea, that she be held by strands of love connected to her children, Declan, and me. Was that a selfish request? Should I have simply had more faith? If that's the answer, then why do we bother with prayer? I look forward to your wisdom on this.

Anyhow, as you know, prayers were answered—she recovered enough to come home. Several weeks have passed and many long sleepless nights, but she is home with her babies and her husband. She is still mending and tires quickly, but she is free to hold her children and watch them as they change minute to minute.

Please continue to hold us in your prayers, Sister, and I will decide soon when it is safe for me to journey home to the abbey.

With God's love,
Sister Clare

"ISN'T THAT JUST MIRACULOUS!" SISTER MIKE EXCLAIMS, HER eyes still scanning the letter she's read aloud. She is glowing, and Sister Edel would like nothing more than to reach out and shake that dippy grin off her face. "Simply miraculous," Sister Mike repeats, head shaking.

"The way you go on, you'd think Jesus himself had just taught an entire colony of lepers to walk on water," Sister Edel says flatly. "The real miracle will take place when Sister Clare returns to the abbey where she belongs, not traipsing around the globe after that dirty-tooth sister of hers. And if I were still Mother Superior, you can be sure I would never have let Sister Clare go. We both know the bad influence the other one can be on her."

Sister Mike's dimming is visible. She steps back, folds the letter as though it were a precious missive from Pope Pius himself. Sister Edel is well aware of how her opinions trample those around her. There is a tiny quiver inside asking her to consider an apology. She brushes it off like lint and continues, "I didn't ask you to come in here and read that letter. Now I'm feeling bothered."

Sister Mike fishes a pack of cigarettes out of her robes and heads for the door. "And when are you not bothered?" she asks. She stops at the bookshelf beside the door and fishes out a silver-framed photograph concealed between two books. Sister Edel stiffens with shame for having held on to a piece of her past. A past she was supposed to be cleaved from after taking holy vows. She despises the fluffy look of nostalgia on Sister Mike's face as she examines the image. She would rather her fellow nun chastise her for such weakness. Sister Mike sets the picture on the bedside table, then spins it to face Sister Edel.

"I believe this would be a good reminder of when you were less bothered by everything and everyone. More compassionate, perhaps."

It is not often Sister Edel is stunned into silence, yet here she is. She flips the photograph onto its belly, not wanting to look through that particular historical window. A prickle of shame courses her body. Sister Mike walks out shaking her head, her sandals clacking down the hall. Her footsteps make a statement, as do everyone's when leaving her room—*I've had enough, and I don't think I'll come back*, they say.

Never would Sister Edel admit it, not even to herself, but she wishes for the sound of Sister Mary Michael's sandals returning. Because now all she can think of is the provoking sound of Isabel McGuire's gimpy gait. Sister Edel plugs her ears. She needs to shutter her mind against the thoughts of all the havoc that prideful girl played with so many lives. But like an invasive weed, Isabel McGuire is sprouting dogged once again.

To Sister Edel the sound of Isabel McGuire moving about the orphanage with her gammy leg had been akin to listening to someone mispronounce the same word over and over. The girl had proven herself time and again to be the petulant and unsalvageable half of the McGuire twins. Drinking the sacramental wine before mass, stuffing socks into the privy, leaving dead rats outside the Sister's bedroom doors, and endlessly sass-mouthing. And then there had been scandalous whispers at the orphanage about a boy and Isabel. About Isabel McGuire disappearing into the trees on the way home from school. No amount of punishment had seemed to bring her into line. Sister Edel's upper lip dampens at the thought of the defiant McGuire girl . . . and of Kathleen. She recalled the pain of being a young woman and having to choose between her love for Kathleen and her love of God. She had not wanted this same anguish for Aelish McGuire, and so Sister Edel had set about doing what was necessary to save Aelish from the moral booby trap that was her twin. Just as the solution for Kathleen had been obvious, so too had been the fix for Isabel McGuire.

She opens and closes her stiff hands; blood struggles to flow into her thickened joints. She stares at her right hand, the empty finger next to her pinky. The plain gold band symbolizing her devotion to Christ was removed with lard when her finger turned a bruised shade of purple.

Sister Edel skims a fingertip over the backing of the picture Sister Mike dropped on the bedside table. She turns it over, caresses the tarnished floral etchings on the frame with her thumbs, expecting a heavy remorse. Instead, for the first time in decades, Sister Edel escapes her spreading flesh, and feels shrunken looking down at herself in the photograph.

"I was fourteen that summer," she whispers. Touching a finger to the grainy image of her face, she connects with that young girl—always a bit rounder, more substantial than the others. *A strapping girl, a healthy lass.* Sister Edel's teeth clench, remembering these words used to describe her as a young woman.

Her eyes move to the other three girls in the picture. One of them appears no bigger than a minute and holding a stuffed toy. Squinting at the stuffed toy dangling from the smaller girl's hand, she whispers, "Mr. Muffin. Where did you get to?"

Sister Edel thinks of how she had let go of childish things easier and earlier than most girls. The call of God came when she took her first communion at age ten. As a teenage girl, only once did she question that vocation, despite the temptations that befell her. She covers herself with the sign of the cross, thinking of Callum Fitzgerald.

Holding the photograph closer, she studies the other young girl standing to her left with thick glasses perched on an upturned nose. Sister Mike and her eternal dirty spectacles.

"She was Fiona then, and she still can't keep those bloody glasses clean."

She shakes her head, a mix of mild disgust and nostalgia sitting at the edge of her heart. Despite resisting, Sister Edel's eyes sweep to the towheaded girl on the right side of the group. The sun catches her golden hair, lighting her up more than the rest. This one is turned slightly away from the cluster of girls, as though something more interesting were happening just outside the frame. A tight wrapping envelops her throat, and she tries to swallow it away.

"I will pray for you, God's mercy." Her words are stilted. Often, the sharpness of her words serves a godly purpose of keeping young women morally unsullied. It did not work with the girl gazing off the right side of the photograph.

"You reap what you sow," she utters as though the young woman were standing sheepish in front of her. She returns the photograph to the bedside table face down. *I'll get Sister Mike to put it back where she got it. Maybe I'll request the handyman incinerate it. That time is through.*

The beat of her heart reaches into the tips of her fingers and the soft indents alongside her eyebrows. Sister Edel is dropped back into her inert body at the sound of faltering footsteps down the hall, hesitating outside the door. Within the novice's faltering footsteps, Sister Edel hears, *This is awful—why me?*

"Go away," Sister Edel barks, despite having a full bladder and knowing it may be another three hours before the next dawdling novice shows up. As the novice walks away, Sister Edel hears her footfalls proclaim, *Thank you, Lord.*

7

AELISH, AUGUST 1955

Aelish cocks her head to the sound of Isabel's uneven pacing in the other room. She is murmuring to one of the twins, who is clearly unhappy. Aelish waits to see if Isabel can settle the little one, but the fuss swells quickly into a tirade. Aelish presses her palm against the wavy glass window in her room. She considers how the daily rituals from the abbey have been replaced. Prayers swapped out for lullabies, the scent of incense for talcum. Aelish now has two tiny altars in the shape of bassinets at which she prays the rosary every day, but only when Izzy is out of sight. Izzy seems to be just keeping her nose above the waterline in her convalescence, having two children and a husband to care for.

"Do you need help?" Aelish calls out, walking toward Isabel's bedroom doorway. It's Paddy making all the ruckus, a brilliant shade of angry as he writhes on the bed. Izzy sits beside him, her eyes puffy and red-rimmed, her hair a greasy tangle. Sar lies on her back, enthralled with her chubby toes. Aelish wonders if her ailing sister came home too soon, if Izzy's stubbornness has trounced her common sense yet again.

"Do you have to wear that all the time?" Isabel snaps, waving a hand at Aelish's robe and veil. A tear slides over Izzy's sallow cheek.

Aelish touches the chest of her robes, self-conscious. She knows her twin is overwhelmed, exhausted, but senses there is more. So much more. Aelish sensed it the first time she saw her in that hospital bed—Izzy's sickness was deeper than flesh. Her hands are unsteady, and her temper is short, even with the babies and especially with Declan. To hear them bickering through walls as thin as tissue often sends Aelish out of the house and down the hill to have tea and watch Lawrence Welk with Gabby Doolin on her new big boxy television. Both relief and luxury.

"Does it help to know I don't wear knickers underneath my habit?" Aelish asks. The attempt to make Izzy laugh works somewhat as one corner of her mouth lifts, then the other. "It's quite freeing, really." Aelish wiggles her hips a little. This loosens the dam, and Izzy's laughter soon turns to sobs.

Taking Paddy's pudgy legs, Aelish moves them as though he is riding the world's tiniest pedal bike. Having watched Mrs. Doolin do this with Sarah, Aelish knows it's magic. After a few moments of peddling, Paddy lets go of his troubles with a gusty little toot, then falls into a soft whimper.

"How did you know to do that?" Isabel looks as though she's just witnessed a miracle, then crumbles again. "I can't do this, Ay," she says and presses her palms into her eyes.

"We can do this together. You've got all of us . . . me, Declan, Gabby." Aelish pauses, wondering if this is a good time to nudge her sister toward the good Lord. "And Mother Mary. Pray to Mother Mary. She knows what you're struggling with."

When Isabel lowers her hands, the bitterness in her eyes makes Aelish sit back. Isabel's bottom lip quivers, transforming her into the ten-year-old girl who rolled up to the abbey in a wheelchair, bereft and incensed.

"Stop hiding and open your goddamned eyes, Aelish," Isabel hisses.

She grasps the bedcovers with each hand. Aelish begins to reach for her crucifix but thinks better of it. Isabel leans forward, her nose nearly touching Aelish's. The inside of Aelish's skull begins to roil with hot sparks. *Is this what it feels like inside of you, Izzy?* she wonders.

Isabel blinks several times and slumps back into the pillows, but not before Aelish catches a faint whiff of something antiseptic.

Aelish suddenly recalls being fourteen and sitting in church next to Isabel waiting for Father McManus to discover the empty glass cruet—the missing Sacramental mass wine that Isabel had drunk—Isabel with a grin stained purple, a sour scent on her breath, Aelish fermenting in guilt.

Aelish asks her now, "Isabel, have you been drinking?"

Not one to lie, Isabel says, "I'm a grown woman, Aelish. I can do as I damned well please." Izzy stares down and absently rubs at her palm with one thumb. She does this more and more lately. When Aelish draws her hand out, Isabel initially resists, then softens.

"What happened, Izzy?" Aelish traces one of the thicker scars on her twin's pink palm. Sarah makes a sucking sound in her sleep, then falls silent.

"They didn't tell you, did they?" Isabel asks. Aelish hears a click in her sister's throat. "No one told you. Not even your precious Sister Mike. What you believe in is a lie, Ay. They're a bunch of liars and thieves. Dark as tar, each and every one of them." Izzy wraps her hand around Aelish's first two fingers, just like the babies do from time to time. Unlike the babes, her grip is fierce. Aelish's breathing grows rapid, shallow.

"Sister Mike is not a liar or a thief." Knowing to speak softly, Aelish hopes to keep the calm, as Izzy is still prone to jags of coughing when excited or upset. Aelish is confused by her sister's words and desperate to change the subject.

"They steal lives, Aelish. I was one of the lucky ones." She holds out her palm, jabs at the pale puckered scars. "I got out."

"What are you talking about? Where did those come from?"

Isabel's eyes widen, and her mouth narrows into an angry white line. Aelish wonders if she herself has ever looked so hurt, so dark, so resentful, then remembers the day she fled from the schoolhouse in the rain, mortified. As the thought of that day traverses her mind the crisscross pattern of scars on her soles prickles.

"Girls? Anyone home, or have you all flown the coop on me?" Declan's chipper voice makes Aelish blink. She bends down and rips her shoes off, rubbing the distant throb across her soles. Isabel is staring at Aelish, head tilted. The sound of his heavy boots comes down the hall. "I feel like the odd man out, what with a house full of twins." He stands in the bedroom doorway, beaming at his babies. His grin falters when he looks at his wife. "Is there a sisterly squabble happening here?"

As though sensing her father's nearness, Sar wakes, reaches her chubby arms into the air. Declan scoops her up and hoists her high over his head. A milky strand of drool lands in the centre of his forehead. When Aelish looks at Izzy, she is smiling. Her resentment is a bear backing into its cave.

"Tell Da what's going on in here, sweet Sar. What's the gossip?" Declan asks, still marvelling at his wee daughter.

"Just a bit tired today." Izzy rubs at one eye. "I could use a rest for a while if you don't mind."

Aelish squeezes Izzy's hand, wordlessly hoping Izzy will let her into whatever dark cage is holding her. Aelish wants to soothe her twin, the way Izzy comforted her after Aelish was whipped across the tender bottoms of her feet, holding a cool cloth to Aelish's soles, bringing her food when she could not walk. But Aelish worries her sister's wounds have festered far too long from the inside; the infection likely seeped into her bloodstream.

As Aelish heads down the short hall, Paddy snug on her hip, Declan ahead of her chatting with Sar about seagulls and fish guts, she steps gingerly. The bottoms of her feet have not pestered her like this in years. Her face and her soles burn and she wonders if Declan ever thinks about that day. She steps to the window and stares out, unable to face her brother-in-law, imagining he and Izzy having a good laugh about it—a laugh about her running away from school. And she is mortified all over again. Izzy's words come round again: *They steal lives . . . Dark as tar, each and every one of them.* And Aelish is unsure why it has never occurred to her to wonder if Sister Edel and Sister Mike remember that day Aelish ran from school and why.

AELISH, 1946

NOT LONG AFTER DECLAN KISSED AELISH IN THE SCHOOLROOM and, in a panic, she'd passed off her feelings about him as Izzy's, Declan and Isabel started teasing each other. Isabel developed a tittering giggle Aelish found ridiculous.

"What's wrong with your sister?" Mean Clare had startled Aelish from behind. Wet leaves scampered across the schoolyard, Clare's presence pushing the misery of the weather deeper into the bones.

After a fortifying breath Aelish turned to square up with the most hateful girl she knew. The same girl she'd slept next to, close enough to touch, for six years.

"Doesn't she know that Declan kid is thick in the head? A real plank. Can't read proper or spell his own name, likely." Clare snorted, then spat on the ground. While shorter than Aelish and Izzy, Clare was all sinew. A nasty badger, always ready to bite.

"He is not thick." Aelish looked to the ground, toed an acorn with her boot.

"Oh, wait a minute," Clare said slowly, tilting her head to get a better look at Aelish. "You're blushin'! You like him too!" Clare pointed a sharp finger. "You like your sister's cabbage-headed boyfriend."

"I do not!" Aelish exclaimed. "Leave me alone or . . ." Aelish's mind sputtered. "Or I'll tell everyone that you're sixteen and still suck your thumb at night."

Clare's eyes narrowed to spiteful slits, the tendons in her neck standing out in thin ropes. She rapped Aelish on the chest with a blunt knuckle.

"You better mind your own feckin' business, or I'll tell Sister Mike *and* Isabel you kissed Declan."

Aelish stepped back, rattled. At the same time, she wondered if Clare was bluffing. There was not a single second of that day Declan kissed her that Aelish had lost. She was certain Clare had pretended to have a dose of something that day and had stayed in bed. She took a chance. Told another half lie.

"That's not true. I never kissed Declan." She stood taller, tried to imitate Izzy's unapologetic boldness.

"Doesn't matter," Clare retorted. "Just keep your mouth shut." She spat again, then turned her vindictive attention on one of the defenceless home babies, dismissing Aelish as though nothing had happened.

Picking up an acorn, Aelish threw it against the stony schoolhouse. She wanted it to bust through the wall and send the whole thing crumbling to the ground, but it bounced off and rolled back to her boot. She watched it totter back and forth on its roundness, wondering how such a mighty tree could come out of something so small and boring. Aelish stomped on it, smashing it beneath her heel. Empty inside—no miracle or magic power to bring out a giant sheltering tree.

"Aelish," Izzy called out, all the while making glad eyes at Declan. "Come stand with me. Let's stay warm together." She knew

Isabel only wanted to stand next to her so Teacher didn't notice her flirting with a boy.

"Don't be loose." The words slid past Aelish's bitten lip before she could catch them.

Izzy looked at Aelish, tilted her head. "What did you say?"

"I said, you're such a goose. It's time to go back inside."

Aelish felt Izzy's fingers slip into hers as they walked up the steps. Aelish squeezed her hand, then pulled her limping twin up the steps.

"Ay, you look a bit cheesed off. Was Clare giving you grief? What did she say?"

"Nothing. She's a lot of hot air."

Just then, Declan ran past, bumping Aelish's shoulder. She stumbled, then fell to her knees with Isabel still holding her hand. The jolt of hitting the floor knocked a great gust of wind from Aelish's backside.

The kids bustling into the room suddenly froze in a silent herd. Then the popping of snickers and giggles began. Clare's jeering laugh cut clean through. Izzy's hand was still in Aelish's, but it soon began to shake. She too joined the laughter. The sounds of all the giggling fluttered around Aelish, a bunch of blackbirds pecking at her pride. Stealing a glance upward, Aelish saw that Declan and a few of the home babies were the only ones not laughing. The pity pouring from Declan's moss-coloured eyes made Aelish's spine want to curl into a tight spiral. He took a step toward her, reaching out his hand. She would rather he had kicked her. Less humiliating.

For Aelish, that shame-riddled moment buried ever having liked Declan Kelly.

"Aelish! Wait!" Izzy called out as Aelish ran down the lane, eyes bleary, her heart pumping shame through her veins.

Aelish had hoped to make it to her bed unnoticed; however,

Sister Bernice nabbed her by the scruff just outside the dormitory and delivered her straight to Sister Edel's office.

"Tell us what happened, Aelish." Sister's Mike's voice was soothing, and for a moment, Aelish thought, *It will be alright,* as she sat in the chair, hair hanging in strings around her burning cheeks. She scratched at her arms, tried to move her lips, but her mouth was sealed with a wax of humiliation. She swiped a trickle of rain or tears from her pointy chin, hoping to free her jaw. The odour of Sister Edel's office was that of a musty barn on wet days.

When Sister Edel smashed her hands together in front of Aelish's nose, her stomach lurched, and she was hurled back into their crumbling home on Donegall Street, under the cracking beams in the ceiling.

Dropping to the floor, Aelish covered her head, anticipating a rain of brick and wood on her back and bare neck.

"Sister Edel, let us remember the Lord's mercy," Sister Mike implored. "Can't you see the child is upset about something? Did someone hurt you, Aelish? Are you okay?" Sister whispered.

"She is truant," Sister Edel barked. Aelish cringed, hearing the explosions. "You need to stop coddling these girls, Sister Mary Michael. Now, unless you can give me a very good reason why you are here, Miss McGuire, I have no choice but to deal with your lack of respect." Mother Superior nudged Aelish's leg with the toe of her black shoe. "Do you have anything to say for yourself?"

Aelish shook her head and planted it between her knees, put up no fight as Sister Edel dug her fingers into her arm and hoisted her off the floor like a bag of sopping rubbish. The lashings across the bottom of Aelish's feet came as a strange and merciful relief, the disgrace in the classroom made smaller with each stinging crack of the stick, each cry that escaped her throat. And she welcomed the punishment for her dreadful thoughts as she had run through the storm back to the abbey. *I wish it was Isabel who died, not Mammy and Daddy. I hate her. I hate her. I hate her.* For a relentless moment, she had understood spiteful Clare.

When Sister Edel unlocked the door, Sister Mike rushed in. Sharp words between the Sisters shot back and forth above Aelish's head, lost in a hazy sky of pain. Feet and heart throbbed in unison as Sister Edel carried Aelish to the dorm room in arms as thick as trees. She set Aelish on the bed, stood tall, then straightened the knotted cord at her waist with her stubby fingers. Aelish stared at each knot and thought about what they represented, repeating it over and over.

Chastity, obedience, poverty, enclosure . . . Chastity, obedience, poverty, enclosure . . . Chastity, obedience, poverty, enclosure.

"I only do this for your good. You have a heart for God, and we must guide that along in any way we can. Have you learned your lesson, Miss McGuire?" Sister Edel's voice came to Aelish from the farthest corner of the heavens, as light as a feather.

"Yes, Sister." All was quiet in her head as she studied the four secure knots.

A heart for God. Chastity, obedience, poverty, enclosure. Those words had fallen like a downy blanket over all her worst fears.

AELISH, AUGUST 1955

"IS ISABEL DRINKING?" AELISH RESTS THE KNOTTED ROPE OF HER belt across her lap, runs one foot back and forth atop the other, itching the scars. She watches Declan's Adam's apple bob as he swallows his lukewarm coffee. He enjoys it lukewarm. Reaching down into the tall neck of his big green boot, he scratches his leg, hesitating, perhaps stalling. He looks wearied; Aelish wonders if she should leave him be and rest before he leaves for the fishing boat. Setting his cup down on the kitchen table, Declan runs a thumb over a chip on the mug's lip.

"Is she, Declan?" Aelish pushes. It is Isabel's well-being, after all, and she needs to know.

"She says it calms her nerves. When she's back to herself, she won't need it. But for now, with two six-month-old babies and all . . ." His voice trails off, eyes flicking from Aelish to the chip on the mug. Her mind asks a hundred questions at once, as it is prone to do. *When, how, and, more importantly, why?*

"What about those scars on her hands? Where did those come from?" Having scoured Isabel's letters for any hints of suffering, Aelish found nothing. The only constant thread was her wanting Aelish to come away from the abbey and be with her.

"I only know bits and pieces," Declan says, rubbing one eyebrow. "I was hoping *you* could tell *me* more. She just showed up on me parents' farm, middle of the night in the freezing cold." Declan spins his mug side to side, shaking his head. "I've never seen anyone in such a mess. Her lips were blue, and she was bloody all over. It was the first time I'd seen her in months. Thought she'd disappeared on me. I was sure my heart broke when she was gone, but that was nothin' compared to seein' her that night. She was a ghost, Aelish. I thought she was going to die, right there on me Ma and Da's front step." Declan lifts his mug halfway to his lips, then sets it back down.

The room around Declan dissolves from Aelish's vision. She is swallowing continuously to keep everything down. How could she not know Isabel was so hurt?

"Ma cleaned her up, found most of the blood was from her hands and knees, and put her to bed. When they found out who she was . . ." Declan scratches at a speck of food on the table, drops it into his coffee, and pushes it away. "Where she was from, what with no folks and all, they told her to go back to the orphanage where she belonged, back to them Catholics, back with the Sisters." Aelish touches her veil, self-conscious from Declan's pained glance.

"When did this happen? Did you ask her what happened?" Aelish's voice is dry. Her memory races back but cannot find a time when Izzy was badly cut on the hands. *It did not happen at the abbey,* Aelish tells herself. *I would have known, I should have known.*

"It took years to get anything out of her, and I know she's not told me the whole story," Declan continues. "When she told my folks that the nuns kicked her out, my folks couldn't see fit to keep her, especially when they saw the way we looked at each other. They were charitable enough to find a lady in the community who needed a house cleaner for room and board. So that's where she went. And when me ma and da refused to let her come round, I went with her, I did." Declan's eyes well. "I love that girl in there, Aelish. I'll love her even after I'm long dead and gone."

Aelish stares at the missing piece in Declan's mug, wondering if it's grown bigger in the few short minutes of their conversation. *Kicked out? Izzy wasn't kicked out, she left,* Aelish thinks as she tugs at the skin on her throat. She pictures the brief note Izzy left on her pillow all those years ago, the rage she poured onto red-headed Clare because of it.

Declan's chair creaks as he leans forward, elbows resting on his thighs, soiled hands hanging loosely. Aelish turns her hands over and back, wipes them together, hoping to shed any imaginary cinnamon-coloured hairs or cobwebs of rage. *My scars are tucked out of sight,* she thinks.

"Everything alright there, Sister?" he asks, then turns toward a rumble of thunder out the window. A brilliant finger of lightning touches the horizon.

"Tell me what she has told you, Declan." Something gauzy starts to lift from Aelish's eyes, and it terrifies her. *Izzy suffered nothing physically beyond bruises on her back and bottom from Sister Edel's stick; however, she's got scars I don't know about, can't reach.*

"I can't do that. Not my place." He shakes his head, and he

holds up his hands. "She's my wife, and I can't go betrayin' her trust. Just isn't right. Besides, you know that temper as well as I do, and I'd like to keep everything attached to me body, ya know. We are trying for number three, after all." He glances down at the front of his pants. This time Declan is the one to crimson when he remembers who he's speaking to. "Oh, Lordy, I'm so sorry, Sister. I just got so comfortable around ya . . . it just felt like you were normal people like . . . not that you aren't normal. Ah, jaysus."

Aelish considers letting him dig a deeper hole, if only because the air in the room grows lighter the more he stumbles and stutters. "You want to keep diggin'? 'Cause I can still see the top of your head," she teases. And for the first time, Aelish enjoys feeling like a young girl again.

"I do remember the temper," she says, letting him off the hook. "And I'm going to be selfish and say I would like more nieces and nephews, so I will talk with Izzy myself." Aelish smiles and scoops her shoes off the floor.

"Best get to the docks, or I'll miss the afternoon boat. Tommy's sure to tear a strip off me if I'm late." Declan tosses his coffee down the drain, and when he turns back to Aelish, he is less red, and relief softens the edges of his eyes. "She needs you, Aelish. She's tough as them rocks out there, but Izz needs you." He slips his hat onto his head and shrugs into his coat. "One down, one to go," he says under his breath.

"Pardon?" Aelish asks, confused.

"One miracle down and one to go." When he opens the door, the wind off the ocean fills the room. Standing in the doorway, he is framed in a background of boiling slate clouds. "You and Izz are made up, and now we just have to get me ma and da to come to their senses. Those wee ones in there need a proper family. I'll make it happen if it's the last thing I do." He steps out the door and, as though he has forgotten something, spins and takes two long steps back into the room. Taking Aelish by the shoulders, he plants a quick kiss on her cheek—proper this time, like brother and sister.

Aelish is frozen on the spot, just as she was all those years ago in the draughty schoolroom.

"Thank you, Aelish, for being so good to Izzy. I know she doesn't make it easy, but she loves you." He presses his lips together, then says, "We love you. You're our family."

Before Aelish can say anything, not that she knows what to say, Declan is clomping down the steps two at a time, headed down the path for the docks, pinning his hat to keep a sudden hand of wind from snatching it away.

"A proper family," she whispers. Aelish's throat clenches at the thought.

Pausing in the bright and dishevelled living room, Aelish holds her cheek; she hovers over the sleeping twins. Sar's lips move as she sucks on an invisible nipple. Paddy has the back of his hand plugged into his mouth, as usual. She notices Declan's blue hanky on the floor, the one he usually has stuffed in his back pocket, picks it up and thinks to run to the door and let him know he's left it. *He's too far gone,* she thinks, and tucks it into her sleeve.

Drinking in the perfection of the babies, she touches Sarah's brow and says, "A proper family."

Once she's prayed over the twins, Aelish plans to head to Isabel's room, where she'll remove her veil and crawl in behind her sleeping sister. Aelish let Izzy slip away once, and she will not do it again.

AELISH, 1946

AELISH'S ITCHY BURNING SKIN FOREBODED SOMETHING WAS NOT right. As she, Sister Mike, and Charlie Rose drove back from cleaning the church rectory in a neighbouring county, the newly healed scars on her feet prickled, her elbow creases burned, and her lower bowel was in a furious twist. They had been gone overnight and Aelish had begged Izzy before leaving: please behave, please leave Clare alone, please avoid Sister Edel. Never did she think to say, *Please don't leave me.*

Aelish shifted about on the stiff vinyl back seat while Sister Mike and Charlie Rose marvelled at the snow falling in hunks unlike anything Northern Ireland had seen. Charlie Rose's mother had predicted it—rather, her crabby hip had. Aelish squirmed, biting her knuckle, worried. Her worst fear was Izzy clobbering Clare for ratting to Sister Edel about her day at the beach with Declan. Her imagination did not stretch beyond that.

Aelish headed straight from the car to the sleeping hall after hanging her jacket and slipping out of her wet wellies. When Aelish stuffed her hands in her pockets to warm them, her fingers wrapped around the dense scone Sister Mike had given her to take to Izzy—"But tell no one," Sister had warned with a wink.

A few girls were making their beds or slipping on wool socks. A new little girl with wide-set eyes, a moon face, and bright red, cracked lips stood at the window, mesmerized by the snow. The back of her white-blonde hair was a snarled nest. She did not yet know the routine, so Aelish held her shoulders and turned the little one gently in the direction of the doors.

"Time to get cleaned up before morning prayers." The stunned girl looked up blinking, then scurried off.

Scanning the cots, she saw Isabel's was empty, her bed made. The muscles in Aelish's back stiffened—bracing against what, she didn't know. *She's likely in the washroom,* Aelish's mind reasoned, even as her bowels coiled tighter.

Clare was bent over, snapping the sheets on her bed up and tight, her tangle of cinnamon hair sticking in all directions. Spotting Aelish, she paused. Clare's smirk was loaded. Her gaze flitted to Aelish's bed for a moment. She swiped a wiry sprig of hair off her face, then turned her attention back to straightening sheets.

A piece of paper poked out from under Aelish's pillow. Her arms went cold, her anxiety alchemizing to lead. Aelish felt miles aways from her hands as they pulled the paper out from under the pillow.

A bird warbled outside, caught off guard by the sudden snowfall. She unfolded the paper; it shook so badly she could barely read the perfect handwriting. Isabel's penmanship had always been impeccable.

Dear Aelish,

Aelish read the first words, then drew the paper to her pounding chest. Steadying her hands, she began again.

Dear Aelish,
I had to leave. I hope to explain it to you someday.
Your life can be good and safe here. You belong at the abbey.
I don't. I'm sorry.

Love,
Izzy

The thin sheet of paper slipped from her lifeless fingers, drifting to the floor and disappearing under the bed. Clare sat on her cot, chewing her fingernails then spitting them to the floor. She looked up, and the corners of her chapped red lips curled down, her grin reversed. She casually swung her feet, one toe worming out a hole in her stocking. Studying Clare's cold marble eyes, every hurt she'd safely tucked away broke loose in Aelish's brain, driving her across the narrow space between the beds. Aelish heard the bird unprepared for winter throw its body against the window.

Clare's eyes flooded with confusion and a bit of marvel as Aelish flattened her to the bed. She bucked under Aelish straddling her chest. Clutching fists full of hair, Aelish banged Clare's head against the thin mattress over and over. The room was a flurry of stars. In the dazed part of her mind, she wondered who had let the snowstorm in. The howling of a wounded animal filled the room.

"This is your fault! She's gone! It's your fault! I hate you! I hate you! I hate you!" Aelish's screams were not enough to sate her fury.

Yanking clumps of Clare's cinnamon hair brought no relief. Clare managed to free her arms to protect herself from pelting blows. Aelish did not feel her pinky finger break as it smashed into a bony forearm. But the sting of the stick across her back suspended everything. Aelish arched her spine, then fell to the floor, her bones relieved of their rigid rage.

In the infirmary, the pale pink curtain around Aelish breathed in and out. Sister Mike's distraught eyes hovered behind black-rimmed glasses. A small sting came as the needle punctured Aelish's flesh, followed by a suffocating heaviness seeping through her skin and into her muscles. She slipped down a sightless hole.

8

ISABEL, AUGUST 1955

ISABEL SINKS INTO THE SAGGING DIP OF THEIR SECONDHAND mattress. The Doolins were so kind, collecting from the small fishing community all the things the young Irish couple would need to start a life here in Canada. Including a job for Declan on Tommy Doolin's fishing boat. Having grown up tending soil rather than sea, four-legged animals rather than fish, Declan finds the work exhausting and challenging. Despite being worn out and telling unnerving stories of Mother Nature's unpredictability, her husband always returns from the ocean looking calm. The salt water seems a poultice drawing out his day-to-day concerns.

Theirs is a small home, the walls a thin skin through which she hears Aelish and Declan talking about her. Neither of them has all the pieces of the story. Only Isabel knows. And as her twin sister and her husband talk, they stack a prison of history around her. Despite knowing it is not true, she sometimes wishes Aelish had never come. It would be safer.

Staring at a long crack in the plaster ceiling, Isabel questions: When will it all fall on them? That misgiving has been circling frantic laps within her since the age of ten. She wonders if perhaps a day—a lifetime—on the fishing boat for her might stop that question. When will it all fall? Over and over, she has gotten her answer.

She turns to her side; the incision down her chest aches. Covering her head with a pillow, she hopes to smother the sound, the light, the memories. But it all wriggles its way out. Soiled images—things Isabel vowed never to think of again after her twins were born—push to the surface. These hauntings fortify the desperation to get Aelish away from Sister Edel, away from the abbey.

She sees the tree that helped her over the wall that night when she was sixteen—a reaching woody hand. She leapt from a sturdy branch to the top of the stone wall, shocked by the waiting fangs of glass embedded in the top edge of the wall. They chewed her palms and fingers to ribbons. That pain, however, was nothing compared to the agony she was leaving behind as she fell to the other side of the high barrier.

Even now, resting in her sagging mattress, after all she has endured, Izzy is not sure how, as a teenage girl, she managed to limp away from that place with no broken bones. It was the only time God was ever watching out for her; she is sure of it.

With her head still turtled under the pillow, she reaches over the edge of the mattress and under its soft cotton belly. Her fingers pause their search, touching smooth glass. *This is the last time—I just need to rest,* she tells herself. Finishing the last few fingers of whiskey, Isabel vows to try and let it all go. As she drifts off she promises to pour her willfulness into getting Aelish to stay.

ISABEL, AUGUST 1955

THE SUN OFTEN SHINES THIS TIME OF YEAR IN NEWFOUNDLAND; however, the constant wind is strangely absent in their U-shaped cove where Izzy sits on the sand, Paddy tucked between her legs. The ocean is offering a show of emerald sparkles unlike any other. Isabel watches Declan, knee-deep in a tidal pool, Sar resting on his hip, his pants rolled up to show his skinny freckled shins. He holds a spiralling shell on his palm for Sar to poke and pet. Paddy topples sideways between Izzy's thighs, and she catches him at the last moment. Isabel pulls his hat back and kisses his rust-coloured curls, then shields her eyes to look up the hill.

"Auntie Aelish is coming, Paddy, see?"

Aelish is making her way down the dirt road from the slanted church. Isabel can see her twin's smile and wonders if her own smile is as bright. Touching her lips, she feels like it might be getting so.

As Aelish approaches, Izzy taps the wool blanket beside her. "We've been waiting for you, Auntie." Dropping down beside Izzy, Aelish pulls beefy Paddy onto her lap, kisses each dimple on the back of his hand.

"Hello, lad. I said a prayer for you in church this morning." Aelish glances at Isabel, tentative. Feeling strangely unbothered, Isabel decides to let it go.

Declan walks across the stones toward them. He bends, plucks Paddy off Aelish's lap with the ease of picking a leaf off the grass. "Come on, kids, let's go home and let the ladies natter. One of ya smells ripe." Declan slips into his wellies as he sniffs his babies.

"Well, aren't you just husband of the year." Isabel leans back on her hands and watches him walk away, balanced by a child on each hip. They shimmer in the bright sun.

"Thought maybe I could pay a visit to the pub later if I'm a good boy," he says over his shoulder. *That grin will never grow old,* Isabel thinks to herself.

She cups her hands around her mouth and shouts, "We'll see about that, Declan Kelly!"

When she turns to Aelish, her sister's eyes are glassy. A wind picks up and floats the black veil off her shoulders; it reminds Izzy of a crow in flight.

"I have to go back to the abbey soon, Izzy."

Isabel picks a round black stone off the beach, squeezes it, then throws it to the water's edge, where it disappears into all the other stones just like it. Aelish stands and brushes sand from her robe.

Picking another stone, Isabel hands it to Aelish and says, "Let's see who can throw the farthest, Ay."

"Did you hear me, Izzy?"

Izzy wishes she could shut her ears against these words, this idea of separation. Something doesn't sound right in her twin's voice.

"You throw farther than me, you can go back. I throw farther, you must stay a while longer. Another month—or two."

Aelish shakes Isabel by the shoulders.

"Izzy, did you hear me?" Isabel blinks. Aelish turns pasty white. Suddenly she is close enough to smell the coffee on her breath. "Something has happened—we have to go to the docks—Isabel!"

The sunny cove, the black stones, the hiss of waves, the bargaining for more time—it is all yanked away by a gale outside her bedroom window—Isabel is back in her bedroom with the cracked ceiling. Aelish's eyes frighten Izzy more than being shaken, more than the words. Even more than the disappearing ocean and cove.

"Declan?" Isabel says, her mouth, her brain gluey. Sitting up, she glances over at an empty amber bottle lying on the bedside table. "Where's Dec?"

Aelish pulls a wool sweater over Izzy's head and says too softly, "There's been an accident, Izzy."

Adrenaline combusts inside. Catching her foot in the blankets, Isabel stumbles then grasps the doorway. Mrs. Doolin rocks side to side in the middle of the living room, a twin on each padded hip. She gnaws on her lower lip, her eyes wide and round.

"Oh, my dear girl," Gabby Doolin says as Isabel bursts out the front door and down the steps in bare feet.

On a good day, the steep hillside path down to the docks is a measured, careful walk for Isabel's lopsided gate. Today is not a good day. Stumbling down, she hears Aelish calling, "Isabel, wait for me, be careful!"

A gale blows clear through a fist-sized hole in her chest. Two things she loved—the scent of ocean brine and the call of seagulls—are ruined for Isabel McGuire.

ISABEL, AUGUST 1955

BOWLINE. CLEAT HITCH. FIGURE-EIGHT KNOT. CLOVE HITCH. Running toward the dock as fast as her feeble leg will allow, Isabel's mind speaks the knots Declan showed her while sitting at the scuffed kitchen table, a chunk of rope snaked to the floor between them. "You're hopeless," he said. She purposely floundered over and over, just to hear his laughter.

Men clad in thick sweaters, rubber boots, and knit caps stand in a close circle on the dock. Fishing boats and little dories scrub against the edge of the pier, held fast by rugged lines. On any other day, this clutch of weather-beaten men might be standing over an impressive cod. For a few blessed moments, Isabel lets herself believe this is true. The men turn to the uneven sound of her feet pounding the planks, remove their knit caps, and look away.

"Izzy!" Aelish cries out, close behind.

Declan's feet are bare. And blue. *Where are his boots?* Isabel wonders. She is always after him to take off those damn boots in the house.

"He lives in those boots," she whispers, then comes to a teetering halt. Her legs turn to pillars, as stiff as the thick wood posts holding the pier above the ocean. Aelish's arms wrap around her sister's waist seconds before those pillars turn to ash. The men, stinking of fish guts and grief, close the circle around the two women huddled together on their knees. Isabel howls, holding Declan's long narrow feet. They're chilled and wrinkled. Isabel rubs them, blows warmth on them. Mrs. Doolin's husband Tommy, the man who gave Declan a job on his fishing boat, turns away and vomits into the bay.

"Isabel. Isabel. Isabel. Dear God in heaven, help us. Mother Mary, I beseech you, help us." Aelish whispers into the side of Isabel's head, rocking forward and back.

"A blanket!" Isabel barks. "He needs a blanket . . . to warm him. We have to warm him up."

Tommy Doolin drops to one knee. "Mrs. Kelly, Declan is gone." He places one chafed red hand on Isabel's wrist, the other on Declan's ankle. A wet, choking sound rises from his throat.

"A blanket," Isabel says again. "A blanket." She speaks louder, as no one is moving. When she finally raises her eyes past her husband's feet and sees his beautiful face, the same shade of blue, she screams, "A blanket!"

Aelish stiffens, clenching tighter to her twin. Tommy Doolin sits back, points at two of the barrel-chested fishermen and orders, "Take 'em off." The men stare back, stunned. "Your goddamn sweaters, you eejits. Take off your bloody sweaters!"

The men scramble out of their heavy layers and place them over Declan Kelly's chest and legs. When Aelish lets go of Isabel, Isabel cannot breathe. It's as though Aelish is doing the breathing for both of them. In her mind, Isabel hears her twin whispering: *Hold on, I'm here, hold on.*

Aelish pulls off her black veil and drapes it over Declan's bare shins and Isabel's hands clasping her husband's toes. When Aelish wraps her arms around her sister once again, Isabel gasps as though rising from the depths of the very ocean that has just taken her sweetheart.

"Our Father who art in heaven, hallowed be thy name." Aelish's lips move against the side of Isabel's head as she prays.

It has been many years since Isabel's parents have appeared to her, shimmering and smokelike. Now they stand at Declan's head. A luminous Sarah McGuire kneels and strokes the space an inch above Declan's wet, dark hair, leaving green light trails. Da stands behind her, looking upon Isabel. His eyes swim with sorrow. A third shadowy form rises behind them.

In that instant, Isabel thinks only of her children—the gaping hole she would have to fill should they be fatherless. She knows that dogged grief, and it engorges her body in a sea of flames.

Isabel scrambles up her husband's body and, despite her husband being twice her weight and lifeless, flips him onto his side.

"Izzy! Stop!" Aelish cries out.

Isabel pounds on his back, fuelled by all the rage she has kept cornered as bombs dropped on her life. The edges of her dainty hands strike a sharp shoulder blade. There is a cracking sound. Isabel's brain does not register the fractured bone in her hand. Da stands over Isabel, shaking his head. Aelish prays between sobs. Isabel grunts and pounds on her sweetheart's broad back. The men step away. Something in them knows better than to step between this woman and her torment.

AELISH, AUGUST 1955

NO MATTER HOW LOUD AELISH PRAYS, SHE CANNOT BLOCK OUT the hollow-drum noise of Izzy pounding Declan's back. It is the desperate sound of someone wanting in, frantic not to be left out in the cold.

"Thy kingdom come, they will be done . . ." Aelish's voice cracks.

She plugs her knuckle between her teeth and bites hard. It has been many years since Aelish has felt the tingling on her skin, her edges disappearing. Isabel's thumping fades. The praying stops. Aelish becomes what, as a scared little girl, she thought of as a God-speck. Declan is surrounded by the same bleary shimmer of heat that rises off a hot road. Every blow from Isabel sends out indigo droplets as though she is slapping a human puddle. *He's gone,* she thinks, hoping Izzy will hear her. *Please stop,* she says again, and the waves around Declan turn a radiant violet.

Isabel curls both of her hands together into a petite hammer and, as if giving the very last of her willpower, swings them into the middle of Declan's back. The pop of another bone in Izzy's hand or perhaps one of Declan's ribs reaches Aelish's ears. The noise, the shot of pain in her own fingers, slams Aelish back to the fish-stained, splintered planks of the pier. As Isabel and Aelish cry out in pain-filled unison, Tommy Doolin shouts, "Stand back, give her some space."

Aelish crawls to her sister, grabs her by the wrists. Declan flops onto his back; a trickle of brackish liquid seeps from the edge of his mouth. Aelish looks away and into the acidity of Isabel's glare, her skin fevered. Aelish fights against the instinct to pull away.

The fight comes before the collapse as Izzy thrashes, yanks, uses her meagre body weight to escape both her sister and the cold blue truth lying in front of them. Praying to her Lord for the strength, Aelish holds on even as muscles in her arms and back threaten to cramp. She prays for the courage to say what needs to be said, knowing it will drain the hopeful venom keeping Isabel upright.

"Izzy, look at me!" Aelish commands. "Look. At. Me." She is staggered to be here again. Once more telling her twin that the centre of her life is gone. First Ma and Da, now her sweetheart.

"Declan is gone." The words sap all her remaining energy. The guilt as she watches Isabel crumple over her husband's wet body is inexplicable. The protective storm of rage runs itself out.

Aelish feels as responsible as the ocean. *The sea took Declan's life,* she thinks, *but I took Izzy's hope.*

The dock shudders and creaks as more people gather at the end anchored to land.

"Why is that man all blue? Where's his wellies go?" A child's questions float by. "Is he a sea monster?"

Her innocent curiosity is a feather next to the iron truth of death. Aelish recognizes the child from the ship. Sofia is the plucky, unafraid little one who pulled her from the rail and reminded her so much of Isabel. The child fights her mother, who is trying to turn her into the folds of her skirt. Protect her from death—from life.

"Mammy, let go! I want to see the blue monster!" The mother stares, uncomprehending, even as her hands work to hold the determined girl.

"Alright, folks. That's enough." The middle-aged priest from the slanted church on the hill rushes through the small crowd and lumbers down the dock. He's still clad in yellow rubber overalls from his morning fishing trip. "I think it would be more helpful if you all head to the church and start praying for this poor family. Go on, now." He waves them off as though they are pestering seagulls, but no one moves more than a step or two. Hands are clasped over mouths and hearts. But not eyes; never eyes.

Tommy Doolin meets the priest halfway and says, "I'm afraid it's too late for last rites, Father. Sister Clare has been here praying the whole time, though."

"I want to see the monster!" The young girl's demand is loud enough to be heard across the island. Every head turns to see the mother attempting to drag the petulant child off the pier, both caught in a twist of determination.

Isabel lifts her head from Declan's chest. Aelish bites her knuckle, slides fingers across the rosary beads in her other hand. Isabel has always been unpredictable, even at the best of times. Aelish is crouched, bracing for the explosion.

"He's not a monster." Izzy's voice is flat, soft. The mother and child stop their wrestling. "He's my sweetheart." Izzy runs the sleeve of her bulky sweater under her nose, blinks several times as she looks at the child. The girl squats, keeping a safe distance, and examines something small in the cup of her pink hand.

"What's wrong? Why you crying?" The girl talks without looking at Isabel, as if she knows better.

Isabel bites her bottom lip. Aelish hears her answer inside before it's spoken, and it makes her cover her mouth to keep from wailing.

"My sweetheart's gone to sleep, and I miss him."

The little girl with dark hair and defiant eyes stands and takes a step toward Isabel. Her mother grabs her by the arm. The girl yanks free. Simultaneously, Isabel and the child say, "Let go!"

The little one walks toward Isabel and Declan with surety. Squatting on the other side of Declan's body, she unfolds her smooth fingers one at a time. Aelish leans forward to see what is nestled in the folds of her palm. The child plucks a white-and-brown-specked spiralling seashell the size of a thimble from her hand and places it on the centre of Declan's unmoving chest, then taps it three times.

"Him want you to have this. Make you feel better," the girl announces as though she knows exactly what she is talking about. Isabel covers her mouth with both hands, and tears pour over her fingers. The child rises, spins, and runs up the dock through the crowd, ducking her mother's grab. A flock of seagulls fighting over fish guts bursts into the air as she charges through the middle of them, giggling.

As Izzy reaches for the shell, Aelish steadies her hand by holding her narrow wrist. Isabel clutches the seashell to her chest. Aelish curls around her sister. Tommy Doolin sends one of the younger fishermen up the hill to fetch blankets and tea from Mrs. Doolin.

9

ISABEL, SEPTEMBER 1955

ISABEL SLUMPS INTO THE PINK-FLOWERED ARMCHAIR NEXT TO the window, staring at the peeling paint around one of the glass squares. Another thing Declan was going to repair before the end of summer. Now September has arrived and he is gone. A book of fairy tales rests in her lap; the first gift Declan gave to the babies. He had always struggled with the way words jumbled and mixed in his head.

"I won't have my kids feeling like eejits in school, not the way I did," he'd promised her and himself. Izzy remembers him holding the book out to her while looking down at his socked feet. She often reassured him he was the smartest man she knew, but nothing could pull that root of self-doubt. "You don't know many men, Izz, so it's not hard to find me clever." And then he'd grin the beautiful way he did, showing all his teeth.

Isabel holds the book to her chest and bites the top edge to keep from screaming and waking the twins. *They're so wee,* she thinks, *only six months and they will never know their da.* They will not miss their father. Not the way she misses her da near daily. Feeling envy for her children's ignorance makes her bite harder on the book of rhymes. The craving for drink is a thousand earwigs crawling on her skin.

"This is my fault," she whispers.

For the past forty-eight hours, Isabel has been telling herself that if she had been awake, she would have sensed something—anything—warning her to stop Declan from going on the fishing boat that morning. Isabel picks at the flaking paint with her ring finger and stares at the simple silver band Declan gave her.

"What is? What's your fault?" Aelish asks.

She stands at the edge of the living room in the kitchen archway, her head tilted, dark hair tucked behind her ears. No veil or robe tonight. She's wearing a pale yellow housecoat. Barefooted. Isabel isn't sure if this is on purpose, but she appreciates it. It's comforting to see her twin sister, not some stranger in a starched wimple, moving through the house, holding the children, trying to cook.

Aelish doesn't wait for Izzy to answer; she doesn't have to. "This was an accident, Izzy. You heard what Tommy Doolin said." Aelish sits on the arm of the pink chair, strokes Isabel's hair. "A storm caught them out, the sea was rough. Declan reached down to untangle a net and got his wrist caught. It could have happened to any one of those men."

"But it didn't. It happened to Dec. To us." Unable to control anything, Isabel hurls the thin book across the room, barely missing their only lamp. Aelish flinches when it hits the wall. "I was asleep," Isabel says. What she does not say: *I was drinking.* Isabel digs into her thighs to keep from lashing out. A mound of confusion forms at Aelish's brow. "If I'd had my wits about me," Izzy says, "I could have stopped him from going to work. If I had been better, he wouldn't have had to work so much." She gathers the cotton of her nightdress in bunches in her fists. "Declan offered to take an extra shift on the boat . . . because of me."

"You don't know any such thing, Isabel McGuire!" Aelish scolds. "That's just foolish talk. You know better than I do, there is . . . there was no stopping that man from doing what he thought was best for his family."

The break in Aelish's voice is more than Izzy can stand, so she gets up and walks to the kitchen. A few strides away from Aelish and a few strides closer to what she needs, Isabel breathes easier. The chair leg puts another scrape into the wood floor when Izzy pulls it to the fridge. Hiking her nightie above her freckled knees, Isabel steps up onto the seat.

"What are you doing?" Aelish asks in her unique high-pitched tone of worry. Isabel grits her teeth.

Even on tiptoes, the stubby brown bottle sits just out of reach on the top shelf. As she stretches her arm, the top edge of their refrigerator digs into her armpit. Izzy wriggles her fingers and hisses through her teeth as a shot of unbearable heat surges through the pink scar on her chest. "Feckin' bajaysus!" Isabel shouts, then grasps her ribs.

"Dear Lord, Isabel! Are ya daft? Get down from there." Aelish stands beside the chair with hands curled on her hips. Isabel sees her ma in the tilt of Aelish's head, the tight line of her lips, the flare of nostrils. The shimmering image Isabel saw of Ma and Da on the pier returns. However, Declan stands behind them this time, a full head taller and a hand on each of their shoulders. The world slows, the floor stretches away, and Izzy's knees give out.

A CHILLED CIRCLE PRESSES INTO ISABEL'S CHEST. SHE FEELS THE mattress's sag under her and wonders how she got back into her bedroom—her and Declan's bedroom. Declan is gone, and the sag they shared is now a sorrowful trench.

"She's fine, Sister Clare. Good thing you caught her before she hit the floor. The incision is fine, well healed. Just a case of nerves, I suspect. Poor thing." Isabel recognizes Dr. Sinclair's voice reaching into her fog but keeps her eyes shut. She cannot stomach the piteous looks.

"What was she doing up on a kitchen chair, anyhow?" he asks.

There is a pause. Isabel's leg muscles tighten. Aelish knows what Izzy was straining—longing—for at the back of the cupboard.

"She was getting something for the babies, I suspect." Aelish's voice is thin, and the grip she has on Isabel's hand tightens as she lies.

"How are the twins doing? Shall I have a little look at them? It's a blessing they are so young." He makes a clucking sound, and without seeing him, Izzy knows he's shaking his head. "They won't even know their father is gone. The Lord works in mysterious ways, am I right, Sister?"

Before Isabel can open her eyes and grab the ageing doctor by his thick shock of silver hair and shake him to pitiful bits, Aelish says in a chilly tone, "The twins are fine. And there is no blessing nor mystery to be found in this situation, Doctor. Now, if you think Isabel simply needs rest, I'll show you to the door."

Isabel cracks one eye enough to see Aelish take the older man by the arm, lift him from the edge of the mattress, and hustle him out the door. He fumbles to get his stethoscope back into his black case as they walk.

Izzy wants to weep. She wants to laugh. She is doing both when Aelish comes back into the bedroom, a sleepy-eyed baby straddling each narrow hip and Sar clutching her auntie's earlobe. Aelish is the only one who does not look on Izzy with sticky sympathy. It's as though she knows something about Isabel's strength that Izzy herself does not know.

"Have you had just about enough?" Aelish asks. Isabel folds her bottom lip into her mouth and bites down. "Because I have. And I won't stand for it, Isabel McGuire. We've had more terrible in our lives than anyone deserves—we don't need to go searching for more. You have decisions to make, and you'll do them with a clear head. Do you hear me?" Paddy reaches his arms out to his mother, grunts and squirms. When Aelish sets the hefty boy on the bed, he scrambles up Izzy's chest, grabs handfuls of her dark, unwashed hair. Perhaps it's because Paddy's a boy that Isabel sees more of Declan in him, especially in his eyes' soft slant.

"I don't know what to do," Isabel whispers into the top of her son's head.

"Well, neither do I." Aelish's eyes well, and she runs a knuckle across her blotchy cheek to catch a tear. "Neither do I," she repeats, sounding defeated.

The bottom of Isabel's tummy drops as an inconvenient truth wriggles to the front of her mind. What if Aelish stops praying? In that question, Isabel discovers that her loathing of and her dependence upon Aelish's love of God have been silently equal. She fights against understanding that Aelish's faith has always been a vicarious blanket of safety, one Isabel never had to hold down when the winds blew. That was Aelish's job. Aelish was the one planted on her knees at the foot of the Mary statue in the dark dormitory, or the chapel, or the stations of the cross circling the backyard of the abbey.

"You're not leaving us?" Isabel feels like a small child; her throat threatens to close. Aelish mentioned a few days earlier that Sister Mike was bidding her return soon, and the thought of it then was hard enough. Now, with Declan gone, it is unfathomable.

"I think we should go together—all of us. As a family." Aelish rocks from one bare foot to the other, the hem of her soft yellow housecoat swaying at her shins. Sarah is intrigued with a bit of lace on the collar and pulls it into her mouth.

The old smells of lye soap and incense fill Isabel's nose, making her cough. Panic presses at her throat.

"To Ireland?" The words are bitter tasting. The thought is suffocating. "Are you feckin' daft?" If not for the children, Isabel would throw something. Paddy startles at the sound of his mammy's raised voice, his eyes growing big. Isabel kisses his mouth, and he decides not to cry.

"I'm not leaving Declan. This is our home."

"All of us need to go back, Izzy," Aelish says softly. "You're not the only one who lost Declan. You're not his only family."

"And you're not his family AT ALL!" Isabel screams. "Not if you're suggesting I take him back to his parents. Maybe you should go back, Aelish. If that's your idea of helping me, then go back."

Isabel watches as, one by one, her words take down the three people left in the world who love her. Paddy's lip quivers and fat tears roll over his lashes; Sar buries herself into Aelish's neck. Aelish tries to blink back tears but fails. She circles her hand on Sarah's back and *shh*'s the baby. Isabel feels the seams of what's left of her heart unravel a little bit more.

"Give her to me," Isabel says, reaching out for her daughter. Aelish hesitates. "Give her to me," she repeats, clamping down on everything and aching to have both babies against her chest.

Sarah clings to Izzy's side when she is set down. Gathering the twins to her body, Izzy smells the soft creases of their necks, their silky fingers, the milky tops of their heads. She is hoping to find some trace of their father. Kissing them, she is desperate to capture the last kiss he laid on their skin. Isabel licks her lips and wonders if Declan kissed her before he left; she can't remember whether she was awake or asleep. Aelish holds her cheek as she closes the door behind her. When Isabel hears her sister's soft crying through the door, the worn threads of her heart undo entirely. As she weeps, she tastes the dirt of her parents' graves back in Ireland.

AELISH, SEPTEMBER 1955

SHARP-EDGED STONES CHEW AELISH'S BARE FEET. SHE IS DRAPED in robe and veil, but the thought of shoes felt like stifling leather caskets. Aelish fears that if her skin does not touch the ground, she might float away on the sorrow—the strange anger—and what lay beneath it all.

Aelish is confused about why she is gripped by such hatred toward Izzy when her heart should have nothing but compassion. The dock dips to one side when she steps onto it; the spongy dampness of the boards is a relief to her soles. *If I lie on my belly, will my heart receive the same solace?*

It has been three days since Declan died. Twenty-four hours since Isabel demanded she go back to Ireland. The silence between them is a thorny bulwark.

"I can do it" is all Isabel says when Aelish reaches for one of the babies, or attempts to prepare some food, or pulls the broom out of the closet. "I can do it myself." Over and over.

Sitting on the edge of the dock, Aelish sinks her feet into the frigid water, turning them golden below the surface. They soon numb. A stubby dory the fishermen use to travel back and forth to the bigger boats rocks beside her.

Reaching into her sleeve, Aelish twines her fingers into the blue handkerchief she plucked off the floor. The one Declan often tied around his neck to keep the cold out and the sun off.

It suddenly has the weight of a stone. She is scared to question why she's held on to it. She fears that her evaporating connection to the Lord may be wrapped up in its faded fibres. The sound of the water sloshing against the dory's belly is made louder with her eyes closed. Every sight, sound, smell is piercing. But nothing more so than what she's desperate to keep out of God's omniscient sight.

The hitching in her chest rises as sudden as the storm that took Declan's life. Before logic can bind her, the dory's ropes are undone, and Aelish is rowing out of the harbour. Her tears draw a bleary curtain over the houses, the slanted church, the rough hillside in front of her. The burning in her lanky arms and thin back go unnoticed as she leans forward, circles the cumbersome oars, throws all her weight back and yanks through the short chop of the bay. Each stroke births a grunt. When the shoreline—Izzy and Declan's tiny home—are nothing but flecks of white against the black rock, her arms stop. Peeling her fingers from the oars one by one, Aelish stares at the pale blisters rising on her skin. The salt water stings when she leans to dip her hand into the ocean. Her anger at Isabel is now as distant as the tiny seaside village. She cannot feel Isabel inside her mind; the rope between them is still and slack. *Does it wait for me onshore? How can I ever go back?*

"Please forgive me, Lord," she whispers, touching a wet finger to her forehead, heart, and each shoulder. "For I have sinned."

When she pulls out the blue handkerchief, it unfurls in her hand, a miniature sail fluttering on the wind. As clear as a photograph, Aelish sees Declan's concerned youthful face among those who laughed at her that day on the schoolhouse steps. She recalls how every morning in the schoolyard he greeted her, smiling as warm as the sun. "Did you have a long sleep, Aelish?" he would often ask, as though it mattered to him. "Are you sure you want to help a thickheaded cabbage like me?" he would ask when Aelish offered to help him read.

A shrill cry cuts the brisk air—a cruciform shadow sails across the floor of the boat. Looking up, Aelish shields her eyes and watches what she thinks, at first, to be an enormous seagull. Several realities collide as she follows the bird's effortless soaring. Declan knew what it was like to be embarrassed, ashamed. She recalls him fumbling over words like sharp thorns, his long body slumped down to avoid being chosen by Teacher to read aloud. Most of all, she remembers his reaching for her when she fell to hands and knees on the schoolroom steps, willing to pull her up from the muck of mortification.

This makes her love him even more than she did as a young girl. And the seabird headed for the empty horizon is an albatross.

Aelish curls the handkerchief into her hand and holds it against her forehead. She dares not press it to her nose, knowing that the scent of him would be a place from which she could not return. *I would have to stay in this boat and drift away,* she thinks. *I could never return to shore, face my sister.*

With her eyes tight, she sees it: the instant she acknowledged Declan was not only a man her twin sister loved but a man she loved. It was the moment Aelish looked down on his lifeless face. Alive, he belonged to Isabel; it made sense. Dead, he belonged to no one, and her heart exhaled its truth. A rockslide of truth that would certainly crush her sister.

"Dear God in heaven, please forgive me my trespasses, my coveting. Dear Lord, please." With no walls to catch it, her pleading drifts away. "Help me, dammit!" Screaming at the sky turns her throat raw. The silence is broken only by the waves caressing the sides of the dory.

Aelish slips to her knees and holds the edge of the boat. Her disjointed reflection ripples on black water. She does not recognize herself in the fragmented pieces. The water is numbingly cold; it's a relief that her hand cannot feel as it dangles in the ocean. Dipping both hands in brings more deliverance. Under water, Declan's handkerchief is a blue swath of kelp pulled by a liquid breeze. The sleeves of Aelish's robe grow heavy, absorbing the salty water. Numb to her elbows, she closes her eyes, leans a little more. She remembers the small child pulling her back from the ship's rail.

A whisper in her head says no one will pull her back this time.

If I could just put my head under water, she thinks, *it might wash all of this away—a second baptism.* In the space from one breath to the next, Aelish leans and is over the edge, upside down under water.

The shock of cold forces her mouth open and her lungs to draw air. Her nose, throat, chest, belly fill with the fire of salt water. Her arms tangle in her wool robe and her veil billows around her. Everything slows. The sound of lapping waves is gone. Her limbs dissolve in frigid waters. Her right hand drifts in front of her face, a tail of blue cloth fluttering from its grip. Her fingers appear fish-belly white, swollen as they lengthen out one by one. The handkerchief hangs in the space of her open palm, then is pulled away. Closing her eyes makes it easier to let it go. Closing her eyes makes everything easier.

AELISH STRUGGLES TO CURL AWAY FROM THE STONES PELTING her back and chest. Everything from her stomach rushes up and out her throat in a briny geyser. Her insides are washed in acid, she coughs, and the pain makes her cry out.

"Sister, c'mon now! Just breathe now, Sister Clare, that's it." The shaking begins as Aelish takes a gasp of fresh air and opens her eyes. She's never been this cold, so cold her bones hurt. Tommy Doolin kneels beside her, his meaty red hands shaking, droplets of water clinging to the silver whiskers on his chin. Aelish feels the rocking under her back; above her, she sees a small canvas sail.

"Ya put the heart crossways in me, Sister. What were ya doing out in that dory by your lonesome?"

He digs through a canvas bag and pulls out a packet of cigarettes. Aelish's throat is far too raw to speak, so she pulls the wool coat covering her body closer to her chin. The cigarette nearly disappears in the hook of Tommy Doolin's thick finger as he lights it. The scent of tobacco makes Aelish want to cry. *Sister Mike would be ashamed of me.* Tommy runs a hand up over his wet eyebrows and into his thin hair and stares out to sea.

"Just imagine, two of ya inside a week. Lucky for you, the weather's fine." He swallows and shakes his head. Tommy Doolin continues to talk as though Aelish were not shivering on the floor of his sailboat. "Can't even imagine what that would do to your sister, or my wife, come ta think of it. Woman thinks of everyone under the age of forty as one of her bloody children."

Leaning back, he shifts the rudder a bit to the right, and the boat lists to one side, then centres itself. Aelish slides a trembling hand out from under the heavy coat to draw her veil tighter under her chin. Instead, she grasps a handful of wet hair.

"I had to take it off ya, Sister. Was weighing ya down as sure as cement in your wellies." His ruddy complexion turns a darker shade. "My apologies. But either that come off, or we both went down."

"Where is it?" It hurts, but Aelish has to ask. She knows the answer will hurt even more.

"Well, I reckon it's at the bottom of this here ocean by now."

He peers over the edge as though he might still spot it drifting downward. Aelish stares at her empty hand; her fingertips are wrinkled and blue. This slaps her with the image of Declan's feet . . . his blue handkerchief. Where is it? She can only hope it's nestled with her veil on the seafloor in inky darkness, never to be found.

"If ya don't mind me asking again, what were you doing' out here? You're lucky I was on my way in from the bay around the point. I watched ya dipping your arms in." Aelish must look away from his hazel eyes, his penetrating stare. "I hollered at ya ta be careful, close enough to be heard, but it was like you were deaf. And lickety-split, you was over the edge like a slippery fish got away."

"Fresh air." It's all she can think to say. It's pathetic.

"Pardon my sayin', Sister, and God forgive my foul mouth, but we live on a feckin' rock. There's plenty of fresh air to be had whichever direction ya head . . . on foot." To make a point, he blows a cloud of smoke over his head and raises a finger as the wind pulls the smoke away.

The sobs rise and are out before Aelish knows to stuff them down. It's as though they were trapped under all the ocean water in her belly. She curls knees to chest and pulls the wool coat over her exposed head.

"Oh jaysus, Doolin, ya gobshite!" Tommy says to himself. "Now you've done it. Gone and made a nun cry." There's a heavy patting on Aelish's back that feels more like a thumping as Tommy Doolin attempts to calm her with ham fists. "Now, Sister. Stop yer cryin'. I didn't mean ta ride ya so. Just worried, that's all. I'm a thick old fool. Mrs. Doolin tells me so every day. Don't mind me."

They sit in a silence broken only by gulls wheeling and calling, more so the closer they near the dock.

"I'm the fool," Aelish says finally from the dark shelter of the coat. Sliding her head out, she sees Tommy Doolin grinning at her wide enough to show he's missing one of his side teeth.

"Ya wanna' know who's gonna be lookin' the fool, Sister Clare?"

Aelish shakes her head and wipes her top lip across the coat's collar.

"The cod down there wearin' your nun headgear."

There is a moment of silence before they both decide it's okay to laugh—to laugh to the point of tears. To laugh to the point where Aelish cannot catch her breath and begins to cough up the remnant of the sea in her belly.

"You're gonna be alright, Sister. The whole lot of ya." Tommy flicks the last unsmoked bit of his cigarette into the water just as the boat's nose nudges the dock. When Aelish sits up, her head spins. The dory she slipped out of is a wooden dog tied and tailing behind Tommy's sailboat. As he goes about tying off the lines, turning knots as deft as a magician, Tommy says, "I reckon you'll soon be taking the young fella back to his family in Ireland?"

Aelish crawls out of the boat, staying on hands and knees, not yet trusting her legs. "Isabel refuses. I feel it's only right, but she doesn't seem to think so." Tommy throws his canvas bag onto the dock, lights another cigarette, stands with one hand on his hip. Without his heavy coat, Aelish can see that the man doesn't often miss out on his wife's home cooking, which explains why he is not shivering, despite being wet head to foot.

"Our boy lives on the other side of Canada. Not even a different country." He raises a palm to the sky. "Heaven help us if anything happened to him, me and Gabby would insist he come back here to be with us for his final rest. Wouldn't have it any other way."

"I can't get her to listen to me." Aelish draws her knees to her chest and stacks her bare feet. She should go back to the house. But she cannot gather the strength to explain what has happened or hide what sits at the bottom of the ocean.

"Declan came down here more than once riled up worse than a fighting rooster because of that little gal up there." He juts his chin up the hillside. "Are you sure she wasn't born a redhead? Before the lung fever took a bit of spit out of her, a few dishes were thrown in that kitchen. In fact, he pitched her off the end of this very dock one time, to cool her off, sober her up." Tommy glances at Aelish and folds his lips over his teeth as though he has let something slip.

Aelish nods her head and asks, "Do you think you could talk to her, Mr. Doolin? She might listen to you. I know taking Declan back is the right thing." She swallows, sparing this rugged fisherman another bout of her crying. "And I can't leave her and the babies here. I have to return to the convent, and I just cannot leave them here."

Tommy extends a hand and hoists Aelish to her feet. The weight of his arm is a log over her thin shoulders. In a way, it plants Aelish back into the earth.

"If ya don't mind an old bugger being nosy awhile longer, where are your wellies?"

Aelish looks down at her purplish toes, wiggles them, and says, "It's a long and windy story with no good ending. Let's go wet the tea." Tommy Doolin chuckles, then helps Aelish up the hillside path.

ISABEL, SEPTEMBER 1955

"YOU'RE NOT MY MA!" ISABEL HOLLERS AS SHE THROWS A TEACUP into the sink. The dainty handle breaks clean from the porcelain body. Isabel stands with her back to the sink, fingernails digging into the counter, glaring at Gabby Doolin.

"And a good thing for you, Miss Isabel. You're none too old to go over my knee. You keep on breaking dishes, and you'll soon be eating off the floor." The trusty anchor that is Mrs. Doolin stands, unflinching, on the other side of the kitchen table, arms crossed over her heavy chest. This should remind Isabel of her battles with Sister Edel, but Gabby Doolin's eyes are too filled with affection. "It's a horrible thing that's happened, and I suspect it's not the first horrible thing," she says, shaking her head. "But you've got to stop thinking about yourself and bring that lad back to his folks. He was a lovable young fella, and I can't imagine how much his ma and da miss him."

Isabel slides down the cupboard to sit on the wood floor and hides in her hands. Mrs. Doolin makes a huffing sound as she lowers herself into a chair at the table.

"I can't go back there, Gabby."

"This isn't his home, Isabel. He needs to be taken home for his final rest. His folks—" When Mrs. Doolin's voice breaks Izzy pulls her hands away from her eyes. "They need to lay eyes on him. If I lost mine and did not see them, I'd dig a hole and crawl right in."

Isabel tastes dirt. She wishes it weren't so, but it happens whenever she thinks of her parents. She did not get to see them before they went into the ground, and she is starting to see, even though she was so young, it may have maimed her—given her an emotional limp to match her gimpy leg.

"I see them," Isabel confesses.

She twists her fingers together, does not look up at the matronly woman in her kitchen. She's never told anyone, not even Aelish. "My parents. And now I see Declan too. Just glimpses sometimes, and other times like floating pictures."

"Well, at least you have that," Mrs. Doolin says, matter-of-fact. "What do his parents have? Some unfinished business and hard feelings. Let them put that to rest along with their son." Gabby Doolin pauses, folds a tea towel sitting on the table, then says, "I don't want to say this, but I get the feeling it's the only way to make you understand how selfish you're being." Isabel's jaw clamps down. Gabby Doolin leans forward, brushes Isabel's cheek. Izzy wants to pull back, slap the woman's hand, but the comfort of her touch, the scent of butter on her fingers is too necessary.

"Imagine if it were Paddy or sweet Sarah," she says softly.

This is the one thought Isabel has been holding off, tucking away. She holds her stomach and fights to catch her breath. Everything about Isabel—her past, her resentments, her need to be angry—falls away. All but her motherhood.

Gabby grabs the tea towel, dabs Izzy's eyes, and then holds it to Izzy's nose.

"Blow," she says.

Isabel obeys and snorts into the towel. *How is it possible to be a lost child and a lost adult all at once?* Isabel wonders.

"Let's have some Red Rose," Mrs. Doolin says as she lifts herself off the chair and heads for the kettle. "Those wee darlings will be up soon, and we best have some tea in us before they do. This quiet time, it's like hens' teeth. Rare and gettin' scarcer, I hate to tell you."

When Isabel stands, she spots Aelish and Mr. Doolin trudging up the hill, Tommy with his arm slung over Aelish.

"What in bloody . . ." Izzy's voice trails off when she sees Aelish is drenched and missing her veil.

Limping to the door, she throws it open and asks, "What happened?" As Tommy Doolin slips out of his boots at the bottom of the steps, Izzy sees he's wet as well. "What have you two been up to?" Aelish walks up the steps on stiff legs. She is shivering, and her lips are near purple. Declan's blue face flashes across Izzy's mind, and she covers her mouth. "Aelish! You're soaking wet."

"Gabby, I think ya best run the good Sister a hot bath," Tommy announces. "And I'll take some of that Red Rose."

The chair creaks when Tommy sets his thick body down. Without question, Mrs. Doolin trundles off, tea towel over her shoulder, to run hot water into the tub. Aelish pulls a quilt from the couch and wraps it around her body.

"Would one of you mind filling me in?" Izzy asks, her heart filling her throat. She searches for the rope, staring into Aelish's red-rimmed eyes. There is silence inside and out.

"'Twas just a silly thing," Tommy says, waving a hand in the air. "The good Sister was looking at something in the water and fell in. Done it myself more times than I've got fingers." He wiggles his thick digits in the air.

Izzy lets go of her held breath. Something about this story makes her back away. *I don't want to know,* she thinks, turning to the whistling kettle. Isabel pours two more cups of tea and thinks about how to ask a question that, even in her worst nightmares, she never thought she'd have to ask. The tremble in her hand spills some of the tea onto the table.

"How do we get him home?" Isabel says.

A surprised glance passes between Aelish and Tommy. Aelish bites her knuckle. Tommy clears his throat, pulls out a cigarette, and sets it on the table. Isabel wonders why he doesn't light it. That is, until Mrs. Doolin comes around the corner and gives him a swat to the back of the head.

"Tommy Doolin, don't you go stinkin' up Isabel's pretty house with that. You don't smoke in our home, yer certainly not gonna start here. Filthy." She gives him a second swat on the head, then kisses his cheek with a great smacking sound. He rubs his head and feigns a hurt look.

Tommy clears his throat, spins his teacup around a few times, and says, "I reckon the same way they brought those young fellas home from war a few years back. He'll be on the ship with you—down below, of course, in a pine box. He's at Carnell's, right?"

Izzy can't answer.

"Yes," Aelish says. "Will they bring him to the ship?" Aelish steps a bit closer to Izzy. "If Izzy decides to bring him to Ireland, will Carnell's bring him to us?"

Tommy rolls the cigarette back and forth under his finger. His eyes well and he clears his throat.

"You don't have to worry about any of that," Gabby interjects. "Tommy knows old man Carnell, don't you, dear? In fact, I believe he owes you a favour for getting him home from the pub more than one time and saving him from being walloped by that surly boot he calls a wife. Tommy will take care of that sure as you like." When she kisses her husband's cheek again, Isabel has to look away. The number of times she kissed Declan while he sat in that same chair. Mrs. Doolin takes both Isabel and Aelish by the hands and sets them in chairs on either side of Tommy.

"Come, girls. Just sit and drink your tea, then this one is getting in the tub." She pats Aelish on the head.

It starts as a hint of a smile on Izzy's lips. Watching Aelish being patted on the head tickles something inside. A nun being patted. Aelish smirks, then Izzy begins to snicker. The two of them clutch at Tommy Doolin's shoulders as they fall into laughter.

"I've had about enough of crazy women for today," Tommy says, unwedging himself from between the twins. He sets his empty mug into the sink, and the unlit cigarette between his teeth wags as he asks, "What happened here?" The broken teacup is miniature in his thick fingers as he examines it.

Mrs. Doolin raises one eyebrow, then looks to Isabel, who stops laughing just long enough to say, "It's a long and windy story with no good ending."

PART 2

10

ISABEL, SEPTEMBER 1955

THE MORNING SEA AIR BITES AT ISABEL'S EXPOSED FINGERS. As she blows on them, the image of her wool mittens comes into her mind. "I know exactly where I left them," she says into the wind. She pictures the frayed red mittens Mrs. Doolin knitted for her resting on top of Declan's pine casket in the ship's echoey belly.

Since the age of ten, Isabel has used her vibrant imagination to visualize the worst. "If I can picture it, I won't be surprised" is her motto. Returning to Ireland with her beloved in a pine box eclipses any dreadful flight of imagination she could create.

Not a day of the sea passage has gone by without an hour or three spent sitting next to or sometimes lying on his coffin, crying, talking about the babies or how hard it was to leave Gabby and Tommy Doolin behind, everyone in tears.

Izzy holds her curled hands to her mouth, then tucks them into her armpits. She wonders if she will see them, Ma, Da, and Declan, in Ireland. *Will they follow me back there? Am I going mad? Is my head broken?* It is not the first time she has feared her mind is pitted with deep dark holes. She's thought of bringing it to Aelish—this business of seeing dead people—but the distance between them is too messy.

"That place did this to me. To us." Her voice is hoarse from days of crying. She touches the cracked rim of her nostrils, winces.

The flesh of her palms and arms itch; her chest flushes. Memories of climbing the wall all those years ago rush in. *It must be noon,* she thinks. *This is when it happens.* She's not had a drink since falling off the kitchen chair, and the drink has always acted as a liquid barrier, keeping the past at bay.

"Those preaching priests don't know their arse from their elbow when they go on about purgatory," she mutters.

It seems even on the open deck in the freezing wind, she is too confined; the itch is inescapable. And so, just as she's done for the past three days, she paces up and down the railing, dodging memories and waiting until the craving goes underground.

Isabel stops in the middle of her step and swing, step and swing, realizing that as much as she despises being trapped on this floating cage, what she must face in Ireland is far worse.

Isabel does not want to recount to Aelish what happened to her after leaving the orphanage. Her stomach churns at the thought. But Aelish needs to recognize, once and for all, the ruthless hypocrisy she has devoted her life to. Selfishly, Izzy had hoped Declan would tell the story, at least what he knew of it, so she wouldn't have to. The churning in her stomach turns to nausea.

Izzy holds her belly and says, "I can't tell her. I just can't say it out loud."

"Say what out loud?" Aelish's voice cuts through the wind.

Startled, Izzy spins to see Aelish standing with a bundled baby in each arm, her head tilted, brown hair flying loose.

Isabel's nausea storms the back of her throat, and she makes it to the rail just in time. Pressed against the steel bar and retching over the boat's side, Isabel notices how tender her breasts are.

SISTER MIKE, SEPTEMBER 1955

SISTER MIKE TURNS INTO THE AUTUMN WIND AND HEADS UPHILL. She likes to get the hard work out of the way and would rather have wind pushing at her back on the way home. A stone fence hugs each side of the thin black road, leaving a plank-sized shoulder to walk on.

Eventually, this road wends to the sea, she thinks, but that would take an hour on foot. An hour she does not have as Mother Superior. She has already wasted an hour this morning reading about the polio epidemic terrorizing Cork. *It seems,* she thinks, *the timeline of my life will be punctuated by a series of plagues—the Spanish flu, then lung fever, and now polio.* Picturing her pack of cigarettes sitting on her desk, she cannot decide if it was wise to refrain from smoking on her daily walks or not, especially today.

Aelish called six days ago with the horrific news of Declan and Isabel and their poor babies. She has three more days to wrap her mind and heart around this catastrophe as the McGuire twins cross the ocean. She had so hoped that Isabel's life had finally found its peaceful path with her husband and two children. And now this.

Reaching out, she plucks a brilliant crimson berry from a hawthorn tree crowding the road's edge. She rolls this tiny ball of perfection around on her palm and wonders: *How much can these young women take? Especially young Isabel.*

Aelish has a home here, a vocation, a comfort. And now Isabel has no husband and two children to care for.

"Those girls and their tumultuous lives were the singular challenge to my faith," she says to the berry, then tosses it into a shallow puddle, its brightness swallowed by dull water.

Those twins were not the only challenge to your faith.

She hears this voice inside her head often, and it sounds like Sister Edel. Recriminating. Unwilling to allow a hair's width of self-deception.

She spins the ring on her right finger and recalls the words upon which everything in her life has turned. "If you go in there, you're dead to me, Fiona. It's me or them." Standing at the top of the convent steps that day all those years ago, Fiona—who would soon be Sister Mary Michael—felt a rupture, a stubborn wound which never quite healed.

She is not sure how her legs carried her down the steps that day, or how she managed to slide the modest engagement ring off her finger. Her ears ring as she recalls the church bells clanging overhead, marking the moment. Celebration or death? Her skull throbbed from those three extra whiskeys she drank the night before, drinks to mark the end of a year-long struggle with God's unrelenting calling.

"Take it, Charlie, please," she pleaded.

Hands stubbornly stuffed in his pockets, Charlie Rose shook his head, vehement. His hat sat crooked, askew from the blow of her rejection. When she bent to set the ring on the step, a trickle of sick filled her throat. Tears slid from behind the rim of her glasses, one falling into the centre of the precious gold hoop.

"Please forgive me, Charlie, please, I do love you." Even the sight of him, humiliated and stricken, could not stop the truth. "This"—she pointed up the steps to the convent—"is more than love." And just as her legs had carried her, mindless, down the steps, they brought her back up, and with numb arms she swung open the convent doors and let herself be swallowed by that something more than love.

A horn blats at her right shoulder, a spray of muddy water paints the lower half of her black habit. The truck passing nearly scrubs her elbow, ruffles her veil. Sister Mike stands with her hands out, palms up, startled and miffed.

"Are ya off yer nut!" she hollers.

"Sorry, Sister!" the farmer yells but does not stop. He sends an apology wave out the window.

The flecks of mud on her glasses blot out certain details in the world around her. As she cleans them with the sleeve of her robe, Sister Mike wishes for a pair of lenses like this through which to look at all life—little pieces blocked out.

"To hell with rose-coloured glasses," she mutters. "Sometimes, I'd rather see nothing at all." She is thinking, once again, of Isabel McGuire. She supposes that even in the reminiscence of her brief engagement to Charlie Rose, she was thinking of Isabel, how Isabel wasn't given the choice of letting go . . . choosing something else, another path, another someone to love. Sister Mike wants to blame the eejit farmer who just muddied her for the grip of anger in her throat but knows it's Charlie she is strangely resentful of—unlike poor Isabel, he had a choice to find another path, another someone else to love when he proclaimed her dead all those years ago. And yet, he did not. She swipes her hand in the air, dismissing Charlie Rose and his muleheaded ways.

"What am I going to do with Isabel and those babies?" The mother and baby home in the next county comes to mind. Sister Mike has never been, but she is sure it would be a place for Isabel to get her bearings.

When Isabel ran off at sixteen to God knows where and Aelish fell into such a bleak place, Sister Mike prayed every morning and night on bended knees that Isabel come back from wherever it was she had run. *Bring her home, Dear Lord, just bring her home,* she would implore.

Closing her eyes now, spotted glasses hanging in her trembling fingers, Sister Mike gulps the brisk wind blowing in her face. She wishes that this wind still held all those prayers so she could suck each word back in. Leave Isabel to her life in Canada with a husband who is alive and children who have a father.

Sister Mike turns around and heads downhill, the wind at her back. She soaks in the effortlessness of this short journey back to the abbey, knowing there is far more uphill and into-the-wind work to be done when the twins return in three days.

AELISH, SEPTEMBER 1955

AELISH WANTS TO RUN TO SISTER MIKE, WHO WAITS AT THE END of the gangplank, arms outstretched. But with Sarah squirming in one arm and a bag slung over her shoulder, hurried walking is all she can safely manage.

"Oh, my dear hearts! Let me take this little one," Sister Mike says, reaching for Sarah.

"No!" Isabel shouts from behind. "Don't you touch her." Sister Mike lowers her open arms, steps back.

"Isabel!" Aelish says, stunned by Izzy's harshness. "Sister Mike was kind enough to come here and pick us up. She wants to meet Sar and Paddy. What's the matter with you?"

"It's quite alright, Sister Clare." Sister Mike pats Aelish's arm, then folds her hands in front of her body. "Isabel has been through quite an ordeal, and it's a mother's right to be protective of her children. It warms my heart to see all of you."

Despite her kind words, Aelish sees hurt in the Sister's eyes. And as though the older nun is a matronly magnetic north, both babies reach their arms out and wiggle their fingers at Sister Mike. The nun raises a hand and returns the wiggle. Sarah laughs, then slaps Aelish on the cheek.

When Aelish glances over Isabel's shoulder, she spots Charlie Rose. He removes his hat as he approaches three of the ship's crew who are walking Declan's pine box across the pier. They too have removed their hats. She tries to look away before Isabel catches her line of sight, but it's too late.

"Where are they taking him? Wait!" she shouts across the docks. She hesitates, then thrusts Paddy into Sister Mike's arms and hurries away. Sister Mike teeters on her heels under Paddy's heft.

"My oh my, what a big lad this one is!" She pulls her head back to get a better look at Paddy. He grabs at the rosary beads hanging around Sister Mike's neck. The Mother Superior chuckles when Paddy stuffs the beads in his mouth.

"What a bundle of sweets!" Sister Mike exclaims. "Mark my word; this one is headed for the priesthood, sure as you like."

Watching Izzy walk lopsided as fast as she can gives Aelish that old powerless sinking sensation. *If I could give her my legs, I would.*

"How is she?" Sister Mike is still grinning at Paddy when she asks about Isabel. "We've included Isabel and these beautiful wee ones in our daily prayers since you left. And then to hear about Declan. We're all heartsick, just heartsick."

Aelish moves a copper curl off Sarah's brow. "She's not well. There's so much anger inside of her, and not just because of Declan's death." As Aelish sees Isabel standing next to Declan's casket resting in the back of the truck, she stops talking—stops sharing about Isabel. *You've betrayed her enough,* Aelish thinks to herself.

"Where is your veil, Sister Clare?" Both the question and Sister Mike's voice startle Aelish from silent admonishments. She reaches up, touches the hair flying loose around her face. Aelish cannot make eye contact with the Mother Superior. She pictures her veil and Declan's blue handkerchief entwined on the ocean floor.

She lies. "We left in such a rush, what with the babies needing attention and Isabel being so distraught, I forgot to put on my veil the morning we left Newfoundland."

Without looking, Aelish can sense Sister Mike's searching stare. "You must not feel yourself without it. Am I right?"

"I don't feel myself for many reasons, Sister." It is the most honest answer she can give. Seeing the men standing away from Isabel, watching her as though they have no idea what to do, Aelish adds, "It's been a long journey, Mother Superior, and I fear we've only just begun the hardest parts."

Sister Mike sticks two fingers between her lips, gives a shrill whistle, and waves a hand in the air. Paddy startles in her arms, then giggles. Like dogs in desperate need of a task, the men standing around Isabel hustle over and grab the rest of the bags.

Charlie walks over, smooths down the sparse spikes of his brown hair, and gives Aelish a sad, tight-lipped smile. "Good to see you again, Sister. Sorry for yer loss. Yer sister's loss, I mean."

"Thank you, Charlie, for everything," Aelish says, squeezing his hand.

"Put the bags in the boot of my car, Charlie. And we'll follow you back to the abbey," Sister Mike says, then pokes Paddy on the tummy. "Do you want to see the abbey, young man?"

Paddy clutches her hand, pulls it to his mouth, and bites her knuckle. Mother Superior wrinkles her nose and pretends to cry. Paddy laughs. Despite the dreadful circumstances, Aelish cannot stop the relief. Sister Mike's playfulness is vibrant pasture in a stark desert.

Aelish looks up and sees Isabel standing next to the truck. *I can't leave him*. Aelish gives the nod. Izzy knows she's been heard and so climbs into Charlie Rose's truck and slams the door.

Tucking the babies into the front seat of the Mother Superior's car, Aelish attempts to contain their squirming. Paddy stands facing the back seat and bounces while Sar slithers down to the floorboards between Aelish's feet.

"Perfect, now you're both contained!" Aelish says as she clamps Sar between her legs and rests an arm against Paddy's backside.

Sister Mike cups the cigarette between her lips and flicks a lighter into life. The satisfaction that softens Mother Superior's eye as she blows smoke out the window makes Aelish wonder what it's like. Her fear has always been a white-knuckled fist. She wonders, *Would it simmer down if I smoked?*

"They're saying these will kill me." Sister Mike studies the orange ember tip, picks a fleck of tobacco off her tongue. "If these don't, then taking care of Sister Edel and Sister Eunice certainly will."

Aelish is fascinated by the smoky ribbon slipping past Sister Mike's top lip and straight back into her nostrils. The car makes a protesting grind and shudders forward as Mother Superior struggles to find first gear.

"Once I get going, we'll be right," she assures Aelish. Just for good measure, Aelish presses her arm and legs a bit tighter around the babies.

"How are they? Sister Edel and Sister Eunice?" Aelish asks.

Having smoothed out the ride, Sister Mike grips the wheel with both hands and leans forward, her chin only inches from her gripped fingers. There is no response for quite some time, and Aelish wonders if she should let Sister Mike concentrate. She's squinting through her smudged glasses as a curtain of smoke rises from the cigarette propped between her fingers.

Finally, she says, "One's cantankerous and getting more so every day, and the other is daft as you like. Sister Eunice's lucid days are strung out like a broke picket fence. Used to be sharp as a pencil. Ageing's not been friendly to her mind." Sister Mike shakes her head. "And poor Charlie."

Aelish is confused, suddenly concerned for Charlie Rose. However, Sister Mike looks to be holding back a smirk with little success.

"What about Charlie? What's he got to do with Sister Edel and Sister Eunice?"

Sister Mike risks a drag off her cigarette, the car swerving slightly, then says, "Charlie found our Sister Eunice in a delicate state." Swallowing keeps the laughter at bay for a moment before Sister Mike begins to giggle and cough. She abandons her smoke out the window.

"Mother Superior, what are you talking about?" Aelish can feel contagious giggles bubbling in her body. It's like a long-awaited exhale. She is suddenly glad Isabel is not in the car with them.

"Oh, you should have seen Charlie's face," Sister Mike says. "The way he sputtered and stammered. You'd have thought he'd seen a ghost." Sister Mike falls into another coughing laugh then says, "A ghost in the nip!" She slaps the steering wheel, and the car lurches left. Gripping the wheel again, she steadies the car. "She was out in the garden with not a stitch of clothing on."

"Sister Eunice? Nude? How, why?" Aelish pictures the tiny old nun digging in the garden just the way God made her.

Sister Mike coughs into the crook of her elbow, then manages to say, "She said that God told her it was good for the vegetables."

Aelish throws her head back and laughs in a way she has never done before. It is a sound that seems to come from someone else's throat. Someone who knows where she belongs.

ISABEL, SEPTEMBER 1955

THE IMMACULATE FARMHOUSE, BACKLIT BY THE LATE-AFTERNOON sun, sits a way back at the end of a narrow lane dividing two undulating pastures. Sheep with nappy coats and muddy bellies lift their heads, half-interested as the truck carrying a wooden box trundles by.

Isabel wonders if Declan helped raise any of these sheep. She presses a palm against her chest, thinking about how wrong it is that some empty-headed sheep should outlive her husband. Isabel's jaw locks with contempt and desire to rip the wool from their backs, pull those dark beady eyes out of their sockets.

"Declan's folks must have been some heartsick to hear the news." Charlie sniffles, slows the truck to navigate a cavernous mucky hole in the lane.

"I don't know. I didn't tell them."

Isabel looks out at the sheep, who have resumed their aimless grazing. *Everything goes on,* Isabel thinks, *everything except me.* She thinks back to the moment she found out she was pregnant with the twins. She was excited to tell Declan but ached to be truthful with Aelish. She was expecting something in her to bloom into a woman as her belly grew and her breasts filled; instead, she felt like a furious little girl parading around in a pregnant lady suit—terrified, confused, and fat.

Charlie's sudden stop sends Isabel jolting forward, reaching for the dashboard. "Mrs. Kelly, what do you mean you didn't tell them?" Charlie rubs two fingers across the stubble on his chin, perplexed. "I can't . . . we can't pull up to these poor folks' doorstep with their son in a box. It ain't right."

"Charlie, Sister Mike did it, she called them. I didn't."

"Oh, praise Jesus." Charlie blows out a puff of air and starts the truck rolling again.

Isabel leans ahead and squints through the dirty windscreen. Two blackened images stand on the front porch, both tall and reedy, like Declan. Her heart pounds a drum in her ears, and the itch rises. Suddenly she realizes what a mistake she has made.

And that it's too late. Declan's folks are watching the old truck bump up the road, a pine box resting in the back. There is no way to turn around, go back to the abbey, get Aelish. *Why did I think I could do this?* Isabel pinches her leg, and it sends a clarifying jolt of pain into her skull. *I took their son away, and now I'm returning him, dead.*

"Stop the truck! Charlie, stop!" Isabel claps a hand over her mouth. The truck stops just in time for Isabel to throw open the door.

"Mrs. Kelly, are ya alright?" Charlie asks after Isabel's stomach is emptied onto the lane.

Isabel takes the hanky Charlie holds out to her, wipes her chin, closes the door.

"Go on, Charlie. Let's get this over with."

Even in the failing light of the day, Isabel can see that their eyes are red-rimmed. Declan's mother is ashen. Declan's father has an arm wrapped around his wife's shoulder. Isabel must look away, not because of their sadness; rather, it is too hard to see what Declan might have looked like in his later years. He was the mirror image of his da. As Isabel walks up to them, she sees the singular and glaring difference between Declan and his father: Mr. Kelly's eyes are as cold as stone, where Declan's were always welcoming pools of mossy green.

Isabel stops short, an awkward distance. Aelish would know what to do, say, how to navigate this bog of grief between them. The silence of Declan's parents is excruciating. His mother stares at the box, resting in the back of the truck. She chews on her lip. Works her hands at her chest. Her longing to run to her dead son is electric on Isabel's mothering skin. Mr. Kelly grips his wife.

"Mr. and Mrs. Kelly, I'm sorry for the loss of yer boy." The sound of Charlie's condolences makes Isabel want to weep. But she will not give them her weakness. Not when the last words she overheard them speak of her were so horrible, calling her filthy and ruined, not fit for their son. They had gotten her a job hoping she might disappear. Anger suffocates any fear she might have had.

"The man in that box is a stranger to us," Mr. Kelly says. His wife makes a mournful whimpering noise. Charlie takes two steps back. "Our son was as good as dead to us the moment he left this house with her." Mr. Kelly juts his chin at Isabel. It is a punch in the gut. Isabel swallows, furious, her throbbing leg acting as an emotional thermometer.

"Then why did you have me bring him out here?" Isabel asks, incredulous. Mrs. Kelly's watery eyes flit from the distant sheep to Isabel to Declan's pine box, unable to focus on anything. For a brief second, Isabel worries about the woman; she looks as though she is teetering on the edge of a spell.

"Just to be sure you know," Mr. Kelly says, stepping past his wife. Isabel's body wants to retreat, but the part of her too acquainted with bullies wielding metre sticks and self-righteous judgements does not allow her to back down. Nor will she ask what exactly it is he wants her to *know*. The longer she stares at Mr. Kelly, the less she sees the likeness of her Declan. A brave relief settles inside her.

"John, please." Mrs. Kelly sets a hand on her husband's arm. He throws her hand back as if it were a foul thing, and she winds her arms together in front of her. Isabel sees Mrs. Kelly's hands shaking and decides to feel nothing for her.

"This. Is. Your. Fault." Mr. Kelly speaks the words slowly, each a nail sinking into Isabel's chest. Any bit of strength she held by clenching her jaw, shoulders, and guts drains into the dirt. A thick arm wraps around her waist, and for a moment, Isabel can smell Declan—a mix of salt water, coffee, and damp wood. Expecting to see him, she looks over her shoulder.

"Now, Mr. Kelly, let's not be like that," Charlie says. "These are tough times for all of ya. Everyone's shattered about yer boy, especially his young wife here. And his two children—your grandchildren—cute as they come, I might add. They're without a da now."

Mrs. Kelly sobs at the mention of the twins. Isabel leans into Charlie's arm around her waist and takes a few deep breaths. The smell of Declan is carried off by the breeze only to be replaced by the odour of wet farm animals. Isabel's stomach rises once more.

"You will never see me again," she utters. "You will never see your grandchildren." When Isabel places a hand to her belly, Mrs. Kelly's eyes follow. Isabel waits for the woman's sorrowful gaze to rise back up. Mrs. Kelly understands what Isabel is only just beginning to believe.

Isabel turns and nods at a pale, striken Charlie.

"Are ya sure, Mrs. Kelly?" he whispers, taking her arm as they walk toward the truck.

"Please, call me Izzy. I'm not Mrs. Kelly."

As Charlie opens the door for Isabel and helps her into the truck, she hears Declan's mother pleading with her husband to reconsider. Pulling the door shut uses the last bit of energy in her arms. She rests them across her stomach, hoping the weight of them will protect this last bit of Declan Kelly.

11

AELISH, OCTOBER 1955

Aelish sits in the abbey's cavernous chapel staring at the threadlike fissure tracing the left side of the Virgin Mother's nose. Where did that crack come from? She doesn't recall it being there. It's not possible for something so solid to simply crack. Before her mind can spool out possible causes for the flaw, Aelish closes her eyes, attempts the rosary, the repetitive circle of petitions that once lulled her into a holy trance.

That lull is miles away at the bottom of the ocean now.

Aelish's eyes shoot open, and she glances nervously around the empty chapel, despite knowing the voice was in her head. The new wimple Mother Superior gave Aelish cuts into her chin. She crams her fingers into the gap at her throat. Stained-glass Saint Patrick stares down at her, staff in hand, a demure lamb huddled at his heel. No light comes from behind or within the patron saint this early in the morning. For the first time in over fifteen years, Saint Patrick's image, his eyes, the hold of his mouth do not extend compassion and comfort. Instead, his gaze is stern, the lamb cowering. Aelish wonders if she has ever really looked at the snakes he fends off. The skin on her ankles crawls, imagining them twining around her. Saint Patrick's hand around the staff is the size of a looming hammer waiting to befall something . . . someone. Aelish's heart feels like a rabbit let loose under her habit. Her body temperature swings wildly—boil to freeze.

"Aren't you a sight that makes my eyes less sore." A startled squeak escapes Aelish's throat at the sound of his voice. She keeps her eyes sewn shut, afraid to look up. Afraid to see Declan despite how frequently he clumsily roams through her thoughts.

"Sister Clare?" His warm fingers wrap over her shoulder, and Aelish screams and bats him away, then scurries across the polished pew. Opening her eyes, she sees Father McManus standing over her, hands raised in surrender. He tilts his head, and his unruly brows draw tight. She wonders how on earth she could have missed the sound of his lumbering footsteps or mistaken his rolling Scottish brogue.

"Whoa," he says. "Is everything okay, Sister? I didn't mean to put the fright into ya." He points a thick finger to the bench. "Can I sit awhile?" He settles himself into the pew; it creaks under his density. His broad body and presence are out of place on this side of the altar—both too imposing for the space.

Aelish nods and manages to say, "Father, I'm sorry. I was . . ." Unsure how to explain that she thought he was her twin sister's dead husband, she says, "I was deep in prayer."

She runs a palm across her thigh. Everything under her robe feels swampy, as though it's just come out of the washtub . . . *Or the ocean*. Aelish's eyes flit away from Father McManus. Her mouth is dry, her tongue rancid with coffee.

"It's nice to see you back, and so early in the morning. Wanting to beat the crowds, are ya?" he says with a genuine cheer that makes Aelish cringe, undeserving. "The children have been missing their teacher. And speaking of children, I heard that Isabel and her wee bairns returned with you. Terrible circumstances." He looks up to the cross hanging over the altar and crosses himself, then kisses his thumbnail.

Following his reverent gaze, Aelish asks, "Is that a new crucifix, Father?" To Aelish, it appears much smaller than before; in fact, everything seems shrunken—less full.

When the priest presses his lips together, his beard and mustache blend into a curtain of rust-coloured hair. "Not unless someone found some extra pounds in the church budget. I've been repairing holes in my vestments for years. I've become somewhat of a seamstress," he announces. He slings his arm over the back of the bench, rests an ankle upon his knee. His casual posture brings a softening to Aelish's belly. Even as a young girl, she appreciated how good this man was at silence.

Just like the balloons she and Izzy used to get at the zoo, the words she needs to say, confessions she needs to make, dark covetous thoughts she needs to release—they all grow fat to the point of bursting. Glancing at the priest's leg resting on his thigh, Aelish notices a stripe of pale, freckled skin and coarse hair the colour of his beard below his black pants' hem.

"You're not as good as you think," she blurts. Father McManus has been resting his eyes at half-mast. He blinks several times, turns to Aelish. Aelish points at his leg, quickly realizing how bold her words sounded. "Your sock. You're not as good a seamstress as you think."

He pokes his finger through the hole at the top of his sock, wiggles it like a fleshy worm, and chuckles.

"It's hard to find good help these days."

Once again, the comfort of his chuckle, the casual hole in his sock—Aelish is overcome with the urge to let the balloon break, knowing it would coat this virtuous man in a mess of poisonous feelings.

Instead, she tucks it down, grasps her rosary, and asks, "How did that crack happen? When?" Aelish points at Mary.

Leaning forward, the priest rests his forearms on the seat-back in front of them. His black shirt strains at the seams under the expanse of his shoulders. His thick dark hair sticks up here and there, as though he's just gotten out of bed.

"Well, would you look at that," he says, thoroughly intrigued. "Hmm?"

Aelish leans forward as well, elbow to elbow. She feels herself fall into the well of alleviating silence once more. Unsure how long they have sat there, resting and staring, Aelish gives a bit of a start when he speaks.

"I couldn't tell ya how it got there, but it makes her even more beautiful, don't ya think?" Aelish doesn't answer, can't answer. "Maybe she's reminding us that perfection isn't possible, that we can break under the strain of it if we're not careful. We've all got flaws—cracks—some of us have gaping holes."

Leaning back, Father McManus pulls at the tear in his dark sock. Aelish hears her soft laugh, but it is hollow—and dry. *Just like the rest of me*, she thinks. *Dry*.

"She's dry." The words slip out before Aelish can stop. Father McManus draws in a deep breath, holds it, then lets it go.

"That's the thing about cracks, I guess," Father McManus says. "They let moisture into places it might not otherwise go."

Feeling unsafe, she gathers questions, arranges them like sticks into a pointy barricade. Keeping herself in and him out. "Shouldn't we do something about this? Find out how it happened? Someone has to know how it happened. What if her face falls off, she just cracks in half one day? In the middle of mass! Then what?"

The priest's ease, which usually soothes, becomes salt against her skin. It reminds her of kneeling in the hall on corn grit, being mistaken for her twin after Isabel drank the wine and ate the communion wafers. Absently, she reaches down and rubs her kneecap. Father McManus shifts his vast body, studying her with a maddening mix of curiosity and compassion, and she slides away from him, more room for the barricade. She tries to forget how he rescued her from Sister Edel and *herself* that day—how he gave her courage to no longer take punishments that belonged to Isabel.

And although it's been nearly ten years since that day and she likes to believe herself a grown woman now, that desire to burrow into his holy density—take shelter from Izzy's pain—is present, forcing her to look anywhere but at the priest with his messy hair and hole-ridden socks.

"Sister," he says, reaching across the gap. Aelish leans forward, avoiding his touch, adjusting an already perfectly placed hymn book. The priest withdraws and falls back into his comfortable posture. "I doubt very much the Virgin Mother's head will crack open in the middle of mass. She's made of sturdier stuff than that, I think. Wouldn't you agree?" Aelish makes a noise that may or may not indicate agreement. Inside, she thrashes her way to some surface, unlike when she dropped over the edge of the small wooden boat, willing to succumb to whatever waited in the liquid depths.

"Maybe we could talk to Mother Superior about this . . ." He pauses, fiddles with the hole in his sock, then says, "This crack. Find out how it happened." Aelish nods. Breathes. Nods again. "And as for you, Sister Clare, I wonder how long it has been since your last confession. Did you go when you were with your sister and her . . ." He folds his hands together between his knees. "God rest his soul—her husband."

Aelish tastes blood. She has bitten into the tip of her tongue, sending a constellation of pain stars into her vision.

"Yes, I went to confession," she lies and bites her tongue again.

There is a crackling sound in her ear. When she looks up, Aelish expects to see Mother Mary eroding right in front of her. At the least, she is sure the fissure will have crept farther down, spidering out, threatening to drop away virginal lips and chin. Not once did Aelish go to confession in Newfoundland. And it wasn't because she was too busy, although she was terribly distracted with babies and caring for Isabel. And Declan. *Caring for Declan,* the voice says. The fact is, not once did it enter her mind to go.

"The babies." Her voice is loud, echoing off the rows of stark wood pews and the stone altar table. "I have to go check on the children, see if Isabel is okay after seeing Declan's parents."

She stands abruptly, and Father McManus's amber eyes first grow round and then narrow. Aelish doesn't give him time to stand and make room. Her haste forces him to twist his thick legs out of her way.

He calls out to her as she heads for the swinging doors. "Sister Clare, we can talk about the statue with Mother Superior, maybe figure out how to fix it."

His words are fingers clawing at her back, threatening to slice through the balloon she is attempting to keep afloat and out of sight.

"There is no fixing this," Aelish whispers.

She presses her palms into the heavy door. When it swings open, the relief of cooler air is fleeting. She stops short of the spot on which, as a teenager, she was made to kneel on corn grit for Isabel for the last time. She wonders aloud, "Would things have been different if I'd kept my mouth shut? Maybe Izzy wouldn't have run away."

AELISH, 1947

THEY WERE SIXTEEN WHEN IZZY SNUCK INTO THE VESTRY BEFORE mass, drank the altar wine, and chewed down all the communion wafers, hoping for what, Aelish had no clue. When Sister Edel sneaked up on Aelish during that mass, hustled *her* and not Izzy out of the church, pinching the thin flesh of *her* arm, not Izzy's, it was a strange relief. She deserved this punishment. *You knew what Isabel was up to, you could have stopped her,* Aelish scolded herself. *You should have stopped her. And now this is what you get.*

The corn grit Sister Edel spread on the floor bore into Aelish's soft knees, and after a few short minutes, the discomfort of grit turned to the stabbing of broken glass. Leaning her forehead against the wall earned her a crack of the Mother Superior's stick on the top of her head. At least it wasn't the wood sandal this time.

"When I was your age, I knew a girl who lost her way when Satan got hold of her heart," Sister Edel lectured, wood sandals clacking as she paced back and forth. "She ended up in a very bad way. Is that what you want? The dark prince to get hold of your heart and lead you straight into the fires of hell?"

A drop of sweat trickled down the back of Aelish's thigh, pooling in the cracked skin of her knee pit. Aelish rubbed her eyes, hoping to brush away thoughts of a boggy stinking hollow in the earth filled with sooty flames, broken bricks, and burned leg bones—her idea of hell.

"No, Mother Superior." Aelish knew to be clear, short in answering. Would there be an eternity of kneeling on glass in hell? Aelish wanted to ask Sister Edel but kept her tongue. She didn't want to hear the answer, not really.

The final hymn floated down the hall, and Aelish's worry turned in a new direction. Father McManus. *He is going to step through the doors and see me all soggy and crying like a baby.*

Aelish wished the floor to open and swallow her whole—even if hell were just below. *He knows I was in the church with Isabel when she ate the hosts and drank the wine. What if he thinks I did it?* Aelish's brain buzzed; sparks in her head made her blink. The more she blinked, the bigger the tears that soaked her white church blouse.

The double doors opened. Sister Edel stopped her pacing. The musky smell of incense drifted past Aelish's face. It did not soothe her like usual. Her shoulders shook as she risked biting at her knuckle. A stifling embarrassment covered her.

"I think that's sufficient, Sister." The sound of Father McManus's voice so close made Aelish jump and cry out, just as she had done during mass when Isabel had pinched her arm—which was what ultimately led to her kneeling in the hall.

"Father, if you don't mind, Isabel is not through with her penance." There was a silence, and Aelish wondered if she'd heard correctly. *Isabel?*

Aelish and Isabel often pretended to be one another, confusing some of the nuns and playing tricks on the other girls. Usually, Aelish took Isabel's scoldings and didn't tell Isabel, hoping her twin would have less reason to run away. This time, however, she was no longer willing to be mistaken.

"I'm Aelish," she said, clearly, unsure whose voice had just spoken. "I'm not Isabel."

The sound of Mother Superior's breathing grew stronger. Aelish pictured her nostrils flaring, her face turning a shade of ripe tomato.

"I was just about to point that out." When Father spoke these words, it sounded to Aelish as though he were smiling. "We have a case of mistaken identity on our hands." As a flower strains for the sun, Aelish's spine lengthened just a bit at being recognized.

There was another strung-out pause. "No matter," Sister Edel maintained, her voice tight. "This is the one who caused the uproar during mass." Aelish winced as Sister Edel jabbed her shoulder with the stick. She prayed for no lashing in front of Father.

The priest's hand, as big as a shovel, slid under Aelish's armpit. He lifted her with no effort.

"I think it's safe to say it was not nearly an uproar, and we most likely don't have the whole story, Mother Superior. Wouldn't you agree?" He spoke to Sister Edel; however, his soft gaze never left

Aelish. "I think if you tell Mother Superior how sorry you are for making noise in mass and agree to do a lap or two around the stations of the cross, everything will be right as rain." He turned to Sister Edel and stood at his full height—a tree standing over a squat shrub. "Isn't that right, Mother Superior?"

Sister Edel lifted her chin and straightened the front of her robes.

"Isabel and Sister Mike are in the church waiting for you, Aelish." He patted Aelish on the head, winked, and said, "God bless you, lass."

If not for fear of being whacked on the behind by Sister Edel's stick, Aelish would have thrown herself into the folds of Father McManus's red robe and held on forever. Finally, someone understood how hard it was to be Isabel McGuire's twin and keep her out of the pits of hell.

Sister Edel steered Aelish back into the chapel by the back of the neck, her grip fierce. The girls filed out of the chapel, taking furtive glances at Aelish—all but brazen Clare, whose smug grin revealed the gap between her front teeth.

"Mother Superior, might I have a word?" Father McManus called out from behind. "We need to have a little chin-wag about the poor state of our altar boys' gowns." Sister Edel's fingernails dug a bit deeper into Aelish's neck, holding her in place.

"This minute, Father? I have some unfinished business with these unruly young women."

"I think Sister Mike can handle these rowdies. Although there won't be a next time, will there, Aelish?" Father McManus tried to look stern, but the glint in his eyes made Aelish scarlet. Mother Superior shoved Aelish toward the chapel doors.

At the sound of Aelish's footsteps, Isabel spun around in the pew, and the worry in her eyes was quickly swept away by the usual storminess. Aelish preferred the concern.

The pew creaked in the holy quiet as she settled beside Sister Mike. The silent nun stared straight ahead, expressionless, hands folded in her lap. Aelish glanced at Sister and noticed a cluster of dark hairs protruding out of her chin. She looked away, embarrassed. *Are women supposed to have beards?* She was unsure if this was her thought or Isabel's. On the other side of Sister Mike, Isabel snorted. Aelish chewed on her lip, fighting to keep Izzy out.

"Isabel McGuire, you best apologize to your sister. And later, when Father McManus comes back, you'll be apologizing to him as well." Sister Mike's usual unhurried voice was brusque. She continued to stare. Aelish followed her gaze to Jesus hanging on the cross. The mercury of guilt started at the bottom of her feet and rose to her scalp.

Aelish leaned forward to see Isabel on the other side. *Say something, Izzy.* Isabel folded her lips tight and swallowed. *Say sorry, for once,* Aelish implored with her mind, knowing Isabel could hear her, feel her.

"Sorry." The small round stone of apology shot from Isabel's mouth.

Sister Mike pulled off her glasses, set them in her lap, and closed her eyes. Her lips moved, soundless. When she opened her eyes, she was soft once again. She held Isabel's jaw, kissed her forehead, then held her away, saying, "I'm not sure how He's going to do it, but I know the good Lord will soften that heart of yours someday."

AELISH, OCTOBER 1955

LEANING AGAINST THE WALL AROUND THE CORNER FROM THE chapel, Aelish listens for Father McManus—the sound of a tree if it pulled up roots and walked. The musk of incense from the chapel mingles with the scent of sweet oil soap.

She reaches down, rubs the phantom bite of corn grit on her knees, and wonders if Sister Mike's petition all those years ago—that the Lord soften Isabel's heart someday—may have fallen on deaf spiritual ears. Aelish cannot imagine how Isabel's losing her husband and being left alone with two babies could lead to anything other than Isabel's spiritual contempt fossilizing.

Aelish had forgotten how the dense silence in the abbey leaves no thought unnoticed. The hush ripples at the whisper of scuffing feet. She sees Sister Eunice for the first time since her return. Aelish had no idea someone could age so severely in a mere six months. It's as though time is swallowing the old woman's spiritual light and her body bit by brittle bit.

Sister Eunice shuffles across narrow islands of the day's first light coming in through the windows. Pausing, the petite withered nun looks up at Aelish. The feel of Sister Eunice's hand curling into her own is confusing. Who is taking care of whom? With their fingers intertwined, they begin to walk down the hall as though finishing a stroll that had commenced only moments ago, stepping from one faint light island to the next. The old nun smells of talcum. Holding hands, Aelish senses that this woman has somehow become more air than flesh and bone.

Sister Eunice speaks first, resuming an imaginary conversation. "The Virgin Mother's got a broken face. Did you see it? I think she's a broken heart as well." The childlike sound of her voice, as much as the poignant words, melt Aelish's frozen turmoil.

Knowing how much Sister Eunice has always adored children and how badly she does not want to talk about the broken Mother Mary again, Aelish says, "Come, Sister, I'd like to introduce you to the twins." The old nun's face turns sunny, and her eyes sink into folds of skin.

"Oh, those darling girls! Isabel and Aelish. I've met them, dear." The nun pats Aelish's hand. "But let's go see what trouble they're into now. I do love how they vex my sister—nasty old boot if ever there was one."

Aelish gently pulls the nun to a stop, momentarily dismissing that Sister Eunice is foundering in a reality that is a decade old. "Your sister?" Aelish leans forward a bit to get a look at Sister Eunice's grin.

"Edel. Sister Edel," Sister Eunice says. "She was Veronica when we were children."

"You and Sister Edel are sisters? Flesh and blood sisters?" Aelish is bewildered, and unsure why; it's not some sinister secret, she supposes.

"And Kathleen," Sister Eunice says, then tightens her grip on Aelish's hand and keeps shuffling. "She's gone now, a long time, I think." A thin veil of sadness falls over the old nun's face.

"What happened to Kathleen, Sister?"

The slight quivering in Sister Eunice's hand, the quick slick of sweat between their palms tell Aelish she's pushed this fragile woman too far. Sister Eunice fingers her crucifix with her free hand, stares at it as though she has no idea its purpose, how it got there.

"Kathleen would have loved the twins. She loved children," she says, sounding wistful. "Can we go find the girls, see what trouble they're up to? They're such fun! Can we?"

Aelish does not remember herself and Izzy as being *such fun*. That time is shrouded in anxiety, panic, and life-long urgency to keep Isabel safe. Aelish squeezes the balloon full of troubles back into the cavern of her belly.

"These are new twins, Sister. Happy little scamps," she says.

Taking Sister Eunice by her twiggy elbow, Aelish guides her toward the nursery, longing for the warm sweet tea feeling of being near the babies.

ISABEL, OCTOBER 1955

IT IS EARLY DAWN—THE TIME OF DAY ISABEL FEELS MOST UNSAFE, unprepared for what might lie ahead. The nursery is as stark as the rest of the abbey. Steel-barred cribs contain her children, lying asleep on stiff mattresses, and she was sure to have her cot set right next to them. The vaporous bleach coming off the blankets that cover their vulnerable bodies raises a nauseous mix of reminders. The laundry. Hours spent scrubbing. A continuous musty chill. The punishments. The memory of standing in that basement pleading Aelish to come away from this place of lies. When she attempts to wrap herself in her protective shell of fury, it disintegrates into a useless musty powder. She is exhausted.

As far as Isabel is concerned, the only person in the entire place with a speck of decency is Sister Eunice. And only because she's always been shy a shilling in her head, which made her friendly. Most importantly, she never raised a hand to the girls or barked orders.

Sister Eunice was often there to soothe Isabel, understand her outrage, not once ask her to be something she was not. Very early on Isabel had decided Sister Eunice was someone she could believe in. Isabel had found that same solid ground of trust in Declan's gentle soul. And now, that was gone.

Reaching up, she grasps a cold steel bar on Paddy's crib. Her ears thirst for the sound of her children stirring, suckling in their slumber. One of Paddy's hands slides and comes to rest against Izzy's knuckles as he rolls in his sleep. The first light of day is moving into the nursery empty-handed, holding no hope. She clutches to the sound of her babies breathing in short even puffs.

With the rage fallen off, Izzy is left holding something she hadn't known she was carrying across the ocean: an anemic wish that Declan's death might come to a sliver of good, perhaps bringing his parents away from their bitterness and into the sweet life of Declan's children . . . maybe into her life, making them her people, people she could believe in. Looking at it now, Isabel sees it as a stillborn dream.

The warmth that is unique to children's skin—comforting and fresh like the flames of a small fire—forces Izzy to cover her mouth so as not to cry out in sorrow and wake the babies. The anguish rolling through her body has the power to shake the entire abbey.

Peering over the edge of her hand, she watches Paddy's back rise and fall. She turns to watch Sar doing the same and is caught in an undertow of panic. It is the thought of her children being snatched from her arms, shipped off to some other family—worse yet, left in that horrible place to wither and die, treated like tiny useless animals.

"I can't keep you both safe," she whispers.

Isabel has been blindly tracing the ragged hole Declan's death has left in her life, but not until now has she stepped deep into that gaping wound with full vision, full comprehension of now having to keep two children safe on her own. To protect them from what she knows happens to a mother with no husband. Declan was her umbrella—the babies' protection from the storms she would doubtless bring.

Using the bars on the crib to pull up from the floor, Isabel groans against the rigidity of her leg.

"Shh, little man," she says, lifting Paddy from the crib. Pressing her lips to the side of Paddy's silky curls makes his eyes flutter, and he gives a half-hearted, confused cry. "Let's get you in here."

Isabel sets the boy next to his sister in her crib. In the dim light, it is impossible to tell them apart. They blend as Paddy nestles into his sister's back and grasps a handful of her curls. Within seconds their breathing is united. Isabel steps left so that her shadow falls over their helpless bodies, sheltering them from the dawning day. Seeing them together, safe in one spot, delivers a cobweb of comfort to Izzy. However, one speck of memory about the black hole in the tall weeds is sure to blow away this flimsy solace.

Isabel startles at the scraping of the swinging door across the hardwood. Light from the hall sends a square spotlight into the room. A two-headed backlit figure pauses in the doorway—one head much lower than the other. Izzy feels Aelish; it's a tuning fork sort of hum in her body. They pad over floorboards, hand in hand like a mother and child. Sister Eunice appears to be the juvenile.

Isabel tries not to see that Aelish is back under her wimple and veil and instead focuses on her eyes, her mouth—the parts that still belong to Isabel. It might be the donning of the veil once again, but Isabel senses something else, another curtain hanging between them. Staring at Aelish's profile, watching how she strokes Sar's back then Paddy's, Isabel realizes that perhaps what is hanging between them are her own dank memories surrounding the hole in the earth, what she saw from the window in the middle of the night. And how she has never shared this with her twin. Sister Eunice coos over the children, traces a finger over Sar's heart-shaped lips.

"I think . . ." Isabel whispers, then pauses, chin-deep in her confusion. Unsure how she should feel, she looks to Aelish to decide, then says, "I'm pregnant."

Everything is suspended. Aelish's breathing, her hand stroking Sar's head, Isabel's heartbeat, the humming between their minds and bodies. Only Sister Eunice's loving whispers are unstopped. Aelish takes Izzy's hand and kisses it. Aelish's dripping sadness lets Izzy know she understands; Declan is the one who should be hearing this news. Declan is the one Izzy wants holding her steady, grounded, on course. *I would do it all again,* Isabel thinks, *every whipping, every humiliation, every battle—just to be telling Declan his family is growing.*

She curls her fingers over the scars on her palm. She wonders if all would be different if, as a younger woman, she had not tried to wait out Aelish's faith-blindness. If, after that battle with Sister Edel, she had stormed out of the abbey and straight into Declan's arms like she was desperate to do.

ISABEL, 1947

WHEN ISABEL WAS SIXTEEN SISTER EDEL COULD STILL STAND, an apathetic tower. And deliver a slap to knock a girl stumbling well into the next week. She used this talent liberally. The rain was a sideways slash against the window that day, making the Mother Superior's office more musty than usual. Despite being sixteen, Isabel was forced to sit on a toddler-sized wood stool, legs folded so close to her face she could study the scars on her knees. When Aelish and Sister Mike stepped into the dim, stodgy office, disgust swelled in Izzy's gut. She'd never felt this way about her twin sister before.

"What happened, Isabel?" Aelish blurted. She was wearing a sloppy brown jumper buttoned to the top. Isabel despised it. When Aelish rushed to her side, Izzy shoved her away so hard she toppled into Sister Mike.

"Isabel!" Sister Mike exclaimed. "Control yourself, child. You're already in enough hot water."

Izzy crossed her arms over her chest, sharpening her words.

"Isabel tells me you were a part of her sinful behaviour." Sister Edel set a verbal trap for Aelish. "You helped her to go out and destroy her purity with a young man. Is this true?"

Aelish covered her mouth, eyes blinking rapidly.

"Izzy." Aelish's voice was splintered by hurt. "Why did you pull me into it?"

Izzy stood, knocking the stool into the panelled wood wall with a startling bang. She was so close to Aelish she could smell the sour fear on her breath.

"Pull you in? You started this, you rat! You're jealous of me and Declan." Isabel shoved with both hands, sending Aelish to the floor with a thump.

"Girls!" Sister Mike stepped between and held a hand toward Sister Edel, who was readying her stick. Sister Mike, flushed and shaken, uttered, "The Lord says, let he who is free from sin cast the first stone."

"I'd like ta cast a stone alright, right at her head!" Izzy pointed around Sister Mike's shoulder at Aelish.

There was a flat *whap* sound as Sister Edel's stick met Izzy's backside. Izzy flinched at the familiar sting. She wheeled around to the Mother Superior, every one of her senses narrowed and pointed at the ruthless woman. Fury buzzed blindly about the room.

"Why are you calling me a rat, Izzy?" Aelish asked from the floor.

"You told them." Isabel pointed at the Sisters as if they were strangers. "You told them about me and Declan!" Isabel swiped at the tears trailing her face, and her voice dropped as she said, "That was our secret."

"No!" Aelish exclaimed, stunned. "I didn't. I wouldn't, I promise. I really do promise, Izzy." Aelish got to her knees, folded her hands together. "Please believe me!"

Isabel knew right down to the smallest bone in her body that Aelish was not lying.

"Who was it, then? Who's the blabbermouth?" Izzy stared at Sister Edel, drilling for truth. "You let me believe it was my sister. Who was it?" Isabel demanded, slamming her good foot into the floorboards.

"That is not your concern, Miss McGuire," Sister Edel said.

"Your only concern should be the state of your soul." She pursed her lips in disgust as though Isabel were a musty washrag. "Letting a boy defile you like that."

"And I loved it. Maybe you should try it," Isabel declared, no speck of hesitation.

The shock of the words from Isabel's mouth sucked the air out of the room. Aelish clapped her hands over her eyes. Sister Edel slapped Isabel hard enough to make her head rock. The stinging heat of it spread on her face. Izzy cupped her cheek, then charged the nun.

"Please," Sister Mike pleaded, stepping between once again. "Let's handle this like God-fearing women, please!"

"It was Clare," Aelish blurted, finally rising from her knees. "Stupid mean Clare. I know it!"

The way Sister Edel blinked then glanced at the floor proved it true.

"That's enough out of you," Sister Edel said, pointing her stick at Aelish. Her hands shook; she turned a sickly shade of bog water. "That's enough of both of you. Straight to the chapel. There will be no supper for either of you. You can spend the remainder of the day on your knees praying that it is not too late for your soul."

"I'll do no such." Izzy spat the words out just before Sister Mike placed a hand over her mouth and spun her toward the door.

"Go. Now. Do as you're told for once, Isabel McGuire," Sister Mike ordered. Aelish pulled at Izzy's arm. The office door slammed behind them.

Aelish's fingers dug into Isabel's forearm. "You believe me, right?" Aelish implored.

"I'm sorry I thought it was you—that old cow in there wanted me to believe it!" Izzy said, more angry than remorseful.

"It's okay, Izz. Really."

"No! It's not, and that's your feckin' problem." Isabel swung her arm around. "None of this is okay!"

"Shh! Izzy!" Aelish hissed. "You'll get us in more trouble." Aelish glanced back toward the door. The battling nuns' words were muffled, but their inflamed tone was clear.

Both Isabel and Aelish turned toward the sound of soft whistling coming down the hall. Sister Eunice walked a lopsided limp as she approached. Were it anyone else, Isabel would be furious, assuming she was being mocked for her crooked gate. Sister Eunice, however, was missing a shoe. When she got to the girls, she stopped, reached up, and touched Isabel on the cheek. Her dreamy smile faltered then, caressing the hand-shaped welt.

"Oh, dear. What has she done now," the nun whispered, shaking her head. Isabel's throat clenched at the tenderness even as the daft nun resumed her whistling and limped away, blowing a kiss to the picture of Jesus hanging on the wall.

Isabel spun and headed in the opposite direction.

"Hey, where are you going? Sister told us to go to the chapel," Aelish called out.

When Aelish caught up and grabbed Izzy's arm, she yanked it away.

"I don't care what that witch said. I'm going to find Clare the rat."

"Please don't do that." Aelish folded her hands over her heart, pleading. "Don't make things worse. Let's go outside, look." She pointed to the window and the breaking clouds. "The rain has stopped."

Isabel stared at Aelish. Tears of worry and guilt dropped from Aelish's chin, and she shifted from foot to foot, scratching at her arms.

"Fine. I need my jumper. I'll meet you under the oak," Isabel said, walking away.

Isabel decided revenge on Clare the rat could be put on hold until after she convinced Aelish they needed to leave the abbey, find Declan, and never look back.

ISABEL, OCTOBER 1955

IZZY SITS THIGH-TO-THIGH WITH SISTER EUNICE ON THE COT next to the cribs. She holds a ready hand behind Sar's back as Sister Eunice balances the squirming girl on her narrow lap. Their delight and fascination with one another is equal as Sar pulls on the nun's stretchy wrinkled cheek. Sister Eunice has laid no less than twenty kisses on Sar's face, and it has become a game of sorts.

Watching Aelish lift Paddy over her head, her black veil pooling at the base of her spine, Isabel thinks about all the waiting Aelish must have done. Not until now has she thought about how this waiting might have bent her sister's path.

"Good morning! And who's my favourite boy?" Aelish asks. Paddy responds with a giggle from the belly. "What do you think about a new baby brother or sister? Isn't that exciting!" Aelish poses this question in a singsong voice to her nephew but glances at Izzy.

Isabel answers Aelish, saying, "I think he's excited, scared out of his mind, and broken down all at the same time."

Isabel is unsure if the lack of responsibility for the children's survival makes her sister so natural and breezy with them or if Aelish indeed carries more mother in her bones than she herself does. If Aelish does not long to know motherhood, Isabel is wishing it for her. Once more, she wonders if the waiting had caused her twin to miss out on something that seems such a natural delight for her.

"And does Paddy know that Auntie Aelish will never leave him and Sar and his new brother or sister?" Aelish kisses Paddy's temple and whispers, "Never. Not ever."

"Don't make such promises, Auntie Ay. We both know better than that."

Isabel studies her sister as she has done for a lifetime—save the four years and fifty-two days they were apart—knowing her every expression, gesture, and sometimes even the words she might speak before they arrive. Suddenly, she sees a stranger. *No,* Isabel thinks, *a stranger has features and shape.* The Aelish Isabel has been studying for a lifetime—the anxious Aelish, the ardent Aelish, the Aelish who carried the world's burdens as her own—has disappeared. To Isabel, not being able to touch Aelish in this way feels as mysterious as what happens to the caterpillar when it disappears into the cocoon. She knows something is happening to Aelish, but she is not privy to what exactly.

"Never. Not ever," Aelish repeats, laying a hand on Sar's head.

"Would one of you girls be a dear and help me find Ronnie?" Sister Eunice asks, letting Sar squirm over to Isabel's lap. "I need to see her before I go."

Isabel's confusion is reflected in Aelish's furrowed brow, tilted head. Rather than unwinding a thread of questions about who this Ronnie is, Aelish stands Paddy in the crib, then helps the tiny nun off the bed.

"How about we go to your room first, maybe have a wee bit of rest before we track down Ronnie? Or a bit of breakfast?" Aelish suggests, leading Sister Eunice toward the doors of the nursery.

"I am quite tired," Sister Eunice concedes. "That sounds like a grand idea, Aelish."

Glancing back at Isabel, Aelish raises her eyebrows, surprised. Izzy can read Aelish's thoughts with ease: Sister Eunice can't remember to wear two shoes most days, yet she remembers Aelish's given name.

Watching her sister's tenderness with the daft nun, Isabel realizes that perhaps there are pieces and parts of Aelish that could never entirely disappear. And if she were a praying woman, she might thank God for that.

SISTER EDEL, OCTOBER 1955

SISTER EDEL IS NOT IGNORANT OF HER ENORMITY. THE EDGES OF her flesh are a river in flood pouring across her reinforced bed. Between prayers, she watches out the window what comes and goes from the top half of the venerable oak tree in the yard. She watches from her corporeal prison as a sparrow hawk holds to a high, swaying perch and scans the ground below for prey.

Kathleen was obsessed with birds. To have thoughts of her younger sister may have been shocking a few years back, but lately, it seems that the spreading of her body has bulldozed walls she once thought impenetrable. Barriers that once kept everything where it belonged. Memories. Resentments. Sins. Unreturned love. Mercy.

Lifting her arm, Sister Edel tries to wriggle her fingers. They've become rigid. The skin is taut, and she wonders when they will simply split open like sausage casings fried on the skillet.

She had one of the young novices relocate Jesus to the wall at the foot of her bed. She insisted that Jesus' suffering, his passion, be the first thing she sees in the morning and the last she sees at night before closing her puffy eyes. It serves as perspective for her paltry pangs of infirmity. And although she cannot see it clearly, she knows the photograph of her and Kathleen has been relocated to the shelf. Also a constant reminder—not of suffering—rather, of disgrace.

Thinking of disgrace reminds her of the news that Isabel McGuire has returned with her illegitimate children, and now no father. It is indeed a sad situation for the children, but not entirely surprising. She is certain of hearing Isabel's uneven footsteps from time to time. The side of her neck throbs each time she thinks she hears them.

There is a tapping at the door. The timidity of it sends frustration marching through her body. She can only assume it is one of the novices.

"Come," Sister Edel orders. She keeps her communications to the barest necessity, saving her words for prayer and supplication. She lost so much that night in the basement when Isabel McGuire sneaked back into the abbey trying to lure her twin from her holy vows. Perhaps the most tragic of losses: her desire to speak.

When Sister Eunice slips through the crack in the doorway, a breathless Sister Edel realizes her lungs do not match the enormity of her flesh. Sister Eunice is without her veil and wimple. A translucent rough cotton beige shift hangs from her minute frame, one bony shoulder exposed, showing a map of connecting brown splotches on milky skin. Sister Edel recognizes the ragged burgundy Bible cradled in one arm. There is an identical Good Book lying on her bedside table; it was a gift from their parents. In Sister Eunice's other arm is a brown fuzzy lump of material. Unlike all the others who enter this room, Sister Eunice does not wince or mouth breathe as she shuffles barefoot to Sister Edel's bedside. Sister Edel knows she smells of wet yeasty dough. She sees and senses the repulsion of all the young nuns who screw up their faces while attending to her humiliating bathing and toileting needs. Sister Eunice's eyes have a sheen to them, a bright blue iridescence. It is the only actual colour in the drab bedroom.

"Ronnie?" the little nun says. The name sends a vibration over the expansive field of Sister Edel's skin. It has been decades since anyone has called her Ronnie. When they were children, Sister Eunice shortened Veronica to Ronnie. Veronica became Ronnie, Kathleen became Leena, and Brianne became Bree.

Ronnie, Leena, and Bree. As Sister Edel rolls this combination of names around and around, they gather like sweet floss on her tongue, which is promptly shoved aside by salty bitterness.

"Sister Eunice, what are you doing in here? Where is your habit? You must put on your robes." Sister Eunice's dark nipples pointing downward show through the worn material. "You're not decent!" Sister Edel clears her throat.

Oblivious of Sister Edel's admonitions, the vaporous nun walks to the shelf at the foot of the bed, tucks the brown material under her arm, and picks up the photograph. Her silver hair is in a messy pile on top of her head, and Sister Edel spots a dead leaf and twig caught in the tangle of grey on the back of Sister Eunice's scalp.

"Where's Leena?" Sister Eunice asks, staring at the photograph. "I would like to say goodbye to Leena. Do you know where she went?"

The stacked round bumps of Sister Eunice's spine push through the thin material of her shift. For a moment, staring at those knuckle-like bumps keeps Sister Edel's world rigid. But when the words *Where's Leena? Do you know where she went?* find their way through the layers of insulation, Sister Edel must raise a distended hand to her mouth. It takes effort—raising that arm and keeping it all in.

"I've been hiding Mr. Muffin in my room. Don't tell." Sister Eunice holds a bent finger to her lips and dangles the brown lump out in front of her. A sly grin smooths the vertical creases around her lips for a moment. As she walks to the edge of the bed, the scraggly bit of material takes on a recognizable shape. Sister Edel's mind falls back on its heels, caught in a current of time.

Sister Eunice—Bree—as a child, always no bigger than a button, carrying that brown stuffed lamb everywhere she went. Screaming, inconsolable should they be separated for minutes. A quivering begins, first in Sister Edel's useless legs, then migrating to her arms. The hand over her mouth clenches, then vibrates.

Sister Eunice climbs onto the bed and burrows into the space once occupied by Sister Edel's arm. The only touch Sister Edel's known for years has been riddled with holy disdain and scarcely hidden disgust.

Sister Eunice—Bree—sighs like that of a contented pup, nestles into the spill of Sister Edel's right breast. A strangled noise rises from within the folds beneath Sister Edel's chin. The tears wanting to fall, however, are buried far too deep.

Sister Edel wants to stiffen against the warmth of the frail familiar body next to hers, memories of three in a bed on damp chilly nights, but her atrophied muscles do not have the strength. More than that, she wants to push away what comes next as she listens to the sound of Bree's breathing. It is the sound of a train rolling into the station, coming to a gradual gliding stop.

"Sister Eunice?" she says brusquely.

There is no reply. Turning her head and looking down over the rise of her cheeks, Sister Edel can only see the snowy top of Sister Eunice's head. A torn, one-eyed Mr. Muffin sits in the middle of Sister Edel's chest, held loosely in Sister Eunice's spotted hand. Sister Edel never dreamed she would come up against something larger, more imposing than her own massive body. Still, when she pauses her laboured existence—the silence in the room, outside the window, in the corridors—it dwarfs her in an instant.

"Bree?" she whispers, knowing there will be no answer.

The frigid waterline of panic creeps up the sides of Sister Edel's inert body. Sliding up the edges of her thighs, arms, across the acreage of her abdomen. When the tip of her nose finally drops below the waterline of dread, the groaning begins, then slowly turns into a wailing prayer.

"Our Father, who art in heaven . . ." The stringent quiet throughout the abbey is crushed under the density of Veronica's petitions.

12

SISTER MIKE, NOVEMBER 1955

SISTER MIKE ISN'T ONE TO BELIEVE IN MIRACLES. IT IS NOT something she voices aloud, but it is true. Instead, she puts her faith in God meeting her or anyone halfway.

"Nodding your head doesn't row the boat," she mutters, unaware she has spoken aloud.

"Beg your pardon, Mother Superior?" Aelish asks. "Did you say something?"

Isabel and Aelish sit across from Sister Mike at a scarred butcher block in the abbey kitchen. They have slid the table closer to the iron stove to stay warm.

"Just remembering something my da used to say." Sister Mike finds the intruding odour of onions rising from the table hard to ignore as she takes a sip of tea. She slides her chair back a bit and sets the cup and saucer on her thigh. "Did I ever tell you my da didn't believe in God? And madder than a wet hen when I told him I was to enter the convent. He did show a little favour though when Father Michael O'Flanagan called the Pope an enemy of Irish freedom."

Sister Mike takes in both young women, less and less identical as the years pass, and sees what she has always seen. Aelish: sweet politeness covering a quivering sea of worry, and Isabel: an open book of incredulity and passion. Mother Superior is unsure which is harder to look upon as she studies their sharply shaped eyes and long thin noses, intensifying whatever expression they might carry.

"Sound like smart fellas, your da and O'Flanagan. But what does all that have to do with this baby?" Isabel rubs her tummy, becoming round with life.

"I guess I was thinking about miracles," Sister Mike says, feeling a bit worried about how distracted she has been as of late. What with Sister Eunice's death and funeral and dealing with Sister Edel's enormous grief that seems to reach far beyond that of Sister Eunice's passing. And then Declan's simple graveside service attended only by herself, his young widow, Aelish, Sister Mary Celine, Charlie Rose, and Father McManus. And now, the baby, yet another child tragically left without a father.

As though reading her mind, Isabel says, "This baby is no miracle, Sister Mike. What am I supposed to do now? It was hard enough to feed the twins . . ." In a flash, Isabel's hard shell falls away; her chin quivers. "When Declan was alive, and we had help. And a house. We had family in Newfoundland."

Never has Sister Mike felt the urge to strike another human being—that is, until she turns to see Aelish's gaze drop to the floor.

"Might I remind you, Isabel, that you have family. Here." Sister Mike grips the thin handle on her teacup with one hand and the saucer's edge with the other. Isabel's cheeks grow two circles of red. Her eyes dart to Aelish, then to the floor. Sister Mike's grip loosens, witnessing remorse in Isabel's eyes.

"It was just different there, that's all I meant. You know how people treat single mothers here in Ireland. Even though I was married, now that my husband's dead, I'm suddenly a fallen woman?" Isabel's hands shake as she takes a sip of her tea, glancing at Aelish.

Aelish returns a sad smile and says, "I know what she means, Sister Mike. Izzy and Declan had a lovely life with lots of good folks looking out for them." Aelish sets a hand on Isabel's thigh, squeezes, and says, "And we can do the same, right here. We can be a family here. It won't be the same for you, Izzy, as it is for mothers out of wedlock."

Sensing where this is headed, Sister Mike leans forward, sets her cup on the table, pausing. Having raised hundreds of children in the orphanage, the Mother Superior knows the look of hope. She is also an expert in placing a soft stone on that rising hope before it gets dangerously high.

"Sister Clare, this is not the place to raise a family." Sister Mike purposely shakes her head as she speaks. It is a thing she does with confused and emotional children to help them better understand her words.

"We raise children here day in and day out. I don't see the problem, Mother Superior. Besides, they've been here a few months now, and that's been no trouble." Aelish shrinks as hope seeps away.

"Yes, we do raise children here . . . with the hopes of sending them out to good families. We don't bring families here. We simply cannot afford to do such a thing. And I thought it would be good for you all to be together for a while until Isabel got settled. And now it's time to think long term."

Isabel shifts in her chair, clearly uncomfortable. A pair of novice nuns bustles into the kitchen, whispering like two thieves. They link arms and freeze after spotting the triangle of women having tea.

Not knowing what they are after, but sensing they are up to no good, the Mother Superior looks over the top of her glasses and says, "If you are looking for the chapel, it's down the hall and to the left. You'll know it by the rather large crucifix holding the body of Christ at the far end of the room."

Wordless, the two young women turn and scamper out the door. Becoming Mother Superior allows Sister Mike to deliver the Lord's work with more mercy, less harshness; however, it does not give her the authority to change the institution's entire vocation.

Returning her attention, she sees that Isabel's toughness has rolled back into place. Isabel pushes her cup and saucer away from the edge of the table and flicks a few biscuit crumbs from her lap onto the floor.

"We'll figure something out, dear," Sister Mike promises. "And in the meantime, you can stay at the mother and baby home."

The clatter of the chair toppling makes Sister Mike gasp. Aelish lets out a small scream. Isabel is standing over the Mother Superior in a flash before there is time to register what is happening.

"Izzy! Stop it!" Aelish exclaims, grabbing hold of Isabel's wrist.

Sister Mike leans as far back as possible, feeling the weight of her chair teeter backward toward the hot stove. The urge to cover herself with the cross is overpowering, yet not as powerful as the need to avoid upsetting Isabel any further. Instead, she watches the embers in Isabel's eyes spark.

"How dare you." Isabel speaks slowly. "Shame on you for even mentioning that hellhole." Isabel's pointed finger is so close to Sister Mike's nose, it blurs through her glasses. "I had no choice the first time, being grabbed up and dropped off in the middle of the night! But you're off yer feckin' nut if ya think I'm going back there. And with my kids? My children would be safer and far better treated livin' under a bridge than in that place. Yer a fool eejit and a far cry crueller than I believed. Shame on you, Sister Mike."

Every word Isabel speaks is bewildering; however, it hurts when Isabel curses her with shame.

"What are you talking about?" Aelish and Mother Superior say at the same instant.

Isabel blinks and, by the look of it, is wrestling confusion of her own. She turns pasty, lays both hands on her tummy. Whirling about, Isabel makes it to the deep sink just in time. Aelish hurries to Isabel's side and holds her long auburn hair aside, whispering. Looking closer, Sister Mike wonders if Aelish's lips are even moving. Nonetheless, she knows they are communicating.

The Mother Superior keeps her distance, recalling that day all those years ago at the edge of a double burial plot. She remembers that she turned away from those little girls then. Although the urge is there once more—a strange twisting that begins in her ankles—this time, she faces them, one hand on her chair, the other wrapped around the beads at her chest.

Sister Mike must witness all the loss they've had, plus a dark welt of some secret rising between them. Sister Mike shudders. Not only does she want to turn away, she wants to run before the ulcerous secret bursts.

ISABEL, NOVEMBER 1955

ISABEL CUPS HER HANDS AND LETS THE COOL TAP WATER POOL. Drawing it into her mouth, she tastes rust and earth. Swishing it in her cheeks brings her back to the kitchen and the relief of Aelish's hand stroking her spine. She spits, then takes the cloth Aelish holds out. A quivering voice inside Isabel's head speaks: *What if Sister Mike really doesn't know?*

"Not possible," Isabel mutters to herself.

Isabel swallows the leftover sour in her mouth. She presses the back of her hand to her lips.

"Please, child, sit. You're worrying me. I can assure you; we'll figure all of this out." Sister Mike slides a chair across the stone floor.

Planted in the chair, she presses the base of her palms into her eyes. Isabel knows Sister Mike is kneeling next to her by the scent of cigarettes and roses. Aelish kneels in front. Pulling her hands away, Isabel stares at the raised lines of pale flesh on her palms. They shake until Aelish steadies them with her fingertips, tracing the lines, stroking the markings Isabel will never be rid of.

"Izzy, where did you get these?" Aelish asks.

Isabel knows there is a part of Aelish that does not want to hear. And Isabel does not want to tell. It will be the second bombing, the second crumbling of walls that once kept Aelish safe. The desperate way Mother Superior searches Isabel's eyes—the middle-aged nun has no idea what Isabel went through. No idea what goes on behind those walls. *She really doesn't know.* A shower of sorrow dampens Isabel's anger; her throat narrows.

All those years ago, Isabel stood at the window in that prison they call a home, not knowing what she was seeing—believing herself stuck in a nightmare—until now. The geyser of her anger has blown the truth clear to the surface.

Swallowing and swallowing does nothing to keep the sobs buried. It does not stifle the remembering of a circle of yellow light moving across the grass and a tiny white bundle being dropped into a black hole in the tall grass. It is a smirched image.

Isabel rocks, wanting to run from this spectral memory faster than her lame leg will allow, farther than the love of her children will extend. Both are impossible, and so the memory long buried clambers up.

She was only sixteen. Alone in the mother and baby home. Standing at a window in the deepest hour of night longing for Aelish, who slept only miles away. A lantern light floats across the high untended weeds in the yard, catching her attention. As the amber light swings, it reveals a white bundle no bigger than a loaf being carried by a darkened figure. The lamplight settles to the earth, an oversized firefly. Its glow reveals a dark mouth on the ground. The cloth bundle is fed into the maw by hands stained golden. Those same hands rise, fall, and reach side to side—a crucifix drawn over the black hole in the ground. The circle of light and the vague figure seem to dissolve. Isabel believes she is trapped in a set of nesting doll nightmares, one inside the other.

The grotesque truth makes her cry out now. "The babies . . ." Isabel sobs.

"They're fine, dear one, your babies are fine." Sister Mike pats Isabel's thigh, trying to soothe. "In the nursery, napping snug as bugs with Sister Mary Celine."

When Isabel locks eyes with Aelish, the cord between them is taut as wire and humming. Her twin knows Izzy is not speaking of Sar and Paddy. Aelish plugs her knuckle between her teeth. Izzy does not begrudge her this nervous habit, not this time.

"There's a hole in the tall grass." Isabel must turn away from Aelish, cannot watch her sister's life fall to pieces, nor can she leave buried what she knows. "Behind the mother and baby home, there's a hole."

"Whatever are ya talking about, child? A hole . . . what sort of hole?" Sister Mike's voice takes an uncharacteristic edge of impatience. "How would you know such a thing?"

Isabel no longer feels the chair under her bottom or Aelish's fingers digging into her forearm. The words come from her mouth in small dry mounds, their sound muffled in her ears.

"They put the dead babies in the hole"—she takes a slow breath in—"in the tall grass behind the mother and baby home. And—" She stumbles on the truth about to come out. "I think the dead babies are better off than the ones who survive."

Aelish's groan comes from far away as if she too is underground—with those dead children. Isabel reaches out for Aelish first with her hand, then her mind. Finding her shoulder, Isabel clutches it.

Sister Mike is mute. Aelish's chin drops to her chest as though her neck has given up. The unseen connection between them does not allow Aelish the luxury of doubting her sister's words, the horror she witnessed, the pain snaking just under her skin. Turning one of Isabel's hands over, Aelish searches her twin's eyes for an explanation.

"They put broken glass on the top of the stone wall around the home. They wouldn't let me out, so I climbed over," Isabel says.

This time the groan comes from the Mother Superior, who has a hand clasped to her chest. Sister Mike stands, then walks the length of the narrow kitchen back and forth. She stops long enough to scrape a match along the rough cast-iron stovetop, light a cigarette, then resume pacing and puffing.

"Who . . ." Sister Mike aborts the question. "Sister Edel sent you there." She is talking to herself, her wooden sandals clacking louder with each lap back and forth. "That's where you went. You didn't run off. She sent you there." Sister Mike stops in front of Isabel, hitting a wall of incredulity. "She took you herself." Isabel nods.

A long chunk of ash floats to the floor as the nun's hand shakes. "My dear girl, were you with child?" Sister Mike flicks her cigarette into the sink, bends over top of Aelish, and grasps Isabel's shoulders. She is so close Isabel can see that Sister Mike's eyes are a startling shade of cornflower blue, always hidden behind the thick dark rims of her glasses. "The hole . . . did someone . . . take your child? Isabel, you need to tell me everything that happened."

In all the years of pushing down on those thrashing memories, wondering if it had all been a nightmare, Isabel never once thought she would feel relief in speaking about it. Not even Declan knew the whole story. Isabel judged him too fragile or, perhaps it is truer—feared he would be ashamed of her.

"Izzy?" Aelish whispers. "Was there a baby . . . before the twins?"

"I don't know," is the only answer she has.

Beads of sweat trickle her spine. There was so much blood, and it had felt as though everything below her belly button were being ripped in two.

"I was there for two months, maybe three, I think . . ." Her skull aches. She presses at her temples. "And one night I woke up feeling like my stomach was on fire, on the inside. Everything hurt . . .

down there." Sister Mike sits in a chair behind Aelish, bouncing her knee, smoking another cigarette. "When I pulled back the blanket, there was so much blood everywhere. Someone . . . a woman . . . not one of the Sisters. . . . she helped me to the privy and . . ." The sweet scent of blood fills Isabel's nose. "It was such a horrible mess. I didn't know what was happening. So young . . ." Isabel shakes her head, wraps her ankles around the legs of the chair, holding tight. Aelish rests her forehead against Isabel's forearm and fingers the beads at her neck. "Such a mess . . . the Sisters made me clean it all up and sleep on the bloody mattress."

Isabel was not conscious when the bricks of her childhood home crashed down, but she feels a different sort of crumbling, choking dust, and cutting debris now as she realizes what happened in the mother and baby home that night. Isabel slides her hands down and looks over the tips of her fingers at Sister Mike.

"I think they made me clean up my own miscarriage."

Isabel is stuck to the chair, buried under the rubble of realization—there was a baby before the twins. And Declan never knew. Aelish is whispering prayers, Isabel is too empty to fight it.

Through the numbness, it is hard to feel Sister Mike behind her, arms wrapped around her, but the side-to-side swaying, the way she strokes the back of Isabel's head, breaks through the wall that has been surrounding and protecting her since the age of ten. Isabel's arms go limp, and everything she has been holding up falls around her.

AELISH, NOVEMBER 1955

AELISH HURRIES PAST THE CHAPEL. THE URGE TO PRAY IS GONE. The desire to seek out that urge, nonexistent. The Mother Superior's door is open, and she is perched on the windowsill. A Bible rests open on her lap, and she cradles a short glass of dark brown liquid in her hand and is staring out the window at the lashing rain. Aelish is uncertain what is in the glass until Sister Mike swallows it in one gulp and screws up her face.

Staring into the empty glass, she says, "One shot of whiskey a year . . . usually a special occasion. Not this year, it would seem." Then she asks, "How is the poor thing?"

"Sleeping in my room. What are we going to do?" Without waiting for a reply, Aelish steps in and announces, "We must go to that mother and baby home, right now. How could this happen? What are they doing to those babies! I always knew there was something wrong with those children."

"Let's not lose our heads in this. We don't know what happened." Mother Superior raises her hand. Aelish curls her toes to keep from making fists. The doubt in the Mother Superior's voice beckons the same pulsing anger Aelish used to attack poor Clare.

"Isabel *told* us what happened. Did you see her hands? They're horribly scarred! She wouldn't lie. She's never lied about anything." Shame coats her head to foot for ever doubting Izzy. Sister Mike closes the Bible, sets it on the edge of the desk, and sets the whiskey glass on top of it.

"Did Isabel tell you anything else before she fell asleep?" Aelish presses a hand to her stomach. Isabel's warmth is still there. They had gone straight to Aelish's room after leaving the kitchen and lay as spoons on the skinny cot. Squeezing Isabel tight was the only way to get the shaking to subside. And when it slowed, Isabel spoke in fragmented thoughts, and somehow, Aelish was able to pull the pieces back together to form a reprehensible puzzle.

"It's a prison, Mother Superior. Some of those women have been there for twenty years or more. They will never leave there; they're not like you and I here. We made a choice, a vow." Aelish's voice cracks.

"It's hardly a prison, Sister Clare." Sister Mike tilts her head, confused. "Those young women are given a place to stay, food to eat, an opportunity to seek forgiveness while they are pregnant. And once their children are born, they might be adopted into loving homes . . . if they're blessed to find a family. That's how it works." Sister Mike sits and slides a second chair next to it. She points, but Aelish shakes her head.

"That is *not* how it works. The children and their mothers are beaten, starved. Sister Mike, Isabel swears she watched one of the mothers eating the moss that grows between the stones, she was so hungry! Those women are forced to stay as penance for a year after their children are born, and only then can they leave." Scratching at her skin inflames the fiery itch in the crooks of Aelish's elbows. "Some never leave even after their babies are given away . . . or die. They've nowhere to go, no way to take care of themselves. Everyone has cast them out! The children, Sister Mike! The children . . ." A bit of acid hits the back of her throat as she thinks of Molly, one of her favourite Bible study children, and how she and all the others have been suffering under her nose for years. Until now, Aelish had never been able to understand why these children had seemed more vapour than solid—tiny anxious mounds of mist. Aelish's shame pushes her down into the hard chair next to the Mother Superior. She scratches at her arms, neck, and chin.

"So, if that's true, Isabel left before the year was through?"

"Of course she did! And you're missing the point!" The disappointment she feels in Sister Mike sits like a stone in her gut. "There are babies buried—and not in proper blessed graves—just in a hole somewhere on that land. Babies, Sister Mike!" Without thinking, Aelish slams her palm on the desk, making the Mother Superior start a little. "How could you not know this? And what about Sister Edel? Surely she must know."

This thought sparks a new depth of confused anger. For so long, Aelish has made excuses for Sister Edel; she's faithful to the Lord, stern but righteous. In an instant, all the excuses turn to mud. And what about her beloved Sister Mike? Taking the bottom corners of her veil, Aelish covers her eyes. The blackness brings the vivid images to life: Izzy covered in the bloody loss of her first child, Izzy stealing over a wall hemmed with broken glass, Izzy watching lifeless babies dropped into the earth.

Aelish pinches the soft web of skin between her thumb and finger, replacing the vile visions with a flash of pain. The radiator by the window ticks in the hush.

"Isabel was shaking so badly. You'd think she'd seen a ghost." Aelish uncurls her toes and folds her hands together on her lap, pleads for Izzy. "Someone has to be on her side . . . for once, Mother Superior. Someone."

Mother Superior holds two fingers to her lips as if grasping an invisible cigarette. Her eyes are closed, her breathing steady. When Sister Mike's eyes open, a soft smile rises but does not reach the sadness in her eyes.

"The good Lord has always been on Isabel's side." Sister Mike leans and places a hand over Aelish's folded fists. "But you, my dear, have been in the way."

The feel of her backbone turning liquid shocks Aelish as much as the Mother Superior's words. Stiffening against both, Aelish sits straight, gripping the arms of the chair.

"In the way? How could I be in God's way?" Aelish shakes her head, incredulous, despite a subtle vibration of truth. "So this is all my fault? *I* shipped her away and locked her in a horrible mother and baby home? *I* told her she was a ruined woman? 'Wanton' . . . I believe that was how Sister Edel described my sister, as some filthy temptress from *The Pilgrim's Progress*."

Aelish runs her palm over the rough cloth of her habit, then covers her mouth. She is recalling the day that she, at age nineteen, told Sister Mike and Sister Edel she intended to join the sisterhood. Despite Sister Edel referring to Izzy as a path to hell and bitter as wormwood, a threat to Aelish's calling, Aelish let them talk of her and Izzy as though she were not in the room. She had handed over her history with Isabel to make room for her new life. Aelish had indeed banished Isabel as much as anyone else.

"Of course you didn't ship her away. And I am certain if you had known . . ." Sister Mike's voice falters, eyes welling. "If I had known what was happening, she would not have been left there longer than a minute." Sister Mike continues slow and soft. "Many difficult things are going on here, and I can assure you I will be asking questions. But at this moment, as much as it hurts me to say this, the Lord has put it on my heart to ask *you* to get on your knees and examine *your* choices."

"What choices? What do my choices have to do with Isabel's suffering now?"

"It's not just her suffering at this moment, Sister Clare. You have spent your life making it okay for Isabel to walk through this world angry . . . at everyone." Aelish's confusion is at boiling point.

"How? How did I make that okay? I hated that she was so mad all the time, biting like a mean cat. I never knew what she would do next or who would get hurt. There was nothing more I wanted than to *not* feel that hatred coming off her skin. It was exhausting." A cold washes over Aelish, a chill she has only experienced once—the welcoming downward push of the ocean the day she slipped over the side of the dory. Clutching at the neck of her habit, she tries to pull it away, let in more air. Her words breathe back into her face: *There was nothing I wanted more than to* not *feel.*

"As a child, you suffered for her. You turned your life into a living, breathing penance. Look at the reason you chose your religious name, Sister Clare. Was that not a form of penance for attacking Clare when you believed Isabel left you behind?" Aelish looks up at Sister Mike, surprised. "And I know how many times you took Isabel's punishments, warranted or not. I know, Sister Clare. I have always been able to tell the two of you apart; to me, you are like day and night. You sacrificed your flesh, and then you sacrificed your heart." When Sister Mike slides a finger under Aelish's chin, her head becomes a dense stone. The whiskey on Sister Mike's breath is sweet smelling. "I know you were young, Sister Clare, but I know a broken heart when I see one." Aelish's legs want to push her up out of the chair, rush her out of the room before Sister Mike says it, but everything has gone liquid again.

"Declan," Mother Superior says, as though that one word is an entire sentence—an entire lifetime of words. She is grateful Sister Mike is still holding her chin up; otherwise, she would fall to the floor. "What I am most concerned about, Sister, are your vows. I'm questioning if you took your vows because it was in your heart to do so or if you did so for Isabel, or in spite of her perhaps? This is what I mean when I say you stand between God and Isabel." Sister Mike runs a thumb through Aelish's tears, leaving a trail of warmth.

The confusion has boiled over, creating a sticky mess preventing Aelish's thoughts or feelings from taking a step in any direction.

"Aelish." The sound of her given name cuts through the turbulent paralysis. Sister Mike is kneeling in front of her, holding Aelish's knees. "Did you believe becoming a nun would somehow protect Isabel? Or protect *you* from your own feelings?"

"It didn't . . . I didn't." Aelish fights the urge to pull up her sleeves and dig at the burning creases of her elbows.

Although quiet and meagre, the knock at the door startles Aelish. Sister Mary Celine stands with folded hands. Aelish will never see her as anyone but sweet Becky, whose fragile nature survived Sister Edel and tuberculosis. Becky coughs into her hand, not to announce her presence; rather, it indicates she has hurried from the far end of the abbey. She is winded.

"What is it, Sister?" Mother Superior stands and steps between Aelish and the dainty nun in the doorway as an act of privacy.

"The twins are awake and wanting Mammy. Could you tell me where to find Isabel?"

"She'll still be resting in my room. I'll take care of the children." Aelish stands, relieved to get away from Sister Mike—from the questions that make her feel as though she is walking under water. Becky glances up, then picks at her fingernail. "What's wrong, Becky?" Impatient, Aelish uses Sister Mary Celine's given name.

"She's not there. I checked, I knocked, and I peeked in. I'm sorry, Sister Clare. I know I'm not supposed to go into your room . . ." Becky looks at her shoes.

"Never mind that," Aelish snaps. Becky back-steps.

"Sister Clare." Mother Superior sets a hand on Aelish's shoulder. "I'm sure Isabel is about. Let's not panic."

"I saw her walking across the lawn after I checked your room, Sister Clare." Becky's voice shakes. "That's why I came here—I thought maybe she went out for a breath and told you first."

Aelish reaches for the rope in her mind. *Isabel, where are you? What are you doing now?* The connection between them is a numb appendage. She would give anything to feel Izzy's anger, sorrow, anything but the deadness of silence. She knows what it means.

"Go back to the babies." Aelish grabs Becky's knobby thin shoulders, spins her, shoves her out the door.

"Sister Clare! What on earth?" Sister Mike's voice falls away as Aelish sprints down the hall for the front doors. Aelish's mind screams, *You can't let her go there alone! Not this time!* She shoulders open the door and stumbles down the rain-glistened steps.

ISABEL, NOVEMBER 1955

ISABEL WIPES RAIN FROM HER EYE. WATER SEEPS INTO HER SHOES, numbing her toes. The two-story wall of the mother and baby home rises in front of her, a stony flashback. Although she cannot see the glass teeth at the top edge, her tingling palms remember. Stopping in the middle of the dirt road, Isabel flicks her hands, trying to rid the crawling on her skin. The iron gate sits open slightly.

Isabel looks down, certain she is knees deep in sucking mud. Her legs are immobile. Unwilling.

"Are ya here for a child?" A wizened woman steps out of the blackthorn hedge growing against the stone wall inside the gates. Isabel startles, back-stepping. "There's no more children today." The woman folds the sleeve of her jumper over her knuckles and sucks at the woollen material. Isabel cringes at the sound of teeth on wool. *She must have been here when I was,* she thinks, but cannot place her amid all the murkiness.

"Do you live here?" Isabel asks.

Isabel takes two steps toward the gate. The woman disappears around the edge of the wall, but Isabel can still hear her nose whistling as she breathes. Isabel pauses, straining to remember this woman.

"They need me." The woman's voice takes a tentative crawl around the wall.

"The women? Mothers?" Isabel takes another step to the gate. It is open enough for her to slip in, or for the strange familiar woman to slip out; however, both stay on their sides—both afraid of what might happen should they cross the imaginary line between here and there.

"Yes. And the angels. I look after the angels. My angel," the woman declares. A shiver courses Isabel's skin.

A small pebble bounces out from the woman's hiding spot and rolls to the muddy nose of Isabel's shoe. The woman is testing her, as someone would test the ice before venturing from shore. Isabel examines the pebble and tosses it back. A mottled hand reaches out and snatches the stone.

"I thought angels looked after us?" Isabel asks. Hunkering down to bent knees, Isabel hopes to draw the woman out, get a better look.

"Not from in there. It's too dark."

The woman sends her open hand around the wall and through the bars. The tiny stone rolls across creases of her palm. When Isabel reaches for the pebble, the woman snaps her hand shut, then laughs with an edge of madness. The sound of it shatters the thin glass wall keeping Isabel's memories trapped.

Leena.

Isabel remembers her name. This woman came to her bed the night she lost the baby she did not know she was carrying. In the dark, Leena had patted Isabel's sweat-soaked brow. "Leena will take care of your angel. Don't you worry. Leena will take good care," she had promised.

The woman duck-waddles out from behind the wall, still giggling. "Did you come back for your angel?" she asks, tugging a thorny twig snagged in her jumper.

Isabel and the woman named Leena are eye to eye, crouched on either side of the iron gate. Leena's question sends a cramp into Isabel's belly. She thinks of the new baby growing inside and wonders if he or she can sense the residue of loss in that warm space.

"No, Leena. That is your name, right?"

"You remember me?" The woman's face brightens; she pushes back the floppy hat slanting sideways on her head. "No one remembers me." The brightness is short-lived, however.

"I do, Leena. Why don't you come out? The gate is open," Isabel says, reaching a hand through the opening. Her arms vibrate as though she's just reached into a sharp-toothed muzzle. "You don't have to stay there. I know what they do . . . I remember what the Sisters do to the mothers and the babies. And to you."

Isabel grabs one of the iron bars, turning her knuckles white. Leena takes off her hat, exposing her stringy grey hair and pale scalp to a fine mist. She chews on the brim of her hat and scratches her head. Isabel is grateful it isn't the wet wool sleeve.

"Oh, no! I can't leave the angels." Leena shakes her head, adamant. "Why don't you come in?" Her watery brown eyes beg. "Maybe you can make them stop, ask the Sisters to be kind." The older woman reaches through the bars, touches Isabel's knuckles, then peels her fingers off the bar one at a time. She turns Isabel's hand over with a gentleness that's been practiced a lifetime. Her scars are burning red crosshatches on pale, wrinkled skin. "I watched you climb over the wall . . . from up there." Leena points to a high window. "You're so strong. They'll listen to you. They don't listen to me anymore . . . say I'm daft."

Isabel curls her fingers around Leena's hand, wanting to hold on forever, and knows the woman's rough and broken skin comes from countless hours of scrubbing floors and doing laundry.

"I can't come in there, Leena. I'm scared I'll never get back out. I don't know if I can climb that wall again. I've got angels of my own to take care of . . . out here. And in here." Isabel pats her belly.

Leena's eyes widen. Her smile reveals yellow stained teeth and two missing on the side. "You have babies!" Clapping her hands, she giggles again, and this time Isabel finds it a warming sound. "Oh, my dear! You have babies!"

"Twins and another on the way."

A peculiar sensation courses across Isabel's chest. At first, she doesn't know what to call it, then she recognizes it from too long ago. Excitement. This is the moment, she realizes, that was missed the first time around. No one knew, no one celebrated, no one was overjoyed.

Isabel's breath catches in her throat as she looks up. Crouched behind Leena is Isabel's mother, stroking the woman's head with a mist-like hand. Ma comes in and out of sight, made visible only by the tiny drops of rain—as though she is the rain. Leena closes her eyes; her smile is pure, crooked, and her lips are cracked and dry.

When she opens her eyes again, she says, "I can't come out there, my dear. I'm scared I'll never get back in. And who would look after the angels?" The rain stops, and Ma disappears with it.

Distracted by Ma appearing then vanishing, Isabel doesn't hear the splashing footsteps until they are right upon her. Turning to look, Isabel sees a world map of worry in her twin, no piece of her untouched by distress. She carries her shoes in her hands, muddy to the shins.

"Izzy! Are you alright?" Aelish drops her shoes, crouches, draws Isabel tight to her side. "What are you doing here?" Aelish moves a wet chunk of Izzy's hair, tucking it behind an ear.

"I don't know." When Isabel turns back to the gate, there is an expanse of weeds and grass, the mother and baby home squatting like a block of brooding sky—but no Leena. Isabel leans forward, presses her temples to the chilly iron bars. "Leena?" Isabel listens for wet wool being chewed, a rustling of crowded bushes, nose-breathing. She is met with silence.

"Izzy, who's Leena? Here, put this on or you'll catch a good dose." There is a comforting weight to the rain jacket Aelish drapes over her.

Am I off my nut? she wonders. *Have I finally lost my mind . . . seeing a strange woman who takes care of angels . . . seeing Ma made of raindrops?* Isabel believes this sceptical voice until she spots a set of shoe prints in the mud on the other side of the gate—headed to the left of the stone building. And then she hears someone call out in a dense French accent.

"Kathleen!" One of the sisters stands in the open doorway at the top of the steps looking efficient and starched, hands nailed to her narrow waist. "Where do you think you are going! We have mouths to feed here. The children need to be put on the potties." Isabel spots Leena at the edge of the building. She had almost made it unseen around the corner but turns slowly and walks back to the steps, a cowering creature. Isabel grasps the bars, furious and stuck. She recalls how the children's small potties were lined up outside in the yard of the home, the children forced to sit and not move, no matter the weather.

Catching sight of Isabel and Aelish, the nun raises a hand and shoos them away like dogs.

"There's nothing to see here. *Veuillez quitter!* Go on!" The slam of the front doors lands on Isabel's chest.

"Izzy, tell me what happened." Aelish hooks a hand under Isabel's armpit, helping her stand. Isabel's sleeping legs hardly hold her; she grips Aelish's forearm.

"She looks after the babies . . . that woman Leena. I think she's been in there her whole life. A whole life—of that."

Aelish spins Isabel, grips her shoulders. "What was that woman's name again? What did you call her?"

Isabel pulls her head back, needing to take in her twin's foreign expression. Aelish's jaw is flexed and set, her chest high and tight. The heat in her eyes reminds Isabel of her father . . . his temper.

"She told me her name is Leena. I remember her. She helped . . ." Isabel does not have the strength to recount the story yet again. "I guess it's short for Kathleen."

Aelish turns to the gates, her jaw still working. Isabel reaches for the cord between them and takes two steps back as though she's just touched a scorching iron. Aelish wrings the knotted rope at her waist. Isabel is unsure if her sister is praying or keeping herself tethered.

"Ay, what is it?"

Aelish's back expands three times before she bends to pick up her shoes. Turning back to Isabel, she takes her arm.

"Let's get you back to the abbey. The twins are awake and missing Mammy."

"Why don't you put those back on?" Isabel points to Aelish's hand.

Aelish holds the mud-laden shoes out, examines them and shakes her head.

"I think better with bare feet." Draping Izzy's shoulder, Aelish says, "We need to talk with Sister Mike." The surety in Aelish's voice, the protective weight of her twin sister's arm permit Izzy to hang down her usual armour.

"Yes, we do," Izzy says, then adds, "That outfit of yours must weigh a fair bit more than a bull calf when it's wet." Aelish hoists her arm; the sleeve of her habit is a dripping blanket. She can hide none of the sadness in her eyes.

"And sometimes twice as much . . . even when it's dry," she replies.

AELISH, NOVEMBER 1955

AELISH WALKS ISABEL BACK DOWN THE ROAD, BACK TO THE abbey navigating mud holes. One hand opens and closes, while the other holds on to Izzy. She struggles to be present. No matter her efforts, she cannot stop her mind from repeating—*Kathleen. Kathleen. Kathleen.* That name is pulling a memory to her, hand over hand, on a long mental rope.

The first time she heard the name Kathleen, Aelish was sixteen. She was standing shaken, transfixed and eavesdropping outside Sister Edel's door.

Isabel had just stormed out of the Mother Superior's office with a scarlet handprint rising on her cheek, a tattoo of rage. Mean Clare had ratted on Isabel's day at the beach with Declan, and Sister Edel was doling out the punishment—Sister Edel being the only one to know it would end with Isabel's banishment to the mother and baby home.

Aelish had overheard Sister Edel say to Sister Mike, "That girl is a danger to Aelish's soul. And heaven forbid she should end up with child!"

There had been a long pause. Aelish was about to run after Izzy, meet her at the oak tree, when she heard Sister Mike speak. "Mother Superior, I think Isabel McGuire is bringing up a ghost for you." Curious, Aelish pressed her face to the door; the heat of ire seeped through.

"How dare you, Sister Mary Michael! If you're referring to Kathleen, you can stop right now. I forbid you from ever bringing up our childhood. Our life before we took holy vows is dead." Hearing Sister Edel stomp toward the door, Aelish ran to find Isabel. She was torn between the deep drive to keep Izzy safe and the itch to learn more about these women—brides of Christ, pasts supposedly erased by holy euthanasia.

Aelish now looks back down the narrow muddy road toward the mother and baby home. At the top of the hill, the road comes to a benign point—as though nothing horrifying is taking place on the other side of the hill.

"I need you to talk, say something. Anything," Izzy implores, pausing to catch a breath. Aelish cannot say what she is thinking. It would scald her throat on the way out. *Did Sister Edel drive you there herself or make someone else do it for her?*

Aelish glances down; Isabel's hand is laced into hers. The long fingers of Izzy's other hand splay across her round tummy, and Aelish knows without asking: she's holding on, protecting. Tears brim and spill down Aelish's cheeks. Everyone within the circle of Isabel is held and protected with ferocity. Squeezing Isabel's fingers, she says, "I've got you, Izzy. I've got you."

13

SISTER MIKE, NOVEMBER 1955

SISTER MIKE LEANS OUTSIDE THE DOOR OF SISTER EDEL'S ROOM, hands hidden in the sleeves of her robe, head lowered. She is not praying so much as gathering herself—attempting to tame all the undomesticated words in the cage of her throat. She thought of waiting a day, maybe a lifetime before speaking with Sister Edel; it would have been the wiser choice. Instead, she is lunging forward, come what may.

The sound of Father McManus's voice on the other side of the door delivering holy communion to Sister Edel is the blessed delay. "Body of Christ," he murmurs.

Sister Mike rests her head back into the wall, slides her glasses off, and shuts her eyes. *They made me clean up my own miscarriage.* Isabel's words—the shame of her story—upended Sister Mike's levelheadedness.

"Mother Superior?" Father McManus looks down on Sister Mike, mischief on his face. She did not hear him step out into the hall. She has known Father McManus far too long to be embarrassed. Sister Mike closes her eyes again, still unravelled—her discernment up and gone away.

"I can think of better places to take a catnap," he says. "The abbey is full of nooks and crannies, especially for someone no bigger than a leaf. Used to find Sister Eunice, God rest her, curled up in a corner with her head on a stack of hymnals at least once a week. I caught a few winks myself behind the altar table just last week." Even with her eyes closed, Sister Mike hears the smile in his voice.

"How is she today?" Sister Mike slips her glasses on and nods toward the door. She pushes her body away from the wall.

"Talking up a storm as usual." The priest shakes his head a little. "She took holy communion, gave her confession, then pointed me to the door. So I would say she's the same no-nonsense gal we all know and love." Sister Mike notices a bit of worry gather at the corner of the priest's eyes. "Have you ever thought about . . ." He pauses, lowers his voice, crosses his arms. "How will we ever get her out of there when the good Lord comes calling?"

"It will take nothing short of a second parting of the sea, Father. That, and a few strong backs," Sister Mike says quietly, glancing around for busybodies.

The storm clears from his face. He pulls a scratched silver pocket watch from his rumpled sweater, flicks its face with his thick finger, and scowls. "I think I'm late. Never can tell with this." Glancing up at Sister Mike, he tilts his head and asks, "Is there anything I can help you with, Sister?"

Sister Mike holds her breath, wanting to unload the rugged confusing cross on her back, but for the moment, the fewer people in this mess, the better. "Maybe later we can wet the tea, have a cuppa. That would be nice. For now, you should go; you may or may not be late."

The priest nods and chuckles. The sound of his heavy footsteps walking away takes with it the short-lived reprieve from all the confusion. She runs after him—after it—her bare feet tapping the wood.

"Father, wait." She grabs hold of the delicate swinging beads at her chest with one hand and the priest's bulky arm with the other, her thin fingers barely crossing the width of his forearm.

"What's got you so bothered, Sister?" He lets her hand remain on his arm.

"What does she confess? Sister Edel . . . what does she say?" The words come out of her, immediately regretted. Sister Mike pulls her hand off the priest's arm, fearful of contaminating him with her lack of faith and propriety. She steps back. Father McManus drops a hand onto her shoulder, planting her to the ground.

"You know I can't answer that, but I can meet you for tea in the kitchen after mass this evening." He taps the pocket of his sweater, then says, "I may or may not be late."

As he turns the corner down the hall, Sister Mike reaches into her robe for her cigarettes. Her hands shake as she lights the match, a cigarette loyal and waiting between her teeth. The flame sways in front of her face; watching it soothes her glassy nerves. The paper sticks to her lip just a bit when she pulls the cigarette out of her mouth, unlit. Sister Mike shakes the match just as heat nears her fingertips.

"I think you've broken enough rules for today," she whispers to herself.

She licks her fingers, pinches the match, and slips it and the unsmoked cigarette into the box, shoves them back in her robes. With one hand on the brass doorknob of Sister Edel's stuffy room, she covers herself with the sign of the cross.

"Dear Lord," she implores, "I'll keep my prayer simple. Help keep my hands off her throat." She then taps the door and steps into stale unaired history.

Sister Eunice took the last of Sister Edel's mettle when she curled up next to her and died. The bedridden nun peers at Sister Mike momentarily, then back out the window, uninterested. Until recently, Sister Mike didn't think it possible to miss this woman's hard-boiled constitution.

Sister Mike drags a chair to the edge of the bed. Before sitting, she lifts the window, disregarding the rain splattering the windowsill, then lights the cigarette she denied only moments ago and takes three purposeful drags, enjoying the crackle of tobacco. Sister Edel does nothing, says nothing. Her breathing is that of a horse. Sister Mike flicks the half-smoked butt out the window and drops onto the chair. Holding her hand up off her thigh, she sees the shake is gone.

"Why did you send that poor girl to the mother and baby home?" The horse breathing halts, then resumes. Sister Mike stares at the woman's fingers, distended so much so that the splotchy skin is smooth, glistening.

"Which one." Sister Edel slides her gaze from the window to Sister Mike, still indifferent.

"Whitehall just over the hill, run by the Soeurs du Saint Sacrement."

"I know which home. Which girl."

Sister Mike rubs the sudden stiffness in her neck and asks, "How many did you send there?"

"Only those that needed to go. This is an abbey, not a nursery. Close that window."

"Never mind the damn window. It's an orphanage as well. It is part of our vocation to care for these children of God."

Sister Edel rolls her head to face Sister Mike. "They are no longer children of God when they open their legs and ruin their virtue. They are fallen women. Fallen women don't belong here." Her vehement stare and coarse words push Sister Mike back into her chair.

Stunned into silence and sorrow, Sister Mike presses her top lip into her teeth with her fingertips. Looking away, she sees the photograph perched on a shelf.

"And what of Kathleen?" Sister Mike accuses. "No longer a child of God? Don't you think it's up to God to decide who his children are or are not?" Sister Mike stands, turns her back, and picks up the photograph.

"Kathleen made her sinful bed," Sister Edel bites back. "And slept in it, in case you have forgotten."

"And you have made her stay in it for a lifetime, at least in your mind and heart. Do you even know where she is? What happened to her? With Sister Eunice gone, Kathleen is all you have left, if she's still alive." Sister Mike turns back just in time to see a fleeting sadness soften Sister Edel's bloated features.

"I don't want to know. She shamed our family, and it sent my mother to an early grave."

"I know the story," Sister Mike says. "I was there. We were all friends, remember? And I also know as well as you that Kathleen was born with a bit of a feeble mind. What happened was not her fault. She thought that boy liked her, she trusted him, and he took advantage of her."

"She knew right from wrong. She knew the nature of sin. And if you cared so much about Kathleen, where were you when my mother passed and I had no choice but to send Kathleen away? Father Walsh came to the farm and said he would have it no other way, not in his parish. What was I to do?" Lifting an arm off the bed, Sister Edel points a finger. "Oh, yes, you were busy with Charlie Rose." The mention of his name—that time in life—sends a flush up Sister Mike's neck and face. "I was surprised it wasn't you instead of Kathleen who was in the family way. And the way that man slinks around here like a beat dog after all these years, it's pathetic." Sister Edel's breathing comes in choppy huffs. A film of moisture slicks her forehead.

There is nothing Sister Mike can say that will not throw petrol onto this fire. She knows Sister Edel's blustering is meant to shift the shame and blame. She lights another cigarette and kneels at the sill once again. She blows a sliver of her anger out with each blue cloud and reaches a hand into the damp afternoon breeze, hoping the rain will wash this turmoil away.

"Kathleen was there one day and gone the next," Sister Mike says. "And you've never spoken of her, and you forbade Bree from speaking of her. That's not good for the soul. People don't just vanish from your heart, Sister. And as for Charlie, you know I made my choice long ago."

There is a trail of moisture running down the side of Sister Edel's face. When it catches in her ear, Sister Mike sees it is a rivulet of tears. Still kneeling, Sister Mike reaches out and touches Sister Edel's forearm. She is clammy. Although she wants to recoil from the corpse-like feel, Sister Mike gives a gentle squeeze.

Sister Edel stiffens and clamps her eyes shut. More tears fall from her puffy face as she sniffles. Although she would never say it, Sister Mike can't help but think, *All this pain you're in is a cage of your own making.* Instead, she closes the window, rests her forehead on tented fingers, and begins to pray the rosary aloud. Sister Edel remains silent, eyes closed, and soon she is asleep and snoring. Looking at Sister Edel's profile, Sister Mike sees her childhood friend Veronica.

She attempts a smile, tries to forgive, then whispers, "That snoring could chase Christ from the tomb."

AELISH, NOVEMBER 1955

AELISH STANDS NAKED NEXT TO THE RADIATOR IN HER NARROW room in the abbey. The only things on her body besides the mud between her toes are the silver crucifix hanging between her apple breasts and the gold band on her finger. She touches the ring, then the dainty cross and, for the first time, wonders what would happen if she took them off. The thought is akin to a snap of frigid air across her bare body. Resting a hand on her belly, she feels the hole of her navel against her palm—something missing in the middle of all that flesh.

She runs her other hand over the curve of her left buttock, lifts the flesh a little and lets it drop. She does the same lift and drop with her small left breast; it's not nearly as heavy. There is no mirror to see who and what looks back at her, what she's kept covered in black robes all these years. And she is not sure what made her decide today to break from the ritual of dressing and undressing while never being fully unclothed—always a piece of clothing covering something.

Izzy crouched at that iron gate, wet and exposed, undid Aelish in a way that she cannot get hold of. There was a shearing across her heart, leaving the upper and lower halves askew.

After bringing Izzy back to the abbey, drying her off, and settling her in with the twins, all Aelish could think about was slipping out of her habit. *And not just because it was rain-soaked,* she thinks.

The knock at the door and its opening happen at once.

"Wait!" Aelish shouts. She uses her hands to cover as much of herself as possible, spinning to scoop the sheet off the bed. Isabel stands in the doorway, and her stunned face quickly upturns into amusement.

"Well, that's your best side now, isn't it." Isabel leans on the doorway, smirking, casual as though she's caught Aelish reading.

"Close the door!" Aelish hisses. When she lunges for the door, the sheet slips aside.

"I wanted to see you, but not that much of you." Isabel steps in, closes the door. She perches on the edge of the bed, folds her arms over the bump of her belly. She takes Aelish in from tip to toe. "Why are you hiding? We're twins, remember. You've got nothing I don't have . . . I hope."

The top of Aelish's scalp is a blister of heat. Embarrassed by her nakedness and Izzy's boldness. She tries to snug the sheet around her without soiling it with her feet. "Can you please leave! I'm changing."

"I see that you've changed. It's been a long while since we've shared a room. You obviously don't remember our show."

For the first time in years, Aelish sees a spark flare up in her sister's eyes. When Isabel unbuttons her jumper and lets it fall to the bed, Aelish glances around, nervous, confused. Isabel stands and drops her skirt to the floor.

"Isabel! What in heaven's name." Isabel is naked before Aelish can get the words out. Staring at Isabel's scarred chest, the map of stretch marks crawling across her stomach, the hang of her breasts and the deep reddy-brown of her saucer nipples, Aelish sees just how different their lives have been. Their bodies, flesh-bound diaries, each tell such different stories. Aelish is shocked by the enormous swell of Isabel's belly. She had no idea a baby could grow so fast in a few months' time.

"The Nudy Judy Show," Aelish whispers, then claps a hand over her mouth to barricade the giggles.

She lets go of the sheet, and it puddles at her filthy feet. Isabel looks Aelish up and down unabashed, then whistles through her teeth.

The entire childhood routine floods Aelish's mind as though it happened only moments ago. The same rose petal pink vibration of silliness fills an emptiness under her skin. Isabel raises her hands high above her head, waiting for Aelish to match her palm-to-palm.

"Come on!" Izzy encourages.

The grin on Izzy's face is a broom sweeping Aelish's shyness aside. Something like freedom takes its place. Clapping Isabel's palms is all that Aelish will remember before she evaporates into a God-speck watching from above as two beautiful creatures dance around the narrow bedroom, ribbons of pink and pearl essence flaring off of their naked bodies. When they laugh, soft sparks rise into the air. They spin, so connected that despite the cramped room, they never once collide.

"Sister Clare!" Sister Bernice's curt voice on the other side of the door sends Aelish crashing back into the box of her nude body. "Whatever is happening in there? It is a quiet time of reflection and prayer."

Another rapid set of knocks brings Aelish into her tight senses, scrambling for the bathrobe hanging on the wall. Isabel is doubled over, one hand on her mouth, the other on the round of her belly. Her back bucks with stifled laughs. Aelish jabs a finger at Isabel's clothes on the floor, but her twin does not attempt to cover herself. Aelish is embarrassed watching Isabel's breasts swing as she giggles silently.

"Sorry, Sister Bernice. I was just moving my bed to catch the sunlight better." Isabel looks up, tilts her head at the absurd lie, then snorts in laughter. Aelish shrugs.

"What time is evening meal?" Aelish asks, knowing full well the rigid schedule of the abbey. She is hoping to distract Sister Bernice with both the thought of food and the foolishness of the question.

"The same time it has been for decades. Right after vespers. You know this. What's going on in there, Sister?"

"What's for supper?" Isabel blurts.

Aelish slaps her on the shoulder, holds a finger to her lips, and points at Izzy's clothing.

"Stop asking such foolish questions," Sister Bernice says. "It's mutton, it's always mutton. Keep the noise down, Sister Clare. And don't be late for stations of the cross."

Aelish presses an ear to the wood door. For a moment, there is silence, then Sister Bernice's heavy steps recede, followed by the closing of her door across the hall. Aelish spins, leans back into the door, and slides down to the floor. Dressed once again, Isabel kneels in front of Aelish, cotton skirt tucked between her thighs. She sits back on her haunches, hands folded across her belly.

"Remember knick-knackin' on Sister Bernice's door?" Isabel smirks, looking all of sixteen again.

"Thunder and lightning," Aelish replies, feeling the warm glow of a good memory.

"Knock like thunder. Run like lightning," the twins say in unison.

"What I remember is that Sister Mary Angela always looked like a bulldog chewing on a wasp." Izzy scrunches up her face and juts out her bottom teeth. "And how furious she was, thinking Sister Bernice was the one who knick-knacked her door! 'Thithter Berneeth, pleeth keep it down. Thith ith a time of thilence.'" Isabel's imitation of Sister Mary Angela's unfortunate lisp is flawless, making Aelish snort. For a time, Aelish is lost on a page of their past worn softer by time.

Aelish ponders, "I wonder what happened to mean Clare?"

"Good riddance to bad rubbish. That girl was dull as dishwater," Izzy says, wiping her hands together. "Becky—who hates to gossip . . ." Isabel rolls her eyes. "She heard that Clare moved to Dublin to work in a brothel. And I told Becky, there's not a brothel between here and Calcutta that would take that manky thing. I imagine having sex with that one would be like getting up on a cracked plate." Isabel chuckles. Aelish cringes, hoping Izzy did not share this last thought with delicate Becky.

Aelish recalls that Clare's hair was always a hurricane of red like her head was on fire and her eyes continually narrowed and glinting like black stones. *Indeed, I've exaggerated her over the years,* she thinks. And then she remembers the fear that tightened her low belly every time Clare got near. As with all people in her life, Aelish tries to soften the girl in her mind. But just thinking of Clare makes Aelish's bowels wring a little. Izzy, however, was unafraid—better yet, amused by Clare's crossness. "Mind yer business, Clare, or I'll give ya some business to mind," Izzy would say, calm as could be, neck long, chest broad, a confident grin on her face. Izzy had sounded so much like Da.

Down the hall from Aelish's room, Sister Bernice, who does nothing without determination, slams her door. It startles Aelish away from mean Clare. Isabel has her head tilted; a gentle smile rests on her face.

The safety Aelish felt standing behind Da's leg as a wee girl sweeps through in a bittersweet breeze.

"Do you remember what Da said about bullies?" Aelish asks.

In unison, they recite Da's wisdom. "'They're weak with no heart and not worth a fart.'" Isabel laughs, falls forward, and buries her face in Aelish's lap. When their laughter runs dry, Isabel sits up, twists her neck this way and that with a few loud pops. Aelish watches her twin—seeing her. Really seeing her.

"What is it, Ay?" Isabel asks, twirling her long hair into a knot on top of her head.

Aelish thinks of all the scarred and broken tissue on her sister's wondrous mothering body, every mark telling a story of loving someone. Then she thinks about the false flawless landscape of her own skin—her only scars hidden out of sight on the bottoms of her feet.

Gathering Isabel's hands between her own, Aelish kisses Isabel's fingertips, then says, "We need to go and speak with Sister Mike and Sister Edel. Something must change."

ISABEL, NOVEMBER 1955

ISABEL TRAILS AELISH DOWN THE HALL, HEADED FOR SISTER Edel's room. The floor glistens underfoot. Her kneecaps ache as she recalls a childhood spent scrubbing and polishing. The pungent chemical mix of beeswax, linseed oil, and turpentine churns Isabel's tummy. As they get closer to the old nun's room, odours and sounds of harsh memories grow fangs.

The suffering in her leg flares, the limp worsens. *I don't know if I can do this—I don't know if I can look at that atrocious woman.* Reaching out for Aelish, two steps ahead, Isabel's finger brushes the hem of her swinging veil. Three steps, then four separate them now.

Aelish, I can't. Isabel is not strong enough to say it aloud. Aelish is straight, strong. The stretch of her shoulders, wide. She thinks of the strength it must have taken Aelish to let her go, move on, ignore all those letters—mistakenly believing herself abandoned, not knowing Sister Edel had dropped Isabel off at that godforsaken home in the middle of the night.

Perhaps this life Aelish has been living has given her something I don't have, a faith in doing the right thing. But Isabel knows that faith has always been in her sister, like an extra bone, it's part of her anatomy.

Aelish turns, curious, as though hearing a distressed bird just outside the window. Seeing Isabel, her brows tip with worry.

"We don't have to do this, Izzy, not now. Or I can go alone," Aelish offers, closing the gap between them, taking Isabel's hand. The touch of her skin tethers Isabel back into a protective bay. "Why don't you go be with the babies? I can handle this," Aelish insists.

As Aelish guides Isabel back down the hall, she glances down at Aelish's bare feet. Isabel stops. Aelish halts against Isabel's planting.

"Why don't you like to wear shoes?" Isabel knows the answer but is not so sure Aelish does. Or will admit it.

"It's more comfortable, I suppose . . . my feet get hot, I don't know. Sister Mike says it helps her think. Does it matter?"

Any fear Isabel had of seeing Sister Edel's face falls away.

Unlike Aelish, who draws her strength from some silent well, Isabel's rises from turbulent waters and crashing seas. She remembers holding a cool cloth to the bottoms of Aelish's swollen, slashed feet the day she ran from the schoolhouse, only to be punished by Sister Edel. Aelish couldn't wear shoes for weeks after that; instead, she had to wear loosely tied rags. All because she was mortified by falling in front of all the other kids—and Declan. Isabel remembers watching the way Aelish looked at Declan that day. Like he was the only one that mattered in that circle of laughing kids—in the world. Isabel's throat thickens.

"Izzy, do you want to go back and be with Paddy and Sar?"

"I know you liked him, Ay," Isabel says, confronting what she's always been too afraid to see. "I took him from you, and I couldn't give him back."

Aelish draws her head back, appears confused. However, in their secret room where there is no such thing as a secret, Isabel knows Aelish understands. Knows she will be hurt.

"You're talking nonsense. Are you feeling alright?" Isabel pushes Aelish's hand away when she reaches to test her forehead for fever.

"Declan," Isabel states. "You liked him . . . quite a lot. I know you, Aelish. I watched you in school when we were girls. I watched you around him."

Aelish blinks, scratches at the crease of her elbow. The spaces between the red patches on her face go stark white. Her mouth opens and closes without sound.

"I laughed at you that day on the steps of the schoolhouse only because I knew you liked him so much and so did I," Isabel recalls. "And then that mean old cow whipped your feet raw." Aelish shakes her head, not wanting to listen. "Because I laughed at you . . . because you liked Declan, she whipped your feet. And now you don't like to wear shoes."

Aelish shifts from one foot to the other as if the skin of her soles has broken open. "Don't be daft, Izzy," Aelish objects. She pinches her top lip, shakes her head even more.

"About which part? That you liked Declan even before I did, or that you can't wear shoes because of that broken-down wagon in there?" Isabel jabs her finger toward Sister Edel's closed door.

"Either. It's all silliness. That was years ago," Aelish mutters, shifting from foot to foot. She fumbles with the knotted rope at her waist. Isabel yanks it out of her hand.

"It's now, Aelish!" Isabel shouts, pointing at her twin's bare and scarred feet. "It's now!" she repeats, this time placing a hand on her belly. "This isn't history."

"That's why we're going to speak to Sister Edel, Izzy. We must make it right. What happened to you isn't right!" Aelish exclaims.

Isabel's hands curl. The growing frustration makes her jaw throb. Aelish's denial is a wall as impervious and even more painful than the one surrounding the mother and baby home.

"What happened to *you* isn't right. None of this is right!" Isabel says, clutching the outside of Aelish's arms. In her mind, Isabel feels her twin trying to twist away from the cord vibrating between their hearts and minds.

"I couldn't give him back," Isabel says, once again. Hoping Aelish will hear, react, become furious. She is willing to sacrifice herself to get Aelish to see that blind faith—even in her twin—only leads to heartache. "I had no one. You had Sister Mike and God. And you didn't need me. I needed someone, so I kept him to myself. I loved him with all my heart, but not at first. At first, I kept him . . . from you."

Aelish looks at the polished floor, the wall over Isabel's shoulder, the top of Isabel's head. For a moment, Aelish's upper lip quivers as she blinks back tears. Then the smell of cigarette smoke curls between them, the sound of soft tapping shoes. Isabel watches her sister retreat back into the refuge of faith blindness, buttoning it all up. Isabel lets her hands drop, exhausted.

"Sister Clare? Isabel? Is everything okay?" Sister Mike asks cautiously. Isabel raises her eyebrows at the copy of *The Lion, the Witch and the Wardrobe* rather than the Bible held to the nun's chest. Sister Mike caresses the gold letters on its blue spine. "It's far more entertaining than the Old Testament."

"Anything is," Isabel retorts. Aelish pokes Izzy's arm, shakes her head slightly.

"We need to see Sister Edel." Aelish's voice is sure once again.

"I left her sleeping a while ago. She's had quite a morning. Can it wait?"

"No, Mother Superior. It cannot," Aelish declares. "You know this has waited far too long. It should never have been at all." The determined Aelish has returned. So too has the Aelish who gave up a boy she might have loved so that Isabel would know happiness and safety in her life.

Sister Mike humbles her chin, closes her eyes for a moment. *Is there a prayer for bloodless hypocrites?* Isabel wants to ask. Instead, she keeps her tongue. Even through the haze of her anger, Isabel sees Sister Mike fumbling to find the head of this moral snake in the grass.

Sister Mike opens her eyes, pushes her glasses up into place. Isabel is uncertain if the adoration flowing from the nun's eyes is intensified by her thick lenses or if it was something in her silent prayer. Izzy must look away. Sister Mike tucks her novel under her arm, steps between Izzy and Aelish, takes both of their hands, and leads them to Sister Edel's door.

14

SISTER EDEL, NOVEMBER 1955

IF NOT FOR FEAR OF ETERNAL DAMNATION, SISTER EDEL WOULD hold her breath until she vanished from the prison of her flesh. *Forgive me, Dear Lord.*

She cries more often now, wondering if this is what happens just before people die—all those useless emotions coming out like the final wringing of a rag before it is hung to dry. Sister Edel rotates her ankles and wriggles her toes. She can feel the moving in her right foot despite not having seen her feet for ages. She has told no one, especially that old crow Dr. Gibbs; however, her left foot is numb and has been for months.

All this talk of Kathleen and the past is exhausting, and she knows Sister Mike is not through with the subject. She has known Sister Mike long enough to know that she's a dog on a bone when there is something on her heart.

"Kathleen," Sister Edel says in a hoarse whisper.

Sister Mike was right about Kathleen. She was feeble-minded, everyone knew it. But it didn't stop her knowing right from wrong and black from white. Nor did it stop her from understanding that, as a young woman, Sister Edel had very much liked the very same boy who got Kathleen in the family way.

The sweet scent of straw and horse manure pull her back there. To the lopsided barn in spring. Stripes of dusty honey-coloured light seeping through the barn board walls as she and Kathleen mucked stalls. Kathleen carries a new bale of straw into the stall—a task Veronica cannot do with her fevered aching hands—and flops down onto it. She wears the May Day crown of snowy hawthorne blossoms she made, intending to place it on the statue of Mary at church that day. She itches at the red straw rash on her forearms, then grins at the beetle trundling across the straw bale.

"Can you keep a secret, Kathleen?"

Kathleen looks up at her older sister, her gold-green eyes bright, simple, and curious. She twists an invisible lock on her lips and throws the unseen key over her shoulder.

"I love a secret this much!" Kathleen exclaims, stretching her arms so wide she near topples off the bale. "Tell me, Ronnie! Tell me a secret."

"Okay, but no telling, not even Bree." Kathleen puffs out her cheeks, holding her breath. It's what she does when she's excited.

"I really like Callum. And I think he likes me." Veronica's smile starts in her stomach and arrives on her face. The butterflies create a fluttering riot inside. She's told no one that Callum Fitzgerald kissed her under the giant elm in the McCarthys' back pasture. Or that she would marry Callum rather than take holy vows as a Sister . . . if he asked.

Kathleen clutches the collar of her cotton shirt and pulls it up over her mouth and nose. She is all round, dancing eyes. Silent.

"Well, say something," Veronica urges after two minutes of solid silence.

Kathleen pulls her shirt collar down, revealing a grin that shows most of her teeth and gums.

She whispers, "You said to keep a secret."

"It's not a secret between us, dummy! You can talk to me about it."

Kathleen shrinks. Veronica knows what she's done.

"I'm sorry, Leena, I didn't mean to call you a dummy, you're not a dummy."

Sitting on the bale beside Kathleen, Veronica slings an arm over her shoulder, adjusts her flowery crown. Her gold hair smells of sweat and spring air. Kathleen is a wilted flower coming back to life under Veronica's embrace. Her smile widens once more.

"I have happy tingles in here because you like him." Kathleen pats her chest.

Veronica kisses her sister's forehead, stands, and extends a hand. "We've got to get this stall cleaned before church and before Daddy comes back with the new mare, up ya get." Kathleen takes Ronnie's hand and kisses each inflamed knuckle with a loud smacking noise before standing. "Remember, though, it's our secret, right?" When Kathleen locks her lips and throws away the key again, earnestness burns in her eyes. Veronica's heart swells at the miracle of Kathleen's innocence.

Sister Edel is drifting in that hazy place where then and now are delicately stitched when the knob on the door to her stagnant room turns. For a moment, she is still coated in the sweet scent of horses and the taste of chewing a stem of straw is fresh in her mouth. She licks her lips, and it all evaporates. Opening her eyes and looking over the rise of her body, she sees three women, one of whom she hoped to never lay eyes on again.

ISABEL, NOVEMBER 1955

ISABEL MUST WRESTLE THE IMAGE INTO THE GROOVES OF HER brain for it to make sense. The woman in the bed is a colossus. Neither Sister Mike nor Aelish had talked of Sister Edel's enormity, saying only, "She's unwell—she's been bedridden for years with rheumatoid arthritis."

Now Isabel wishes she'd been forewarned, because a few small fragments of her protective bitterness have been flecked away by pity—the last thing Isabel wants to feel for the woman who dropped her into that grim prison.

This woman is not the volcano of righteousness she once was.

The grinding of Isabel's teeth is loud inside her skull. Isabel touches her cheekbone. The fossil of their first battle is still there in the shape of Sister Edel's handprint.

"What is it you want, Sister Mike?" The chafing of Sister Edel's voice brings Isabel back into the bedroom, back to the stink of overripe vegetables. "I've had about enough for this week."

Having just gotten over her morning sickness, Isabel is angry to be revisited with a push of nausea. She breathes through her mouth, refusing to let this woman chase her away once again. Sister Mike draws back the curtain, cracks the window. The biting November wind pushes the stagnant air around the room.

Isabel fights the urge to take the glass of water on the bedside table and throw it against the wall. Her arms and legs sizzle. The scars on her palms pulsate, wanting to be noticed—acknowledged—paid for. Isabel steps to the foot of the bed. Much worse than no eye contact, Sister Edel looks through Isabel—an inconsequential ghost.

"Look at me!" Isabel clutches the footboard and shakes it. The stony woman does not flinch.

Aelish then steps shoulder to shoulder with her twin. Isabel feels the rope between their minds being held steady, without restraint by Aelish.

"These young women need some answers, Sister." Sister Mike settles into the tall-backed chair at the bedside, smooths her robes, and folds her hands in her lap.

"I have nothing to say other than she does not belong here." The old nun jabs a bloated finger at Isabel. "This is a house of God.

She was forbidden from ever setting foot here again a long time ago."

Before Isabel releases the hateful cyclone inside her, Sister Mike says, "I'm afraid you're not privy to making those sorts of decisions any longer, Sister. And you're right about this being a house of God." Sister Mike reaches into her robe and sets a package of cigarettes on her lap. "Sister Clare, Isabel, ask your questions with the grace of God in your heart and on your lips."

Isabel watches both Aelish and Sister Mike cover themselves with the sign of the cross. Refusing, Isabel bolts her arms to her sides. Sister Edel stares at the ceiling, huffing in choppy snorts.

"There was no grace the night she dragged me out of here. Why should I offer grace now?" Isabel rebukes Sister Mike, pacing at the foot of the bed, two steps left, then two steps back to the right. Aelish steps out of the way, slipping behind Sister Mike's chair.

"'Twas the best thing for you. For you and your sister." Sister Edel juts the mound of her chin toward Aelish. "Look at her now. At least one of you is a woman of God. I had to make a choice."

Isabel presses her hands to her ears, closes her eyes, trying to keep the woman's callousness from getting in—and her own incensed rage from getting out. It has been weeks since the itch for the bottle has risen under her skin. Isabel places a hand on her round tummy, and the itch subsides slightly.

"Do you have any idea what happens in that godforsaken place you decided was best for me? Have you ever set foot inside those walls?" Isabel tries not to meet Sister Edel's cruelty with her own but fails. "Of course not—look at ya."

"Isabel, child," Sister Mike says, imploring Isabel for kindness.

"Have you, Sister Edel?" Aelish asks as she steps into Sister Edel's line of sight. "Have you ever been to Whitehall mother and baby home?"

Isabel watches Aelish—her accusing eyes, tight lips—and thinks, *How is it possible that I've never once seen her look at someone like that, with such suspicion, contempt even?* Isabel touches the rope, sensing something vibrate its way through.

"That is not your business, Sister Clare. That's nobody's business," Sister Edel protests, glaring at Aelish, trying to reduce her on the spot. It does not work this time.

"Between you and God, then," Aelish notes, her head tilted.

Isabel is the one to step aside this time, wondering where the strange chill on her skin is coming from. Sister Mike sits silent, leaning toward the open window, nursing a cigarette.

"Or is it between you and God and Kathleen?" The cigarette stops halfway to Sister Mike's lips.

Isabel's thoughts race in circles. Kathleen? Leena? She pictures the woman at the gate, the pebble in her hand, her childlike giggle. This is the only Kathleen she knows. The Kathleen who mopped her brow, rubbed her back in soothing circles, helped clean up the miscarriage.

Isabel stares at Sister Edel. All the pieces of a tattered puzzle force themselves together.

"You know who Kathleen is?" Isabel asks, confused and unsure who to bring this question to. Sister Edel digs her fingers into the blanket straining to drape her wide body. The rise and fall across the mountain of her belly cease.

"How dare you speak of my sister," Sister Edel hisses.

Isabel's mouth, her whole body turns dry. She is unable to move or blink; her mind fumbles.

"Do you know she is still living in that prison?" Aelish asks as she cups her hands together at her chest. Then begs, "I pray to the good Lord you did not know this. Please, Sister, tell me you did not know this, that you didn't leave her there to rot all these years."

Sister Edel's paled skin blends with the starched white sheet across her throat. Her thick hands shake. Sister Mike steps to the bed, rests the back of her hand across the nun's forehead.

"Sister Edel, you need to calm down." Sister Mike turns to Isabel and Aelish, shaking her head in confusion. "Whatever are you talking about?"

Isabel laces her fingers into Aelish's hand. There is heat and strength in their grip.

Isabel's chest and throat contract as she says, "A woman named Kathleen . . . Leena took care of me the night I . . ." When Aelish squeezes her hand, the words find their way out. "I had a miscarriage. And I saw her again today."

Sister Edel has all but fallen out of the conversation, stricken.

"Today? Where?" Sister Mike looks back and forth between Isabel and Sister Edel, her lips tight.

"The mother and baby home," Aelish explains. "That's where Isabel was when Sister Celine couldn't find her."

Isabel's thighs weaken at the haunting mention of the mother and baby home. Isabel knows Aelish feels this in her own legs. She pulls a chair over for Isabel to sit. Refusing, Isabel stands and grips the back of it.

"A woman with a childish mind was at the gate when I got there, I remembered her name was Leena," Isabel manages. "I remembered because she helped me . . . she told me that night she would take care of my angel. She refused to come outside the gate today because she needed to take care of all the angels. That's what she said." Isabel points her finger at Sister Edel. "And do you know the angels she was goin' on about? The babies buried in the tall grasses behind that terrible place! Your sister is taking care of children who die in that place and the poor mothers who suffer the loss." The flame in Isabel rises, needing to set fire to the inert woman in the bed. "And you . . . all you've been doing is beating young girls senseless your whole life, and now you lay here like a whale washed up on a miserable shore."

Sister Mike wraps an arm around Isabel's shoulder and says gently, "Isabel, this is not good for anyone. You must think of the baby and calm yourself." Isabel fights the desire to turn and burrow into the safety of Sister Mike's neck, into the scent of smoke and rose water.

"I am thinking of the baby," Isabel insists. "All the babies. And Leena."

Sister Edel blinks at the sound of that name. Isabel walks to the edge of the bed. The body odour, the heat coming off the old nun is unbearable; however, the impulse to speak for Kathleen is a bitter, potent force. The confusion—the shock in the nun's eyes makes satisfaction well in Isabel.

Isabel holds her stomach, overcome with protecting the child inside her, as she says, "No matter how many times you say that rosary or do those bloody stations of the cross"—she points to the door behind her—"no matter how many hours you spent on your knees in that stuffy old chapel praying for us sinners, your sister Kathleen has been more a woman of God than you could ever hope to be." Watching Sister Edel recoil into her pillow makes Isabel lean in, cornering the nun in her own pen of cruelty. "You know nothing of God or mercy. I hope you rot in hell."

The grip on her upper arm sends an ache into the bone. She tries to twist away, but Sister Mike does not relent her grasp as she pulls Isabel to the door yet again.

"That's enough out of you." Sister Mike's voice is tight, sharp. "I'd tell ya to leave before you regret what comes out of your mouth, but that horse has left the barn. For your own good, go to the kitchen, have some tea, and tend to your babies. Go on, now."

Isabel twists back, expecting Aelish to follow. Sister Mike raises a halting hand to Aelish and demands, "Sister Clare, you stay here. We'll pray on this, then discuss it with a level head."

Isabel's eyes fill, then run over. A flash of the night in the laundry rises—being rain-soaked, the acrid scent of lye, the desperation of needing Aelish to leave with her. She scrambles for the rope strung between them, both hands clasping the front of her sweater.

Aelish shakes her head and says, "Please forgive me, Mother Superior, but a level head is not what's needed here. Truth and humility are." Aelish steps around Sister Mike. "I agree Isabel needs to calm herself, but that won't happen if she leaves this room alone. I'll not have her sent away again like she doesn't belong."

Aelish steadies her gaze on Isabel. Isabel stops breathing for a moment, startled to see Ma in her twin sister's narrowed eyes and determined jaw. When Aelish twines her arm through Isabel's, the tether between them courses. She hears: *Teaspoons.*

15

AELISH, NOVEMBER 1955

Aelish settled Isabel with Sarah and Paddy, then went to the chapel intending to pray, but the threshold was insurmountable. Standing in the chapel doorway, she found herself with the taste of brick dust coating her mouth and the sensation of earth shuddering beneath her feet, her mind dragging her to the narrow living room on Donegall Street, swallowed in darkness and explosions of orange and ash. Worst of all was the phantom feel of her mammy's lifeless, severed hand in hers. All of this turned her away from the chapel, running for the most solid thing she knew: the foot of Sister Mike's smoking tree.

Aelish sits on the damp earth, her tired back against the trunk. The cold cannot reach her through the numbness. Resting her head against the bark, she notices shapes and letters suspended in the leafless branches above.

Aelish closes her eyes and murmurs, "I don't know. I just don't know." Her fidgeting hands fall quiet and settle to the hard-packed dirt at her sides. The cool of the soil is a balm that slides up her arms and across her chest.

"I don't know," she whispers again. The bottom of her stomach swings low and heavy, subdued by not having to know the answers.

Is this what prayer is supposed to feel like? she wonders. *Is this the serenity I see on Sister Mike's face after quiet solitude?*

Aelish's prayers have always been fits of intensity, begging, lamenting, asking forgiveness for every transgression. At times, forgiveness for simply being alive, it seems. But this—this isn't prayer, Aelish knows that. Rather, she feels herself stepping onto a thin branch of surrender. Isabel's words from their discussion before entering Sister Edel's room—the ones Aelish could not swallow—finally belly-land.

I had no one. You had Sister Mike and God. And you didn't need me. I needed someone, so I kept him from you. I couldn't give him back.

"I don't know . . ." The loose hammock of her stomach begins to tighten as she finishes the thought. ". . . if I can do this anymore."

The scratch of a match makes Aelish's eyes open. Sister Mike stands, her head cocked, holding a flame to the cigarette between her lips. She hands Aelish a wool blanket to cover her legs.

Blowing out the first drag of smoke, she asks, "What is it you can no longer do, Aelish?"

The sound of her given name sends Aelish's fingers digging into the dirt, clutching for a root, a rock—anything to keep from being thrown out of the life she struggles to hold to. Sister Mike lowers to sitting in front of Aelish, her large eyes and all their burden framed by the dark rims of her glasses. She pulls a portion of the blanket onto her thighs.

As though attached to someone else's body, directed by someone else's mind, Aelish's arm extends. She watches her hand reach for Mother Superior's cigarette. Before she can pluck the cigarette from Sister Mike's dainty fingers, the Mother Superior leans in close enough to kiss Aelish's nose and blows a cloud of smoke into her face. An incinerating explosion follows the heat in Aelish's throat and lungs. The hacking cough is instant, her body trying to rid itself of the sudden mound of coal in her chest. Through watering eyes, she watches the world spin.

"That ought to cure ya," Sister Mike declares, sitting back, looking quite pleased. "Now, why don't ya tell me what's on your heart, Sister. And don't give me some story about it being all about Isabel."

The spinning comes to a slow turn. The world Aelish sees around her steadies, but the landscape inside her continues to convulse. Aelish has no idea what to say. Her thoughts and heart-sick feelings are a fraying tangle of rope with no beginning.

Aelish asks, "Have you ever thought about . . . not being here?"

When this question pops past Aelish's lips, it jars her like a missed step in the dark. Sister Mike twists her cigarette into the dirt, then wipes her hands together. Aelish knows by asking that question she has stepped through a crack in her reality.

"Are ya referring to not being *here* in *this* world"—Sister Mike glances at the abbey standing silent watch beside them, then spins a finger above her head, saying, "or *this* world?"

Aelish was not talking about wanting to die. She never wanted to talk about that. It was, after all, a mortal sin. Despite that fact, she suddenly feels damp, ocean soaked. Her back remembers the bruises left by the ribs in the bottom of Tommy Doolin's boat the day he fished her from the sea.

"I was in love with a man once," Sister Mike reflects mildly as she tucks her robes tighter under her. "A very good man." Picking a twig from the earth, the Mother Superior plays with it and looks across the lawn to the front gates. Aelish closes her eyes so as not to see this woman she loves and holds high as fallible. History-ridden.

"And I did." She pauses, exhales as though she still has smoke in her lungs. "I do, more recent than I care to confess, let myself think of leaving here . . . what that would be like. What life would be like with him and not this." Sister Mike touches the crucifix at her chest, pulls the knotted rope onto her lap, and holds it. Aelish reaches down for her own rope and, where once she felt the security of those knots holding her to some holy anchor, she now feels their twisted tightness. She drops them and itches at the crook of her left elbow.

Sister Mike carries on, her eyes soft and looking up into the branches. "And then I remembered what put me here. It might seem strange to most, but thoughts of a life of marriage, perhaps children and grandchildren, well, it all seemed . . ." Pausing, the Mother Superior squints and tilts her head as though spotting something high in the tree. "Predictable. Yes, that's it. Predictable. More important is that, in my heart, this life of doing God's work—it's lively. Wouldn't you agree, Sister?"

Aelish's fingernail breaks from picking at a thin root at the surface of the dirt. Pulling knees to chest, she curls her toes. Rocking, Aelish buries her face into the wool blanket stretched across her knees.

"Child." Sister Mike rests a palm on the back of Aelish's bowed head. "God knows what's on your heart; you might as well be out with it. And then maybe we can go indoors where it's a reasonable temperature."

Aelish sips breath through the course weave against her lips and confesses, "I don't belong here." She wants Isabel here as she steps off this limb. "I don't think I ever have."

Sister Mike sighs. Aelish is terrified to look up and see disappointment, paralyzed by the thought of facing an unrecognizable world if she were to peek out of her makeshift shelter. Sister Mike slides two fingers under Aelish's tucked chin.

"Look at me, Sister," Mother Superior says in a whisper.

Aelish cracks her swollen eyes open to find the world has not changed. Sister Mike in her dark framed glasses, the brick abbey planted on the lawn over her shoulder, the breeze tapping thin branches together . . . all unchanged.

"How long have you been feeling this way?" she asks.

Aelish reaches, blind and groping for the moment, for the single thread that broke first. "I don't know *how* I feel. All I know is that I don't think I feel how I *should*." She pauses for a hitching breath.

"Which is?" Sister Mike rests a hand at her heart.

"Content," Aelish says, uncertain. That word doesn't have the weight. Closing her eyes, she petitions with her whole heart. She's not done this in a very long time.

Please, Virgin Mother, give me clarity.

In her mind, like a picture show, she sees Ma and Da and she and Izzy as girls all caught in a warm summer rain at the shore. She sees Izzy, Declan, herself, and the babies in their colourful cottage those few precious peaceful days they shared in Pouch Cove.

Aelish breathes slowly within the silent, waiting space Sister Mike offers. And when the answer comes, it is a velvet leaf settling on her lips.

Aelish blows it into the air by saying, "Whole. I want to feel whole."

Sister Mike's glance drifts skyward again as though watching what Aelish has released into the air. A line of tears slips from under the edge of her glasses. When Sister Mike takes her hand, it reminds Aelish of all the worry she felt on Ma's skin before the bombs dropped.

AELISH, NOVEMBER 1955

AELISH IS SEATED NEXT TO SISTER EDEL'S BED, ATTEMPTING TO say the rosary. Sister Edel's snoring reminds Aelish of the big lorries that rumble past the abbey from time to time with a burden of livestock. Following Isabel's attempt to exhume Aelish's buried fondness for Declan and then cracking open under the tree with

Sister Mike, Aelish now hopes the heft of Sister Edel might somehow pin her down into her life, her vows, her commitment once again.

She shifts in her chair, of half a mind to leave quietly.

"Can't a person get any peace around here?" Sister Edel croaks. "Did you come to accuse me of nailing Christ to the cross with my bare hands? Because I'll hear no more of accusations and fool-headed talk of what goes on at that mother and baby home."

Thin blue veins crisscross the woman's closed eyelids. Aelish's earlier infuriation with Sister Edel is now deflated. As she sat under the tree, a wisp of clarity took hold, showing Aelish that Sister Edel was genuinely ignorant of the atrocities happening only a few miles down the road. It was an entirely different order of nuns, autonomous, mostly French speaking. Aelish even doubted that the old nun knew her own sister Leena was still wandering the halls of that place. And that was the more challenging piece to let go of—that Sister Edel had never tried to find her own sister.

Aelish wiggles her fingers before they clutch and cast the first stone. What confronts Aelish's mind: the stack of Isabel's stubbornly unopened letters that grew under her bed. She reminds herself: *I didn't come here to hold this woman accountable.* Then wonders again, *What am I doing here?*

"Speak, Sister Clare. Speak or leave me in peace."

"I don't believe I can continue as a nun," Aelish says, coming out with it.

"I don't believe that either," Sister Edel retorts without a hair's width of pause.

Aelish grabs the edges of the chair, bewildered by her abrupt admission and Sister Edel's brusque agreement. Sister Edel turns her head with the slowness of a ship turning about on the sea and, locking watery grey eyes on Aelish, stares. Feeling almost hypnotized, Aelish notices a few wiry chin hairs and the smattering of age spots across the Sister's high forehead.

"I had my doubts about you since that day you walked into my office asking to join the order. But I let Sister Mike and her predilection for sentimentality cloud my judgement." Sister Edel takes a heaving breath. "And I am ashamed to say that perhaps . . ." The elderly nun steers her head back to the middle, stares at the ceiling, silent. Aelish leans in, needing to hear what this righteous stronghold could possibly feel ashamed of.

"My"—Sister Edel searches the ceiling—"opposition to your sister." Aelish knows the words are being cautiously chosen. "It clouded my instincts in that matter. In so many matters. She was my cross to bear, and I did not bear it with grace." Sister Edel turns back to Aelish once again. The room is so silent Aelish hears the nun's thinning hair scratch against the pillow. Exhaustion and sadness transform the old nun's gaze. "I fear I failed you, Sister Clare. And God willing, I hope to make it right by telling you now: you do not belong here. If you came here to get my blessing to leave this life, you have it."

She takes another gulp of air, closes her eyes, rolls her head back. Aelish's skin crawls with static, losing her edges just as she did all those years ago, kneeling at the foot of the Virgin Mother. She feels transparent enough to pass through the pane of glass in the tall window and drift into the barren treetop. When she looks down, she sees her own pale, freckled hand is intertwined with that of Sister Edel, with no recollection of how it happened. Reaching for the sensation of their finger webbing connected, she feels the warmth of bathwater. When Sister Edel squeezes her creaseless puffy fingers into Aelish's she slides back into her body.

"Sister Edel, I don't know how to *not* be here," Aelish whispers.

The Sister takes her hand away; the thin moment of tenderness disintegrates.

"Between you and that sister of yours, I'm not sure which of ya is more frustrating. I'd like to put you both in a box and give you a good shake. Just because you don't know any other way to live is no reason to stay. Just go where you've always been. Your sister has bitten off more of life than she can chew, and I suspect she'll continue to do so. She's got none of your common sense." Sister Edel lifts a heavy arm off the bed and shoos Aelish away like a pesky fly. "Just go where you've always been."

All the moments of Aelish's life that were muddied by concerns of Isabel now rustle and scratch. The intrusive wonderings about Izzy during compline or vespers. The silent meditations interrupted by imagining the landscape of Isabel's life. The piece of Aelish that has been with Isabel all these years returns to her now—an exhausted wanderer. Aelish wraps her arms around her shoulders, wanting to curl herself around this familiar bone-weary stranger.

"Will I ever find God's favour again . . . if I leave?" Aelish asks from the cave of her veil.

"Not likely," Sister Edel pronounces.

This is not what Aelish hoped to hear. She lifts her head to see the nun's heavy lids are shuttered once again. Her voice sounds scratchy and worn as she continues. "But better to take a chance and be truthful than try and fool the Lord Almighty. Remember what happened to Adam and Eve."

Aelish recalls the weeks of childhood nightmares, the Garden of Eden quaking with thunder and lightning, Adam and Eve ashamed, a mountain of snakes roiling around them. Aelish shudders her way out of the memory.

Sister Edel's mouth hangs open in an O, headed toward snoring. Aelish rises from the chair and slides it back against the wall. Sister Edel's foot poking out from the blanket is a deep purple from the ankle to the tips of her swollen toes. She covers Sister Edel with the blanket and heads for the chapel.

SAINT PATRICK'S STAINED-GLASS EYES TRACK AELISH AS SHE steps into the pew, kneels, and rests her backside onto the edge of the bench. She nestles her chin into her folded arms. The skeleton of what matters in her life has been rearranged into some unrecognizable creature. She lets her eyes close halfway; the chapel blurs, the crack marring the Virgin's porcelain profile disappears.

"I know I don't deserve your help, Mother Mary, but I'm asking for strength," Aelish murmurs.

Dropping her forehead into the cradle of her arms, she feels a hood of exhaustion slide over her head. The vision of a woman comes to her. The delicate scents of sweet lilacs and soda bread filling her nose let her know this woman she sees is one of motherhood. *A* mother, *the* Mother, *her* mother? She cannot be sure.

All of Aelish's burdensome questions and confusion disperse weightless as dandelion seeds in all directions around this Mother. The Mother reaches her fingers, playing with the drifting bits of Aelish's torment, sending it all into a high dance above her head. This woman appears bathed in a delight that fills Aelish with a bone-deep thirst.

Licking her lips, Aelish tries to muster saliva to soothe a dry throat, but nothing comes. No relief, no soothing, no answers. The Mother is a wavering mirage, holding all the answers just beyond the parched fringe of Aelish's heart.

The vision of the Mother fractures when Aelish slaps the edge of the pew. The sound of her frustration echoes through the chapel. Several of the nuns kneeling in silent prayer gasp, startled. Others cluck their tongues in disapproval, shushing Aelish.

Rising, Aelish flips the kneeler up with a brazen bang and heads back down the aisle. Some Sisters glare; others, like Becky, have eyes saturated with empathy. Before leaving, she stops at the holy water font. Another mirage of relief. Denying the reflex built into her since childhood, she walks past the shallow ceramic bowl without submerging her fingertips. No catastrophe befalls her as she steps through the double doors because she dared not wet herself with blessed water. She pounds up the steps to her room and is halted mid stride by a sudden realization. A percipience that weakens her bones with relief and agony.

Catastrophes have been happening regardless of her spiritual toiling. Weeds of despair grow heedless of her prayers and petitions, holy confessions, and daily communion, trying to control them, pluck them out. Still, they grow vibrant with life. Sister Mike, even Sister Edel in her stringent piety—they fold these weeds of tragedy into the soil of their faith as nourishment. Letting it all come to pass is the root of their calling. It is their being, as much as the hearts that march in their chests.

Aelish is not built this way. She hasn't this faith.

She stops and presses her hand against the pitted plaster wall, steadying herself. With her eyes closed, a vision of the Mother returns. This time Aelish sees what she did not notice, perhaps refused to see in the chapel.

Floating above the Mother's all-knowing smile are eyes filled with a lifetime of fantastic sorrow, windows to a soul that knows doubt. Doubled over, hands on her thighs, Aelish's eyes, mouth, and nose flood with moisture and relief.

16

SISTER MIKE, DECEMBER 1955

SISTER MIKE MOVES FROM THE SECOND STATION OF THE CROSS to the third on her knees. The stone statues portraying Jesus' torment and death are strung out in a half circle in a garden behind the abbey. A narrow dirt path connects one sorrowful vignette to the next.

"I've failed her, Lord. I've failed them all," she utters, her head pounding as she thinks of all the young women, the children, the infants, and lastly, sweet Kathleen. "How could this be happening only a stone's throw away?" She reaches for Jesus' suffering but cannot get around the anger. Crawling to the fourth station, Sister Mike stretches out a finger to the hem of Mother Mary's stone dress. "How could you let it happen? Those suffering young women and their children . . . how could you!"

She thinks of Isabel's telling, and how she wanted to disbelieve all those babies were cast off like useless husks. She knows Isabel McGuire is many colourful things; however, a liar is not among them.

As a girl growing up, Sister Mike heard stories of young women in the community—fallen women—being sent away to these mother and baby homes to avoid plastering the family in shame. Yet, somehow in her mind, she had imagined these girls finding a life elsewhere after their time of penance. She feels such a heartless, unthinking fool.

Cupping hands over glasses, Sister Mike doubles over and sobs at the base of the statue of the Mother Mary watching her beloved son tormented.

Although it has been decades since she has felt his broad warm hand on her back, it is still known and comforting.

"Don't want to interrupt, Sister, but you looked more than a little bothered," he says. "And cold."

Sister Mike unfolds herself, pulls her glasses off, and takes the handkerchief from a bleary Charlie-shaped figure in front of her. He smells of sweat and oil; familiar.

"Is everything okay? Should I fetch one of the others?" Charlie asks, his body half-turned, ready. He points to the abbey.

"Something horrible has happened," Sister Mike confesses. She blows her nose, slides her glasses back into place. "Has been happening, I mean. And right under our noses."

Charlie pulls up the collar of his jacket, buries his hands into his pockets, narrows his eyes—his look of concentration. She knows he is not one to pry, but she cannot bear this alone, and the silence from God in her prayers is maddening. *Perhaps God sent Charlie to the garden as a mercy for my burdened spirit?*

Glancing at the enormous cross on Jesus' bent back, she stands and walks to a wood bench in the centre of the statues. Charlie built the bench, declaring mockingly that all that suffering deserves a sit-down from time to time. He was right.

Charlie takes up the far end of the bench, sits back, and sets an ankle on his knee. "Am I the person you should be talking to, Sister?" he asks, picking at a scabbed-over cut on his knuckle.

"Not likely, but it looks like the good Lord put you here for a reason." Sister Mike twists the hanky around her fingers, hoping to bind the urge to smoke in front of Charlie.

"Trust me; I'm no miracle. I was just on my way to the tool shed for a pail. Blasted roof is leaking again in the kitchen. The place is a bucket full of holes . . ." Charlie trails off.

Holes, she thinks to herself, shuddering. Sister Mike swallows, and her tears begin again. She hesitates in burdening this man with such a horrendous thing. Charlie grips the edge of the bench, his thick shoulders raised to his ears.

"Should I fetch you one of those buckets or are you gonna tell me what's on your mind? I don't have all day. And me arse is gettin' a chill." Sister Mike knows Charlie's impatience is as deep as his loyalty. He adjusts the brim of his hat.

"Sister Clare . . . Aelish may be leaving the sisterhood," Sister Mike explains.

Charlie's shoulders soften; he sits back on the bench. "Well, I can see how that might be troublin', but she can't be the first one to smell freedom and fly the coop. You're acting like she's killed someone." He holds up a calloused hand and says, "No disrespect, Fiona, but would it be the end of the world if she left?" He pauses. "Did she kill someone?"

The Mother Superior glances across the bench to see if Charlie realizes he's used her given name. He is oblivious, deep in his assessment of the circumstances. She shakes her head at his ridiculous question, then, given what she's learned, wonders how silly that question truly is.

"It would not be the end of the world, Charlie, if she were leaving for reasons that weren't so incomprehensible." Sister Mike wraps her arms around her chest, trapping her frigid hands in her armpits.

Sister Mike knows that Charlie tapping his scuffed boot marks his impatience. There is no one else who would know what to do. Not even Father McManus would be as plainspoken, as pragmatic as Charlie. Sister Mike unravels the hanky, runs the sewn edge between her fingers.

"Fiona, for the love of God, speak your piece," Charlie demands. "Sorry, Sister, it's just that I've got a repairs list as long as me arm and one twice that for tomorrow."

"Have you ever done any repairs at the mother and baby home?" Sister Mike blurts.

"Only the one time. The kitchen sink burst a pipe, and old Hamish MacIntrye needed help with it." Charlie shakes his head and scratches at his throat. " 'Twas a sad sight, all those young girls no older than babes themselves and having children . . ." Charlie trails off again, his Adam's apple dipping. "Let's just say I made quick work of that job. Too much sad in that place," he reflects. "Those Frenchie nuns were none too friendly either." Charlie points to Sister Edel's window. "Made that one in there look like a pussycat. Don't tell me you want me to go back there and fix somethin'." Charlie's brow furrows.

Sister Mike feels poorly knowing that he would go do repairs if she asked him. She feels even worse knowing she may have to ask him to do something even more unimaginable. Charlie is the only person she can trust with such a dark task.

CHARLIE'S HAT IS DROPPED IN HIS LAP. HIS BARREL CHEST IS collapsed, and he is the colour of oatmeal except for the two red splotches on his cheeks. Sister Mike has never seen the man so still. There's always some part of him moving about, but that frenetic movement is stunned.

"Charlie, say something," she begs. "Tell me what you're thinking."

Sister Mike slides closer to him on the bench. *I've made a grave mistake in telling him Isabel's story. How could I have been so careless?*

She has forgotten how sensitive this man is under his shield of practicality—how he cries at every funeral and gets misty over the suffering of small children. *How could I forget that?* She answers herself: *A careless, selfish need to unburden my heart.*

Charlie turns his head. His eyes are round, glassy. "A hole in the ground?" His voice cracks. "Can't be." His disbelief is flattened. Sister Mike sits back a little when Charlie's eyes narrow, and he crams his hat onto his head. "And what exactly do you expect me to do about this, Fiona? Tell me, what? I'm the fool eejit handyman, and that's all!" As though proving his point, Charlie waves his grimy hands in front of Sister Mike's glasses. She blinks and pulls back farther.

"I'm sorry, Charlie. I should not have told you. I don't know what I was expecting."

The wimple bites into Sister Mike's chin. She digs into her robes, and before she knows it, there is a cigarette between her lips and a burning relief in her chest. When Charlie snatches the smoke from her fingers, she expects he'll throw it to the dirt path and flatten it under his boot. Instead, he places it between his lips and inhales, turning most of the cigarette to ash instantly. Leaning back into the bench, he blows a funnel of blue into the air over his head, then hands the cigarette back. Sister Mike knows he is dizzy when he closes his eyes.

"Were you expecting me to go in there with a shovel and start diggin'?" he asks, incredulous.

"No! Of course not, Charlie," Sister Mike insists, but even as the words stumble from her lips, she knows that is precisely what she wanted. Proof. She needs proof, and there is no one else to ask. No one that she trusts like Charlie Rose. She looks around at the stations of the cross, all the suffering and sacrifice made for her soul, then concedes to what they both know to be true.

"Fine, yes, now that you say it," she confesses. "I was hoping you would help. I just can't see any other way of knowing the truth."

"Ah, bajaysus, Fiona! You said you believe the girl."

Sister Mike feels as though she herself is digging an inescapable hole. She does believe Isabel, with her whole heart, and at the same time, it is not enough to let the story be true and do nothing about it.

"Sometimes believing is not enough," she says, crestfallen. She examines the pebbles at her feet, moves a few aside.

"Well, those words coming from a nun are as rare as hens' teeth," Charlie exclaims.

His smile is weak, and Sister Mike recognizes it as an attempt first to distract then dissuade her. It's too late—she knows it, and by the worried droop at the edges of his eyes, Charlie knows it too.

"If I did nothing, the thought of those tender souls thrown into an unblessed grave would haunt me every single day. No amount of prayer or faith in the good Lord could quiet that thought." Sister Mike unwinds her fingers and examines the small red indents left by her fingernails.

"And ya don't think I'd be haunted . . . if I said no to ya?" Charlie blows a puff of air, exasperated. Folding his arms over his barrel chest, he leans into the back of the bench. "Just hearing about it gives me the heebie-jeebies, true or not true. Ya know me ma raised me to believe in ghosts. I've not been the same since she took me to see the mummies of St. Michan when I was a boy." Charlie shudders, then asks, "Who does that to a young lad?"

Sister Mike knows Charlie's changing of the subject is another attempt to divert the matter. Although it is the last thing she wants, Sister Mike offers Charlie a way out, an open door.

"I can ask for someone else's help, Charlie, if you're set against this."

"Are ye half eejit? Of course, I'm set against it! About as set as a retired mule on a rainy day."

Charlie runs a thumb under one of his coveralls' shoulder straps and pulls his cap down tighter, so his ears stick out just a little. Sister Mike's heart sinks. She had not realized how invested she was in having Charlie's help in this crazy search for truth.

"I'm sorry, Charlie. I should not have pulled you into this mess. I need to spend more time in prayer and less time interfering with God's plans."

Her embarrassment is sticky. She rubs the crucifix hanging around her neck, hoping to feel something familiar. The bench under her thighs seems to take a breath as Charlie stands up. He is halfway across the semicircle of granite statues before he turns around.

Shaking his head, he declares, "We can't go in there in broad daylight and just start diggin' a hole. We'll have to go in there at night." His words are clipped, full of frustration. "No use disturbing everyone if there's nothing to be disturbed about in the end. You best be on your knees praying that young Isabel was dreaming all this malarky. I'll come by tomorrow night and fetch ya. Tonight, I'll be in the pub with several pints and wondering what in God's name you've gotten me into." As Charlie walks between the fifth and sixth stations, he removes his hat and nods respectfully to Simon helping Jesus with his cross.

Sister Mike's heart pounds. At night? In the dark? Charlie has given her no room to annul what she has started. She had not thought of what might happen and how, when she began speaking to Charlie Rose. She dares not argue with the man she has corralled into this mess.

She calls out, "While you're in the pub, I'll be in the chapel prayin'."

It is all she can think to offer. And although she knows prayer is all-powerful, now she would give most anything to disappear into a boisterous pub with a pint, maybe a shot of whiskey, and loyal Charlie Rose.

ISABEL, DECEMBER 1955

ISABEL MARVELS AT A CLEAR NIGHT SKY, THE UNCOUNTABLE stars, and a thumbnail moon. The chill of the stone step seeps through her thick coat and cotton skirt as she sits. She can picture the blanket she meant to bring outside after getting the babies to sleep; it's hanging over the edge of Paddy's crib. Too tired to fetch it, Isabel lifts her body, rearranges her coat under her bottom, and sits again. She wonders where Aelish is, not having seen her all afternoon or evening.

When she stuffs her hands into her pockets, her fingers touch a familiar shape. The seashell goes everywhere with her, transferred from one pocket to another. It has become a comfort rather than a token of sorrow, helping Isabel remember the tenacious little girl who gave her this treasure more so than the scene of Declan's death.

"Thank you," Isabel says to the stars, squeezing the shell between her thumb and finger, hoping the young girl somehow hears her gratitude across the sea.

A circle of light spreading on the lawn at the edge of the building catches Isabel's eye. Low voices follow, curling around the bricks. She leans forward, squints into the blackness. A tiny, dark figure follows on the heels of a bulky shadow. When the two step past a low window laying a square of light onto the grass, Isabel recognizes them.

She stands and walks down the stairs. The sound of her left foot dragging makes the two shadows stop, the light swinging between them.

"Sister Mike?" Isabel says in a low voice. "Charlie?" The two-headed shadow freezes. "I can see you," she says, a little amused. "Clear as day."

"Go on inside, Isabel." The tremble in Sister Mike's voice dampens Isabel's tenuous entertainment.

"What are you doing?" Isabel's questioning and her knowing arrive in unison. Her eyes adjust to the dark, she spots the shovel resting over Charlie's shoulder. "Oh no!" she demands, walking toward them. "Not without me." She shakes her head and adds, "And not without Aelish."

Isabel gets near enough to smell the beer on Charlie's breath, and the wave of itchy craving floods her skin. It saddens her to know it is a monster that sleeps but refuses to die.

"Isabel," Charlie says quietly, glancing around. "This is makin' me nervous as a cat in a room full of rockers as it is. It's best if ya let us go and see if there's even anything to be bothered about."

"I know what I saw, Charlie. There's plenty to be bothered about." Something about the earnestness in the caretaker's eyes keeps Isabel's usual outrage at bay. She remembers his awkward tenderness the day Declan's parents sent her and their dead son away. "Please don't make me wait here. Let me fetch Aelish. Please." Squeezing Charlie's arm is all it takes to melt the man's thin wall of conviction. He stabs the shovel into the earth, shaking his head.

"Dammit, Fiona!" he says. "Now look at this mess. We're going to traipse down there like a herd of cattle. We'll never get away with this, and you know it."

"Charlie, you can go back to your pub right this minute. You're a free man." Sister Mike tries to take the shovel from Charlie's grip, but he pulls it back.

"Am I? Am I, Fiona? A free man?" Charlie turns away, walks into the dark a few steps. If not for the heavy scent of stout in the air, Isabel would have believed him gone.

"He's had a few too many pints, I fear." Sister Mike lowers the lamp, hiding in the darkness. "Go on, then, fetch Aelish and be quick smart about it."

The edge in Sister Mike's tone warns Isabel to button her lip, do as she is told. For once, she obeys. But her bottomless curiosity has her wondering why Charlie Rose is calling Sister Mike Fiona.

Hand on the front door, she pauses, remembering that Aelish's room is on the second floor above the front steps. Isabel walks back down the steps, turns, and cups her hands around her mouth. The first owl call is soft; too soft, she thinks. By the third call, Isabel is practically shouting. *Whooo! Whoo! Whoo!*

From across the darkened lawn, she hears Charlie Rose say, "That girl is daft! She's gonna wake the whole place."

A window scrapes open.

"Isabel?" Aelish hangs out to her waist, peering into the night. "What in heaven's name are you doing out there? Come inside! It's freezing!"

"Come down here! Meet me at the front step." Knowing that the abbey is full to the rafters with meddlesome women, Isabel says as little as possible. "I need to talk to you."

"Outside? Why outside?"

Isabel growls up at her sister in frustration and says, "Bajayzus, Aelish! For once, stop asking questions and get yer arse down here."

Aelish stands for a few moments. Isabel can feel her debating, and so she adds, "My gammy leg is giving me grief. Don't make me walk up all those stairs to see you. And ask Sister Mary Celine to keep an eye on the twins."

When Aelish sighs, Isabel knows she has her. The window slides down, and within minutes Aelish steps out the front door wrapped in a coat. Handing a blanket to Isabel, she shakes her head.

"What's going on, Izz?" Aelish whispers. Isabel sets the blanket on the steps, takes Aelish by the hand, and leads her out to the circle of lamplight by the front gate.

"Mother Superior? What are you doing?" Aelish asks, and then, just as Isabel did a few moments ago, she notices the shovel in Charlie Rose's hand. Aelish takes a step away from the circle of four. Although Isabel cannot see well in the dark, she hears her twin scratching at her skin. Before Aelish can ramble out her fears, Isabel links arms with her sister and pulls her through the gate. Looking over her shoulder to Sister Mike and Charlie, she waves them forward.

To Aelish, she says, "We need this." The heady ribbon of Sister Mike's fresh lit cigarette curls over Isabel's shoulder.

From a few steps behind, Charlie Rose grumbles, "What *I* need is me arse back on that barstool."

ISABEL, DECEMBER 1955

THE IRON GATE GUARDING THE MOTHER AND BABY HOME SITS slightly open, just as it was the day Isabel spoke with Leena. Isabel is surprised to feel it give when she pushes. *Was it locked the night I climbed the wall?* Her memories from that night, her time in this place, are a tangle of rusted wire. Misgivings crawl about in her guts.

What if none of this is true? What if the gate was unlocked, and I ran away from something in my imagination? Her legs want to turn her around, go back to her sleeping babies.

"Izz, are you sure about this?" Aelish asks, reading Isabel as only she can.

"You can go back to the abbey," Sister Mike offers.

"*We* can go back," Charlie adds.

"Dear girl, are you sure about all of this?" Two balls of wavering light dance on Sister Mike's glasses as she holds the lamp up.

Isabel opens the miniature glass door on the lamp and blows. The group is dropped into blindness. Aelish reaches out and clutches Isabel's arm.

"Don't want anyone to see that light," Isabel says. "I can find our way around to the back of the building if we follow the wall." She walks ahead, pulling Aelish. Isabel runs her fingers across the map of stones and pauses at the spot where she made her escape. Peering skyward, she touches her scarred palms.

"I know the gate was locked that night. It was always locked when I was here," Isabel says low and mostly to herself, but Aelish hears.

"I'm sure it was, Izz."

Reaching the end of the north-facing wall, Isabel turns left and traces the short walk down the west wall past the slanted tool shed to the back of the building. Isabel hears a clicking sound and soon realizes it's Aelish's teeth chattering.

"This is as mad as a box of frogs!" Charlie Rose grumbles from the back of the line.

"One more word from you, Charlie Rose, and Lord help me, I'll clobber ya with that shovel," Sister Mike hisses.

Any other time, any other circumstances Isabel would be doubled over with laughter. Instead, she notices the crawling on her skin—that part of her which has always been able to see the terrible coming. Even as a little girl on the night the bombs took her parents, or as a young woman that evening in the laundry when the abbey took Aelish, or as a wife and mother when the sea took Declan. She's never had a language for it, but that mould of dread spreading over her skin never lies. It grows thicker as she leaves the wall and steps into the overrun grasses.

"Do you need the light?" Sister Mike's voice comes from some distant place. Isabel shakes her head.

"No. She knows where she's going," Aelish says.

After a few minutes of stepping through the grass and avoiding the thorny teeth of gorse, Charlie Rose whispers, "This is a wild goose chase. How can she even see where she's headed? Someone's bound to bend an ankle in these weeds."

Before Sister Mike can turn and put Charlie in his place, the toe of Isabel's boot meets wood. Stopping suddenly causes the others to bumble into one another.

Charlie drops the shovel into the weeds. "Ah, shite! Now I've gone and lost the shovel."

"Use your foot to find it, Charlie. I'm sure it's not grown legs and walked away. Here." Sister Mike lights a match, holds it above the grass, and after Charlie finds the shovel, she lights a cigarette and snuffs the match with her shoe.

"It's right here," Isabel whispers through suffocating dread. She flicks her hands, then holds them to her mouth to keep from crying out. Aelish whimpers, feeling all this pain once removed.

"Girls?" Sister Mike lights the oil lamp and sets it in the grass. Placing a hand on Isabel's shoulder, she asks, "Do you need to sit, Izzy?"

Sister Mike has never shortened Isabel's name. The endearing sound of it drops Isabel to her knees. She sets a burning hand on the square of wood hidden in the grass. The suffering held under this lid seems a poultice drawing the agony out of her skin.

"Under here. They're under here."

Charlie Rose sucks in his breath. Aelish is on her knees beside Isabel, jaw hanging strengthless. The ribbon of flame inside the lamp makes the shadows of the grass and gorse slither on the wood lid. A hand of wind pushes at Isabel's back.

"Are you sure, child?" Charlie Rose asks, all his gruffness smoothed. "Are you sure you want me to look in there?"

Isabel does not need to look into the hole to find the truth. It's alive and crawling on her skin. What is in the hole will change so many things for the people she loves. Aelish is regressed, a ten-year-old biting her knuckle. Sister Mike rocks from foot to foot, smoking and clutching her rosary. Charlie Rose has removed his cap and has it balled up in his grip. The gathering wind tousles his hair.

Isabel has had the seams of her life torn apart. She knows the strain of trying to bring those tattered edges back together. *How do I stop this without hurting more people?* She touches the square of wood, listens with her skin for an answer. Isabel longs to see her mammy and daddy, craves the silvery sight of Declan letting her know what to do. Instead, there is only night. And wind.

"Did you come to visit the angels?" A childlike voice rises out of the grass a few steps away. Aelish lets out a cry, scrambling backward, forcing Isabel to topple. Sister Mike side-steps and trips over Isabel's leg, stumbling to the ground, losing her glasses.

"Feckin' bloody hell!" Charlie hollers, shovel raised, ready to strike.

The oil lamp teeters, then lies sideways, spilling fluid and flames into the weeds and gorse.

AELISH, DECEMBER 1955

WIND TUGS AT THE FLAMES, INFUSES THE NIGHT WITH THE ACRID scent of kerosene. Aelish's eyes and nose sting. The fire sprawls as a blue and orange pool across the ground sloping toward the mother and baby home. The crisp gorse forms a map of wicks, fire leaping one to the next.

"Get back!" Charlie hollers. He bangs the flat of the shovel onto the flames. As he snuffs one patch, another rises.

"Aelish!" Isabel screams. Aelish is mesmerized, floating above the heat. "Your robe!" Aelish stares at the bottom edge of her robe, a strip of orange eating black. Sister Mike slaps at the flames, and her glasses fall off.

"Get up. Aelish! Get up!" Sister Mike and Isabel dig fingers into Aelish's armpits and drag her backward, half walking, half running along the brick wall toward the front gate. Aelish wakens when she hears sobbing somewhere in the grass that is being swallowed by fire. Did one of the children get out? Her mind clambers, and adrenaline prickles her arms and legs.

"There's someone in the grass!" She points to a curled figure surrounded by flames.

The fire's limbs reach too broad and too fast for Charlie Rose and his shovel. One of the rickety outbuildings is engulfed, and the wall of fire rushes toward the simple chapel behind the brick building. Windows in the mother and baby home slide open, lights flash on. Startled cries float out above the low ceiling of smoke.

Charlie runs for the front door, shouting, "Someone call the fire brigade!"

Aelish hears the crying once again. Pulling her veil off, she holds it to her mouth and nose and gathers her robe high.

"Aelish!" Isabel calls out as Aelish runs back toward the huddled figure.

Although the flames are staying low to the ground where she is running, the heat bites at her bare shins, and the blisters rise instantly. She is thankful to be wearing shoes. The smoke seeps through the weave of cloth across her mouth. The wall of grey and the tears leave her disoriented and groping. Clawing memories threaten to stop her . . . mounds of ash, concussive explosions, broken parents.

"Where are you? Say something!" she shouts.

"Aelish, get back here!" Sister Mike calls out from far behind.

Panic grips Aelish by the gut, questioning, *Did you really see someone?* Too far in to turn back, she trips on something, stumbles to hands and knees. Even the dirt is hot. She rubs her hands on the front of her robes, reaches down to feel what has tripped her up. Silky hair and the bumps of an adult spine meet her palm. Anxious whimpering rises from the ground.

"Oh, dear Lord!" she utters.

She drapes the veil over herself and the person crouched on the burning earth. Aelish peeks out, hoping to find a path back to safety, to the shouts of Sister Mike and Izzy. She spots a narrow charred, flameless corridor.

"Get up! Now!" she commands. The woman rises without question, the sleeve of her sweater plugged into her mouth. "Put your arm over your nose and mouth."

The woman lets Aelish pull her along. The wind becomes an ally, pushing the fire away from them. Sister Mike and Isabel appear through ropes of smoke. They run to Aelish, hustle them to the gate, higher ground, and clear air.

Isabel pulls the veil off their heads. "Leena?"

"God, have mercy," Sister Mike whispers, then kisses her crucifix. She grabs the shivering woman, rocks her, and kisses the side of her neck. "Sweet Leena," she says over and over. Leena is a head taller than Sister Mike; her gaze is unfocused over the nun's shoulder.

"It's me, Fiona," Sister Mike says. Leena blinks, grinds the base of her palms into her eyes, then runs a dirty hand under her nose.

"Fiona, will the angels get burned?" Leena asks as though never having missed a single minute of life without her friend. "I'm supposed to take care of them."

Leena wraps herself around Sister Mike, clinging, shivering. Aelish feels the tide of adrenaline going out, leaving behind a stretch of depletion. Isabel uses her sleeve to wipe the soot from Aelish's chin, forehead, hands. They sit together, arms entwined, their backs against the stones of the high fence. The sirens crest the hill just as the small chapel crumbles inward. Charlie runs back and forth, shuttling women and children to the front gate.

"*Dépêche-toi! Maintenant! Allez, allez!*" the nuns shout, corralling the frightened young mothers.

A nun with a baby in her arms shouts, "*Venez ici!*" at one of the shivering mothers straying from the herd.

Turning to Isabel, who is streaming tears, Aelish pulls her into her bare neck, away from the heartbreaking chaos. The mothers crying out to hold their children, the pregnant ones holding their swollen tummies—hardly out of childhood themselves. Sister Mike steps between Aelish holding Izzy and the frantic scene in front of them. There is a Y crack in the lens of her glasses. Leena clings to her, a nervous leaf on a sturdy tree. The firemen spray water on flames headed toward the building. The chapel is a heap of smouldering charcoal.

"We should go now," Sister Mike says. "The fewer people there are milling about, the easier it will be for the firemen to do their jobs."

"What about all of these women and children?" Aelish asks. "What about Leena?" Reaching out, Aelish strokes Leena's shoulder. Leena is playing with the beads around Sister Mike's neck.

"Leena is coming with us. As for the others, I will let the Mother Superior here know that we can make space if they cannot get back into their building tonight."

Sister Mike scans the crowd for the nun in charge. Charlie approaches the group of women, taking a head count. His hands are blackened, his brow slick with sweat. He smells of destruction.

"Chief Doyle says the building is safe. They just need to spray down the gorse a bit more and be sure the chapel is good and wet before anyone is allowed to go back inside. Are you ladies alright?"

"We will be once we get back to the abbey," Sister Mike says.

"John Doyle will want to know what happened here," Charlie says. He stares at Sister Mike, then points to a man with a folded bundle of hose on his shoulder, barking orders to the firemen. "And what tale shall I tell him, Sister? Why were we here nosing around in the night?" Even in the low light, Aelish can see Charlie Rose's jaw chewing on frustration.

"I don't know, Charlie. Tell him to come see me in the morning and I'll explain it then. Or take him to the pub and drown him in whiskey, make him forget about it. That's what you boys usually do, isn't that right?"

Charlie's nostrils flare. He twists his hat, then slaps it against his thigh. "If only it were that easy." His gruffness makes Leena flinch away. Aelish wraps an arm around her waist, tries to absorb her shivering. Leena examines Aelish, her stare penetrating deeper than Aelish has ever experienced. Somewhere in Leena's mind she deems Aelish safe, pivots, and clings to Aelish, setting Sister Mike free.

"I'm sorry, darlin'," Charlie says, "I didn't mean to frighten you." He squints at Leena, his brow creased. "Is that . . ." His words trail off as his eyes widen in recognition.

"Never mind with that right now, Charlie." Sister Mike shakes her head. "Like I said, send the chief my way, and I'll take care of it. We've had enough excitement for now. Wait here, ladies."

Sister Mike heads toward the nun spewing commands in French. Aelish's skinny knowledge of French is just enough to know the woman's words are not kind. Izzy rests her back against the stone wall; she is running something small between her thumb and finger. Aelish knows it is the seashell. She has seen Isabel do this nearly every day since Declan died. Isabel's eyes are glassed over as she stares out to the place where the wooden lid once covered the hole in the ground. The lid burned as quick as paper in the fire.

As Sister Mike walks back toward them, determined as Aelish has ever seen her, the nun in charge squawks at her in French. Sister Mike spins, covers herself with the sign of the cross and shouts, *"Elle n'est pas prisonnière!"*

Charlie chuckles as Sister Mike marches by, then he says, "But you might be a prisoner when you explain how you almost burned the place down." Sister Mike pivots back to Charlie, yanks his hat from his hand, swats him on the shoulder, and then throws it to the ground.

"Since when do you speak French!" she says. "Come, girls. That's enough for one night."

Sister Mike stands at the gate, now wide open from the fire brigade. Isabel kisses the seashell before tucking it in her pocket, then limps toward the gate. She has aged ten years in the span of one evening. *I imagine I look the same,* Aelish thinks as she rubs the sting in her eyes.

When Aelish steps forward, Leena pulls back, hesitant. Sister Mike holds a hand out to her, nods a little, as though asking the frightened woman to trek across a wide river.

"We'll get you into a nice warm bath and a hot cuppa before bed. How does that sound?" Aelish promises as she places a hand on the small of Leena's back.

"With a biscuit?" Leena's eyes brighten. "And can I wear that?"

She points to the limp veil Aelish holds in her hand, having forgotten that her head is uncovered. Aelish holds the dark swath of material up. It is smeared with grey ash and dirt and reeks of smoke. It looks as though it has given up. *Spiritless* is the word that comes to her mind.

"This one is worn out, I'm afraid; we'll get you a fresh veil after your bath, and as for the biscuit . . ." Aelish rubs her chin, feigning deep consideration. She turns to Isabel, who is slump-shouldered and rubbing her thigh. "What do you think, Izz? Can we scare up a biscuit for Leena?"

Izzy pushes herself tall, loops her arm through Leena's. She lifts one corner of her mouth in a tired smile and says, "Three biscuits. You can have mine and Aelish's too."

Leena whistles through her teeth and hurries through the gate, dragging Aelish and Izzy away from the mother and baby home.

17

AELISH, DECEMBER 1955

RIBBONS OF STEAM SWAY ABOVE THE WATER IN THE CAST-iron tub. Aelish leans into the tub's density, the sleeves of her nightdress pulled up to the elbow. She lifts the cloth out of the water and lets the warm liquid cascade over the hump of Leena's back. Tonight, she doesn't allow herself to wonder about the puckered scars across the woman's shoulders.

"You're very nice. I'll bet you get lots of goodies from Santa Claus," Leena says from behind the curtain of her wet hair.

"As are you, Leena. So very good." Aelish bites her lip and swallows. If she lets herself imagine this woman's life, she'll turn as liquid as the bathwater.

Instead, she asks, "Do you remember your sisters?"

Leena itches the side of one sagging breast, then taps the water, creating small splashes that make her grin. "Bree and Ronnie. Those are my sisters." Turning to peer at Aelish, Leena's eyes widen as she asks, "Do you know my sisters?"

"I do. And I have a sister too."

"I know that!" Pride brightens Leena's expression. "You and her are the same." Her brow tightens as she searches her brain. She drops both fists into the tub with excitement and sends water up into Aelish's face and onto the floor. "Twins! That's what you are! You're twins!" she exclaims. She cowers away immediately, covering her head when she sees the water dripping from Aelish's sharp nose and the damp spots on the floor. "I'm sorry," she whispers.

Seeing Leena cower and the marks on her back resurrect the sting of Sister Edel's stick across Aelish's spine all those years ago.

"Are you mad at me?" *There is no way this timid thing can share blood with Sister Edel,* Aelish thinks. She lays the damp cloth across the back of Leena's neck.

"Of course not, Leena. And yes, Izzy and I are twins; some people can't tell us apart. You're very observant." Aelish speaks softly.

Leena looks cautious out the corner of her eye, then turns open and childlike once more.

"What does that mean? 'Ob-ser-vant' . . ." The word comes out in steps.

"You see many things. You're keen."

"Like a bird!" Leena chimes. "I do love birds!"

She hooks her thumbs together, flutters her thick-knuckled fingers, and sends her hands above her head. If not for the brown spots on sagging skin, the dull grey of her wet hair, the folds of melted flesh on her tummy, Aelish would believe Leena to be a child overflowing with vibrant colour. The greatest part of her still is, she realizes.

Aelish tenderly rubs a smudge of soot off Leena's arm. There is a light tap at the door. A grin blooms on Leena's jowled face when she hears the babbling of Sar and Paddy. Sister Mike pokes her head into the room, smiling and red-eyed. She squints through the wishbone crack across her glasses.

"May we come in?" Sister Mike asks.

Leena nods, slaps the water, her nakedness of no concern.

When Isabel steps into the cramped room behind Sister Mike with her children riding on her hips, Leena covers her mouth with dripping hands. A sound of delight slips between her fingers. She turns to Aelish, eyes wide enough to show white above and below the hazel. She points an arthritic finger at the babies.

"Twins!"

She stretches both arms out, her pendulous breasts hanging into the water. As though caught in Leena's tidal pull of enthusiasm, the twins squirm like slippery fish. So as not to drop them, Isabel sets them down at the tub's edge. Leena traces a wet finger over Sarah's nose, leaving a glistening drop that falls onto her heart-shaped lips. Then she lifts her wet hand above Paddy's head and lets a few droplets fall into his copper curls. They crawl through his hair and trickle down his temple. He shudders and grins.

"This is Sarah and Paddy," Isabel says.

Just like Sister Mike's, her eyes are red-rimmed. Within minutes, the twins are damp head to toe, with all the splashing. Aelish looks to Isabel, who nods. The babies are stripped and plunked into the warm bath in front of Leena.

Sister Mike sits on a short stool, her robes pulled up to her knees, revealing her forest green woollen socks. She rests her chin on one fist and watches Leena. The Mother Superior is a changing sea of joy and sadness.

"She may be simple of mind," Sister Mike whispers, "but she knows children."

Aelish and Izzy nod in unison as Leena holds one curled hand just below the water and squeezes to make a tiny geyser shoot up in front of the captivated babies. The twins—prone to screaming bloody murder to have their heads washed—have no idea Leena is soaping them up and rinsing them down with her free hand.

Sister Mike leans close to Aelish and asks, "Did you tell her about Sister Edel?"

"I felt that was your place, not mine."

"She doesn't deserve to see Leena," Isabel interjects.

Sister Mike rests a hand on Isabel's shoulder and nods toward the woman in the tub.

"Leena deserves to see her." Sister Mike pulls off her glasses, runs a thumb over the broken lens. "She knows children, and she knows love, Isabel. Her mind is not strong enough to carry around grudges. We could all learn from her."

Isabel picks the cloth out of the water and squeezes it onto Leena's arm. Leena takes only a fraction of a second to beam at Isabel before turning back to the babies.

Without words, Isabel and Aelish reach in unison for towels stacked on a shelf below the sink. Sister Mike pulls out a third, stands, and lets it unfurl.

"Just a few more minutes, please!" Leena begs. Her worry ages her.

"You can help Isabel look after these babes as much as you want." Sister Mike glances at Izzy. "Isn't that right, Isabel?" Isabel nods as she plucks Sar from the water. "But right now, Ronnie is waiting to see you." Aelish is surprised, then saddened to see that Leena is keener to stay with the babies than to reunite with her sister after decades of being apart.

Leena points a finger skyward, a bright idea dawning. "After that, I'll help put the babies down for nap time. I know so many lullabies!"

Leena begins to sing.

I see the moon
And the moon sees me
Shining through the branches of the old oak tree
Oh, let the light that shines on me
Shine on the one I love

The sound of Leena's voice in the small bathroom brings everyone to a stop. The children cease their squirming. Isabel holds her chest. Every nerve in Aelish's body swoons like seagrass. Sister Mike closes her eyes, pauses her drying of Leena's back and shoulders. When the singing stops, the silence is a torture.

"My dear," Sister Mike says, wrapping Leena in a robe, "I have never forgotten that voice of yours. The angels breathed it into you when you were born."

"Can we go see Ronnie now, so I can come back and help with the babies?" Leena asks, impatient.

Aelish clings to Paddy's round towel-wrapped body. The feel of him keeps her from floating away on the beautiful truth that is coming to her.

Leena is the catastrophe *and* the blessing, the unrelenting weed *and* the precious flower, the smoke *and* the fresh air. She is the crack in the porcelain. *And* the porcelain itself.

Leena turns her brightness to Aelish and Paddy, then caresses the boy's cheek with the backs of her cracked fingers.

What floats above Leena's all-knowing smile are eyes filled with a fantastic sorrow.

She is the Mother. The Mother is she. Aelish touches Leena's shoulder for a tender moment before Sister Mike walks her out into the hallway, an arm secure around her waist.

SISTER EDEL, DECEMBER 1955

SISTER EDEL'S FINGERS LEAVE MOIST PRINTS ON THE BIBLE RESTING on her chest. Her full lips move in silence, reciting scripture, reminding herself of the Lord's great mercy.

Blessed are the merciful, for they shall obtain mercy.

Clamping her eyes and hands and jaw does nothing to keep out the words Sister Mike spoke to her in the night. Words of Kathleen—here, under the roof of the abbey. Sister Edel runs a palm across both eyebrows.

She was, in a groggy state of being woken in the middle of the night, shocked to hear of her sister. That shock took a swift twist into a refusal to see Kathleen. Sister Mike would ignore this refusal; that she knew. The exasperation she felt for Sister Mike, however, wasn't as considerable as the very old anger toward Leena or the clattery bones of fear buried below that anger. *What could I possibly say to her after all these years?* She's been so near and yet so far away. Lifting the sticky corner of that old emotional scab produces a cringing sting. Sister Edel shakes her head, bolsters her resolve against guilt.

Opening the Bible randomly, her eyes adjust to a passage. The passage which chafes her most—that of the prodigal son. No matter how many times she has read this story of forgiveness and acceptance, or asked for a better understanding, all she sees is weakness and a falling away from the narrow path of righteousness. She closes her Bible again and huffs out her frustration.

"Where are they?" Her voice is raspy, and it seems to shrivel the bigger she gets.

When Sister Edel was a girl, the choir director had assigned her as contralto—the lowest of the female voice—and it only grew stronger as she aged. During compline in the abbey, Sister Edel's voice was a sturdy floor holding up all the other lighter voices dancing above it.

With her eyes closed, she can hear the prayers rising in song, a memory of sound. One soprano voice stands out, cutting through like a determined beam. She realizes it is coming from just down the hall. Recognition suspends her, weightless for a brief second.

A child's lullaby of the moon floats under the door and up over the end of Sister Edel's bed. The limpid stream of Leena's voices trickles through her. She smooths the fold at the top edge of the sheet across her chest, then attempts to tame her unruly hair. Not since she lay down in this bed near five years ago has her urgency to sit up—be prepared—been so loud. For the first time in Sister

Edel's long stringent life, she feels spun about by uncertainty. Her heart is a hammer. She groans while lifting her head and pushing elbows into the scanty edges of the mattress. Sweat floods the creases of her neck even in this small attempt to hoist herself to sitting. The thump of her heart hits the sides of her throat. A frustrated sob escapes her. She flops back to the bed. The drop is no more than a book's height; to her obstinate spirit it is a cliff. A wave of nausea bustles through her, and saliva floods her mouth.

"Breanna?" she whispers.

Sister Edel blinks several times, hoping to make the image of her deceased sister disappear from the far corner, hands folded, eyes clear and youthful. A shard of pain shoots through her back and down her arm. Her lungs contract into two bricks. Clutching the edge of the mattress, she gasps for air. *What is happening? Dear Lord, help me!*

Her Bible slides off her stomach, landing with a blunt thump. Her right hand searches for the rosary beads she keeps tucked under her pillow. It is the rosary that belonged to Sister Eunice—to Breanna. She pulls the beads out and holds them to her chest, and the drumming in her ears softens to a swish. Her nightdress and the sheets beneath her are damp with sweat. Already she is loathing the humiliating change of clothing and sheets—the averted eyes and frigid hands. Lifting her head from the pillow, she squints into the now-empty corner.

As if it's not enough being captive in this bed, now I'm losing my marbles and seeing dead people. Not prone to self-pity, Sister Edel is caught off guard by the hot well of tears, the gum in her throat. Glancing sideways, she sees the Bible on the floor, remembers Jesus' anguish on the cross.

"My God, my God, why have you forsaken me . . ." A milk of guilt, anger, and fear swirls inside her chest. She hears murmuring voices and padding footsteps coming down the hall. For the second time, Sister Edel commits the mental sin of wanting to die this minute. She holds her breath as long as she can before it explodes from her mouth and silver stars expand and shrink in her vision. She would rather die than confront this—her biggest mistake—the sticky residue of which she has worked a lifetime to scrub away.

Sister Edel clamps her eyes again when Leena and Sister Mike step into the room.

"Ronnie, why are you so fat?"

The sound of Leena's innocent voice, unchanged from girlhood, pulls the single thread that causes the unravelling. Sobs surge from Sister Edel's throat.

"Shhh," Sister Mike says to Leena, then leads her to the bedside. "Sister Edel, you need to calm yourself," she continues as she strokes the nun's thinning silver hair.

"Ronnie?" Leena leans in close enough for Sister Edel to feel breath on her wet cheek. "Are you in there? Santa will be here soon, you know."

Just as she did as a child, Leena uses her thumb and finger to pry open one of Sister Edel's eyes. Sleep like the dead and try not to giggle—it was a game all three sisters played in the early mornings in their tiny bedroom before church and school. In the months that Bree has been dead, Sister Edel has not allowed herself the luxury of missing her deceased sister. With Leena now so close, the grief and the longing to have Bree in the room with them is unstoppable.

Opening her eyes, Sister Edel hardly recognizes her simple-minded Leena—save her gold-flecked hazel eyes, as clear as ever.

"Leena," Sister Edel whispers. Her name comes out like a long-held exhale. "Bree is dead." She's not sure why these are her first words; perhaps it is because Leena knows nothing but honesty.

"I know that!" Leena states. She stands tall and waves off this information as though it is yesterday's news. "We have a visit from time to time. She feels much better and wishes you would feel better too." Leena picks up the rosary coiled on Sister Edel's chest, and her eyes swing side to side, tracking the beads' swaying. She pokes her head through the loop and beams with pride, wearing the rosary as jewellery. "Better," she says, patting the crucifix against her chest.

Rock-hard layers of resentment and bitterness, principles and piousness made it easy for Sister Edel to forget how uncomplicated time with Leena could be.

"Is it time for breakfast?" Leena wonders aloud, peering out the window. The morning sun turns her pale skin a light shade of rose.

"I suppose it is," Sister Mike replies, dabbing at her eyes with a hanky.

She offers a second one to Sister Edel. When Sister Edel blows her nose, she makes a loud honking noise. Leena's eyes go round, and she claps a hand over her mouth and falls into a fit of giggles. Sister Edel gives a second loud snort into the hanky, her unpracticed smile hidden behind the cotton barrier.

"Perhaps if it's alright with . . . Ronnie"—Sister Mike glances at Sister Edel—"you could have your breakfast in here with her." A gentle squeeze on the thigh from Sister Mike dissolves the instinctive wall of isolation.

Sister Edel nods and adds, "And then we'll pray the rosary together." She reaches out a finger and strokes the beads hanging around Leena's neck. "It's been a while since we've done that." Sister Edel wants to touch Leena's cheek, feel how she's aged. Instead, she lets her heavy arm fall back to the bed and asks, "Will you join us, Sister Mike?"

Sister Mike raises her thick eyebrows. Sister Edel notices the crack on Sister Mike's lens and thinks to ask after that later. Right now, she is feeling something moving inside—a rusted hinge of hope.

"That would be lovely." Sister Mike removes her cracked glasses, dabs her eyes. "Just lovely."

"And tell those sheep-headed Sisters in the kitchen to stop putting cream in my tea. It's wasteful," Sister Edel orders. Fatigue is rolling up her body. She closes her eyes and listens to Leena's voice receding down the hall.

"No cream for Ronnie! No cream for Ronnie. Fiona, why do the ladies in the kitchen have sheep on their heads?"

Although Sister Edel's eyes remain closed, she sees Breanna in the corner, weightless and much like a firefly, benevolently lit from within.

AELISH, DECEMBER 1955

BALANCING THE CUP AND SAUCER IN ONE HAND, AELISH KNOCKS, then opens the door to the Mother Superior's office. She walks into a wall of cigarette smoke. Stacks of paper, reminders of unattended duties, hide all but the top of Sister Mike's veiled head. A shallow white dish has become a cemetery of bent cigarette stubs. Aelish makes a note to remind the Mother Superior of the latest news on smoking; it's now considered detrimental to one's health. At the moment, there are bigger things to fret over. Aelish doesn't know where to begin.

"Sorry to bother you, Mother Superior."

Sister Mike looks up from the papers splayed out in front of her, sets her glasses on the desk, and twists her spine, creating a series of disturbing pops. Her eyes are heavy-lidded, with dark half-moons sagging below. What Aelish prayed did not happen—Sister Mike has not gotten sleep in the past twenty-four hours. Aelish sets the cup of tea and the three biscuits she nipped from the pantry on the desk beside the short glass of whiskey in front of Sister Mike.

Hesitant, Aelish glances at the glass, thinks of turning around and leaving Sister Mike in peace. The Mother Superior greets the steaming cup like a dear friend, pours a dollop of the whiskey into the tea, and points to a chair in front of her desk. She slides an unruly mound of paper aside. When it topples off the desk, Sister Mike sighs, defeated by another mess. Aelish bends to pick it up.

"Leave it, Sister Clare. It's a chaos only I can clean up. Please sit, I could use some company. It is still Sister Clare, isn't it?" The Mother Superior's question has density.

This is not what Aelish came to speak about. Avoiding the subject for now, she says, "It is, Mother Superior. And I thought whiskey was once a year?"

Sister Mike sits back in her chair and lifts the cup to her lips for a sip. She sighs again, this time welcoming the tea as the answer to all the problems piling up around her.

"We've lived several tough years in this one, wouldn't you agree?"

"I saw the fire chief leaving a short while ago," Aelish says. "Is everything okay at the mother and baby home? Is everyone safe?" She suddenly wishes she had brought herself a cup of tea—perhaps a shot of that whiskey. It would give her something to do with her hands. Instead, she peels the skin at the side of her fingernail, making it raw yet again.

"The ladies and their children are safe. The building is unharmed." When Sister Mike sets her tea down and covers her mouth, Aelish's heart quickens.

"What is it, Sister Mike?" Aelish asks, sliding forward on the chair.

"I asked Charlie Rose to explain to the Chief what we were doing there last night, and Charlie asked the Chief to look in the area where Isabel claimed there was a hole . . ." Sister Mike trails off.

Aelish stiffens against Sister Mike's use of the word *claimed*. Instead of defending Izzy, she sits silently waiting for Sister Mike to continue. Sister Mike stares at the biscuits on the plate, swallows, and moves one across the shallow dish with her finger. She looks far beyond tired. She looks ill.

"Mother Superior, are you feeling unwell? Perhaps you should lie down. We can talk about this later." Aelish rises, prepared to take the petite nun by the forearm and lead her to her room. Sister Mike waves a hand, directing Aelish to sit.

"Poor Charlie." Sister Mike shakes her head. She slides aside an errant paper and lands her gaze on Aelish. "Isabel was right."

Aelish is startled. As deeply as she trusts Izzy's inability to lie, tangled inside was the hope that all of this had been a genuine nightmare.

"Poor Charlie? Why poor Charlie?"

"He and several of the firemen were standing around the hole after discovering it, trying to figure out a way to see into it." Sister Mike pauses. She glances at the tiny heap of dead cigarettes, bites the tender inside of her cheek. "I guess it was the weight of all those men. The dirt gave way with Charlie Rose kneeling, looking in."

Aelish sucks in a breath. The bottom of her stomach lurches to the top.

"Sister Mike, no," Aelish utters, then clasps a hand over her mouth. It is all Aelish can do not to lose her stomach. She doesn't want to hear the entire story; her body coils, prepared to run to the giant tree in the yard, hold fast to its knuckled roots. For Isabel's sake, however, she must stay. She presses her feet into the floor. The tender creases of her elbows flare into a maddening itch.

"What was in there?" Aelish asks quickly before losing her nerve.

Sister Mike's tears brim and spill onto the biscuits in front of her. She attempts to slide open a drawer to her right. When it sticks, she jiggles the handle, and when it does not cooperate, Sister Mike slides back and kicks it with her heel. It succumbs. Aelish folds her lips together, silenced. Sister Mike fishes out a cigarette, her hands unsteady while lighting the tip. Aelish waits for the Mother Superior to exhale.

"It is an unblessed grave. Lord, help us all." Sister Mike covers herself with the sign of the cross; the cigarette acts as a small incense-filled thurible.

Aelish's imagination conjures a knot of horrifying images. And Charlie—poor Charlie. No longer able to hold her stomach, Aelish lurches for the stout wastebasket beside the desk. It feels as though everything she has put faith in ejects from her body, leaving her empty of all but the heartache. Sister Mike remains in her chair, doing what she does best—giving space and time. Aelish pulls out the hanky Sister Mike gave her so many years ago and holds it for a moment, feeling how silky age has made it before bringing it to her mouth.

"How . . . how many?" Aelish stutters, knowing that even one deceased infant dropped into a hole is too many. "How long has this been happening? Who is responsible for this? What happens now? All those poor mothers! Did they know their babies were buried so near? So horribly!" These questions and so many more have been trapped beneath the sick in Aelish's gut. She stands and pushes her chair back. "I have to tell Izzy. She needs to know."

Sister Mike snuffs out her smoke and holds a hand up. "Sister Clare, I agree Isabel needs to know right away, but I think we should tell her together. Calmly. You see how upsetting this was for you and I, but let's remember your sister is with child, and she's had quite a lot of excitement lately. Go for a walk outside, gather yourself, and I will go find Isabel."

Aelish pulls her sleeves down to keep from digging farther into her angry skin. Even though she knows Sister Mike is right, it does not stop the clamouring of questions in her head. There is one that will not wait.

"And what about Leena?" Aelish asks, heartsick. "How could they make someone so innocent do something so . . ." Aelish's stomach threatens again. "Gruesome?"

Sister Mike walks to the window. She waves Aelish over and loops her arm through Aelish's. Pointing to a sparrow, she recites, "'Look at the birds of the air: they neither sow nor reap nor gather into barns, and yet your heavenly Father feeds them. Are you not of more value than they? And which of you, by being anxious, can add a single hour to his span of life?'"

"Matthew six," Aelish whispers.

Sister Mike rubs the outside of Aelish's arm and says, "Leena deserved a far kinder, gentler life all these years. No one is more deserving. All I keep telling myself is there was none better to care for those children in their time of death." Sister Mike reaches under her glasses with a fingertip to catch a tear. "She was their blessing. And I pray I'm correct when I say she holds no ill will. I've witnessed the miracle of her innocence."

Aelish walks to the door. When she opens it, a river of sound floods the room, stops her mid-step. A woman's deep voice melds in song with a flawless high soprano singing "O Holy Night."

ISABEL, DECEMBER 1955

ISABEL SITS ON THE NURSERY FLOOR, SAR BETWEEN HER LEGS tapping a spoon on an upended cup, enthralled. Leaning in, Isabel smells the soapiness of her little girl's head. The child in her tummy kicks. Isabel rests a hand on her stomach.

"Well, hello there," she says.

"I beg your pardon?" Becky asks, looking up from the book she is reading to Paddy.

Isabel has known Sister Mary Celine as Becky since childhood and refuses to call her anything else. Nothing about Becky has changed; she is no bigger than a doll now buried beneath a habit.

"The baby kicked," Isabel says, taking Becky's hand, pressing it into her tummy. As if obliging, the baby creates another ripple on the side of Isabel's stomach. Becky withdraws her hand and stares at her palm in wonder.

"Have you never felt that?"

Becky shakes her head, eyebrows arched. "That's a true miracle!" She holds both hands to her heart. "May I?" she asks, reaching again for Isabel's swollen belly. Isabel nods, welcoming the warmth of Becky's dainty hand. "I've never told anyone, but I've always wanted to be a midwife." Her eyes flutter to her hand resting on Izzy's tummy. "I want to be part of this miracle since I won't be having babes of my own." Her milky skin flushes at the hint of procreation.

Isabel touches Becky's arm. "You can start with this baby." Becky's eyes turn to saucers. Isabel laughs. "You can be with me when the baby comes, and someone else will do the dirty work. How does that sound?"

Becky exhales. "Miraculous. Just miraculous. Thank you, Isabel."

Leena snores from a cot tucked into the corner. Refusing to be away from the twins, she's dragged a narrow bed close to the cribs in the nursery. She fought as long as possible against sleep, worried that if she slept, the twins would not be there when she woke. Knowing the roots of this woman's fears, Isabel promised that they would be there to greet her after some much-needed rest. Becky giggles as Leena lets go the snore of a man twice her size.

"She's a lovely soul." Becky sighs. "It's a tragedy that she and Sister Edel were not together all these years. And to think she was just over the hill all this time." When she looks back at Isabel, she bites her bottom lip. "Please forgive me, Isabel. I didn't mean to gossip. Sometimes my mind is not where my heart wants to be."

Isabel wants to reach out and shake loose whatever binds this young woman to hopeless virtue. However, she is far too tired to fight that battle yet again. Becky does not know the entire story of the mother and baby home—the unimaginable bits—and Isabel is not about to share, then be responsible for mopping sweet Becky up off the floor.

"It's quite alright, Becky," Isabel assures. "You'll just have something to talk about in the confessional today."

There's a twinge in Isabel's chest as she watches Becky nod enthusiastically. Once again she reminds herself, *I'm far too tired.*

They turn to the sound of someone coughing. Sister Mike stands in the doorway, holding a hanky to her mouth. It reminds Isabel of her time with lung fever, and Becky's wide eyes and hand on her chest speak of this same fear. The Mother Superior's cough, however, is self-inflicted.

Sister Mike crouches, kisses both babies on the forehead. With darting little claws, Paddy grabs the beads around her neck and yanks them toward his open mouth. Knowing it's a losing battle, she surrenders the beads over her head. Like a predictor of bad news, a flicker of heat rises in Isabel's leg.

Not one to wait for troubles to arrive Isabel asks, "What is it, Sister Mike?"

"Walk with me, Isabel." Sister Mike stands, offers a hand.

"You go; we'll manage," Becky assures. She waves Isabel away, then reaches out and slides Sarah into the corral of her outstretched legs.

Joining Sister Mike in the open doorway, they walk to the front doors.

"Grab your coat. It's being reasonable out today, but there's a chill. We'll go sit under the tree." When Sister Mike takes Isabel's hand, she feels not much older than her own children.

Outside, Isabel spots Aelish resting her head back into the tree. She walks to her sister as quickly as she's able.

"What is it, Ay? What's happened?"

Aelish opens her eyes, uses a hand to shield them from the daylight. Aelish pats the blanket laid out on the ground. Isabel sits, stretches her leg out, flexes her ankle.

Sister Mike kneels beside her and, wasting no time, says, "Charlie fell in the hole." Sister Mike's words are lifeless. Aelish is a limp flower. She must already know the story. "You were right, Isabel. Not that I doubted you or what you went through . . . what all those young mothers and their innocent children have gone through . . . but I thought you should hear it from me." Sister Mike lays a hand on Isabel's aching thigh. "Did you hear what I said, my darling girl? Do you understand?"

Isabel's gaze is locked in with Aelish's. The rope between their hearts and minds hums with sorrow. Aelish nods. It makes everything Isabel hears from Sister Mike—everything she experienced, bore witness to in the mother and baby home—as real as the deep etching of worry on her sister's forehead. Isabel traces a fingertip over Aelish's worry and down the long bridge of her nose. Aelish's lids close. She's never noticed how long and dense her sister's lashes are.

She sees Aelish now as the ten-year-old girl who ran to Sister Mike's car the day Isabel was brought from hospital to the orphanage. Aelish in ratty clothes, Aelish tripping on sloppy brown boots several sizes too big, Aelish promising that Mammy and Daddy went straight to heaven, no purgatory . . . good people killed in wars got straight into heaven. Aelish was forever trying to make it all okay for Isabel. *Now it is my turn.*

"I understand," Isabel says through the sudden numbness. She secures the top button of her coat snug across her throat, then turns to Sister Mike and asks, "Now what?"

"There's only one course of action here," Sister Mike explains. "Those children must be placed in blessed graves. I'll have to speak with the bishop after Christmas."

Aelish leans away from the tree and asks, "And what about the mothers? And the mothers and babies to come? Who will care for them?"

Isabel and Sister Mike retract slightly from Aelish's pelting accusation. Sister Mike picks a dried leaf from the ground, rolls it between her fingers, turning it into grey dust.

Aelish retreats back into the tree, stares at the ground, and says softly, "I think putting this into the church's hands alone won't do. What if they cover it up . . ." Aelish pauses, then says, "Again."

Isabel feels a quiver in the rope. She understands how terrifying it must be for her sister to speak such distrust aloud, much less to the Mother Superior—a woman of God whom she loves and admires. Never has her love for Aelish been more crystalline.

Isabel leans forward, tilts her head down to make eye contact with Aelish, and promises, "Aelish, there is no way to cover something like this up. Not anymore." The bony part of Isabel's heart is sceptical. The softer, pulsing part, the piece that is more like Aelish, needs to believe.

Isabel did not stay long enough in the mother and baby home to befriend any of the young mothers; nonetheless, their hollowed-out stares cling like lichen to the walls of her memory. These young mothers were empty husks, and when she clambered over the glass fangs atop the wall, Isabel felt them begging at her back to be saved. Forgiven. Loved. Thinking of it now, sitting in freedom under the oak tree, Isabel rubs the goose flesh on the nape of her neck.

Isabel attempts to sit up on her knees and winces; she forgot her leg does not work that way.

"What will the church do?" Isabel asks.

In all the years she's known Sister Mike, the woman has been a clear window, unable to conceal anything. Today is no exception.

The Mother Superior bites at the inside of her lip, takes a deep breath, then says, "Only the good Lord knows the answer to that, my dear. But we will soon find out."

18

SISTER EDEL, DECEMBER 1955

SISTER EDEL'S PRAYER THAT THE GOOD LORD TAKE HER IS no longer a source of guilt. Fatigue has become a deafening shriek. This morning, however, she woke to a holy silence. The tiredness that leaches life from her bones is dormant. Despite being unable to move her stovepipe legs and arms, inside she feels as though she could run a rolling country field from one fence row to the next.

"Sister Edel, can you hear me?" Father McManus's voice startles her.

Frowning, she is sure it is too early for communion. The priest doesn't usually show up until half-past ten and sometimes not until noon, blaming it on his watch, which interferes with her lunch. *Men these days are a lazy lot,* she thinks.

"I'm bedridden, not deaf," she reminds him.

"She's not lost her sense of humour," he says.

Sister Edel turns to see who Father is speaking to. Sister Mike is leaning forward in a chair, elbows resting on her knees, fingers fanned out over her mouth. Pain in the arse Dr. Gibbs hovers in the corner, shirtsleeves pulled up, his pale, hairless head catching the sun like a tin roof with rust spots. *Waiting for the carcass, no doubt,* she thinks.

"You look sick as a small hospital," Sister Edel comments,

noticing the dark circles under Sister Mike's eyes. "What's wrong with you?" She commands rather than asking kindly.

"We came to say goodbye, but you didn't go yet. Thought you might miss baby Jesus being born," Leena explains from her chair at the foot of the bed. Over the hill of Sister Edel's belly, Leena's face is a pleasant floating moon.

Goodbye? There comes a quiver of worry across the newfound lightness in her body. Now, instead of delighting in spaciousness, she is wary, sensing its temporal nature, the trickery of it.

"What's going on here?" she demands. "Why are you bothering me so early in the morning? Get about your business," she tries to bark. It comes out much weaker than the frustration pushing it. Why are they staring at me so piteously? Their sympathy closes in on her. All except Leena, who may as well be watching spring lambs playing in a meadow.

"This abbey does not run itself." She narrows her eyes at Sister Mike. She glares at Father McManus. "It's Christmas Eve. Shouldn't you be preparing for mass?"

"It's best you're not alone." Dr. Gibbs' superciliousness grates.

"And if it's all the same to you, we'd like to stay with you," Father McManus adds, patting the back of her hand. "Besides, Christmas Eve mass speaks for itself. Don't want to steal the spotlight from the main attraction."

In all the years he's been placing the body of Christ on her tongue, she's never noticed how hairy his knuckles are or his fingers being as thick as the sausages her ma used to serve on Sunday afternoons between church services. Closing her eyes brings close the aromas of fried fatty meat, the soda bread, the crackle of eggs in the cast iron pan. When she opens them again Bree is standing at the far corner of the room, a slight tilt to her head. Sister Edel wasn't able to get out of bed for Bree's funeral mass and wants to apologize. Leena twists her body nearly all the way around, looking in the same direction. When she turns back to Sister Edel, she is grinning.

"Shhh," Leena says, holding her finger to her lips, then she turns an invisible key in front of her mouth and throws it over her shoulder.

"Is everything alright, Leena?" Sister Mike asks.

Leena nods several times, then tucks her hands under her thighs, sitting on a secret.

"What's happening here?" Sister Edel asks, despite knowing the answer.

"You had a spell last night," Dr. Gibbs explains in a coddling tones. When he attempts to press a stethoscope to her chest, she glares him back from the bed.

"Spell? What sort of spell? Be out with it, would ya." Sister Edel turns and glares at Dr. Gibbs. "Speak," she commands.

"One of the young novices came in to see if you needed anything before bed, and you weren't breathing—hadn't been for some time," he says. "You were a particular shade of blue. By the time Sister Mike got here, you were on this side again and breathing. I came right away."

"He told Sister Mike to call me," Father McManus says.

The thought of Dr. Gibbs fluttering around her room, poking and prodding her while she lay unconscious or whatever the heck she was, is maddening. *I might not ever die, to spite this hovering fool.*

"He wanted you here for last rites, then," she states. The lightness she had woken to is withering, the fatigue takes its place.

The priest nods. He does not look away. *He's never been weak-kneed; I'll give him that.* When Sister Edel was Mother Superior, Father McManus was still wet behind the ears, unconventional straight out of the gate with his booming laughter and casual, overly friendly ways, which irked her to no end, but never was he spineless like most.

"Well, did you administer them—my last rites?"

"Yes, Sister, indeed, I did." He smirks. "And I must say, it was some of my best work. Wouldn't you agree, Sister Mike? I'm not sure I can do a repeat performance."

When he crosses his arms over his chest, Sister Edel wants to reach out and slap the irreverent grin off his broad face. When Sister Mike starts to giggle, she wishes she had the strength to shove them both out into the hall and slam the door. When Leena joins the giggling, having no idea what she is laughing at, something in Sister Edel's ears crackles. A strange sensation rolls up her throat from her enormous belly, a giant air bubble rising from the ocean floor. When it breaks, she cannot hold it.

Sister Edel has not laughed in decades. It hurts. Every bone in her bedridden body throbs. But she cannot stop it. Her laughter is a booming wave to carry others away. Tears blur the sight of Leena at the end of the bed clapping with excitement, Sister Mike throwing her head back, Father McManus clutching his round knees, and her dead sister Bree tucked like a silent thin lily in the corner of the room. As she continues to laugh, the pain grows. It is a welcome discomfort, reminding her of a sleeping limb returning to life with pins and needles. Mostly she feels it in her chest, her left arm, her sick belly.

The ruckus of her baritone laughter goes silent when she comes to the end of her breath. She is an open mouth, no sound. The veil of tears falls away out the corners of her grey eyes. Bree is standing at Leena's shoulder. Leena goes quiet, still, presses her lips to the palm of her hand and blows the invisible kiss.

"Sister Edel? Ronnie?" Sister Mike's worried face floats over her own, and a silky, warm palm rests against her cheek. Dr. Gibbs lays two fingers at her wrist.

Sister Edel wonders why she has never noticed the flecked blue of her childhood friend's eyes. They are lovely. The lightness is back. It's more than lightness; it is a sense of snowy air filling all the spaces once crowded by fat, callousness, and piety.

"Dr. Gibbs, should I call an ambulance?" Father McManus stands, blocking the sun coming in the window. Sister Edel shakes her head—the doctor leans over her, checking her eyes—an action that would otherwise warrant a stiff bawling out. She no longer minds the pesky doctor; in fact, he and everything else in this perishable world is now a neutral thing to her. She refuses the ambulance because she knows what is happening, as does Leena, who is leaning on her elbows, chin rested in her palms as though watching a large setting sun. Looking at Leena, open and guiltless, suffuses Sister Edel's body with more vitalizing air.

"Leena," she whispers. "Show Fiona the paper I gave you earlier. It's not a secret. Give it to Fiona and Fiona will be happy, and Fiona will know what to do."

Leena bites her bottom lip, raises her brows. She mouths the word *Okay*. Her eyes sparkle as she nods. This is the last thing Sister Edel sees before closing her eyes and letting go.

SISTER MIKE, JANUARY 1956

LEENA HOLDS OUT A WRINKLED STACK OF PAPERS TO SISTER MIKE and shakes them, impatient and eager to be rid of them. Sister Mike knows these sheets are meaningless to a woman who cannot read. She is enthralled by the colourful array of books with pictures lining the Mother Superior's shelves. When Sister Mike takes the wrinkled paper from her, Leena is set free to wander over and caress the book spines.

Looking at the document confirms what Sister Mike believed it to be—the deed to Leena and Sister Edel's family farm.

"Leena, what did Sister . . . your sister say when she gave you these papers?"

Silence. Leena is riffling through the pages of a book, searching for pictures.

"Dear heart, did you hear me?" Sister Mike asks, trying not to reveal her frustration and weariness.

Without taking her eyes from the pages, Leena replies, "Ronnie said, 'Leena, show Fiona the paper. It's not a secret. Give it to Fiona and Fiona will be happy, and Fiona will know what to do.'"

Sister Mike had forgotten the vault-like nature of Leena's memory. While her grasp on the literal often tripped her up, her ability to follow instructions to the letter was astounding.

"Are you happy, Fiona?" Leena inquires, worried as she peers over the edge of the book. "You don't look happy. You're supposed to be happy now." She chews at the side of her fingernail and spits a small piece of skin to the floor.

"I'm happy, Leena. I just miss Ronnie, and that makes me a bit sad."

Leena blinks, mulling the contradiction, then goes back to her book, pretending to read. Sister Mike holds her knuckles to her mouth and turns to the window. She had no idea Sister Edel was sitting on this deed, still holding on to her family's farm. And now she is left with what to do. *Ronnie thought this would make me happy? That I would know what to do? Why didn't she mention this? And what of Leena?* The questions are thorny sticks. Grabbing hold of any of them draws a little angry blood.

Sister Mike restrains the motions to smoke. Since Sister Edel's funeral mass last month just after Christmas, Sister Mike has been trying to smoke less, having decided this while watching Charlie and several local firefighters break a ragged hole in the abbey wall—a brick mouth large enough to extrude Sister Edel and her bed from the building. Charlie was white as flour, the firefighters stone-faced as they worked. Had a heart spell not taken her, Sister Edel's humiliation certainly would have. Sister Mike holds a hand to the heavy woolly sensation in her chest and reaffirms her vow to take more walks and fewer cigarettes.

"Do you know what these papers mean?" Sister Mike asks softly. Leena has switched books, leaving her first choice splayed out on the shelf.

"Ronnie said it was the story of Mammy and Daddy's home." Her face screws up in distaste. "It doesn't look like a very good story. What with no pictures."

"Leena, come sit with me." Sister Mike pulls two straight-backed chairs together. Leena clutches the book to her chest and takes a seat, knee to knee with the Mother Superior. Sister Mike sees the title, *The Lion, the Witch and the Wardrobe,* through Leena's wrinkled, splayed fingers.

"That is a fine choice for a book. I will read it to you if you like, but first, we have to have a little talk about very important things."

Leena's sits tall, the tips of her fingers go white, gripping the cover. Sister Mike holds the deed between her palms. The inked history of a family presses against her skin.

"Do you remember the farm? Where you and Ronnie and Breanna grew up?"

Leena nods and says, "The horses the most." Leena inhales through her nose and closes her eyes. "They smelled like hay, and their noses were soft, just like the velvet ribbons Mammy tied in our hair on Sundays."

"That's right. You had horses. And sheep. Your da was a farmer. And this paper says that the farm is yours now."

Leena tilts her head and twists her mouth a bit. "But Mammy and Daddy are gone. They're angels now, like Ronnie and Bree."

"They are," Sister Mike agrees as she lays a hand on Leena's knee. She prays for some of Leena's simple grace to absorb into her skin. "But the farm is still here, and it's yours."

"Are the horses still there?" Leena asks, her eyes growing round with worry. "They will be awful hungry!"

Unsure if what she's about to say is accurate, Sister Mike reassures Leena that another good farmer has cared for the horses, the sheep, and the entire farm. Relief softens Leena's tight brow. Sister Mike's mind is busy, tired from grasping after all the unravelling threads of what to do next.

She realizes now just how often she sat at Sister Edel's bedside seeking counsel. While certainly no shoulder to cry on or warm heart to sit next to when forsaken by life, Sister Edel's pragmatism was solid and ever-present. She would have known what to do, which is exactly why Sister Mike wants nothing more than to give her deceased friend a tongue-lashing for not leaving an iron-clad set of instructions—and for never mentioning this uncut tie to a life before the sisterhood.

Trying one last time, Sister Mike asks, "Are you sure Ronnie said nothing else about this piece of paper?"

Leena sets the book in her lap, closes her eyes tight, brings closed fists to her ears. Sister Mike remembers this from childhood, and there's a nostalgic ripple through her heart. When Leena's eyes pop open, they are clear.

"I'm very sure. The box is empty." Leena taps her temple, then holds the book out. "Can you read to me now?"

Sitting back in her chair, Sister Mike lets her shoulders fall, weighted by the unknown. She stares at the stout brown couch, a recent addition brought over from the rectory, resting in the corner. Each time she flops into it, the thing exhales pipe smoke. She hoped it would bring comfort to her rigid schedule; she daydreams of catnaps that never happen.

She gets up and kicks the radiator on her way by, it needing a little encouragement at times. She removes the pile of papers from the couch, sets them on the floor, and sinks into its depth, tapping the seat beside her. Leena plops down, and a spring groans deep inside the old piece of furniture. *I know how you feel,* Sister Mike thinks. Leena readies herself, tucking her legs under her, smoothing the pleats on her wool skirt, and squashing an old velvet cushion to her chest.

Sister Mike opens the book to the first page and, without having to look, reads aloud, "*Once there were four children, whose names were Peter, Susan, Edmund and Lucy. This story is about something that happened to them when they were sent away from London during the war because of the air-raids.*" Glancing up, she sees Leena's eyes as big as marbles, her mouth slightly open.

Sister Mike is halfway through the second page when Leena speaks as though daydreaming aloud, "Me and Isabel and all the babies can live on the farm with the horses."

Sister Mike pauses, silenced by the miracle of an answer coming through such a simple vessel. Continuing to read, Sister Mike knows Leena needs no confirmation on her inspiration; she hasn't the mind to question what comes to her heart. Sister Mike reads on around the warm lump in her throat. "'*We've fallen on our feet and no mistake,' said Peter. 'This is going to be perfectly splendid.*'"

AELISH, MARCH 1956

AELISH SITS ON HER NARROW BED, LEGS STRETCHED OUT, BACK against the wall, her chapped hands stuffed between her thighs. She tried kneeling at her windowsill to pray as she has for years. It no longer feels like her spot. Everything outside the window looks distorted. And the draft coming through is intolerable.

Aelish grabs the beige pillow beside her, hugs it for warmth, comfort perhaps. She recalls the only play she's attended in her lifetime, shortly before becoming a novice. When the lights in the cosy little theatre went down between acts, shadowy shapes moved the landscape on the raised stage, sliding, scraping, a susurration of directions. Perched on the edge of her maroon velvet seat, her ears, eyes, and skin were eager for the new scenery, the lights to rise on the next enchanting act. Now, sitting on her bed, looking out the window, she considers all the shuffled scenery of *her* life. Her fear-stricken mind wants the shadowy stagehands to restore all the pieces of her world to act one. Her heart, however, is ready for act two.

Wrapping the pillow over her face and ears, Aelish hopes to drown out Isabel's question to Sister Mike: *What will the church do? What will the church do? What will the church do?* It's a fly bumping around in her head.

Sister Mike had gone to the bishop with the mother and baby home story eight weeks ago, just after Sister Edel's funeral. And each time Aelish asks, "Is there any news from the Bishop?" the answer has been a consistent solemn shaking of the head from Sister Mike.

The door swings open, no knocking. It's Isabel, of course. Aelish lets the pillow fall.

"Sister Mike wants to talk to us," Isabel states, holding the door and rubbing her hip. Her belly has grown so quickly, and Aelish knows that, Izzy being eight months pregnant, the added weight bothers her leg.

"Why?" Aelish asks, feeling the urge to stall.

She scratches at her forearm. Isabel looks to Aelish's arm, shakes her head. Aelish pulls down the sleeves of her robe. Isabel turns to step into the hall and bumps her distended stomach into

Sister Mike, nearly knocking the small nun over. The Mother Superior's eyes are glassy, distracted, and the ever-deepening vertical lines around her lips are tight. Aelish grips the edge of the mattress to keep from digging at the burn on her skin.

"May I come in, Sister Clare?"

Isabel steps aside and lets Sister Mike in. The Mother Superior pulls the wood chair tucked into the desk, slides it to Isabel, and then sits with Aelish. Aelish suddenly feels ten again, seated on the edge of her cot in the all-white dormitory, scared of mean Clare who sucks her thumb at night, terrorized by yet another bomb falling. Aelish takes up her pillow once again, a soft shield for her heart.

"I have heard from the Bishop," the Mother Superior begins; her voice is hazy and far away. "The mother and baby home will remain open."

Aelish's toes curl, the arches of her feet tense as if teetering on a sharp, high ledge. Sister Mike stares out the window. Her eyes brim and spill. The last braided threads of Aelish's hope, faith, and conviction disintegrate.

"The Mother Superior in charge has been moved to another parish. She is being replaced by another Sister from her order out of France."

The sound of Isabel cracking her knuckles brings Aelish out of the gummy place where spoken words are slow and stretched out.

"That Mother Superior is not the only one responsible. They should all be punished," Isabel insists. "I don't know how, but they should *all* be punished. But I guess an eye for an eye doesn't apply to the church."

Aelish waits for Isabel to remember one critical truth. One innocent, simple-minded participant. As she watches Izzy's anger rise, something doesn't look or feel quite right about her twin.

Hoping to slow Isabel's sweeping crusade, Aelish speaks softly,

"For everyone to pay for their actions would be to include our dear Leena in this terrible thing."

With eyes closed, Sister Mike nods her head, then explains, "The Bishop has assured me church representatives will closely monitor the home. Frequent visits from various agencies will ensure the young mothers and their babes are cared for. What we need to pray for is a kind and generous Mother Superior to take over."

"What have they done with . . ." Aelish swallows back the words, unable to finish her thought aloud.

Sister Mike rests a hand on Aelish's thigh and says, "There will be a quiet service next Sunday. The Bishop himself will be blessing the grave, and a headstone will be placed."

Isabel pushes her pregnant body up from the chair, slams a palm on the desk. Both Aelish and Sister Mike flinch. A flash comes to Aelish: a younger Isabel lying belly down in the fresh dirt of their parents' grave, clawing at the earth, her wheelchair on its side with one tire spinning slowly. The heartache is fresh; the smell of grave dirt clings to her memory. Aelish knows that these smells, this pain, and the sensation of grit packed under her nails do not belong to her—these are Isabel's. Just like the sudden gripping in her low belly also belongs to her twin.

"Have they gone feckin' mad!" Isabel hollers. "They'll leave those children in that pit? Bless the grave? What in bloody hell does that mean? What good does that do?" Isabel grips the bottom of her enormous stomach and grimaces. The burning stitch in Aelish's tummy prevents her from standing, from speaking.

"The church feels it best to handle this quietly," Sister Mike says. "So as not to cause an upheaval in the community. This would cause a great deal of heartache for the families." The quivering uncertainty in Sister Mike's voice is a strange note in Aelish's ear.

"So that's it," Izzy says, incredulous. "Bury all those children again. Forget about them all over again."

Tears drop from her jaw as she leans forward. The fallen tears join the puddle between her slippers. Aelish stares at the tiny pond forming on the wood floor. Isabel hisses through clenched teeth. The water crawls out on the floor in narrow rivers. Isabel looks down, then closes her eyes.

"Aelish, run and call Dr. Gibbs," Sister Mike orders.

"And Becky," Isabel says between panting breaths. "Get Becky."

The farther down the hall Aelish runs, the slap of bare feet echoing, the less she feels the ache in her belly. What replaces it is the sound of Izzy groaning as a contraction grips her body, preparing to bring another child into the world.

Aelish covers her mouth as she runs. Stopping to steady herself, she is caught in the jarring collision of joy and sorrow. She will welcome this new child, help Izzy raise him or her up in love. Declan will not.

Something solidifies her spine just then, a liquid warmth in the centre of her back, spreading down her arms. She closes her eyes, takes a deep breath, and smells ocean. This scent is all the benediction she needs to navigate the shuffled scenery in act two of her life.

19

AELISH, MAY 1971

AELISH LOOKS OUT THE HAZY FRONT WINDOW OF THE OLD farmhouse, tracing a corner-to-corner crack in the glass with her finger. She pulls off her glasses, breathes on them, rubs the lenses with the hem of her cotton blouse. "A frying pan would come cleaner," she mutters, holding them up to the low afternoon sun.

The eyeglasses are a recent thing after turning forty. She wonders how Sister Mike could tolerate the things for an entire lifetime. Aelish chuckles, thinking of the moment she donned her new glasses. Isabel took to calling her Specky Four-eyes. Loving how it makes Leena giggle, Izzy uses the nickname any chance she gets.

As if beckoned by thought, Izzy walks into the big square living room. Isabel goes to their secondhand record player, fingers through a short stack of vinyl, pulls out an album, kisses the cover. It's Diana Ross's "The Long and Winding Road," and it has been playing daily for two weeks straight. No one tires of hearing it. Especially Leena, who memorized every line after listening to it one time.

"When can we expect Sister Mike?" Isabel asks, falling back into a well-worn chair, the arms faded from maroon to pink. She taps her thigh to the beat of the music.

"You look simply racked," Aelish comments, noting the hollowness of her twin's cheeks.

"This is a tough place to get a good night's sleep. You know that." Izzy flicks some food debris off her paisley pants. "I always wanted to be a zookeeper." Izzy sweeps her arm out. "Welcome to the zoo." Izzy grins, looking up into the ceiling. "Do you remember the day Sister Mike and Leena told us about this place?"

"Leena asked if we wanted to go live with the horses," Aelish recalls, warmth spreading over her chest. It was shortly after baby Declan arrived. And it was the very moment Aelish knew where she belonged and permitted herself to go there.

"I suspect Sister Mike will be here within the hour." Aelish glances at her watch. "She'll have that new young mother-to-be in tow from over County Cork. Poor thing's just days from giving birth."

"Is Becky ready for the birth? And Leena?" Izzy asks, pulling her thick hair back and wrapping it into a knot. Streaks of silver reveal themselves at her temples.

"Sister Mary Celine . . . Becky is always ready. You know that. She was born to do this, no pun intended." Isabel groans at Aelish's limp humour. "As for Leena, she has the blanket she knitted folded and ready—been carrying it around for days now. "

Over the years, Aelish has watched in wonder as Sister Mary Celine, under the mentorship of Izzy, has transformed from a nervous little mouse to a sturdy rock of comfort and capability during labours.

"She was a good student, our Becky," Izzy reflects. "She knows how to pull up her socks and get the job done. Funny how she still looks twelve even though she's what now? Midthirties?" Her tired smile sparkles with pride at her mentorship.

Pride goeth before destruction. Proverbs 16:18. These words pop into Aelish's head. But that is as far as they travel. She has learned through several bouts of Izzy's ire to no longer preach the Good Word to her twin or anyone else.

Taking advantage of this interlude between all the necessities and mini storm cells of drama, Aelish lies down on the rug, her peasant skirt fanning out amongst the toys. She takes off her headband and scrubs at her scalp. *Even my hair is tired*, she thinks. She drapes a forearm over her eyes and ponders the decade and a bit she's spent since leaving the abbey—grieving at times, yet mostly blessing the truth that set upon her when Leena entered their lives.

Aelish came to the arduous understanding that the abbey walls, the rituals and daily direction of a sequestered life were not the only way to feel loved and safe under God's eyes. Unlike Sister Mike, Sister Mary Celine, and all the others in the abbey, Aelish could not find God in that spiritual huddle of sisterhood.

A baby's hungry cry drifts down from the second floor, mingling with Diana Ross's honeyed, dulcet voice. There are six mothers and their children in the old farmhouse at the moment. Izzy and Aelish look to one another.

"Your turn! Called it!" Izzy declares before Aelish can get the words out. Aelish stomps her foot in mock frustration.

"Sounds like little Josephine," Izzy says, cocking an ear. "Molly is having a hard time getting her on the tit these days." Izzy smirks. Aelish still cringes at her sister's crudeness.

Deciding not to give the satisfaction of a reaction, Aelish peels herself from the floor without comment. On the stairs, she instinctively avoids the creaky outer edge of the fourth step. Halfway to the second floor, the babe's crying softens to whimpers, then goes silent. Young Molly is humming along with "Ain't No Mountain High Enough."

Aelish sits on the stairs, choosing not to interfere. There is a large water stain on the floral wallpaper beside her; it looks like a map of Ireland. She touches the spot on the stain map where they now live. Not far from the abbey—just a county over—but nearer the ocean. She wonders if Sister Edel, Sister Eunice, and their parents are looking down upon what was once their home, now filled with women and children in need of a safe and nurturing place to stay. Would they approve?

"Sister Me-me!" Sarah's delight is a siren from the front yard. The popping of gravel under tires announces the arrival of Sister Mike, or Sister Me-me, as Izzy's children have taken to calling her. Aelish meets Izzy on the front porch.

"Fiona!" Leena calls out, matching Sarah's enthusiasm despite the decades that separate them.

"I guess she finally gave up driving," Izzy says.

"Not a minute too soon," Aelish replies. "She's seventy-five this year. Sister Mary Celine told me Sister Mike backed square into Charlie Rose's new truck last month. Caused quite the show right there in front of the abbey—him yellin', and her prayin'." Aelish shakes her head and smiles, picturing it all.

"Do you miss it? Life in the abbey . . ." Izzy wonders, sliding her arm around Aelish's waist. Izzy asks this question periodically, and with a little less flinching as time goes on.

Aelish uses her thumb to spin the gold band she moved from her ring finger to her middle finger many years ago, recalls the expansive silence, the rolling waves of compline. The defined edges of black and white, right and wrong.

"Compared to working in a zoo?" The cacophony of life in their old farmhouse—babies crying, music playing—plus knowing she can help in such a muscle-and-bone sort of way sends a lively hum through Aelish's body. "Let's just say you're stuck with me, my dear sister," she concludes.

Izzy leans on Aelish's arm as they walk down the porch steps together. They watch Sister Mike refuse Charlie Rose's helping hand as she hoists herself off the passenger seat. Once again, Aelish cannot help but hear Proverbs 16:18 echoing. The matching frustration on their aged faces announces: *We've been bickering all the way here*. Probably over Charlie's wounded truck and Sister Mike's wounded pride.

"Stubborn as the day is long," Charlie declares, raising his hands in surrender. "Isn't stubbornness one of those deadly sins there, good Sister?"

"I believe you mean pride. And I'm certain the good Lord balances my sin of pride with my virtue of patience." Sister Mike pushes her glasses up the bridge of her nose and charges past Charlie Rose as he shakes his head.

"That poor girl," Izzy says as Charlie lends his hand to the pregnant young woman pouring out of the back seat, belly first. "Almost nine months pregnant and having to listen to those two nattering at one another the entire way."

Sarah runs to Sister Mike. Despite being a gangly fifteen, Sar instantly regresses to a small child when nestled under the wings of the old nun's black robe. Sister Mike buries a hand into Sar's mop of ginger hair. Leena waits her turn, a youthful grin with fewer teeth lighting her face.

"Sister Me-me! Where are they?" Sarah digs around in Sister Mike's robe, comes out with a wrapped butterscotch and pops it in her mouth, then hands a second to Leena. Sister Mike reaches up and holds Sarah's cheek, admiring. She then kisses Leena.

"It's so good to see you, sweet Leena." Leena links an arm into one of Sister Mike's.

"Come, Sar." Sister Mike peels Sarah away, takes her hand. "Let's show this young lady her room. This is Abigail."

The young woman looks to the ground as though wishing for the earth to swallow her. The mix of confusion and shame on her face is painful to witness and tragic in its repetition. Stepping in, Aelish draws the girl into her arms, separated from her only by an enormous belly.

"Welcome, Abigail. I'm Aelish, and this is Izzy." Kissing her on the cheek, Aelish hands her off to Sar. Aelish feels the wrestle of heartache and wonderment as Sar takes the petrified pregnant girl by the hand and leads her to the steps. Sar is pure certainty. The young woman's face eases as she looks to the girl, not much younger than herself, marching ahead.

"Mammy, Auntie Ay, which room?" Sar asks, then, distracted by the laughter happening in the circle she's abandoned, Sar looks to Isabel for permission to flutter back to the group of little girls she is entertaining under a hawthorn tree dripping with the blush-coloured blooms of May.

Isabel nods permission to her daughter, takes the young mother by the hand, and says, "Let's get you settled, dear."

Sister Mike presses her cottony cheek to Aelish's, then looks in Charlie's direction. "Lord, help me. That man is my cross to bear," she grumbles. Charlie leans against the car, sullen and picking at something in his teeth.

"Charlie Rose," Aelish calls out. "Can I interest you in a cuppa tea and a biscuit?"

"I'm not one to turn down a biscuit. Besides that, I'm so hungry I could eat the twelve apostles!" Charlie's face grows sunny once again as he taps his generous belly. A button is missing from his work shirt, as it strains against his stomach.

"It shows," Sister Mike mutters.

"Be kind, Sister," Aelish whispers, trying not to grin. "You know we'd all be a little worse for wear without that man around."

"I suppose you're right." The nun's tone holds an amusing ornery edge.

"The twelve apostles!" Leena repeats, giggling. "You can't eat the apostles! They're dead, silly Charlie Rose."

Sister Mike fishes into the folds of her habit and pulls out another wrapped candy. Popping it in her mouth, she sighs. "I swear to the good Lord himself that quitting smoking is making me cranky.

Do you think it's possible?" She glances at Aelish for confirmation, and for the first time, Aelish notices the grey haze in Sister Mike's once-bright clear eyes.

"Got nothin' to do with it," Charlie chimes in from a step behind. "I quit as easy as you like—gentle as a spring lamb, I was."

He struts past and up the front steps to greet Paddy and young Declan. Sister Mike crunches the candy in her teeth and immediately pops another into her mouth.

"Come on, then, let's wet the tea." Aelish takes Sister Mike by a delicate elbow. "You can tell me what they will do with the old mother and baby home now that it's closed," Aelish says.

"First things first." Sister Mike holds up a finger. "I need to squeeze that young Declan and deliver a butterscotch to Sir Paddy."

"I'm giving this to the girl now!" Leena announces, holding up the knitted blanket, then disappears inside.

Sister Mike holds Declan at arm's length and comments on his likeness to his father. "Especially around the eyes," she notes, looking back at Aelish. "Do you see it?"

Aelish nods. "I see a little bit of him in each of them." She thumbs a bit of jam off young Declan's chin.

Aelish still feels a twist in her heart and a salty ocean dampness on her skin at the mention of Declan. The once malignant shame for a selfish girlhood want, however, has faded, gone into remission. She and Isabel have never talked about that day in the abbey when, on the way to confront Sister Edel, Isabel confessed to keeping Declan for herself. It has become a silent identical scar of shame on both their hearts—Isabel for taking him and Aelish for wanting him back.

Young Declan, not one for too much of anything—words, attention, focus—smiles, then plants a quick kiss on Sister Mike's cheek, says a polite thank-you, and, spotting a barn cat, dashes into the yard. Paddy stands, a head above the stooped nun. He hugs her, kisses the top of her veiled head, and asks if she needs any help around the abbey. Much to Izzy's dismay, her eldest son is quite fond of the abbey, spending hours in the gardens, helping Charlie, sitting quietly at the stations of the cross.

"Aelish!" Isabel yells from inside the house, more than a bit nettled. "If you're quite through visiting, I could use your help fixing this crib. It's gone arseways! Again!"

When Charlie offers to take her place and help out, Aelish gratefully accepts, relieved to get space from Isabel's conniptions. Besides that, the more she looks at Sister Mike, noticing the opacity in her eyes, the way stairs have become a chore, and how often the elderly nun repeats her stories, she is glad for the time with her.

"Did I tell you I got a lovely letter from Father McManus?" Sister Mike asks. "He's thrilled to be back in Scotland, retired and with his family and home parish." Aelish does not mention the three previous times she has shared this news. Nor does she talk about how broken the priest was, never quite the same after Sister Mike told him of the mother and baby home. Instead, Aelish relishes time in the present, in Sister Mike's presence.

AELISH, MAY 1971

AFTER WETTING THE TEA AND SETTING OUT BISCUITS, AELISH joins Sister Mike in the living room. The steaming surface ripples from a slight tremor in Sister Mike's left hand as she lifts the tea to her pursed lips. She looks around the farmhouse's large living room, a proud smile deepening the age around her eyes and mouth.

"You girls . . ." She trails off, nodding her head.

Aelish watches as Sister Mike takes in the collection of worn chairs and couches ringing the outer edge of the room, the rug rubbed thin in the middle, a soot-covered stone hearth waiting for tonight's fire, and a few errant toy wood blocks on the floor.

Izzy walks in and flops onto the couch beside Aelish, crosses her arms over her chest. Dust motes take flight into the last of the day's sun.

"Where's Charlie?" Aelish asks.

"He kicked me out!" Isabel exclaims, blowing a loose lock of hair off her face. "Can you believe that! Said I was as useless as a cigarette lighter on a motorbike. He asked Leena to help instead." Aelish covers her smile. Now is not the time to provoke Izzy. "Don't know how much longer we can fiddle with that old crib," Isabel reflects. "It's banjaxed and getting worse by the day. We're gonna walk in there one morning and find some poor wee one rolling across the floor."

Aelish knows Izzy is serious; however, the image of a child rolling helplessly across the floor hits a funny spot, and she begins to giggle. Sister Mike catches the laughter and sets her tea aside to save a mess from shaking hands.

"It's not funny!" Izzy mutters before succumbing to the laughter.

"If you'd like, Charlie could bring over a crib from the mother and baby home," Sister Mike says as she dips her biscuit. "Bloody shame for all of those things to go to waste."

"Let it rot," Izzy says. "It should have burned to the ground that night." Izzy twists a loose thread on the cuff of her knit jumper around her finger and yanks. Izzy's words still sound angry, but there is less bitterness after a year of the home being shut down.

"Izz, we could use all the help we can get," Aelish reminds her. "Some good can come out of that place if we use what's left for these young mothers. Sister Mike, we'll take whatever you see fit from the home," Aelish announces, then turns to Izzy, adding, "Cribs included. And it will be greatly appreciated, won't it, Isabel?" Isabel's silence is as close to conceding as she'll get.

"Very well," Sister Mike says, rubbing her fingers together, depositing crumbs into her cup. "The abbey has permission to remove anything we might need. Between us, I can't see any harm in extending that generosity to you and these girls. I'll speak with the fella who's keeping watch over the building until the church decides what to do with it. He'll let Charlie in, and he'll bring whatever can fit in his fancy new truck."

Izzy leans forward and picks a raggedy cloth doll off the floor. Running her finger over the space where a button eye used to be, she asks, "Why did the church finally decide to shut it down? Was it conscience?" In Izzy's measured pause Aelish senses the acidity of what's about to come. "Or was proper care for these girls and their children costing too much?"

Sister Mike takes another slow sip of her tea, then asks, "Who is this lovely lady singing? Her voice is divine. We could use her talent at evening vespers."

"I don't think Diana Ross would fit in at the abbey," Aelish says, grinning at the image of Diana Ross among the Sisters. "On second thought," she says, "the Sisters would most likely find her absolutely grand."

As though not hearing Aelish's words, Sister Mike turns to Isabel.

"Isabel, my dear, it's time you laid all of this to rest. Aren't you tired of pulling the heavy load of unforgiveness through life?"

Sister Mike has always been the one to disarm Isabel's ire. In the way the elderly nun sets her hands open in her lap, the subtle tilt of her head. One cannot help but fall into the pools of compassion in her eyes. Sister Mike also knows that a change of direction lets Isabel out of the corner.

"How are you girls doing?" Sister Mike asks. "Money wise, I mean."

Aelish follows Sister Mike's gaze to the far window, the one with a crack running from corner to corner. She wants to feel embarrassed for the endless list of things in disrepair but knows that being prideful will not keep the old farmhouse running.

"We sold the highland pasture to Mr. Murphy last month," Aelish reports. "That helped, as do the funds and supplies donated by the local Women's League. Tommy and Gabby Doolin, you remember them, from Canada? They send money with their Christmas letter every year, although I'm not sure where they get it from—they're modest people, and ageing's not been good to Tommy." Izzy bites her lip and looks away at the mention of her lovely friends. "The large garden that all the girls help grow keeps us in vegetables most of the year, and last spring, Declan's father and mother started showing up with mutton and pork every few months. They don't stay long or say too much. They spend some time with the children, then leave, but it's a start." Aelish looks to Izzy again. "Right, Izz?" Aelish can sense the grip of resentment that holds Izzy.

"I'd like Charlie to take a look at the kitchen sink," Izzy says. "The tap is leaking again."

Despite the businesslike tone, Aelish is relieved her sister is willing to ask for help. Aelish thinks, *It's little wins that count when it comes to this life we are living.*

"You know Charlie Rose loves a problem to solve," Sister Mike says. She rolls her eyes. "Besides, you'll be doing me a favour keeping him out from under our feet. Ever since his mother passed, God rest her soul, he's been a bit of a pest at the abbey."

Isabel walks to the window, pokes her finger through a hole in the yellowed lace curtain. Her back expands, and when she exhales, her shoulders drop. Aelish feels a swelling warm wave in her chest.

"Thank you, Sister Mike," Izzy says. Her throat makes a clicking sound when she swallows. "Thank you for everything."

Aelish exhales. She recalls the oak tree in the yard at the abbey;

the feel of its fleshy roots drawing her down. And the soft marble eyes of the Virgin Mother pulling her up. She remembers the reassurance of Saint Patrick glowing in stained glass. On her cheek, she feels the worn comfort of the linen hanky she still keeps tucked under her pillow entwined with the wooden rosary beads which she reaches for when nightmares of falling powerless to the bottom of the ocean come haunting.

Aelish exhales once again, momentarily relieved of the uncertainties she still tussles with. Uncertain if Isabel will ever indeed be free of distrust and the ache of loss. Uncertain when her beloved Sister Mike will pass and leave another love-shaped hole in their lives, just as their parents did. Uncertain whether the God she still prays to on her knees every morning and night followed her away from the abbey.

Abigail, the young mother Sister Mike and Charlie Rose delivered to the farmhouse that morning, steps into the doorway, her eyes in a frantic search, clawed hands gripping the underside of her belly. Leena, her shoulder-length silver hair pinned back in turquoise barrettes, stands with an arm draped over the girl's shoulder, grinning and ready.

Leena announces, "The baby's ready to say hello!"

Aelish takes one more breath before rising, stepping into the free-for-all. She wonders, *Will I ever get used to living this life of continual blind twists in the road?*

There is no other choice.

When she hears this whisper in her mind, she knows it to be the Mother. These words settle on her as a comforting shawl.

As Aelish walks across the worn rug, her heart aches for the young labouring woman whose life is about to be disfigured in the most miraculous way. And in the same breath, Aelish is relieved at being certain of what God has intended for herself, Izzy, Leena, and Sister Mike, at least for this day.

Epilogue

AELISH, EASTER 2016

AUNTIE AELISH?" THE YOUNG WOMAN'S VOICE IS A CARESS. It leads Aelish back into the church pew and her wilted eighty-five-year-old spine. The Easter Sunday morning light is in full flood through tall windows. A few early parishioners are scattered throughout the church, tranquil spiritual islands enjoying the silence before mass.

"You fell asleep. Are you feeling okay?"

Aelish blinks over the grit in her eyes—and, for a grief-riddled second, sees Isabel, her twin, sitting beside her. This, however, is not Isabel. It is Izzy's granddaughter, Izzy-two-too. They share a name and a face constructed of striking angles, but that is where the likeness ends. The nature of this Isabel seated next to her is yielding, soft around the edges, and prone to attacks of a worrisome imaginary future.

"Oh, my dear Izzy-two-too, this business of getting old, it's a dreadful holy show."

Aelish glances at her age-stained hands. *I look like a leopard,* she notes. The nails are bitten to the quick and are angry red around the edges even after all this time, and with so very little left to worry about. The singular blessing God has bestowed upon Aelish's fossilizing: a mind and memory that remain blade-sharp.

Because of this, she can recall her great-niece's troubled questioning prior to her spontaneous slumber.

Aelish says, "I'm not sure why God has put this calling on your heart, my dear, but I do know that it would not be there if it were not meant to be considered." Aelish licks her dry lips and, by the dusty feel of her mouth, knows she was snoring like a beast in front of this lovely young thing. *What a sight I must be,* she thinks, re-adjusting the rowdy pewter bun on top of her head.

"Your granny Izzy; God rest her mulish soul"—Aelish kisses the cross around her neck, looks to the painted ceiling of St. Patrick's cathedral—"never considered taking on the life of a nun, not for a single moment. And look at how the Lord moved through her tenacious bones—taking care of all those forsaken mothers and their wee ones. First in the farmhouse and then, God love her, in the mother and baby home. Your granny and Leena, they brought life to that place. I suppose it was their way of making things right, doing the right thing." Aelish recalls how Leena chose her final resting place. They found her one sunny afternoon curled up like a child in the grass in her white nightie, right over the top of where all those babies had been buried. She was with the angels.

Pulling a hanky from her sleeve, she dabs her eyes. It's more a series of holes held together by tired threads. She had thought to place it in the casket with Sister Mike but found herself feeling so small and helpless at the idea of letting it go. She tucks it back into the sleeve of her jumper.

"Nodding your head doesn't row the boat," Aelish says, mostly to herself.

"Beg your pardon, Auntie?" Izzy-two-too tilts her head in curiosity. Aelish notices the tender skin at the edges of her great-niece's fingernails. It is frayed and angry looking.

"Oh, it's just something Sister Mike believed, and Izzy proved to be true." Aelish continues, "One morning over tea, just before Christmas, Izzy declared she was going to find a way to open the mother and baby home after it had been closed for a few years."

"I thought you opened that place, Auntie? You and Sister Mike," Izzy-two-too says.

Aelish shakes her head. "We helped, but it was your granny Izzy's idea. As usual, I just clung to her fearless coattails . . . and for dear life, I might add. Determined to make it right, she was. I thought she'd gone mad. Turns out she was heeding her unique calling. I wasn't about to stand in the way, so we went about it." Aelish's chuckle floats into the arches. It is something else she's not done much of since Izzy left her behind. "Oh, the battles the between us; Sister Mike refereeing, Leena clutching her ears and singing as pots were thrown, shouting to raise the roof—always followed by tears of laughter, and a call to Charlie Rose to fix the damage. It was a wild ride at times. Some folks didn't take kindly to the idea of fallen women and their babies being truly cared for." Aelish pauses for a moment, then reflects, "Bringing that place to life with love and lots of rowing, well, I suppose it was like watching a river of clean water flow into a desert."

"Sounds like you and Granny and Leena were quite a team. I bet Granny wouldn't have done it without you," Izzy-two-too says.

"Perhaps that's true. Only the good Lord knows." The moisture in Aelish's eyes is a relief, and she realizes she has not cried in a very long time—not since Izzy died two Christmases ago of pneumonia and was buried with a tiny seashell in her curled fingers. Not surprisingly, Izzy went first; she thinks, *She always went first.*

"I think I get why you didn't end up married, but what about Granny?" Izzy-two-too shifts to face Aelish, her hazel eyes direct and earnest. "Why didn't she remarry? Grandpa Declan died so young."

This question—the sudden turnabout in subject—surprises

Aelish, as does the swelling of an ancient sadness. She stretches one leg out under the pew, and her knee grinds. With her not having much meat on her bones, the seat beneath her shows no mercy to her backside. She shifts to better to admire Izzy-two-too and her curiosity. Aelish understands this conversation is one of those exotic flowers she's read about which blooms only once in a lifetime. *Mother Mary,* she says silently, *give me the words.*

She begins slowly, gaining her own clarity as she speaks. "We—your granny and I—both only had one true love. I guess we knew better than to make anyone else try and live up to that."

"But you left the convent. You left your true love," Izzy-two-too replies, scratching at her elbow and looking far too concerned about something long gone by. Aelish is relieved that her great-niece does not fully understand her meaning and sees no wisdom in opening that old door.

It dawns on her that this young woman is not so much a reminder of her beloved twin but a foggy mirror of herself—her years of uncertainties, being batted about by confusion and questioning.

It is then that a hushed clarity cloaks Aelish. A clarity she knows has been eagerly biding its time for this moment, this conversation. Waiting for the stone to be rolled back.

Aelish pulls the threadbare hanky from her sleeve once again, folds its tattered edges together and flattens the small square on her bony thigh. She senses Izzy-two-too's gaze, as ardent as her desire to have an answer . . . all the answers.

Izzy-two-too's wrist is silk soft under Aelish's touch. She turns the girl's hand open to the flat angels on the sky-high ceiling. Thoughts of a pearl-white dove come into Aelish's mind as she nestles the hanky onto Izzy's unmarred palm. Picturing her mammy whole and serene, Aelish slips the gold band off her middle finger and rests it into the centre of the gossamer material. One by one, Aelish folds the girl's delicate piano-playing fingers over the band and timeworn cloth. *If this handkerchief could talk,* she thinks. Closing her eyes, Aelish lifts Izzy's hand to her lips and breathes in, not at all surprised this child smells of ocean minerals.

"The convent was only one piece of my journey, my dear heart. It was only one choice, one step on a very long path." Aelish swallows, wishing she had a mint to soothe her parched throat and lubricate her words. "It was one of many places that showed me truly loving often means letting go. And it hurts like the dickens. When I left there, I doubted for a very long time that God would meet me outside those walls. But I was very wrong." She pats Izzy's hand. "Your granny Izzy showed me this. She was the good Lord's fierceness and fire in action everywhere, every day. She showed me that love and light could live alongside scars of resentment, bitterness, and grief." Aelish thinks of how Charlie Rose died asleep in his recliner precisely one week after Sister Mike died. She thinks to tell Izzy-two-too that there are also times when we cannot outlive our grief. But she keeps this to herself.

Aelish's heart feels far too large for her chest as young Izzy touches the worn cloth and ring on her palm, regarding them sacred relics. Looking over Izzy-two-too's thin shoulder, she sees a translucent image of her twin sister standing next to the marble statue of Mother Mary. Blinking several times does not clear it from her vision. Squinting does not bring it into focus. Aelish's mouth fills with the moisture she has been missing. Her heart floods with the love she's been anguishing over since Izzy left. The spark that lights Isabel's translucent eyes is that of their childhood—spirited and playful—free of secret sorrows and shames.

Izzy is home, Aelish thinks.

Returning her gaze to Izzy-two-too's fresh and worried face, Aelish says, "In fact, all of that heartache, all of that letting go can become fertilizer for the strongest of loves."

Leaning forward, Aelish uses the pew in front to hoist herself. Her left hip replacement, the one she thinks of as a robot, clunks into place when she stands.

"Aren't you staying for Easter Mass, Auntie Ay? You've never missed. Mammy and Daddy, Uncle Declan and his kids. Everyone will be here soon. Uncle Paddy is saying mass today. Won't that be nice?"

Aelish uses the toe of her orthotic shoe to lift the kneeler out of the way.

"It sounds lovely, sweetheart." Stepping into the aisle, Aelish bows her head and covers herself with the sign of the cross. She gave up kneeling when the robot hip came along. She looks to the statue of the Virgin Mother. No Isabel in sight, although she can feel her nearer than when she was alive, stubborn and refusing to come to Easter Mass with the family. For once, there is no lump in Aelish's throat. No grip around her chest. No itch on her skin. She feels free of all that. Her hope no longer strains backward; it has come to rest.

She reaches for the youthful sturdiness of Izzy-two-too's arm and turns to the doors at the back of the church.

"I would like to go home," she says.

And to herself, Aelish thinks, *It is time to go home.*

Acknowledgments

MY IMMEDIATE ACKNOWLEDGMENT, RESPECT, AND PROFOUND appreciation go to the fifty-six thousand mothers and the fifty-seven thousand babies of Ireland who suffered the atrocities of mother and baby homes explored in this book. And to each of the Forgotten Angels—the thousands of children who died in these institutions only to be buried in unmarked graves—I pray peace for you.

All of the characters, the orphanage, and the mother and baby home held in the world of this novel are fictional. The injustices and marginalization, however, are heartbreakingly real. I wish to thank Catherine Corless, a historian from Tuam, Ireland, who uncovered the dark truth of hundreds of children banned from consecrated ground and buried without record or blessing. Thank you to all the journalists who gave me a concise, striking picture of what transpired over eight decades of Irish history.

The writing of this book over five years has seen many seasons and supporters. My heartfelt thanks go out to my writing mentor, Suzanne Kingsbury. This book would not be without your encouragement, craft genius, writing industry expertise, and wisdom.

My deepest appreciation to my coven of literary witches and first readers: Laura Freeman, Janet Bertolus, Laura Richitelli, Steph Jagger, and Sandra O'Donnell. Thank you for your valuable feedback and cheerleading when the weeds got thick. Also, great thanks to my Gateless Community and writing friends for giving me such a safe place to explore words. So much thanks to you, Amber Krzys. You and I met so long ago at the starting line and I was blessed by your support in crossing the finish line.

Much of the research for this novel came from articles, newsreels, and journals, however I am forever grateful to Kathleen Delahaunty for sharing with me in person your experience of choosing to leave the religious life of a nun.

My agent, Sara O'Keeffe, of Aevitas Creative Management—I am so grateful for your loving, brilliant support. You held a clear literary vision of what this story could be. Your steady encouragement and insightful editorial feedback helped me get it there. I am forever grateful that you managed my expectations and then far exceeded them by guiding this book into the safe harbor of HarperCollins.

This book has been fortunate to have two top-notch editors. First, Mary Gaule, and then, Sara Nelson, my editor at HarperCollins. Thank you, Sara, for championing a book that landed in your lap. I am grateful for your observant editorial eye and encouragement to hone my craft—less is more. Thanks to all members of the HarperCollins team, especially the creative design team, who produced a cover that brought me to tears with its perfection. To the copyediting team, who cleaned up my grammatical mess, my apologies and warmest thanks.

Thank you to my inner circle. Martha Towers, I am blessed to have a friend as loving and unwavering as you, never questioning the years of writing and everything in between. Thank you, Boop Boop. Deep appreciation to my mother, my aunt Carol, and my aunt Susie. The three of you demonstrated the calming power of reading as you often sat in silence, immersed in separate literary worlds while connected in a shared sisterly heart. And to my sister Beth Maure, whose steady love I drew upon when creating the sister-bond of the McGuire girls. To my grandmother, Carmen Ennett, thank you for demonstrating feminine strength and giving me the best line for a novel: "I'd like to put you in a box and give you a good shake."

Thank you, Jim, my canine Boo, for your sacrifice of precious fetching and swim time. You are my heart. Most of all, thank you to Pierre Kaufmann—my rock, my Taurus, my great love. I have never known a steadier being, a more loving, openhearted, and generous man. Your support and you simply being yourself grounded me daily as I wrote this book and sent it out to find a home. You knew when to ask and when to let it be. Everything is made easier, more delightful, and truly loving because of you.

About the Author

MELANIE MAURE HOLDS A MASTER'S IN COUNSELLING PSYCHOLOGY. She is a writing coach, life coach, and a psychotherapist, and lives in central British Columbia. She is second-generation Irish; her travels throughout Ireland are an enduring source of inspiration for her work. *Sisters of Belfast* is her debut novel.